PENGUIN BOOKS

THE MERRY-GO-ROUND
IN THE SEA

Randolph Stow was born in Western Australia in 1935; his roots go deep into Australia, to pioneering in South Australia and to the land into the Geraldton district of Western Australia. He is an Arts Graduate of the University of Western Australia, and has lectured in English at the Universities of Adelaide, Western Australia, and Leeds. He studied anthropology and worked on a mission in the far north-west of Western Australia and also as a patrol officer in the Trobriand Islands. He is at present living in the U.K.

Randolph Stow has published five novels, *A Haunted Land*, *The Bystander*, *To the Islands*, *Tourmaline*, and *The Visitants*, as well as books of verse and the highly successful children's book *Midnite* (in Puffin). He has been highly praised by critics in England, the U.S.A., and Australia. Passionately concerned with the primitive peoples and the landscape of Australia and the South Pacific, Stow is deeply versed in the subtleties of the old civilizations and in their impact upon a fast developing Australia.

D0743965

RANDOLPH STOW

The Merry-Go-Round in the Sea

Kỷ vật từ xứ Kangoaroo,

từ một người bạn —

Đại diện hiệp hội
Nông dân Úc Châu —

Hạ Quốc Thái
1989

PENGUIN BOOKS

Penguin Books Ltd,
Harmondsworth, Middlesex, England
Penguin Books,
40 West 23rd Street, New York, N.Y. 10010, U.S.A.
Penguin Books Australia Ltd,
Ringwood, Victoria, Australia
Penguin Books Canada Ltd,
2801 John Street, Markham, Ontario, Canada
Penguin Books (N.Z.) Ltd,
182-190 Wairau Road, Auckland 10, New Zealand

First published by Macdonald & Co. 1965
Published in Penguin Books 1968
Reprinted 1970. 1971, 1972. 1974, 1976 (twice), 1977, 1978, 1979, 1980,
1982, 1983

Copyright © Julian Randolph Stow, 1965

Made and printed in Australia by
The Dominion Press–Hedges & Bell, Vic., Australia
Set in Linotype Times

For my sister

and all the cousins

Acknowledgments

Thanks and acknowledgments are due to The Society of Authors as the literary representative of the Estate of the late Laurence Binyon for permission to quote from Laurence Binyon's *Poems for the Fallen*.

Also to their publishers and copyright owners for permission to reprint lyrics from the following songs:

You Are My Sunshine by Jimmie Davis and Charles Mitchell. Copyright 1940 by Peer International Corporation, New York, and Southern Music Publishing Co. Ltd., London.

Move Along Baldy by Tex Morton. Copyright 1939 from Nicholson's Sydney No. 7 Song Album.

There's A Long, Long Trail A-winding by Stoddard King and Zoe Elliot. Copyright 1914 by West's Limited, London, and M. Witmark & Sons, New York.

The quotation from the song *Bless 'Em All* by Jimmy Lake, Frank Kerslake and Fred Godfrey, copyright by Keith Prowse Music Publishing Co. Ltd., is reproduced by permission of the publishers.

The wartime parody of *Deep In The Heart Of Texas*, original words by June Hershey, music by Don Swander, copyright 1941 by Melody Lane Publications Inc., New York, and Southern Music Publishing Co., London, is resurrected with apologies to all concerned.

I would like also to express my gratitude to the "cousins and strangers" of the Commonwealth Fund, New York, but for whom a book about Western Australia would certainly not have been written in a snowed-up New Mexico orchard; to Lester and Jean Downey; and to a number of people who have checked or provided material used in the book: in particular, my mother and sister, and Messrs. Russell Braddon, William Grono, Robert Testaferrata, Olivier and Silas Wade.

R. S.

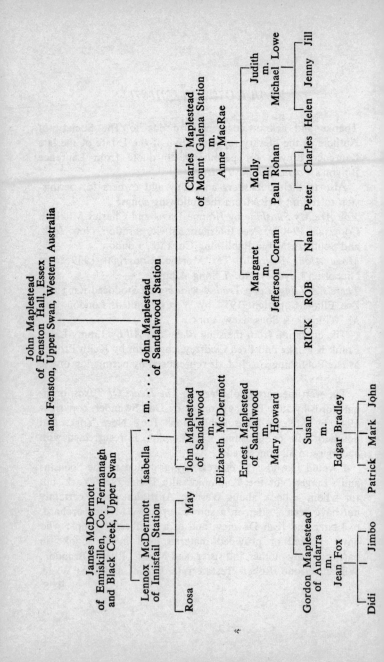

1
Rick Away
1941-1945

The merry-go-round had a centre post of cast iron, reddened a little by the salt air, and of a certain ornateness: not striking enough to attract a casual eye, but still, to an eye concentrated upon it (to the eye, say, of a lover of the merry-go-round, a child) intriguing in its transitions. The post began as a square pillar, formed rings, continued as a fluted column, suddenly bulged like a diseased tree with an excrescence of iron leaves, narrowed to a peak like the top of a pepperpot, and at last ended, very high in the sky, with an iron ball. In the bulge where the leaves were, was an iron collar. From this collar eight iron stays hung down, supporting the narrow wooden octagonal seat of the merry-go-round, which circled the knees of the centre post rather after the style of a crinoline The planks were polished by the bottoms of children, and on every one of the stays was a small unrusted section where the hands of adults had grasped and pulled to send the merry-go-round spinning.

When the merry-go-round was moving it grated under its collar. But now it was still, there were no children playing about it, only the one small boy who had climbed out of the car by the curb and stood studying the merry-go-round from a distance, his hands jammed down inside the waistband of his shorts.

Under his sandals, leaves and nuts fallen from the Moreton Bay figtrees crunched and popped. Beyond the merry-go-round was the sea. The colour of the sea should have astounded, but the boy was seldom astounded. It was simply the sea, dark and glowing blue, bisected by seagull-grey timbers of the rotting jetty, which dwindled away in the distance until it seemed to come to an end in the flat-topped hills to the north. He did not think about the sea, or about the purple bougainvillaca that glowed against it, propped on a sagging shed. These existed only as the familiar backdrop of the merry-go-round. Nevertheless, the colours had entered into him, printing a brilliant memory.

He went, scuffing leaves, to the merry-go-round, and hanging his body over the narrow seat he began to run with it, lifting his legs from the ground as it gained momentum. But he could not achieve more than half a revolution by this means, and presently he stopped, feeling vaguely hard-used.

His mother was in the Library, getting books. He could see her now, coming out on to the veranda. The Library was a big place with an upstairs. It used to be the railway station in the Old Days, which made it very old indeed. In fact, everything about the merry-go-round was old, though he did not know it. Across the street the convict-built courthouse crumbled away, sunflowers sprouting from the cracked steps. The great stone barn at the next corner was Wainwright's store, where the early ships had landed supplies. That, too, was crumbling, like the jetty and the courthouse and the bougainvillaea-torn shed, like the upturned boat on the foreshore with sunflowers blossoming through its ribs.

The boy was not aware of living in a young country. He knew that he lived in a very old town, full of empty shops with dirty windows and houses with falling fences. He knew that he lived in an old, haunted land, where big stone flour-mills and small stone farmhouses stood windowless and staring among twisted trees. The land had been young once, like the Sleeping Beauty, but it had been stricken, like the Sleeping Beauty, with a curse, called sometimes the Depression and sometimes the Duration, which would never end, which he would never wish to end, because what was was what should be, and safe.

He stood by the merry-go-round, watching his mother. She went to the car and opened the door, putting her books in. Then she looked up, anxious.

'Here I am,' he called.

'You're a naughty boy,' she said. 'I told you to stay in the car.'

'I want a ride,' he said, 'on the merry-go-round.'

2

'We haven't time,' said his mother. 'We're going to Grandma's to pick up Nan and then we're going to the beach.'

'I want a ride,' he said, setting his jaw.

She came towards him, giving in, but not meekly. 'Don't *scowl* at me, Rob,' she said. She had curly brown hair, and her eyes were almost as blue as the sea.

He stopped scowling, and looked blank. He had blue eyes like hers, and blond hair which was darkening as he grew older, but was now bleached with summer. Summer had also freckled his nose and taken some of the skin off it. When he squinted he could see shreds of skin on his nose where it was peeling. *Have eyes turned in different directions —*

'Lift me up,' he said.

His mother stooped and lifted him to the seat of the merry-go-round. 'Oof,' she said. 'You are getting heavy.'

'Aunt Kay lets me ride on her back,' he said, 'and she's old.'

'Aunt Kay is very naughty. You mustn't let her give you piggybacks.'

'You're not as strong as Aunt Kay,' he said.

'Do you *want* a ride?' asked his mother, dangerously.

'Yes,' he said. 'Push me.'

So she heaved on the iron stay that she was holding, and the merry-go-round started to turn. It moved slowly. She hauled on the other stays as they passed, but still it moved slowly.

'Faster,' he shouted.

'Oh, Rob,' she said, 'it's too hot.'

'Why don't you run round with it,' he called, 'like Mavis does.'

'It's too hot,' said his mother, with dampness on her forehead.

The merry-go-round revolved. The world turned about him. The Library, the car, the old store, the courthouse. Sunflowers, Moreton Bay figtrees, the jetty, the sea. Purple bougainvillaea against the sea.

'That's enough,' his mother said. 'We must go now.' The merry-go-round slowed, and then she stopped it. He was

3

sullen as she lifted him down.

'Mavis made it go fast,' he said. 'She ran with it.'

'Mavis is a young girl,' said his mother.

'Why did Mavis go away?'

'To get married.'

'Why don't we have another maid?'

'People don't have maids now,' said his mother.

'Why don't people have maids?'

'Because of the war. People don't have maids in wartime.'

He was silent, thinking of that. The war was a curse, a mystery, an enchantment. Because of the war there were no more paper flowers. That was how he first knew that the curse had fallen. Once there had been little paper seeds that he had dropped into a bowl of water, and slowly they had opened out and become flowers floating in the water. The flowers had come from Japan. Now there was a war, and there would never be paper flowers again. The people in Japan were suddenly wicked, far wickeder than the Germans, though once they had only been funny, like Chinamen. For days and days he had heard the name Pearl Harbour, which was the name of a place where the people in Japan had done something very wicked. It must be a place like Geraldton. The sea he was looking at was called the Harbour. At a place like Geraldton the people in Japan had done something very wicked, and nothing would ever be the same again.

His mother had almost reached the car. She turned and looked back. 'Come along,' she called, 'quick sticks.'

He followed, crunching the big dry leaves. He was thinking of time and change, of how, one morning when he must have been quite small, he had discovered time, lying in the grass with his eyes closed against the sun. He was counting to himself. He counted up to sixty, and thought: That is a minute. Then he thought: It will never be that minute again. It will never be today again. Never.

He would not, in all his life, make another discovery so shattering.

He thought now: I am six years and two weeks old. I will never be that old again.

4

He climbed into the car beside his mother. The car jerked and moved, turning down the street between the courthouse and the store. The street was sandy, barren. The houses looked old and poor. Only the vacant blocks offered splashes of colour, bright heads of sunflowers, the town's brilliant weed.

He thought, often, of himself, of who he was, and why. He would repeat to himself his name, Rob Coram, until the syllables meant nothing, and all names seemed absurd. He would think: I am Australian, and wonder why. Why was he not Japanese? There were millions of Japanese, and too few Australians. How had he come to be Rob Coram, living in this town?

The town was shabby, barren, built on shifting sandhills jutting out into the sea. To the north and south of the town the white dunes were never still, but were forever moving in the southerly, finding new outlines, windrippled, dazzling. If ever people were to leave the town the sand would come back to bury it. It would be at first like a town under snow. And then no town at all, only the woolwhite hills of Costa Branca.

To the north and south the dunes moved in the wind. Each winter the sea gnawed a little from the peninsula. Time was irredeemable. And far to the north was war.

Mrs Maplestead's house was an old station homestead sitting in a town. This was because to Mrs Maplestead, and to Miss Mackay MacRae, her sister, and to the late Charles Maplestead, her husband, a house meant a homestead and nothing less. The house was really two houses. At the front, there was a house for living in, a stone house of the convict era with massive walls and dark small rooms. At the back there was a wooden house composed of store rooms, some of which had highly specialized functions, among them an apple room, where big yellow-green Granny Smith apples lay about on tables, smelling sweetly. Joining the two houses was a covered cemented place, darkened by the rainwater tanks. And hung from the beams over the cement was a swing, which dated from the days when Rob had been the only grandchild.

As the years passed, Mrs Maplestead's homestead had

5

become more townified. The underground tank was unroofed and filled now, and Miss MacRae grew chrysanthemums inside its round wall. The cowshed sometimes stabled a horse, but no longer a cow, since the last Maplestead cow had got drunk on bad grapes, and walked round and round the paddock in circles, and died. But the contents of the house had never changed. Anywhere in Mrs Maplestead's store-rooms one was likely to come across an odd stirrup, a bit, part of a shearing-piece, a lump of gold-bearing quartz. The late Charles Maplestead had thrown nothing away, and some of his leavings were inexplicable. No one could explain the two copper objects Rob had found in the wash-house, but everyone was agreed that there was only one thing they could be. They were false teeth for a horse.

He was satisfied with that. Sometimes when he asked what something was they would say: 'It's a triantiwontigong. It's a wigwam for a goose's bridle.' That made him furious.

Mrs Maplestead's house had a garden. At some time in the past load upon load of rich loam had come from one of Charles Maplestead's farms, pockets of red soil had been imbedded in the sand, and things grew. But the best thing in the garden had been there always. It was the giant Moreton Bay figtree that arched over the stone house, carpeting the ground with its crackling leaves and dropping its dried fruits, clatter clatter, on the iron roof.

Mrs Maplestead hated the tree. It choked up the gutters and buried the lawns. It pushed up the footpath in the street with its roots and tangled electric light wires in its branches. But the boy and his Aunt Kay loved it. At dawn and sunset the butcher-birds came, they warbled under the great dome of the tree, and their voices echoed as if they were singing in a huge empty rainwater tank, which was something that the boy himself liked to do.

Now the southerly had come in, the tough leaves of the tree were making a faint clapping. The boy followed his mother through the side gate in the plumbago hedge. The flowers of the white oleander beside the gate were withered and browned by the hot easterly that blew in the mornings, and in the heat

6

the bigger flowers of the red oleander smelled overwhelmingly, sickeningly sweet. They walked the path beside the veranda, under swaying date-palms that were softly scraping the veranda roof. The dates were green, on stalks that were bright yellow. He reached out and pulled one off the tree and bit into it, and instantly his tongue dried up and shrivelled in his mouth and he stopped in the path and spat, and kept on spitting, spitting among the fallen jacaranda flowers, which were a colour he had no name for, neither blue nor purple, but more beautiful than any colour in the world.

'You silly boy,' his mother said. 'They might be poisonous.'

He knew and she knew that they were not. But that was the sort of thing she always said, and he accepted.

Now they came upon a strange sight. Behind a clump of plumbago tangled with red tecoma was a lady with no face, only hair. She was bending over a basin, which stood on a small table, which stood on the lawn. Her hair was as white as the white basin. She was wearing an old flowered wrapper over her dress, and held a towel to the place where her face should have been.

'Grandma and Aunt Kay are always washing their hair,' said the boy.

'Is that you, Rob?' his grandmother asked, still bending, covering her weeping hair with the towel. 'Is mummy there?'

'Yes,' he said, watching her hands rubbing with the towel. There were dark marks on the skin of her hands, because she was old.

She straightened, drying her face, and said: 'Oh, hullo.' When she was not wearing her hair in a bun it was very long, it reached almost to her waist, and it was pure white. Once when she was in the garden moving a sprinkler a willie-wagtail swooped on her and pulled her hair, trying to get some to make a nest with, because it was whiter than wool. That was one of the funniest things that had ever happened. He teased his grandmother, who was frightened of birds, she said, since that day.

'Are you going to the beach, then?' Grandma said to his mother. She had sat down on a kitchen chair and reached for her hairbrush, sweeping the brush down the long white hair as it dried in the sun. She had a nice face, and nice hair. She was looking at her face in her mirror. The back of the mirror, of beaten silver with patterns of flowers and cherubs, flashed in the sun.

'I suppose so,' said his mother, long-sufferingly. 'I'd love a cup of tea.'

'Well, there's time,' said Mrs Maplestead.

The water in the basin was sharp in his nose. He knew what the smell was. It was ammonia. He could not think why Grandma would want that smell in her hair.

He moved away from it, into another smell, a sweetness, Stephanotis grew all over Mrs Maplestead's rustic lavatory, and a penetrating fragrance spread out from the waxy flowers.

'Grandma,' he said, 'where's Aunt Kay?'

'She's in the play-room,' his grandmother said, 'she's with Nan.'

'Oh,' he said. He had not much time for Nan.

'Can you whistle yet, Rob?' asked his grandmother.

'No,' said the boy, keeping his mouth almost closed. He was being teased, because he had no front teeth.

'Say: "Six thick thistle sticks".'

'No,' he said. 'That's silly.' But it made him think of Aunt Kay again. In winter Aunt Kay was always picking thistles in the paddock and taking them out to the street to give to the baker's horse or the milkman's horse or any other horse she could find. Aunt Kay was mad about horses. On the corner near his house there was a horse-trough with a plate on it saying that it was a present to the horses from George and Annis Wills. Nobody knew who George and Annis Wills were, but Aunt Kay said they must be very good people, and he supposed that if Aunt Kay were rich there would be horse-troughs all over the town with plates on them saying that they were a present to the horses from Miss MacKay MacRae.

He decided that he would go and talk to Aunt Kay after all, and went away, walking across the covered cement and into the second, the wooden house. The first room was the pantry, hung with big black preserving pans, its highest shelf a regular folk museum of Colonial household gear. There were silver lamps there that he would have liked to get down, because they looked like Aladdin's; but even standing on a box he could not reach them. The pantry smelled. It smelled of spice, and onions, and stifling heat.

His sister Nan was sitting in the doorway between the pantry and the play-room, her dark head bent over an album of ancient postcards. He stepped over her. Nan was four, and beneath contempt.

The window of the play-room was propped open with a board, letting in a little coolness, though the southerly could hardly penetrate the jungle of date palms outside. Half swallowed in the palm thicket, a figtree shot out from its rough leaves sudden volleys of greeneyes that were tearing at the ripe fruit.

Aunt Kay was sitting at the sewing-machine, but she was not using it. She was darning men's socks. Aunt Kay was always darning men's socks, because she loved men. She went about the Maplestead clan soliciting men's socks to darn, and when she was not darning socks she was knitting socks, or picking grass-seeds out of socks, or asking for news of the sock situation in outlying parts of the family.

At the moment she was darning a khaki sock. He stood looking at her. She was a little deaf, and had not heard him come in. She was wearing a grey-blue dress and a gold-and-opal brooch on her left breast. Aunt Kay had different-coloured dresses and different-shaped brooches, but the dress was always the same dress and the brooch was always in the same place; and on her left hand, hidden now in the sock, she always wore a big man's ring with a bloodstone in it. She wore her hair in a bun, like his grandmother's, but it was grey, and she had showed him once that it was still dark at the roots, although she was much older than Grandma, nearly seventy.

He stood looking at Aunt Kay. She was very thin, and strong. She still carried him on her back across the paddock to his own house, and when she needed firewood she put on a big pink frilly sunbonnet that almost covered her face and went out and chopped wood like a man. She carried buckets of water and killed snakes. He somehow knew, and knew that other people knew, that Aunt Kay was not like anybody else in the world.

'Aunt Kay,' he said.

She jumped, though he had tried not to startle her. 'Oh, Jeff,' she said. 'I mean, Gordon. I mean—*Rob*.'

Aunt Kay was always getting his name wrong, and always referring to his grandmother as 'your mother'. She lived a good deal in the past, and her past was full of little boys. The names she called him by were the names of little brothers and little nephews, little boys to whom she had been governess, brothers-in-law and nieces' husbands, or simply male Maplesteads, Charles Maplestead's kin. Often she could go on for a long time getting his name wrong, fumbling her way through three generations. Usually she called him Jack, after her youngest brother, who was forever nine years old, and forever sneaking into bed fully clothed and with his boots on, so that he could go off shooting at first light.

He liked hearing her talk about Jack. He could not think of Jack as his great-uncle. Jack was a boy a little older than himself. He was called Little Jack, or Iain Vicky, to distinguish him from his cousin Big Jack, or Iain Mor. The names, Iain Vicky and Iain Mor, astonished him. They were words in a foreign language, called Gaelic, which was Aunt Kay's father's language. Aunt Kay and Grandma and Jack and all their brothers and sisters were Australians, like himself, but their father had had to go to school to learn English. This meant that in them and in himself there was something foreign and enchanted, something that connected them with the barely credible places where there was snow. He kept the names in his memory as a sort of password to the fatherland, his blood's speech.

Aunt Kay had even been to Scotland. Aunt Kay and his Uncle Paul were the only people who had ever been so far away. Nobody else had ever been farther than Singapore, except Gordon, who was at the war. Aunt Kay talked about snow and skating, and a lot about Bonnie Prince Charlie. His

10

grandmother said that Aunt Kay was 'fearfully Scotch'.

'Scots,' Aunt Kay would murmur. She considered that people ought not to say 'Scotch', and she thought that Grandma at least should know better.

Aunt Kay's left hand, with the bloodstone ring, was hidden in a sock, a khaki sock. 'That's one of Daddy's Garrison socks,' he said.

'No,' said Aunt Kay, 'it's one of Rick's.'

'Oh,' said the boy pleased, 'is that Rick's?'

Rick Maplestead was his second cousin, whom he and Aunt Kay worshipped from afar.

'We're going to Sandalwood tomorrow,' he said, 'we'll see Rick.'

'That will be nice,' said Aunt Kay. 'I hope he'll come and say goodbye to us before he goes.'

'He'll have to come, to get his socks,' said the boy.

He was poking around in Aunt Kay's sewing basket. It had funny things in it: bits of chalk, a candle-end, a pair of scissors shaped like a stork. And Aunt Kay had no less than ten thimbles. He fitted one on each finger, then leant down and drummed a tune on the top of Nan's head.

Nan screamed.

'Rob,' said Aunt Kay.

He took the thimbles off and dropped them in the basket. No matter what he did, he felt assured that Aunt Kay would not be cross with him, because he was a boy.

The door was open from the play-room into the big dark wash-house where the galvanized tubs sat in a row on the pinewood bench. Aunt Kay and Grandma had no taps in their wash-house or in their kitchen. They carried water in buckets and jugs from the rainwater tanks, and they were mean with water, because they came from a sheep station in western Victoria. Sometimes they filled the tubs days before they used them. They had done that this week. He knelt on the broad bench and looked at his face in the water. He brought his face down towards his other face, and merged his two faces, plunging his head in the water. Then he went back to the play-room, and stood over Nan, and dripped on her.

11

Nan screamed.

'Rob,' said Aunt Kay.

He meant Nan no harm, but suddenly she bit him in the leg, so he had to kick her.

'I'm going now,' he said. But he had hardly reached the pantry door before Nan streaked past him, off to lay a complaint.

On the lawn his mother and his grandmother turned and looked at him. Nan pointed and howled.

'Rob,' his mother called, 'did you kick Nan?'

'She bit me.'

'What did you do to make her bite you?'

'I dripped water on her,' he said, 'that's all. That didn't hurt her. She's coming for a swim, isn't she?'

'How did you get wet?'

'I put my head in the washing water.'

'You're *not* to do that,' his mother said, 'you'll fall in and drown.'

The boy stopped feeling guilty and felt merely bored. His mother knew of an infinite number of ways to die. Once, one hot day at Sandalwood, he and his cousin Didi had got into the big Coolgardie safe on the back veranda and closed the door. It was very cool in there, water seeping continually down the clinker-packed walls. They shared the safe with half a sheep, and amused themselves by swinging the meat back and forth on its hook like a punching-bag.

Suddenly the door swung open, and there stood Rob's mother.

'Come out,' she said, 'this *instant*, before you both get consumption.'

After that the boy had stopped listening to his mother's warnings of doom. But because no catastrophe was possible which she would not have foreseen, he felt secure with her, he felt that she could thwart any danger, except the one danger he really feared, which was made up of time and change and fragmentary talk of war.

'Well,' he said, 'if we go to the beach now, and you teach me to swim, then I *can't* drown, can I?'

'Pig of a boy,' Margaret Coram remarked to her mother. 'I think he's going to be a lawyer like his father.'

He could never beat her. She might give in, but not meekly.

The beach where the small children swam was called the West End. The water was shallow there, and the sand white and hard, so that cars could drive right to the edge. On hot nights there used always to be lines of cars there, before the war; and fish jumped out of the sea and shone in the headlights. The boy, in those days, would try to get his father to leave the headlights on; but his father, who liked to be invisible, never would.

It was on the beach that the boy liked his father most. He would cling to his father's freckled back and his father would swim away, out into the deep water, where it was dark blue instead of pale green. He would slip off his father's back sometimes, and swallow a lot of water, and choke with excitement. He was in love with the sea, and more than anything wanted to swim.

Or to go in a boat. Once Uncle Paul had taken him in a dinghy right to the end of the breakwater, and he had looked back and seen the town transformed, another town completely, rising out of deep green sea, below high sandhills which became flat-topped rock hills to the north. There had been a big ship at the wharf, and a fishing-boat had passed them, bound for the Abrolhos. The ends of the two grey jetties had seemed a short dog-paddle away. Because the whole world had been changed he had thought that then, at last, he might go to the merry-go-round. But on that day too there had been something to prevent it, and so they had come back again to the everyday shore.

Now Uncle Paul was away in the Air Force, and his father was in camp for the weekend, and he paddled listlessly in the warm shallows. He had been playing by himself in a circle of sandbags among the beach-olives, which had something to do with the war. His legs were caked with white sand. He bent to wash them.

The sun was going down behind the breakwater, gold and orange. Now more than ever the black merry-go-round was real.

His mother sat by the water, on a red towel, in blue bathers. He went and sat beside her, hugging his knees, staring at the merry-go-round. Sand kept falling on the towel as Nan dug canals with her spade.

'Mummy,' he said.

'Yes, Rob?'

'Can't I go to the merry-go-round? Just once?'

'You've had one ride on the merry-go-round today.'

'Not that one,' he said, impatiently. 'The other merry-go-round. The merry-go-round in the sea.'

'Oh, Rob,' she said, laughingly, 'won't you ever believe me? It's not a merry-go-round.'

'It *looks* like a merry-go-round. It *must* be a merry-go-round, Mummy.'

'It's a big boat,' Margaret Coram said. 'It's a big sort of barge that was carting rocks to build the breakwater. And one night there was a storm, and it sank. What you can see is the mast and the iron things that hold the mast up. It just happens to look like a merry-go-round.'

He stared at it. It was very far away, but he could see the bulge where the iron leaves would be, and the collar from which the iron stays descended to support the seat. It could be nothing else but a merry-go-round in the sea.

'Have you been there?' he asked her, sullenly.

'Yes,' she said, 'I've seen it.'

'Well, can't I go then? Can't I go there with you?'

'No, we can't, Rob. We can't go there.'

'Why? Why can't we go there?'

'Oh—because of the war,' his mother said.

Somehow he had foreseen that answer. He would never reach it, because of the war.

'Darling,' his mother said, 'you know that that end of the beach is where Daddy's camp is, and no one can go there now except the Garrison. There are barbed wire fences there to keep people out. So we just can't go to the merry-go-round —I mean the wreck—not till after the war. But you'll go there someday, if you really want to see it. The war won't last forever.'

14

He listened to her with deep cynicism. The war always had been and always would be. The barbed wire would never come down.

'When I'm big,' he said, slowly, getting up, 'I'll *swim* there.' It was a threat.

He went back to the ring of sandbags, he lay in the sand. He thought how he would swim far out into the deep water, past all the fences, so far that looking back he would see the world transformed, as it had been from the dinghy. He would swim miles and miles, until at last the merry-go-round would tower above him, black, glistening, perfect, rooted in the sea. The merry-go-round would turn by itself, just a little above the green water. The world would revolve around him, and nothing would ever change. He would bring Rick to the merry-go-round, and Aunt Kay, and they would stay there always, spinning and diving and dangling their feet in the water, and it would be today forever.

2

The sunflowers followed the road a long way out of town. When the road ran by the white sandhills they were still there, they stood up tall and yellow against the dunes, which were dazzling, like Scottish snow. Sometimes they were framed against a broad triangle of bright sea. But as the coast fell away and the road cut across the river flats the sunflowers thinned out and vanished. Now the land was pale and flat, littered with empty farmhouses, tobacco-bush leaning in through glassless windows. Here and there clumps of gumtrees and palms sheltered houses where people still lived. But there were many, many empty houses, big houses too, like the tall, staring shell of the Old Brewery, a ruined castle.

'Look, Rob,' his mother said, taking her hand off the steering wheel and pointing. 'What are they?'

He followed her finger, and saw the familiar gumtrees, crippled and stooped by the southerly, bowing northward and trailing their leaves on the ground.

'Oh,' he said, with a sort of embarrassment. 'The ladies washing their hair.'

That was something he had said when he was very small, and he supposed that they were teasing when they reminded him. But it was still true, and the bent trees always would look like Grandma and Aunt Kay washing their hair; like Grandma and Aunt Kay trailing their long weeping leaves in the basin.

'Why are we going this way?' he asked.

'We're going to Innisfail,' his mother said, 'to take some of Grandma's jam to Aunt Rosa and Aunt May.'

'Oh,' said the boy, laughing. 'Like Little Red Riding Hood.'

He was pleased by that, because they would be leaving the flat land with the empty houses. On the road to Innisfail there were hills and straight trees, and the Pool, and it was nearly

16

to Sandalwood. He was bored by the farmed, fenced plain of the Greenough.

Nan was in the back seat, leaning forward to look over him. She was eating something, sucking a sweet, making a noise near his ear. It was driving him mad. He felt hot and bored, and it was a long, long way to Innisfail.

'Let's play a game,' he said. 'Let's play "I Spy".'

'All right,' his mother said. 'You go first.'

So they played 'I Spy' all through the flat land, the boy making a lot of mistakes and giving his mother wrong clues because he could not spell very well, but it passed the time. Nan could not spell at all and could not play. She just leaned on the back of his seat and breathed down his neck.

At last they came to blackboys. 'Blackboys!' he said, pointing out along the stony ridge the road was climbing. Their spears thrust up from the rough-smelling scrub, their black bodies leaned, their green hair hung straight from the crown. They were only plants, but he was almost afraid of them. They looked as if they might move.

Now they were really in the country, among hills and gullies, among clumps of York gum. Beside the road the land dropped steeply down to a dry riverbed, and he looked back and followed the line of it with his eyes, among the smaller hills. The hills and the soil were red-brown and stony, brownish-purple in the distance. Pushing Nan aside he could see, through the rear window, miles and miles away, the sea. Then the car was going downhill again, bumping on the dirt road, between rough-barked dark-leaved trees.

The car pulled up at a gate, and he got out and fumbled with the chain. Now that he was out of the car everything was terribly quiet, the trees were still, and the world seemed huge because the *ark ark* of the crows echoed in the sky as if the sky were the roof of a vast room. He breathed the hot air, breathing the smell of wilting gumleaves, breathing the smell of dead grass and the smell of dust that was settling around the car. The gate was hot under his hand and scraped along the ground. He held it open while the car passed through, breathing petrol fumes and dust.

17

Aunt Rosa's and Aunt May's house was very strange. Part of it had an Upstairs and part had not. In front of the part with the Upstairs grew spiky aloes, and the veranda of the other part was hidden behind roses and tecoma. When the car stopped again he smelled roses. He smelled roses and dust and heat.

His mother was getting out of the car. She was reaching for a basket on the back seat beside Nan.

'Can I get out?' he said.

'Oh—' she said. 'No, you stay with Nan. I won't be a minute.'

But he did get out, and stood by the car watching the house. The front door was opening. Aunt Rosa was standing there. He went towards the house, timidly.

'Margaret,' said Aunt Rosa. 'And—and—?'

'Rob,' said his mother. Then she started telling Aunt Rosa about the jam, and that Grandma and Aunt Kay sent their love.

He stood staring at Aunt Rosa. When his mother and Aunt Rosa went into the house he followed, staring. In the hall of Aunt Rosa's house little narrow stairs climbed up and turned a corner. Aunt Rosa's drawing-room was big and dark, the door was open on to the veranda, and it smelled of roses and heat.

He stood in the doorway, staring. Aunt May was in the drawing-room. She turned and saw him and said: 'And here is—here is—?'

'Rob,' said his mother.

Aunt May came and kissed him. Aunt Rosa had not kissed him. Aunt Rosa and his mother were sitting down, and then Aunt May sat down. He stood and stared.

Aunt Rosa and Aunt May were immensely old. They were cousins of his grandfather, who was dead, and even older than his grandfather. They were so old that Aunt Rosa remembered wild blackfellows attacking Innisfail, which meant that Aunt Rosa must be as old as the shearing shed at Sandalwood with the slits in the walls for rifles. Their house was so old that his own great-grandfather Maplestead, with the spear-scar on his

18

hand, had helped their father to build it. Their station had been founded on the first day of his world's creation. And their Pool was older still, and full of bunyips.

Aunt Rosa was taller and straighter than Aunt May. Aunt Rosa's hair was yellowish-white and smooth, Aunt May's was grey with little curls on her forehead. Aunt Rosa's face was broad across the cheekbones, with tight skin. Aunt May's was small and wrinkled. Aunt Rosa talked quietly, and little. Aunt May talked quickly, and laughed. They wore black dresses, and round each of their throats was a narrow, black velvet ribbon.

He had heard his grandmother say that they had been admired for their white skin. Aunt Rosa in particular had been admired. Once, in the dawn of his world's creation, Aunt Rosa and Aunt May had been young. Nowhere in his memory could he find an image to fit them.

Already his mother was getting up to leave, though Aunt May was pressing her to stay. He moved back from the door before they reached it. Through the front door he could see an odd, untidy tree: a fir tree, a tree from Scotland.

They were all going to the car. His mother was lifting up Nan and they were kissing her. He trailed behind them, silent. The age of Aunt Rosa and Aunt May always struck him dumb with awe.

'Come along, Rob,' his mother called. She was already in the car, holding the door open.

Aunt May kissed him again, and so, this time, did Aunt Rosa. 'Goodbye,' he said, in a small voice, and Aunt May slammed the door on him. They waved, they stood in front of their funny house, waving, black ribbons round their throats. They were so old that they used to go to Perth by ship, that they used to ride sidesaddle, that they used to drive a sulky. It was only after he had closed the homestead gate that he recovered from his awe.

The car followed the winding road through the York gums. Ahead, he could see green rushes and smooth-barked river gums. Then they were crossing the ford, and he smelled the river.

19

'Can we go to the Pool, Mummy?' he said. 'Can we, please?'

'Not today. We're going to see Rick.'

'Just for a minute.'

'No.'

He sulked for a while. He and Aunt Kay loved the Pool, and when his mother was little she and the other children used to play there on rafts made of aloe-pole. He thought it was mean of her not to take him to the Pool where she had had so much fun.

But he could see the cliff, at least, as the road climbed. He could see the tall pink cliff that fell down into the water, and kept on falling forever. The Pool was bottomless, and under the dark water there were bunyips, or perhaps only one bunyip, that had been there always. No one knew what a bunyip was, but it had been there before there were any white men, before Aunt Rosa's and Aunt May's father had claimed the Pool, and it was the oldest thing in Australia. The water was hidden behind dense thickets of dryandra, but he could see the cliff, he followed it down with his eye, and knew that somewhere near the roots of the cliff lay the bunyip. Whatever happened, the bunyip would always be there.

Nan was breathing down his neck again, and complaining. 'Mummy, when will we be there?'

'Soon,' his mother said.

'When you count to how many?'

'When you count to a thousand.'

Nan started counting.

'Oh, shut up,' said the boy.

'Rob!' said his mother. She reached over and slapped him on the leg.

'Well, she doesn't have to count out loud.'

'Don't you ever say shut up to your sister.'

'Sister,' he said. 'Huh.'

He brooded over the passing country. They were coming near Sandalwood, to the bare hilly paddocks from which scrub had been cleared by four generations of Maplesteads. Ahead was a clump of dead grey trees. 'Oh, look,' he said, sitting up straight, holding his breath. The trees were white with flowers,

20

with birds; the flowers, the birds were rising in the air; the air was full of screaming flowers. He sat tense on the edge of his seat as the car drove through the snowstorm of cockatoos, as the white storm divided and fell back in the slipstream of the car. 'Oh, look,' cried Nan.

'You're slow,' he said. 'I saw them ages ago.'

'Don't be disagreeable, Rob,' said his mother.

The car stopped at a gate. The gate said Sandalwood Station. He got out and opened it, leaned on it as the car passed through, looking across the tawny silvery-brown paddocks, the rocky hills of Sandalwood.

In the huge sky two crows were calling. Now he was in Rick's country.

'Mummy,' he said, in the car again, 'will I sleep in Rick's room?'

'I don't know,' his mother said. 'That depends on Rick.'

'I want to,' he said.

'I expect you will. But you're not to be a nuisance to Rick.'

'I'm not a nuisance,' he said, indignant.

'But you're only a little boy, and Rick's a grown-up man.'

He was somehow surprised. 'Is Rick a grown-up man?'

'He's nearly twenty-one.'

He could not think of Rick as grown-up. Rick and Aunt Kay were neither grown-ups nor children, but something other.

'He's nearly as old as you,' he said, wickedly.

'Cheeky thing,' said his mother, smiling. Whenever he asked her age she said she was twenty-one, but he knew how old she was; she was thirty-two.

The car followed the winding up-and-down road through the paddocks. In a far corner a man in a blue shirt, on a chestnut horse, was rounding up other horses.

'Look!' he said, sitting up, pointing. 'There's Rick.'

'Where's Rick?' said Nan.

'There,' he said, 'there.'

'He must be bringing in Goldie,' said his mother, 'so you can ride.'

'Oh good,' said Nan.

'*You* can't ride,' said the boy.

'She can so ride,' said his mother, 'if she wants to.'

'Well, she can't hold the reins.'

'Nor could you, when you were four.'

'I could so,' he said.

'You don't even remember.'

'I do so remember,' said the boy.

'Don't contradict,' said his mother. And he shut up. When she said 'don't contradict', she was dangerous.

There was another gate to open, beside the shearing shed. The shearing shed was old, old as Aunt Rosa, it had rifle-slits in stone walls. Inside, it smelled overpoweringly like a shearing shed.

When he had closed the gate he started running, racing the car to the house. He ran in the middle of the road, and the car crawled behind him. He ran past the tall palm tree and under the olives, he ran behind a trellis of climbing roses, and dropped to his knees on the ground. He dropped on his hands and knees and bent over the water. In the little pool three waterlilies were flowering.

'Oh,' he said, a long sigh.

The water and lily-leaves had their own smell. He gazed into the heart of the flowers. He reached out, just touching the smooth petals. 'Oh.'

Beyond the roses people were talking, Aunt Mary and Susan and his mother. 'But didn't you bring Rob?' Aunt Mary was saying, and his mother·said: 'Oh, he's there, he's gone to find the lilies.' 'I don't *like* that pool,' Susan was saying. 'I'm always afraid one of the smaller ones will fall in.' 'Well, perhaps we should have it filled,' said Aunt Mary. 'Really, it does nothing but breed mosquitoes.'

The flowers floated on the water, and he stared into their yellow hearts.

'Rob,' his mother called, 'it's not polite to hide from Aunt Mary.'

He came out from behind the roses, brushing dirt from his knees. 'Hullo, Aunt Mary,' he said, and held up his face to be kissed. Aunt Mary's cheek was soft. Aunt Mary was Rick's mother.

22

Susan was Rick's sister, and had the bluest eyes he had ever seen. All the Maplesteads had blue eyes, but Susan's were like the darkest part of the sea. Susan was holding a baby in her arms, and could not kiss him, but she reached out her hand and he shook it. The baby in Susan's arms was his cousin, and the two little boys at Susan's feet were his cousins. He had so many baby-cousins that between the times he saw them he forgot their names. He did not say hullo to them. They were too small.

'We saw Rick,' he said to Aunt Mary. 'He was bringing in the horses.'

'I expect he was getting Goldie,' said Aunt Mary, 'for you children.'

'Are *they* going to ride?' he said, meaning the cousins on the ground.

'Patrick is,' said Susan; 'aren't you, Patrick?'

'What?' said Patrick.

Patrick was eating dirt in large handfuls.

'Look!' said Aunt Mary. 'Susan, look!'

'Oh, lord,' said Susan. She gave the baby to Aunt Mary, and dragged Patrick away to the bathroom.

'He'll get sand,' Rob said. 'He'll die.'

'Don't be silly,' said his mother. 'Only horses get sand.'

She was never consistent. If Rob had been eating dirt, she would have told him straight away that he would die of sand.

The other little cousin had just finished wetting his pants and was studying the damp patch on the ground.

'Poor Susan,' said Margaret Coram. 'Three, of that age. Shall I take him? Come along, Mark.' She stooped and lifted the wet and earthy cousin, who screamed with rage.

'The baby's wet, too,' said Aunt Mary.

'I want to do weewee,' said Nan.

Suddenly the whole family had gone to the bathroom. The boy was alone in the garden.

He found that he wanted to do weewee too, and did, standing in the path. Then he started running, running out of the garden and up the road he had just arrived by, towards the stables near the shearing shed.

Rick was standing in the stableyard. He was brushing down Goldie with a big brush and puffs of dust were coming up. Goldie's back was clotted with dried mud. She had been rolling, down by the dam.

The boy looked at Rick's back. Rick was wearing a blue shirt and pale moleskins, he was wearing boots and a big hat. His arms were brown, with golden hairs, and he whistled between his teeth.

The boy slipped between the rails of the yard and came quietly across the churned-up, straw-littered ground to where Rick was and stood beside him. Goldie knew he was there, but Rick did not. After a while he said: 'Hey.'

The brush stopped moving, and Rick turned. 'Hey,' he said. 'It's my young cousin. Coming to get his hair done.' He reached out with the brush, and the boy ducked back, covering his hair with his hands.

'Don't,' he said, laughing. 'Don't, Rick.'

Rick leaned against Goldie and took off his hat. His brown hair was ridged by the hat and damp at the edges, and he rubbed at it with his wrist, still holding the brush. Rick's face was brown, which made his eyes look very white where they were white and very blue where they were blue. There was a little bit of gold in one of his teeth.

'Well,' he said. 'Where have you been?'

'Home,' said the boy.

'You didn't come and see me. I had your swag laid out on the bed, and you didn't come.'

'I've come now,' said the boy.

'It's too late. You've hurt my feelings.'

'Oh, bulldust,' said the boy.

'Hey, who taught you to say that?'

'You did.'

'Did I?' said Rick. 'You ever heard me talk like that, Goldie?'

'She has,' Rob said. 'She nodded.'

'She's a lying bitch,' said Rick.

The boy laughed and laughed, looking up at Rick's face, which he loved. 'You shouldn't say that.'

24

'Ah, but you won't tell, will you?'

'When I swear Grandma puts mustard on my tongue.'

'Does she do that?' said Rick. 'Your grandma's a fierce old lady.'

The boy was breathless, he had the giggles. There was nothing on earth less fierce than his grandma. Rick's blue eyes were fixed on him with interest.

'If everyone thought I was as funny as you do,' Rick said, 'I could go on the pictures and make a million dollars.'

'You're just goofy,' said the boy. He looked at Rick's slow smile, and the little glint of gold.

'Well,' Rick said, pushing himself off Goldie, 'this won't get the old girl's hair tidy.' He went back to brushing Goldie, raising puffs of dust out of the tawny hide, while Goldie stared into space. All the time she had not moved, she was so resigned and so old. Rick and Susan had learned to ride on Goldie. She was so old that she was the first horse Rick's brother Gordon had had for his own. She had lived through all those years, the boy supposed, in the same way: staring into space, pretending that human beings did not exist.

The saddle was standing upended by Rick's feet. 'Fish the blanket out of there for me, will you?' said Rick.

The saddlecloth smelled of horse and was covered with hairs. Held high in the boys arms it draped his head, so that he breathed horse. Then Rick reached down and lifted it, and he breathed air again.

Rick was stooping, lifting the saddle. Then he was ducking under Goldie's belly, grabbing the girth. He was buckling the girth, hard, with his tongue between his teeth and his mouth grinning.

'Right,' said Rick, and he turned. He reached under the boy's arms and lifted him high in the sky. 'Wow, you're getting heavy.'

The boy looked down from the sky into Rick's upturned face, which he loved.

'I'm six,' he said.

'Are you really six?' Rick said. 'Then why aren't you in the Army?'

'I'm going in the Navy,' the boy said, 'when I'm seven.'

He looked down at Rick laughing at him, he looked at Rick's brown throat under his chin. 'Aren't you a little wit,' Rick said. 'Well, do you want a ride?'

'Yes,' said the boy.

'Yes what?'

'Yes, Rick, I want a ride,' said the boy, cheekily.

He sat in the saddle, very high in the sky. It was a kid's saddle with leather cups instead of stirrups. Rick's arm was reaching up, handing him the reins. He took them, trying to hold them as Rick had taught him, but they were too wide for his fingers and he needed both hands.

Rick was walking to the gate, and Goldie was following. The boy looked down from the sky. He looked down on Rick holding open the gate, and closing it while Goldie waited. He looked down on Rick walking ahead in the road, being nudged now and then by Goldie's nose, but not turning. The hairs on the back of Rick's neck were golden. Two crows were crying in the sky, and everything was asleep. The day, the summer, would never end. He would walk behind Rick, he would study Rick forever.

The tennis balls were going *pong! pong!* against the racquets, and galahs were screeching over the orchard, wheeling in the late sun, eyeing the nectarines. Aunt Mary was sitting on a rug under the gumtree, surrounded by children. The gumtree reached right over the tennis court fence and dropped small nuts on the court just in front of the bench where the boy was sitting. He was sitting forward on the bench, bending over, watching the bull-ants swarm among the gumnuts.

The court was between the house and the orchard, on the slope of a long gully which sliced through the hills almost to Innisfail. The gully and the hills were rocky and dry, but the orchard was a bog, dangerous to children, a green bog of grass and reeds and cress where one might sink down in the black mud and drown. In the orchard was a crumbling cottage full of swallows' nests, but children were not supposed to go there. It stood in the bog inaccessible, like a moated castle.

All kinds of fruit grew in the orchard, planted there by Great-grandfather Maplestead, who had come from the Swan, where farmers cared about fruit. But the grapes were planted by Uncle Ernest. The grapes grew in a cage. One went in to the grapes through a door, and shut the door after. It was like being in a huge birdcage, except that this cage was to keep birds out. And near the birdcage grew the biggest figtree in the world; not really one figtree at all, but a whole family of figtrees that were constantly trailing their branches to the ground and starting new figtrees, making green tunnels and green rooms where, every now and then, one would come upon a panting sheep. Children could play hide-and-seek in the figtree and get lost. It was like a green town, with streets and houses under the rough leaves.

At the edge of the orchard grew tropical jungle. The boy did not know what was in the middle of the jungle. It was oleander and tecoma and bougainvillaea and gumtrees on the outside, but no one could go to the heart of it. From the fringe of the jungle grew the tall gumtree that was overhanging the court.

The balls went *pong!* against the racquets. His mother and Rick were playing tennis against Susan and Uncle Ernest. Uncle Ernest was old, he was old-fashioned like the boy's own father and played tennis in long white trousers. Rick was playing tennis in shorts, and his legs were brown and hard.

It seemed to the boy that he had spent a lot of time watching people play tennis: on the tennis court at home, when his mother gave the ladies the yellow drink with the passionfruit in it, and at Susan's, and at Sandalwood. In summer they played tennis, and in winter they played golf. Everybody's house was full of silver cups and silver spoons for playing tennis and golf: and Andarra, which was Gordon's house, was full of even bigger cups for playing cricket. Rick and Gordon had so many cups between them that Aunt Mary had told them not to win any more, she was sick of cleaning them. Gordon was famous for playing cricket. Even now, when he was at the war, they remembered that.

The boy looked across the court towards the garden, and went suddenly quiet inside. Frank was standing in the garden, watching the game. He was wearing his big squashed hat and a ragged waistcoat over his shirt. His old trousers were held up with string, and tied with string around his boots. His beard was shining in the sun.

Everybody loved Frank: Aunt Mary and Uncle Ernest and Rick and Susan and everyone. He was part of their childhood. He was part of everyone's childhood. He was so old that he could have been part of Aunt Rosa's childhood. But the boy was awed to silence by him.

Frank had been at Sandalwood since he was nine years old. When he was nine, he had walked to Sandalwood from Perth, walking the three hundred miles quite alone because he belonged to no one. And he had stayed. Once he had gone away to war and earned some land of his own. Then for a while he had gone everywhere, looking at land. And at last he had come back to Uncle Ernest, of whose childhood he was a part, and said there was nowhere he could live, no land he could want, but Sandalwood.

He lived in his camp, among foxskins and rabbitskins. He carved things, he made toys, even, out of gumnuts and skins. He had taught himself to read by reading the labels on jamtins, and now he had a dictionary that he had sent away for to a newspaper in Perth. To Rick and Susan and the boy's mother he was part of their childhood. But the boy turned dumb when he saw Frank, and hid behind Rick.

Now the set was over, Rick and his mother had won. They were leaving the court and going to where Aunt Mary sat in the shade.

The boy got up from the bench and followed. Rick was lying on his back in the dry grass, his arms behind his head. The boy jumped on him.

'Hey, kid,' Rick said, 'fair go.' Rick smelled of sweat.

'Stacks on the mill,' the boy chanted, lying on Rick. 'More on still.' Nan piled on top of him, and then the two boy-cousins. Rick was lying buried in children, groaning piteously.

'Rob,' said his mother, 'don't bother Rick.'

'Help me,' Rick pleaded. 'Sue, help me.'

Susan reached down and picked off her two sons. Then Rick

bucked like a horse, and Rob and Nan fell over.

'Oh, boy,' Rick said, 'you give me a rough life.'

'You're hard,' the boy said, poking Rick in the solar plexus. 'Gosh, you're hard.'

'Hit me,' Rick invited.

Rob hit him in the midriff. It hurt his hand.

'Gosh,' he said.

'Now let me hit you,' Rick said, sitting up and doubling his fist.

The boy got up and ran. 'No bloody fear,' he said.

'Rob,' his mother said, 'did you say that word?'

'What word?' said the boy.

'That thing you say. You know what I mean.'

'He said: "Come over here",' said Rick.

'Oh, Rick,' said Margaret Coram. 'You're worse than Mother and Aunt Kay.'

'I think he should have mustard on his tongue,' said Aunt Mary.

'I *like* mustard,' said the boy.

Uncle Ernest asked, in his deep voice: 'Are we going to play another set?'

'Not me,' Rick said. 'I reckon I've earned a beer.' He stood up, stooping for his racquet, and Uncle Ernest got up beside him, standing very tall in his white trousers. Sun filtered through the gumleaves on to Uncle Ernest's grey hair and Rick's brown hair. They looked alike, brown and strong.

Aunt Mary sat on the rug among her grandchildren, talking to her grandchildren, her voice soft and kind. His mother and Susan were pretty, with blue eyes. In the garden stood Frank, who had belonged to no one, who had come to Sandalwood because he belonged to no one, who had stayed forever.

At night he lay in his bed in Rick's room, in the yellow glow of the kerosene lamp that glinted on the silver cups, on the gold letters of Rick's books that he had had when he was a law student, before he was a soldier. He lay in his bed and waited for his mother.

When she came she had the book in her hand. He said:

29

'Can Rick read to me?'

'We-ell,' she said. 'You've had all day with Rick, and he wants to talk to the grown-ups now.'

'Will you ask him?' the boy said.

'Oh, all right,' said his mother, and went out, taking the other lamp that she had brought with her.

He lay watching the door. After a while the door shone with the lamp coming back, and Rick was in the doorway, holding the lamp and an apple.

'I've been told off to read to you,' he said. 'What'll it be? How about Dicey on the Law of the Constitution?'

'I've got a book,' the boy said. It lay beside him on the bed, open at the page.

Rick put down the lamp on the chest of drawers and sat on the bed. He cleared his throat, reaching for the book. 'Mm,' he said, reading. *The Adventures of Mr and Mrs Vinegar.*

The boy loved Mr and Mrs Vinegar. They reminded him of Uncle Paul's farm, the smell of bread rising by the wood-stove, the smell and hiss of the Aladdin lamp, Aunt Molly reading. Now Aunt Molly and Uncle Paul were in the Air Force. But there was still Mr and Mrs Vinegar; there was still Rick to read to him, by the fainter, yellower light, in the room that smelled like a man.

Rick was chewing, crunch-crunch, on his apple. He swallowed. 'Right,' he said. 'Here goes.

One day Mr Vinegar said to Mrs Vinegar: "We must go on a journey, Mrs Vinegar. We must go to market."

"Yes, Mr Vinegar," said Mrs Vinegar. "Our old red cow is dead, and we must go to market to buy a new cow, so that we shall have milk and butter and cream and cheese for our supper."

('Some diet,' said Rick. 'I'll bet they weighed a ton.')

"It is a very long way to the market," said Mr Vinegar.

"Yes, Mr Vinegar," said Mrs Vinegar. "And tonight I shall bake some bread so that we shall have fresh bread and cheese for the journey."

So Mrs Vinegar baked her bread, and in the morning Mr

and Mrs Vinegar rose very early, and wrapped the bread and the big red cheese in a fresh white cloth, and prepared to go on their journey.

"We must lock the door, Mr Vinegar," said Mrs Vinegar, "because of robbers."

"Yes, Mrs Vinegar," said Mr Vinegar, "we must lock the door so that robbers may not come into our house and steal our big red cheeses."

So Mr and Mrs Vinegar locked their big green door, which Mr Vinegar had freshly painted on the previous Friday, and prepared to go to market.

Just then Mrs Vinegar stopped, and said: "Mr Vinegar."

"Yes, Mrs Vinegar?" said Mr Vinegar.

"If the robbers wish to steal our big red cheeses," said Mrs Vinegar, "they will break down our big green freshly-painted door."

"Yes, Mrs Vinegar," said Mr Vinegar, "I fear that that is what they will do."

"Let us leave our big green door open," said Mrs Vinegar, "and then it will not be broken."

Mr Vinegar considered what Mrs Vinegar had said, and at last he said: "Mrs Vinegar."

"Yes, Mr Vinegar?" said Mrs Vinegar.

"I have heard," said Mr Vinegar, "that robbers are very wild and rough, and I fear that they will break our big green door even if it is open."

Mrs Vinegar considered what Mr Vinegar had said, and her heart grew heavy.

Then suddenly Mrs Vinegar smiled.

"Mr Vinegar," she said.

"Yes, Mrs Vinegar?" said Mr Vinegar.

"Let us take our big green door from its big black hinges," said Mrs Vinegar, "and carry it with us to market, and then it cannot be broken."

"You are a wise woman, Mrs Vinegar," said Mr Vinegar. And together they lifted the big green door from its big black hinges, and tied it to Mr Vinegar's back with a big white rope, and set out on their journey.'

Rick was laughing, making little high-pitched *huh!* sounds. 'This is *mad*,' he said. He stopped reading aloud, he forgot about the boy, he was enthralled by the adventures of Mr and Mrs Vinegar.

The boy was quite happy. He lay and listened to Rick munching an apple, to Rick's *huh!* noises of amusement. He would remember always the sound of Rick eating an apple. The sound made him sleepy, he closed his eyes, he fell asleep, in the dim yellow-lit room where Rick sat laughing at robbers.

In the morning Rick's footfall on the floorboards woke him. He lay in bed and watched Rick, who was coming back from the shower in his pyjama pants and starting to dress.

He was standing in his white underclothes, opening a drawer. Then he was putting on a khaki shirt with coloured things on the sleeves.

The boy sat up in bed. Rick was pulling on khaki trousers and buttoning them. He was sitting down on his bed and putting on khaki socks.

'Those are your soldier's clothes,' said the boy, with dread.

'Yup,' said Rick. 'Do they make me look brave?'

The boy stared. The boots were red-brown and gleaming.

'Are you going, Rick?' he said, very still.

'I'm afraid so, kid,' Rick said.

'Where are you going?'

'Well, I couldn't say. The big boys don't tell me their secrets.'

'Is it in Australia?'

'I don't know. It's a secret.'

He was standing up now, in his big boots. He was leaning to look in the mirror, combing his hair.

'I wish——' said the boy. 'I wish——'

'Hey, fella,' Rick said, turning, 'don't do that. I don't like to see a man cry like that, with real tears. If a man's got to cry he'd do better to bawl his head off.'

'I'm not crying,' said the boy, with a stiff mouth.

'And I'll be back,' Rick said. 'I'll be back, and all you'll be able to see will be two eyes peering through gongs and fruit salad.'

'I wish you didn't have to,' said the boy.

'Well, I do.'

'I wish it wasn't today.'

'But you knew I was going. That's why you came, to say goodbye.'

He leaned on the chest of drawers, looking at the boy. The boy was rising, standing on his bed, so that he was almost as tall as Rick.

'I want to say goodbye now,' he said. 'Here.'

'Well, goodbye,' said Rick; the slow smile showing the glint of gold.

'Goodbye,' said the boy. And they stared at each other.

'Oh, kid,' Rick said. 'Baby. It's all right.'

'I know,' whispered the boy. 'I know.' For the first and last time he kissed Rick, crying soundlessly.

3

The boy's life had no progression, his days led nowhere. He woke in the morning in his room, and at night he slept: the wheel turning full circle, the merry-go-round of his life revolving. There had been a jolt, with Rick's going, but the grief faded, as if, when he was riding the merry-go-round, another child had climbed aboard and the merry-go-round had bumped, jolting a little on its iron stays, and then grown steady again and gone on turning. He woke in the mornings and lay watching the shafts of sunlight that fell through the vineleaves. He watched dustmotes climbing and sliding, gold in the slippery light. Down in the tennis court the windmill clanked in the easterly, and the grey-brown doves roocooed on the tennis court fence. In the grain of the shining bookcase were patterns like faces. The sea sounded gentle and far, because it was morning.

He could stand on his bed and look out of the window on to the tennis court, watching his father. When his father was at home he walked round and round in the early morning, he walked up and down the tennis court, eating an apple. The grass of the court was long and dry, because it was war, and drying weeds grew tall about the big roller. But the windmill clanked, drinking water from the well, the tank gulped, drinking water from the mill, the sprinklers turned, pattering water on the grass, and his father walked on the lawns.

The horizon was spiked with windmills, turning and turning, their broad tails shifting, meeting the easterly. The town was a town of wind, horizons of windmills, a sky for kites, a harbour white-petalled with sails. In his grandmother's house the wind sang in the keyholes. On the windswept flats, crippled gumtrees washed their hair.

The boy's life had no progression, his days led nowhere. It was summer, and he did not go to school. His life was the sea.

the merry-go-round and the swings. It was the twisting path through the scrub to the gate in his grandmother's jungle of palms. It was Aunt Kay singing *Lord Randall*, Aunt Kay at the piano. It was Aunt Kay reading, the bright rainbow on *Cole's Funny Picture Book*, the poems in the funny picture book which made him cry.

Lucy Gray took her lantern and died in the magical snow. Or did not die, but lived as a child forever, singing, a magical child. Beth Gelert savaged the wolf and rescued the baby, and died on Llewellyn's spear, a canine martyr. The boy's throat would swell, and the tears would start springing. *Blood! blood! he saw, on every side! But nowhere found his child.*

The pictures in *Cole's Funny Picture Book* were old. Aunt Kay and Grandma had had *Cole's Funny Picture Book*, and his mother and Aunt Molly and Aunt Judith had had it, and now he and Nan and all the cousins had it. Sometimes it made him laugh, although it was so sad. There was a picture called *Our Tottie, Having Seen The Gardener Plant Potatoes To Get More Potatoes, Has Planted The Pussy To Get More Pussies, Just As Mama Comes Along.* That made him laugh, because the Pussy's feet and tail were sticking up. It made him wonder, too. Grandma and Aunt Kay must have looked like Tottie when they were little, with long skirts and great big boots right up their legs. And their Mama must have looked like Tottie's Mama, with a funny cap and a great big bustle on her bottom. How could they?

He had another book full of poems, poems that did not make one laugh or cry or anything, but were simply magic. His head was full of these poems. When his grandmother sat in the garden drying her hair, he would chant to her:

> Queen Anne, Queen Anne, you sit in the sun
> As fair as a lily, as white as a wand.
> I send you three letters, I pray you read one . . .

and she would say: 'Cheeky thing.' Her name was Anne.

Sometimes, rarely, black swans would pass over the town, and the boy, looking up, would say a poem. There were no poems about black swans, but he would think of other skies, other birds, a land of snow. Words possessed his mind: a meaningless magic.

> Grey goose and gander
> Waft your wings together
> Carry the good king's daughter
> Over the one-strand river.

And there was one poem that Aunt Kay read from the book that terrified him, and he would scream.

> A man of words and not of deeds
> Is like a garden full of weeds.
> And when the weeds begin to blow,
> It's like a garden full of snow.
> And when the snow begins to fall,
> It's like a bird upon the wall.
> And when the bird begins to fly,
> It's like an eagle in the sky.
> And when the sky begins to roar,
> It's like a lion at your door.
> And when the door begins to crack,
> It's like a stick across your back.
> And when your back begins to smart,
> It's like a penknife in your heart.
> And when your heart begins to bleed,
> You're dead, and dead, and dead indeed.

That was darkness, like the dreams from which he would wake screaming, and keep screaming until his mother would come in and take him to her own bed. That was darkness like his waking dreams, like a dream he had had lying awake in his mother's bed, watching shadowy ladies trooping away from her wardrobe with all her dresses, and through the door of his father's dressing-room shadowy gentlemen with feather dusters. His mother said they were shadows, the peppertrees in the moonlight; but he had watched them half the night, and they were real. They were simply avoiding his mother, like the bear that had looked through his bedroom door, and run when his mother appeared, and come back when she went. They hid from the grown-ups, they waited to find him alone. The grown-ups did not understand. In their sheltered lives there were no such revelations of darkness.

These revelations were called nightgowns. 'Get away, you nasty old nightgown,' he yelled at them.

In the boy's memory his own past took on the enchantment of poems, so that already his uncle Paul's bleak farm at Dartmoor was transformed, was a poem, a piercing nostalgia. Anything might bring it back to him: the smell of yeast or of a certain soap, a smell of petals like the big New Guinea beanflowers sweetly wilting. He remembered a century, a whole era that he had spent with Aunt Molly, teasing wool, picking burrs from wool and teasing it for a quilt. He remembered the *ark-ark* of the crows from the ringbarked trees, the kangaroo dog he used to ride, the savage turkey gobbler he had humiliated and tamed by stripping it of a tailfeather. The farm was a smell of chaff, a taste of saltbush, a sound of water swishing in square tanks on the back of a truck. The farm was summed up in one perfect image, like a poem: a morning of mist, himself at the door, saying: 'What, look at what?' and then seeing, and sighing: 'Oh.' Sighing: 'Dawn's got a foal. Oh.'

His days revolved, they moved towards no culmination. His mother turned out the light and he lay in the dark. At night the windmill clanked in the sky and the sea roared to the southward. The sea moaned through his childhood, a morning sighing, thumping in winter rains. In the country, trees took the place of the sea, trees sighed him asleep. But the seasound to which he was born was the first sound, the beginning and ending of all his circling days.

It began to be nearly Christmas, and the boy's Aunt Judith came to stay with Grandma, bringing two girl-cousins too small to be interesting. Aunty Judith had a soothing laugh which made him feel comfortable. Now Grandma was cooking things all the time, making cakes and biscuits, and when she had finished with the basins she put them on a table out on the lawn, so that Rob and Nan and the cousins could 'lick the basin', running their fingers round the basins and licking them. They were a trial to Grandma, who was hot in front of the wood-stove, but she let them make dough-men and bake them in the oven. And when she got tired of the children she would give them each a biscuit with a face on it, made of currants, and say: 'Now, run away laughing.' They called the biscuits run-away-laughings. 'Grandma, can I have a run-away-laughing?'

In the mornings Aunt Kay made toast in front of the wood-stove, holding a newspaper before her face to keep off the heat. Aunt Kay's face got red in the light from the jamwood logs. The wood smelled like raspberry jam when it lay on the hearth, and like toast when it was burning.

On Christmas Eve the boy could not sleep. The pillowslip hung at the bed-end gaping for presents, and he lay listening to the sea. Then he heard his father and mother coming, creeping, or trying to creep, but his father's big boots made a noise like chopping wood. He heard the rustle of presents going into the pillowslip, and lay with his eyes closed, giggling inside, thinking: 'Father Christmas wears Army boots.' He had half a mind to tell them that he knew about Father Christmas.

The morning was rustling parcels, the smell of new presents, the soap-smell that Grandma Coram's presents always had, bright string and paper. They went to dinner at Grandma's, the big table in the dining-room surrounded by relations. The cousins compared presents, coveted presents, offered to swap presents, and fought. The cousins belonging to Susan had presents from Rick, and the boy was jealous. He only had a present which said: 'From Aunt Mary and Uncle Ernest and Rick.'

In the evening the grown-ups sat in deck-chairs in the cool, and the children crawled and rolled on the fresh lawn. Rob sat in the grass beside Aunt Kay and played with a toy merry-go-round which made music as it turned. It belonged to his cousin Jenny, and he did not intend to give it back.

The grown-ups were talking, a quiet sound in the background of the tinkling music. One word they kept saying again and again. He repeated it to himself. 'Hong Kong,' he said, listening to it. 'Hong Kong.' He giggled inside. It was such a goofy sound.

One night the boy woke in the dark, and the world had gone mad and screaming. There were roaring, screaming sounds in the night, then shriller, sharper, multitudinous screaming sounds closer at hand. From the drawing-room came loud voices.

He got up in the dark and ran, running towards the lighted drawing-room, which was full of ladies and men and soldiers, standing up and drinking from glasses and kissing each other.

He stood in the doorway in his pyjamas, and his mother came towards him, with blue eyes.

'What's the matter, Rob?' she said, bending down to him. 'Did you have a nasty old nightgown?'

'No,' he said, breathing shakily. 'It's the noises.'

'Oh, that's just grown-ups being silly,' his mother said. 'The ships are blowing their sirens and people are tooting their car-horns because it's New Year.'

'What's New Year?' said the boy, still trembling.

'Well, it's a different year from last year, with a different number. Yesterday it was 1941, and today it's 1942.'

'Happy New Year, Robbie,' someone called .

He stood in his pyjamas thinking about it, until it seemed to make sense. Happy New Year. 1942 was a happy new year, and people were tooting their horns, getting ready to be happy. 1941 was a sad year, when Rick had gone away. Now they were going to be happy, and Rick would have to come back again, because there was only one place to be happy, and that was here.

Aunt Kay was reading a poem by her sister, Aunt Margaret, very sadly. It was called *The Old Wool Shed*, and it was about their station in Victoria. It seemed that Aunt Margaret had had a lot of fun in the wool shed, but now it was burnt down, and the white ants were eating the posts of it, and there were very mournful birds in the bush that chilled her heart. Aunt

Margaret's poem went on getting sadder and sadder, until at last she said:

> So I leave thee in the gloaming—
> But in dreams I'll see thee still.

And that was the end. The boy felt unsatisfied. It was sad, but not sad enough to make you cry.

'No,' he said, thus removing it from Aunt Kay's repertoire. 'Now sing *Lord Randall*.'

'How you love *Lord Randall*,' Aunt Kay said. 'I don't really think it's a song for little boys, but still.'

'Did you sing *Lord Randall* to Rick when he was little?'

'I don't remember,' Aunt Kay said. 'I expect so. He and Susan were often here, with the girls.'

'Where is Rick now?' said the boy.

Aunt Kay was quiet for a moment. She looked shy, with her eyes down. Then she said: 'I really don't know, Rob.' She drummed with her long fingers on the dark red cloth that covered the dining-room table, looking shy. The gold of the bloodstone ring shone under the low light.

'Poor wee lad,' she murmured.

'Who? Rick?'

'He's far from home, on his twenty-first birthday.'

'Is it Rick's birthday?' said the boy, pleased. 'Did you send him a present?'

'Oh—no,' said Aunt Kay, looking shy. 'But when he comes home, we'll give him one. We'll give him one for every birthday he's missed.'

'Will he miss many birthdays?'

'I really don't know,' said Aunt Kay, vaguely. Then she began to give him a ride, and he forgot. She bumped him up and down on her knee, reciting:

> This is the way the farmer rides:
>   Jig jog, jig jog.
> This is the way the lady rides:
>   Trit trot, trit trot.
> This is the way the gentleman rides:
>   Gallop-a-trot, gallop-a-trot . . .

40

And he screamed with laugher. It was a rough ride, riding like a gentleman.

When he was at home, in his bed, he sang for his mother to come. He sang:

Mother, make my bed soon,
For I'm weary with the hunting, and I fain would lie doon.

And she came, carrying the book, and sat down by the shining bookcase, under the shining bindings of the late Dr Coram's unread books, and told the story. He listened with his eyes closed.

' "Let us take our big green door from its big black hinges," said Mrs Vinegar, "and carry it with us to market, and then it cannot be broken."

"You are a wise woman, Mrs Vinegar," said Mr Vinegar. And together they lifted the big green door from its big black hinges, and tied it to Mr Vinegar's back with a big white rope, and set out on their journey." '

'Rick laughed at that,' said the boy. 'He said it was mad.'

'Well, don't you think it's mad?' said his mother.

'Oh,' he said, 'ye-es.' But he could not see what else Mr and Mrs Vinegar could have done to protect their door. 'They should have stayed at home.'

'But then,' his mother said, 'they wouldn't have got all the gold when their door fell out of the tree on top of the robbers.'

'But they didn't need the gold,' the boy said. 'They had all that cheese.'

'Oh, you unadventurous old thing,' said his mother.

The boy laughed. He had no wish to be adventurous.

'It's Rick's birthday,' he said.

'So it is,' said his mother; and her voice had suddenly got quiet and remote. 'How did you know?'

'Aunt Kay told me.'

'Aren't you and Aunt Kay a pair of old gossips.'

'She doesn't know where Rick is,' the boy said. 'Where is he?'

Margaret Coram looked down at her hands smoothing the pages of the book. 'Come on,' she said, 'let's get on with Mr and Mrs Vinegar.'

'Where is he?' said the boy, suspicious.

'I don't know, Rob. Let's——'

'Where *is* he, Mummy?'

'Don't raise your voice to me,' Margaret Coram said, raising her voice. Then abruptly she closed the book, and said rather quietly, as if she were sulking: 'He's in Malaya.'

A man appeared in the starlit rectangle of the doorway. He stood swaying for a moment. Then he stumbled forward into the hut, he let himself fall, and lay with his face against the dank floor.

The hut was pitch-dark, steam-hot. It stank of men and the tropics.

The man by the wall, whose eyes were accustomed to the hut, looked at the shape of the man who had fallen beside him. After a while he said: 'Okay?'

The man on the floor said nothing. His mouth was in the dirt.

'You all right?' whispered the man by the wall. He reached out to the other man. 'Hey, mate.'

The man on the floor said nothing.

'That's blood,' said the man by the wall. 'Hey. What did they do? Are you hurt?'

The voice of the other man came out of the dirt muffled. 'Not mine,' he said. 'Not mine.'

'What happened? Are you hurt?'

'I'll live.'

'The blood——'

'I don't know his name,' said the man on the floor. 'We were tied together. They cut his head off.'

'Oh, Christ,' breathed the other man.

'He said: "Sport, we can't be worried".'

The man in the dark by the wall was hardly breathing. He said: 'You, what about you?'

'I'll live.'

'You need help?'

There was no answer from the man on the floor, who seemed to be sleeping, his face in the dirt.

After a time, the man by the wall said: 'Listen.' He touched the other man. 'Listen, do something for me.'

The voice in the dirt said: 'Yes.'

'You a 'Groper, too?'

'Yes.'

'If the torch shines on me—or one of the firing squads finally fires—and you get back—tell the folks.'

'Yes.'

'Hugh Mackay,' said the man by the wall. 'Midland Junction.'

'I'll remember.'

The darkness stirred and sighed, and stank of men. The man on the floor did not seem to be alive.

'What about you?' whispered Hugh Mackay. 'What's your name?'

The voice in the dirt seemed hardly certain. 'Richard Maplestead,' it said. 'Geraldton.'

'Got it. So—good luck, mate.'

'Mm,' said Rick Maplestead.

Outside, beyond the wall of the hut, people were moving. 'Wish me luck, Dick.' Hugh Mackay said, 'this could be——'

'Yeah. Luck. The best of British.'

He turned his head at last, laying his cheek in the dirt, looking at the shape by the wall. 'This is my twenty-first,' he said, slowly. 'I've come of age.'

'I hope you've had a very happy day,' said Hugh Mackay; and called out towards the starlit rectangle: 'Hey, you horrible little bastards. A man here wants the key of the door.'

4

Now the name grown-ups were saying was 'Singapore'. Singapore, where people went for holidays, bringing back extraordinary presents. Singapore belonged to the Japs.

When Aunt Molly came back from Singapore she brought a great box which was carved all over with trees and Chinamen. It had a brass latch, and it smelled strange. The smell was called camphor. Aunt Molly was not married when she came back from Singapore, and the box was called her glory-box.

Singapore belonged to the Japs.

Now the words grown-ups were saying were 'Batavia', 'Surabaya'. Extraordinary boats were coming into the harbour. Extraordinary women and children were living in the town, with extraordinary clothes, extraordinary birds in cages. They were coming from the Dutch East Indies, in funny boats. Some others never came. Some died, they sank under the blue water, far to the north.

Now the name grown-ups were saying was 'Darwin'. Darwin was in Australia, very far.

Then they were saying 'Broome'. And the boy was afraid. Broome was a name from his own world. The big misshapen pearls in his grandmother's drawer came from Broome, his grandfather had brought them home. Broome was a part of his grandfather's world, of his world. It was Western Australia.

'Why are they talking about Broome?' he asked his mother, with dread.

'Who is talking about Broome?' said his mother.

'Does Broome belong to the Japs?'

'No,' said his mother. 'And it never will.'

'*Why* are they talking about it?'

'Oh, if you must know,' sighed Margaret Coram, 'the Japs have dropped some bombs there.'

44

'Then they're coming,' said the boy, frightened.

'No, no,' his mother said. 'Don't be silly, Rob. The Japs can't come to Australia. God wouldn't let them.'

'Why wouldn't He,' said the boy, 'if Rick lets them drop bombs on Broome?'

One morning he saw Matthews in the tennis court with a spade. Matthews mowed the lawns, he lived in a tent by the sea and rode on a bicycle carrying his lawnmower over his shoulder. But one morning he was using a spade.

'Why is Matthews digging a hole in the tennis court?' he demanded to know.

'It's a trench,' said his mother.

'What for?' said the boy.

'It's an air-raid trench.'

'What's an air-raid trench?'

'Well, it's a hole in the tennis court. And we have to sit in it sometimes. Just in case the Japs drop bombs.'

'On *us*?' said the boy. 'Drop *bombs* on us?' He was incredulous.

But they did have to sit in it, when the air-raid sirens blew. He hated the sirens, the sound of them did something to his body, worse even than the drums of the Garrison band, which seemed with each thump to hit him in the stomach. When the sirens blew they went down the steps to the tennis court and climbed into the hole and waited. The hole was roofed with titree which let the sun in. It was hot, and the grey sand smelled strong and sour. Always they took a green bottle full of water, which grew warmer and warmer until it made the boy's tongue shrink in his mouth. There was nothing to do, and he and Nan grizzled and whined. There was nothing to do but play 'How many eggs in the bush-bush-bush?' holding snail-shells in one's closed hands while the other two tried to guess how many.

The boy had a steel helmet of his father's which he would wear in the trench, though it was too hot and too heavy on his neck to wear for long. One day when he was wearing it planes flew over, and he went to the mouth of the trench and stuck out his head to look at them.

Suddenly his mother said: 'Rob!' and grabbed him by the belt, dragging him back. 'You stupid boy,' she said. 'If those are Japs they'll see the helmet and think we're soldiers and drop bombs on us.'

He took off the helmet and went and sat by the end wall of the trench, and was quiet a long time. *If those are Japs . . .*

One night he woke up in a coffin in a grave. He woke in the dark and stretched up his arms, yawning, and felt his knuckles bang on the lid of the coffin.

He went quiet inside. Then he screamed. Then he could not scream any longer, his heart was so quiet inside him. He knelt in the coffin and pushed with his hands at the coffin lid, but he could not move it. He pushed at the coffin lid, sobbing, his tongue between his gapped teeth, his mouth grinning.

Then suddenly there was a dim yellow light. He looked down and saw beside him the fat green foot-cushions that Grandma and Aunt Kay called creepies. Beside him the dark-red curtain of the table-cloth lifted, and Aunt Kay was stooping in.

Slowly, his heart returned to beating. He was kneeling under the dining-room table. He had been spending the night with Grandma and Aunt Kay, and there had been an air-raid siren, and they had put him, still sleeping, under the table.

That was the night that a lady rushed from her house stark naked and ran for the sandhills, screaming: 'They're coming!'

His world had changed. His father was in the Garrison all the time now and hardly came home. Everywhere there were soldiers, fifty thousand soldiers, somebody said, and soldiers called Yanks with flying-boats called Catalinas took up more and more of the beach, putting up more and more fences, pushing farther and farther back the merry-go-round in the sea. The Japs bombed farther and farther down the coast, and everyone was agreed that it was the boy's town that they wanted: it was the boy's blue harbour and the silver petrol tanks and the great camouflaged wheatbins that they most desired to wreck or win.

Everything was changed. And then suddenly everything was as it had always been. Because one day his mother said that they were going to live at Sandalwood.

The boy waved his arms and cheered, and Nan copy-catted. But his mother had a funny word for going to live at Sandalwood. She called it evacuating.

That was when the boy's country, his threatened innocent Costa Branca, was seen to be again what it had been in the beginning and never really ceased to be: a frontier. His country was where the small farms ended, where the winter-rainfall ended, where the people ended. Beyond lay the open North: unpeopled, innocent.

At Sandalwood, Frank watched the small girls come back. The small girls were women, with small children.

Ernest Maplestead stood straight and tall among his acres. He thought of the land, the land rescued from Depression, the land under war. By the domed rosetree in the dam paddock dead Maplesteads lay. He walked straight and tall to the sheds in the mornings, stooping with his pocket-knife, grubbing up Guildford grass, which was threatening an invasion.

Mary Maplestead moved, secateurs in her hand, in her garden: courteous, vague, believing that life was to be lived with decorum, a certain grace.

Anne Maplestead smiled on her grandchildren, on Mrs Ernest Maplestead's grandchildren, on her daughter and Mrs Ernest Maplestead's daughter, on Frank. She had never been angry, she had never been unkind, she was a woman with no weapon but a smile. Her sister, her husband, her daughters had guarded her life: she would never, as long as she lived, sleep one night in a house alone. Anne Maplestead smiled, unthreatened, on the Maplestead clan.

Susan Bradley blossomed with sudden enthusiasms, looking again at the house that she had left to marry. She found things to paint, to alter, to plant, that had not been painted or altered or planted before. She lit the bath-heater, and stooped above the bath full of howling sons.

Margaret Coram longed for her own house, blushed for her children, and rediscovered in the garden and country around her the landmarks of her own childhood. She was shy and dry and sardonic by turns. She washed her husband's khaki clothes, and laughed at the huge old mangle in the laundry.

At Innisfail, Miss MacKay MacRae, aged seventy, climbed the hills. She stood on the flat-topped hills and opened her eyes to the country. She anatomized the past with Miss McDermott and Miss May McDermott, accepting their ferocious prejudices with their kindness. The hands with the bloodstone ring caressed horses and dogs, caressed treetrunks and flowers, and wandered on the keys of the silk-fronted piano which the deaf ears strained to hear.

Above one of the windows opening on the drive at Sandalwood were characters scratched in the plaster.

'What's that, Aunt Mary?' asked the boy, pointing. He had been staring at the characters, where their rough edges caught the sun through the peppertrees.

'That?' said Aunt Mary, looking up from cutting back geraniums. 'That's Chinese writing.'

'Who wrote it?'

'The Chinamen who built the house. I don't suppose anyone noticed them doing it.'

'What does it mean?'

'I've no idea,' said Aunt Mary. 'We hope it means: "Good luck to this house", or something like that.'

That was nice, thought the boy. Good luck to this house.

Then he thought of something else, and laughed. 'Funny if it means: "Mr Maplestead is mad",' he said.

The Easter lilies had opened, their delicate pink throats had opened around dusty stamens. A clean, clean sweetness was about them. They had no leaves. Red stems rose clean from the hard ground.

Lilies and oranges and roses. Each scent was distinct in the late summer garden.

Peppertrees smelled sharp, like ants. Berries lay on the ground, beads of dry red lacquer.

48

'I am very happy here,' he said, gravely.

'Then you must be happy,' said Aunt Mary, 'if you know it.'

'Because I know it now? Not later on?'

'Usually one knows afterwards. Long afterwards.'

'Will the war be happy,' the boy asked, 'afterwards?'

'Perhaps,' said Aunt Mary, snipping leaves like green pursed lips. 'For some people. Some people's memories are always happy.'

Two twenty-eights flashed fire, green fire, in a gumtree. 'My memories are always happy,' said the boy.

Around the corner, in front of the house, small children were laughing. The rope swing swooped in the shade of the dark olives. Ripe olives smeared the face of a small boy cousin. And another cousin flew over him, propelled by Nan.

The waterlily pool was a barrow of fresh-turned earth. The flowers were gone, for the safety of the children.

He walked round the house, in the path by the wide veranda. Beneath the veranda lay cellars of ancient treasure, where Nan had found a windchime, a tiny tinkling chandelier.

He climbed the steps in the shadow under the olives, and stood in the cool alley between the house and the kitchen block, and took the white mug from the sweating waterbag and drank. Water, rainwater, tasted like itself. His eyes looked back at him from the bottom of the drained mug.

A tall begonia grew in a pot by the waterbag. Its leaves were dark-green taffeta spotted with white. He touched it. I am happy here, he thought.

The back veranda was cool, it was green, shadowed in with feathery fern. He stood beside the dark begonia and looked down the veranda.

On the veranda were boxes and cartons ranged by the wall. His mother and Susan came out of the house with another carton and placed it beside the others. The cartons had writing on them. He read: *E. C. Maplestead, Bogada Station, Mount Magnet.*

He walked down the veranda and stared at the cartons. 'Do all those boxes belong to Uncle Ernest?' he said.

'No-o,' said his mother, evasively. 'They belong to everyone.'

'What's in them?'

'Oh, clothes and things. Toys and books.'

'My toys and books?'

'Some of them.'

'Where are they going?' he demanded, indignantly.

'To Bogada. Don't ask so many questions, Rob.'

'Where's Bogada?' he insisted. 'Why are they going to Bogada?'

'Bogada's a station,' said his mother, tiredly. 'It's a long way away, it's inland, and we might all be going to live there.'

'I don't want to go away. I want to stay at Sandalwood.'

'You can't, Rob. There'll be nobody here.'

'Where will Grandma be? What about Aunt Mary and Uncle Ernest?'

'If we go, they'll come too. We'll all be evacuating together.'

The boy was red with rage. 'But we *are* evacuated!' He was aware that Aunt Mary had appeared on the veranda with her secateurs, and somehow also aware that she was sympathetic. 'I want to stay, Aunt Mary,' he said, plaintively.

'But it will be *fun*, Rob,' his mother was saying. 'We'll take all the cars, and some sheep, and some cows, and we'll just drive and drive until we get to Bogada, and then the nasty old Japs will never find us.'

'I want to stay with Aunt Mary,' said the boy.

'But Aunt Mary's coming,' said Margaret Coram. 'Aren't you, Aunt Mary?'

'Well, I don't know,' said Aunt Mary. She snipped off a piece of fern. 'After all,' she said, mildly, 'somebody has to bury Frank.'

The boxes went away, but the people did not. The boxes lay on an inland siding, and the black ladies opened them and tried on the white ladies' clothes. At some point that the boy did not observe, the Great Trek was scrapped. It became family history, slightly comical.

At the head of the table in the big dark dining-room Ernest Maplestead carved and carved. Children's plates came back for second helpings, and he was still carving.

Above his head the horses of Rosa Bonheur plunged and reared.

Anne Maplestead bathed her grandchildren and Mrs Ernest Maplestead's grandchildren. Blackboy popped in the bath-heater, smelling of resin. The bathroom breathed of resin, and jamwood bark, and a certain soap.

The boy and Nan and their cousin Patrick sneaked to the orchard. They picked their way through the green bog and stood in the cottage. Through the empty windows swallows swooped to and from their brown mud nests.

Rabbits thronged to the dams at sundown, and Ernest Maplestead trapped them with fences. The rounded furry bodies milled in the traps, and the children shouted. 'I want a black one,' Rob cried; and they gave him a black one, which scratched him. He put it in a birdcage, and lost interest, and forgot to feed it, so they let it go. But it would not go. It stayed round about, like Frank.

The hens cackled in the morning and in the evening. Their suspicious heads turned from side to side. The warm eggs lay just showing under their breast-feathers. Their beaks darted unconfidently at children's hands.

'Chook-chook-chook-chook,' called the children, scattering wheat. 'Come along, chookies. Chook-chook-chook-chook.'

The smooth eggs nestled in billycans of chaff.

In the shearing shed, the wood of pens and tables and press was slick with wool-grease. With awe and affection they stroked the smooth old wool-press. 'You could fill that up with Japs, and then squash them flat.'

And Jock danced and danced around them. They were not allowed to pet him, a working dog. But wherever they went, Jock danced from side to side.

They rode on sheep, fingers deep in the greasy wool. 'Giddup, giddup,' they shouted, kicking the wool. But the sheep stood still, and made lost, unhappy noises.

'I want to ride Goldie,' the boy said. 'I want to trot.'

'Not now,' said his mother. 'Later, when you're bigger.'

'When Rick comes home, he's going to teach me to *gallop*.'

'Well, wait till then. Wait till Rick comes home.'

The nights grew cool, and the summer that had lasted so long, since before Pearl Harbour, merged in the perfect neutral season of autumn-spring. Between summer and winter, between winter and summer, came these days of cool, sharp mornings and midday warmth, when cold wind and hot sun worked together to shake loose the odours from the earth. Dew wet the dead grass, and sun dried it, drawing up a smell of hay. When the sun went down behind the hill copper-sheened with rye-grass, it went down in a bushfire of cloud.

The first May rain was acrid in the nostrils. Falling in the warm afternoon, it bounced in the dust; it splashed on dry woodwork and dry bark, and the summer-shrunk fibres relaxed with a bitter smell. At night, the iron roof over Rick's yellow room roared with rain.

Now the paddocks grew green, and the disc-plough sliced up the fallow. The hard-packed clods shone where the plough had sheered them. Pale shoots veined the clods, struggling to put out leaves.

Crows were the summer's sound, and the winter's was plovers. The children went to the paddocks with billies and table-knives. They hunted, among cowpats and sheep droppings, the new white mushrooms, while the plovers cried *tew-tew-tew-tew* above them.

The hard, sharp land grew soft under green. Sourgrass sprang in the garden paths, and the children chewed the acid stems.

Even the milk came home in the buckets a different colour. 'Winter is very different,' said the boy, staring into the frothing buckets, by the whirring separator.

The cream dripped into the basin making slowly subsiding coils.

Aunt Mary was planting flowers, planting vegetables: trowels and forks in her hands, bags under her knees. The children's knees ground in the dirt, their hands scooped up earth, assisting Aunt Mary.

In the garden paths, piles of weeds bitterly rotted.

'Isn't Sandalwood *interesting*?' said the boy.

They chased one another in the rain, wet wheat-sacks hooding them.

'Where does Daddy live?' asked Nan. And the boy did not know.

'Where's Uncle Rick?' asked their cousin Patrick.

'Uncle Rick is winning the war,' replied Patrick's mother.

Rain fell, and they stomped the verandas on stilts made of jamtins. 'I can run,' said the boy. 'I'm taller. I'm six.'

They fought in the bathtub, dark-rimmed with rich Sandalwood loam.

'Really,' said Mrs Charles Maplestead, 'what dirty little grubs you are.' She soaped their smooth backs, and rubbed at their hair with harsh towels. They laughed, or screamed with rage, depending on mood.

The boy lay in bed in Rick's room and noticed that he smelled of a certain soap. He lay in the yellow glow of the kerosene lamp listening to his mother read to himself and Nan. He did not like sharing Rick's room with his mother and Nan. He would not let his mother move Rick's ebony brushes from the chest of drawers or put anything there of her own.

Yet he was somehow surprised that on this point she was so easy to manage.

'Doesn't Rick write letters?' he said. 'Doesn't anyone *know* where Rick is?'

'Oh, yes,' said his mother: vaguely, coldly. 'We know that Rick is in Malaya.'

'He's very lazy,' said the boy, virtuously, 'not writing letters.'

'I expect he's busy now,' said Margaret Coram.

The boy was older than the other children, and allowed to go farther, and that was how he came to go with Uncle Ernest to a far place. It was so far that he could not tell where it was, somewhere miles and miles beyond Sandalwood, beyond even Andarra, in a fold of the smooth green hills. It was a white two-storied house with sagging verandas, and nobody lived there. Thistles grew in the windowsills and knocked against windows where nobody lived.

The boy stood by the kitchen door where Uncle Ernest had left him, among kerosene tins and basins falling to pieces in the weeds. He stood in the weeds and looked up at the windows. And from the windows a face looked down and vanished.

It is somebody dead, thought the boy, quiet with excitement. Now he knew for certain that this land was haunted.

'Were you there, Uncle Ernest?' he asked; breathless, hopeful. 'In the window, up there?'

'Mm?' said Uncle Ernest. 'Up there? No. No.'

So the boy knew, with elation, that in an unknown house he had seen somebody dead.

He could hardly wait to tell Aunt Kay.

When he told Aunt Kay was when they met for a picnic, she coming from Innisfail and the others from Sandalwood. They were walking on a steep rocky hillside, clutching at trees, when he told her.

'Well,' said Aunt Kay, and she was laughing at him, 'perhaps you have the second sight, like our grandmother.' Aunt Kay never said 'my' grandmother, but always 'our'.

'I sometimes feel that I have the second sight,' said Mrs Charles Maplestead. 'After all, our grandmother had it, and I *am* the seventh child of a seventh child.'

'Susan,' whispered Margaret Coram, 'listen to the Weird Sisters.'

'Oh, you girls,' said Mrs Maplestead, blushing. 'You don't believe in anything.'

'Mummy believes in something,' said the boy. 'She thinks she's a water-diviner.'

'So I am,' said his mother. 'And so is Gordon.'

'And there's no question about that,' said Susan. 'We all saw you two divine a forty-foot well with a windmill on it.'

The boy perceived that nobody wanted anybody else to be good at anything. He clung, nevertheless, to his ghost.

They were walking along the steep side of a gully, high up, near the ridge of fox-holed rock that marked a flat hilltop. Their feet slithered on small stones, and Mrs Maplestead and Miss MacRae stumbled, light black coats flapping, hands reaching out for support from wattle and jamb. Their progress was marked by sudden clatterings, as sheep leaped to their feet and pranced away. Down below in the gully grey-green trees looked soft and cloudy, so diffused was the winter light.

'Where are we going?' Nan asked. 'When will we be there?'

54

'We're going to the Hand Cave,' said her mother.

'What's the Hand Cave?'

'Just you wait and see.'

The trees above the Hand Cave were sheoaks, and sighed continually in the breeze. Closing his eyes, the boy imagined a grey moor, where no foot of man or sheep had ever trodden. The sound of the sheoaks was a sighing mixed with a razor-sharp whistling. It was the speaking voice of utter desolation.

They stopped at the open front of the cave, below the keening trees.

'Are we there?' asked Patrick.

'What's here?' asked Nan.

They were standing in the rust-coloured rock shelter, curiously fretted by water into little galleries.

'Hands,' said the boy, wondering.

The walls of the cave were covered with hands, silhouettes of rock-coloured hands on a background of clay.

'Whose hands?' said the boy.

'Look, Mark,' Susan was saying. 'The old blackfellows' hands.'

'Are they dead?' said the boy.

'Oh, long ago,' said Mrs Maplestead.

'Look, Rob,' said his mother, taking his hand and fitting it over one of the prints on the wall. 'It's a little boy's hand.'

'Gosh,' said the boy, softly, his hand on the cold rock. 'Gosh.'

The sheoaks sighed overhead. It was the loneliest place that had yet been found in the world.

'They put their hands on the wall,' Susan was saying, 'and filled their mouths up with clay and water, then they went *prrrmph!* like a horse, and sprayed it all over their hands, and left the marks on the wall.'

'Why?' asked the boy, very far away. But nobody heard or answered.

He felt lonely, even with all these people.

'It's a pity Ernest has such a down on the blackfellows,' Mrs Maplestead was saying. 'I used to think the Sandalwood stockmen were so colourful, with their bright shirts.'

'I think Dad's quite right,' Susan said. 'I wouldn't have one on the place, if it were mine. They've been enough trouble up at Bogada.'

'Poor creatures,' sighed Aunt Kay.

'Are they like the blackniggers in town?' the boy said. 'Did the blackniggers in town make the hands?'

'No,' said his mother. 'Quite, quite different. These ones lived in the Old Days.'

'What's *wrong* with the blackniggers?' the boy asked, curious.

'Oh—nothing,' said his mother. 'They've got bugs in their hair, that's all.'

He felt the cold rock under his hand, where a dead boy's hand had once rested. Time and change had removed this child from his country, and his world was not one world, but had in it camps of the dispossessed. Above the one monument of the dead black people, the sheoaks sounded cold, sounded colder than rock.

From the road outside the homestead paddock came the constant low complaint of sheep. The farmhand, Bryn, emerged from the kitchen, and set out across the paddock with long strides.

'Where are you going?' the boy called.

'Movin' sheep,' said Bryn.

'Can I come?' shouted the boy.

Bryn said nothing, striding the green paddock in the bright sunlight.

As the boy began to follow, the sunlight changed. Something came over the sun, a kind of dusk. Bryn was passing through the gate by the long stone building where the garages were, and from the middle of the paddock the boy could hardly see him. As he himself reached the gate, night fell.

The night lasted an unreckonable time. When it began to lift he was aware of Rick's face bending over him, but Rick's face curiously distorted, sometimes having three noses, so that he wanted to laugh, although he was scared. Other faces came and went beside Rick's, similarly distorted, his sister's and the small cousins' among them. Then all the faces dropped away and gave place to one normal face, the face of his grand-mother, who stood by the bed where he lay.

His grandmother looked old. Turning his head a little on the pillow he could see his mother, and she, too, looked old.

'Am I——' he said and stopped, because his voice sounded funny. 'Am I sick?'

He tried to sit up, and that hurt him. His grandmother pressed him back, gently.

'Where's Rick?' he asked, after a time.

They would not answer.

'Rick was here,' he said. 'He looked funny. Where is he?'

'He wasn't here, darling,' his mother said. 'You were dream-ing.'

'I saw him,' the boy said, feebly. Weak, silent tears ran down his battered face. 'I want Rick. Please. Where's Rick?'

'You were dreaming, Robbie,' his grandmother said. 'You were delirious.'

'I want Rick,' he said again, faintly; and then fell asleep, tears drying on his scored cheek.

He had nearly died. Frank had said over and over: 'The boy won't live the night.' But the boy had confounded him.

Following the sheep, he had stopped to climb a gumtree down by the creek. Then Uncle Ernest had called in his deep voice: 'Rob, come down,' and he had made the descent of twenty feet by the quickest route.

That was why night had fallen at the paddock gate, twenty minutes before. He had walked into the darkness of amnesia, spreading out like a stain from the moment of his fall. Time, therefore, was more mysterious than he had guessed. It seemed that once, the first time, he should have crossed the paddock in bright sunshine; only on a second crossing going to meet the spreading darkness which should not have had existence before then. Time confused him and possessed his mind, like a riddle which might have the answer to every riddle.

He began to take some pride in his scratched and scabby face, the mark of near-death. But he was quieter now. On a grey day, he and his mother made a melancholy pilgrimage to the trees by the creek, to look for his memory.

He remembered nothing, nothing at all.

'Perhaps it's that tree,' said his mother, 'with the big hole, where you hit the ground.'

'I don't remember,' the boy said. 'I just don't.'

He stood by the hole, which pigs had dug, and which smelled of pigs and wet gumleaves.

'Did I really dream Rick?' he said. 'Wasn't he there?'

'You know he's away, darling,' said his mother.

'I was sure he was there. I think he was, really.'

His mother scratched lines in the leafy ground with the stick she was carrying. She said: 'Rob——'

'Yes?'

'Please, don't talk about Rick. Not here.'

'Why?' said the boy, staring at her. *'Why?'*

'It upsets Aunt Mary. Just forget him.'

'I can't,' the boy said, indignantly. 'I can't forget *Rick*.'

'Well, don't talk about him, except to me.'

The grey sad day dulled the gumleaves and gave them a smoke-blue tinge. Presently it would rain. To the north the sky was almost violet.

The boy said, very slowly, and looking his mother in the eye: 'Did Rick get killed in the war?'

'No!' said Margaret Coram. 'Well—we don't know.'

'If he got killed, someone would tell you.'

'Not—where Rick is, in Malaya. He might be a prisoner. The Japs might be keeping him——'

'They'll torture him!' cried the boy, with staring eyes.

'Rob! Don't talk like that!'

'I want Rick home,' the boy said. 'I want him home.'

A faint patter of rain came on the leaves above them, and Margaret Coram moved. 'Let's go back,' she said. 'Quickly, or we'll get soaked.'

'Can I write to Rick?' the boy asked, very quiet. He was not crying. He was too still inside for that.

'Yes,' said his mother, 'yes, we can keep sending letters, and hope that he gets them. Aunt Mary and Susan do.'

'If I *think* to him,' the boy said, 'he might hear me thinking.'

Fat drops were falling on the dead leaves around them. The smoke from the house spread out directionless in the rain.

'Yes, think to him,' Margaret Coram said. 'That's what all the rest of us are doing. And perhaps, when you thought you saw him——'

She had enough of the Celt in her not to laugh at what she was saying. And the boy, who was all Celt, believed utterly.

'I know,' he said, grinning now, gap-toothed and scab-faced. 'I know. He was thinking back.'

The small car stood in the drive with the boot open. Margaret Coram leaned into the boot, stowing a suitcase.

'Why are we evacuating again?' asked the boy, idly.

'Oh, just to give Aunt Mary a rest from us. We've been here for three months—and you've been quite a worry.'

'Yes,' said the boy, rather proud of himself.

The garden smelled of wet orange-blossom and roses.

'Well, goodbye, Sandalwood,' said the boy.

People were coming with boxes and children and farewells. The wet sunlight smelled of orange-blossom and roses. On the lintel above the office window were undeciphered characters, meaning perhaps: *Bless this house*, or perhaps: *All the Maplesteads stink*.

5

In the winter sunlight, warm out of the wind, the boy sat staring down the street from the back of a battered pick-up. He was bored. He was counting up all the things he could see that began with H, and they were running out.

Just then he saw old Mrs Thickbroom. *'Hag,'* he said to himself.

From the bar-window across the foothpath came a constant roar of voices, punctuated with huge laughs. He found it soothing, rather. He looked towards the window and saw a soldier looking out. *'Hat,'* he said to himself, looking at the slouch hat by the man's elbow. Then he remembered that he had counted that one.

'Hey, you,' the soldier said to him.

'What?' said the boy, feeling shy.

'Don't just sit there. Come an' 'ave a drink.'

'I'm not allowed to,' said the boy, 'thank you very much.'

He felt that he must sound like Aunt Rosa, who had refused a bag of sugar from a soldier because her Papa had told her never to accept gifts from gentlemen.

'Whatcha doin'?' asked the soldier.

'I'm waiting for my mother,' Rob said, politely.

'You a bush kid? Yeah, y'are, I can tell by that scrap'eap yer sittin' in.'

'I'm a bush kid now,' Rob said, 'but I used to be a town kid before the war.'

'Where d'yerz live?'

'Andarra.'

'Where'zat?'

'It's a house,' Rob said. 'It's my cousin's house.'

'I'm a bush kid,' said the soldier in the window, grinning vaguely into the street, and blinking, because he was drunk. He had thin fair hair and crooked teeth.

'You're not very old,' said the boy, 'are you?'

'How old d'yer reckon I am?' said the soldier.

'You're not grown-up,' said the boy.

'I'm eighteen,' said the soldier. 'Eighteen, an' never been pissed.' He belched, and laughed. Then he turned back into the bar and shouted at the top of his voice: 'I'm eighteen, an' never been pissed.'

Another soldier came and pushed him up against the windowsill and said: 'Save it, willya?'

'I got a mate,' the first soldier said. ' 'E's a bush kid like me, an' 'e never let a drop past 'is lips.'

He leaned out of the window, the other soldier leaning on his shoulder. 'Washa name, kid?' he said.

'Rob,' said Rob.

'My name's Reg,' said the drunk soldier, 'an' this 'ere's Tom, the deadliest murphy-peeler in the Forces.'

'How do you do?' said the boy.

'Whatcha doin' 'ere, kid?' Tom asked.

'Just waiting for my mother,' said the boy.

'Whyn'tcha go an' buy yerself an ice-cream or somethin'?'

'I haven't got any money,' said the boy, embarrassed.

' 'E 'asn't got any money,' Reg said. 'The poor kid 'asn't got any money.'

'Here, kid,' Tom said. 'Catch.'

Something fell on the floor of the pick-up. It was sixpence.

'Gosh,' said the boy. 'Thanks.'

' 'E 'asn't got any money,' Reg was shouting at the bar at large. 'The poor kid 'asn't got any money.'

Something else fell in the pick-up. It was a penny.

'Gosh,' said the boy.

Then he was hit on the head by a halfpenny. After that, the storm broke.

He scrambled about the pick-up grabbing at coppers. They fell like a long burst of hail. Hairy arms were reaching out of the window, flinging largesse, and Reg was still shouting: 'The poor kid 'asn't got any money.'

'I've got lots of money,' the boy shouted back, still raking it in.

It was like a dream. He was going to be a millionaire.

Then slowly the shower eased off. After a time the window was empty, except for Reg blondly and muzzily grinning into the street.

'You got enough for an ice-cream, kid?' he asked.

'Gosh,' said the boy, breathless.

He counted it up. Apart from the sixpence, he had one-and-ninepence-halfpenny in coppers. The coins were sticky with beer.

'I've never had this much money,' he said.

'I'll tell yer somethin', kid,' Reg said, 'just for yer own good. Don't spend it on women.'

'No,' said the boy, who had no intention of spending it on women. He meant to spend it on the soldiers.

'Hey, Reg,' someone called inside the bar, 'yer gunna let me drink this?'

'I'll see yer kid,' Reg said, and disappeared.

The boy climbed over the side of the pick-up and made off down the street, the weight of the money in his pockets dragging at his pants.

Then he ran into the blue skirt and bulging shopping-bag of his mother.

'Where are *you* going?' she demanded. 'I told you to stay in the Bug.'

'I was going shopping,' he said. 'I was going to Snells to buy some presents for the soldiers.'

'What with?' she said. 'Why?'

He could see that there had to be explanations, a thorough hearing, and grudgingly he dragged the money out of his pocket. 'They threw me all this,' he said, 'while I was sitting in the Bug. So I was going to buy them something.'

She was laughing at him. 'That won't buy many presents for a bar full of soldiers.'

'Well, something. Ice-creams, or something.'

Now she was giggling, like a little kid. 'I'd almost give a donation, just to see a line-up of soldiers licking ice-creams at the bar.'

'Well?' he said, hopefully.

'No, Rob—they don't want anything. They've got plenty of money to throw away.'

The boy felt mean. He followed his mother back to the Bug, and he felt more and more like Scrooge. The men he had failed were making happy noises in the bar, but there was no one at the window. And no way, it seemed, that he could explain to his mother that all private soldiers were Rick.

Now that the boy lived at Andarra, he lived in an enchanted place.

Andarra lay cut off from the world (and the world was uninhabited) by a forest of gums springing out of mysterious ground in which an underground creek came and went without warning, at times undermining the road to the house, and then vanishing. Among the gumtrees were pools and mud-holes smelling sometimes of pigs, and always, hauntingly, of rotting gumleaves and the tender new leaves of saplings, so that the boy and his cousin Didi on some days would throw back their heads and sniff the air with pure pleasure, like dogs. Or harrumph, like horses, since Didi was usually pretending to be a horse.

Past the thicket began an avenue of gums and ficus and kurrajong and dark unfamiliar trees with fragrant leaves, in which lay smooth gumnuts, felt by the children to be in some way valuable, although they could find no use for them. The avenue was a green tunnel leading nowhere. At the end of the avenue was the closed gate of the wild garden.

The garden was a riot, a jungle, which could not be comprehended in its entirety. It was a tall palm tree rattling high in the sky above the gate. It was dark clumps of olives and oleander. It was a hedge of sour, clean-smelling citrons. It was a stone well in a thicket of curtain-pole bamboo. It was Geraldton wax plant grown into trees, and flowering, where children could perch like birds and talk very seriously. And for the boy, it was above all the roses.

The white roses had taken over one side of the veranda. They engulfed shrubs at the front of the house, and clothed the dead stump of an old palm. The fragile scent of them was everywhere, mixed with citrus and eucalyptus. The flowers, the dark neat leaves, became the boy's image of perfection.

He held the flowers in his hand: small white flowers opening up on a small green heart. The petals were faultless, crisp with life. They were almost too faultless to be real flowers, too alive: faultless as china or marble, alive as painting. The flowers were a scented painting he held in his hand.

'Why aren't there roses anywhere else?' he asked, curiously.

'Those are very old-fashioned roses,' his mother said. 'I suppose people have just stopped growing them.'

He thought very cynically of people then, looking at small perfection in his hand: a jungle rose.

If one went past the rose-covered stump, and up the front steps, and through the unused front door with **ANDARRA** written on it in stained glass, if one went through the big empty porch strewn with toys, one came to the children's territory. There was nothing in the huge ballroom but toys and tricycles. There was nothing in the huge dining-room but saddles and a warm-smelling incubator. There was no traffic in the broad passages but tricycles riding round and round, round and round the tomb of departed elegance.

The boy thought that Andarra must be very old, but they said it was not. They said it was Edwardian, and had been beautiful, before the Depression, before Uncle Ernest bought it for Gordon. Still, to the boy it seemed ancient and enchanted, and he stared in fascination at the glass boxes on the veranda walls where gaslamps had burned, at the diamond panes of the windows on the disused drive. It was old. It felt old. And the garden felt even older. And if it should have a ghost, then he knew who that would be. She would walk in grey silk in her garden. She would walk with some peculiar grace that made people remember her with awe. She would be Aunt Mary's dead sister, and she would walk with grace through the rose-and-citron-scented garden, holding a small white rose in her long hand.

Didi was about nine months younger than the boy, which was a vast gulf, but not unbridgeable; and although she had golden curls and long white socks, she was as good as a boy any day. Not that Didi would have wished to be a boy. Her ambition rose higher: she wanted to be a horse.

The ballroom echoed as Didi cantered around it, dragging Nan behind on the reins of a harness of string. 'Prrrrrrmph!' snorted Didi, tossing her palomino mane, and stamping and pigrooting. 'Wheeeheeheehee!' she whinnied in the resounding ballroom.

The boy was sometimes bewildered. This girl was mysterious.

In the house, aunties and children came and went. Every woman of childbearing age was an aunty, it was easier that way. Most were young mothers evacuating with their children, whose children played in the ballroom for a while and then vanished. Many of these transitory aunties brought furniture to be piled up in the middle of the ballroom, this pile steadily growing and making passage more and more difficult for tricycles, until eventually it ceased to be a ballroom at all, or even the children's territory, and became known as Mr Joseph's Room. Mr Joseph sold secondhand furniture in town.

The chief of all the aunties was Aunty Jean, because it was her house. She was Gordon's wife, and Didi's and Jimbo's mother. Of all the aunties in the known world Aunty Jean was the most accomplished rouser. The boy's mother was no mean hand at rousing children, but nobody could match the performance of Aunty Jean as she waited, hands on hips and eyes flashing, for mud-covered children to come within range. 'My-y-y *word*!' said Aunty Jean; or: 'By-y-y *Jove*!'

The children blenched, but giggled inside. They knew what Aunty Jean was doing. It was called playing to the gallery.

She played at being a tiger as Didi played at being a horse. 'Where's that bloody Harry?' she would call, storming around the veranda. And the children would giggle behind their hands.

The other two permanent aunties were Aunt Jean's sisters: Aunty Janet, who was tall and dark with a quiet voice, and Aunty Dode, who was small and dark and laughed. They were so different that it did not seem to the boy that they could be sisters. They were more different than himself and Nan. When the kids sang in the empty passages, singing ;

Bless 'em all, bless 'em all,
The long and the short and the tall . . .

it was Aunty Janet and Aunty Dode that the boy thought of.

Aunty Janet was very quiet because of something to do with the war. Aunty Dode talked goofy talk to the cats, and the kids giggled. She loved all the cats, and especially the battered Hammerhead. When Hammerhead disappeared Aunty Dode was prostrated with grief, and then raised up with joy, after the children, penetrating the moraine of furniture in the ballroom, discovered on Aunty Somebody's sofa a transformed Hammerhead radiant with motherhood.

The animals at Andarra were almost people, thought the boy, waking at night to hear a sociable horse clump round the veranda.

Certainly the pigs were people, in the pigs' opinion. When the transport came from the Army camp with a cargo of fresh vegetables and half-bags of sugar to be dumped in the paddock, the pigs and the aunties competed on equal terms. Squealing, the pigs rushed from the gum thicket. Hungrily, the aunties rushed from the house. But it was the pigs who almost always won the vegetables. They did not feel that they had to wait till the transport was out of sight.

Even so, they took no chances. They began to meet the transport farther up the road and to run with it, squealing, to the dumping-place. Gradually they came to look on any soldier as a source of food, and took to chasing even motor-bikes, so that an innocent soldier called Ian, coming to call at Andarra, was terrifyingly pursued up the sandy road, weaving and swerving in the soft ruts, by a screaming horde which finally toppled him and nosed carnivorously about the body.

' 'Struth,' said Ian, 'it's like wolves in Russia. If I'd had a baby to throw them, I'd have thrown it.'

One of the pigs was so fat that she drew little railway lines in the sand with her tits. 'Look,' said the children. 'Jemina went that way.'

With mothers and aunties they went for long walks in the winter sun. On the road to the siding, in the yellow sandplain, they stopped to talk to the Barbed Wire Boys. The Barbed Wire Boys wore only shorts and boots, and had whiskers all over their faces, which made them look more grown-up than soldiers ought to look. They lived securely defended from the enemy, first by barbed wire, and then by a rampart of bully-beef tins.

'What do they *do*?' the boy asked. But nobody knew. They were just playing.

He thought of them at night, lying out there in the dark sandplain. They were homeless, like old blackfellows.

'Does Rick live in a house?' he asked.

'I don't know,' said his mother.

'Am I allowed to talk about Rick now?'

'No,' said his mother, 'better not.'

'Why not? Aunt Mary's not here.'

'No, but—Aunty Janet's husband is with Rick, and—well, better not.'

The boy was pleased. 'Aunty Janet's husband will look after Rick, won't he?'

'Yes,' said his mother. 'I expect so.'

Outside the room, he heard her talking to Aunty Jean. 'It wouldn't be so bad,' she was saying, 'if only all the kids didn't have such a thrill on Rick.'

'They won't remember long,' said Aunty Jean.

He would, thought the boy. Nan seemed to have forgotten Rick already, but he would remember. He thought to Rick, thinking jokes and messages.

Sometimes at night, from Harry's room next to the wash-house, came sad strains of music from Harry's squeezebox. Harry played to himself, sitting on his hard bed with the grey blanket. Harry was seventeen, and was only working at Andarra while he was waiting to join the Army. This made him, in the boy's eyes, already half a soldier.

The boy admired him with a silent, wistful devotion. Harry never spoke much, but did not mind being followed. Sometimes Harry even told him things, such as that if one put one's ear against a telephone post one could hear people talking, which was not quite true, the boy found, and yet in the fibres of the wood there was a humming and throbbing as if there might be in the post some almost audible speech more interesting than anything ever spoken into the telephone. It seemed to flow up the post from deep underground, like sap.

The telephone line was nearly always down, and one of Harry's jobs was to sit up the pole holding the wires together, until some aunty waved a tablecloth at him from the house. While Harry sat up the pole, the boy stood below, and listened to the mysterious conversations of the wood.

Harry was neither a grown-up nor a child, and lived according to special rules. He ate in the kitchen, and sat with his chair tilted on its back legs, which no one else was allowed to do. Sometimes he even wore his hat. On days when Harry was feeling sociable the children would follow him to his own room and sit on the bed, and Harry would play the squeeze-box and sing to them, yodelling like a real hillbilly singer. He sang very sad songs, like *Old Shep*, and tears would swell the boy's throat, more even than for Beth Gelert, because Old Shep was not a far-off poetic dog like Beth Gelert, but an ordinary farm dog like Paddy in the yard outside. Harry's songs were about dying stockmen and deserted drovers' wives, sinking or battling on, far away in the heart of stark, bravely yodelling Australia.

Now that he had no Aunt Kay to read to him the boy was discovering Australia. He would not let his mother read the poems Aunt Kay used to read, because he could not tolerate the slightest departure from Aunt Kay's manner of reading, and so his mother was free to choose the poems that she liked. And the poems she liked were poems about Australia, about sad farewells at the slip-rail and death in the far dry distance, where the pelican builds its nest. Gradually Australia formed itself for the boy: bare, melancholy, littered with gallant bones. He had a clear idea where Australia began. Its border with his world was somewhere near his Uncle Paul's farm, in the dry red country. Once past the boundary fence, the bones would start. He built in his mind a vision of Australia, brave and sad, which was both what soldiers went away to die for and the mood in which they died. Deep inside him he yearned towards Australia: but he did not expect ever to go there.

Only Harry and the soldiers could go to Australia. He would say the poems, thinking of Harry and the soldiers.

> Tall and freckled and sandy,
> Face of a country lout,
> That was the picture of Andy,
> Middleton's rouseabout.

He did not know what a 'lout' was. But Andy had the face of Harry and all the soldiers.

And Andy, another Andy. was also Rick, to whom the boy thought, thinking:

> And may good angels send the rain
> On desert stretches sandy;
> And when the summer comes again,
> God grant 'twill bring us Andy.

But his own world was a different world, and on the road to the siding, turning at the pink gash of the cutting, he would stop and look over it: a green gentle country. The chimneys of Andarra barely showed above their sheltering trees. Paddocks stretched out to the far hills, bright with pasture, dark with wheat, silvery with young lupins in the wind. In the winter sun the hills were golden-green and blue-dark, and the air smelled of fresh pasture and the warm oils in the leaves of gum and wattle, a rough sweetness. His world was in summer a spare, bare, clean-smelling country; and in winter, a soft green fire.

The winter drew towards spring, and horses and dogs and children rejoiced in the sun. They pranced and frisked and were told to behave themselves. Impossibly far away, the war kept on happening.

It seemed that even with the war Didi and Rob needed education of some kind. And so Aunty Janet and the boy's mother became governesses, and the children were dragged to tables in separate rooms and set to learning by correspondence.

They practised pothooks and figures and wrote in copybooks, and laboriously they read the story of the Poor Wee Bairn and the Faithful Dog. But somehow nothing that they did was right. Their work went to Perth and came back with red-inked corrections. There were three ways to write the figure 4, and whichever Didi and Rob chose was the wrong way. There were also three ways of drawing a house: with the curtains down, with the curtains looped back, and with the curtains looped back in front of a half-lowered blind.

'They're all so damn suburban, anyway,' said Margaret Coram, piqued at being always wrong.

With the corrected work came the work of two paragons whom the children were to emulate. Didi was to walk in the footsteps of a little girl called Lynette White, and Rob's inspiration was a boy called Murray Long.

'Those kids didn't do that,' Aunty Jean fumed. 'Of *course* their mothers did it.'

Suddenly all the aunties were united against Lynette White and Murray Long. When there was a rush to catch the mail they drew houses themselves, and sent them off to Perth, receiving in return new houses from Lynette White and Murray Long, with encouraging notes.

'It's a pity you can't draw as well as Rick,' the boy said. Rick drew magnificent horses.

'I hope you meet that Murray Long some day,' said his mother, brooding.

'Why?' asked the boy; still wondering, years later, when he found Murray Long at Guildford, a middle-aged farmer of thirteen.

'What a *horrible* little boy he must be,' said Margaret Coram.

Spring came, and Didi and Rob spent more and more time away from the house. Day by day the paddocks grew yellower with capeweed, the sandplain turned yellow with scrubby wattle, and the hills pink and golden with heath and guinea-flower. The children trailed across the paddocks towards the hills, stopping in drifts of pink and white and yellow everlastings to pick the papery flowers. In the warm sunlight their skins tingled with the cold wind. They crawled on hands and knees through rough stems of pink-frosted heath, and sat in the sun and wind on a flat hilltop, breaking open curious round stones which were hollow inside and contained a red powder with which they painted their faces to look like Indians. The far paddocks were stained with pink and white and yellow, and on the sandplain they collected tangy flowers. The air was sweet to breathe, and the haystack musty-sweet in the sun. By a ruined cottage in the pig-paddock an almond tree flowered, twenty-eights haunting it, flashing green fire from their wings.

The peppertrees and the gums put out small green-white flowers that hummed with bees, and the blackboy spears flowered white and fuming. In the sandy paddock near the road a Christmas tree made a loud drone.

'There's a hive in there,' Harry said. 'Now, I wonder.'

The piled sticks crackled around the treetrunk, and bees went mad in the smoke. Harry reached into the belly of the tree and pulled out the scorched dripping combs. The honey tasted of smoke and banksia and gumblossom, sweet and rough like the tang of the whole country.

The huge draughthorse that Harry rode galumphed round its paddock, and Didi copied it. She galumphed through the trees, and flopped in the mud of what was called a pig wallop.

'Oh, shit,' said Didi, with mud in her flaxen hair.

'You shouldn't say that,' said Rob, shocked.

'Why shouldn't I?' demanded Didi, belligerently.

'It's a dirty word.'

'It is not a dirty word,' said Didi.

'It is,' said the boy, 'I know it is.'

'What does it mean, well?'

'It doesn't *mean* anything, it's just a dirty word.'

'It's not a dirty word,' said Didi, haughtily. 'Do you think *I* wouldn't know what's a dirty word?'

The boy gave in. She quelled him, with her yellow hair and long socks. But he brooded. He went in search of Harry, who was chopping wood, and said: 'Harry, is 'shit' a dirty word?'

'Shit,' said Harry, dropping the axe, 'where did you kids pick that up?'

Soldiers came to the house, and sometimes among the soldiers was one called Lieutenant Coram, who was the boy's father. He kissed the boy on arriving and on leaving, and the boy felt a certain awe. Lieutenant Coram was the most grown-up man he had ever seen. Even Uncle Ernest, who was also awesome, had one un-grown-up habit: he spat in the paddocks. But the boy's father was totally, flawlessly, grown-up.

The boy rather liked the look of his father, who was tall and had a face like the King. Watching him from a distance, he decided that his father was probably a nice man. But they kissed one another with great reserve, and had nothing to say.

Spring merged into summer, with green almonds and oleander. In the evenings the air was sweet with drying grass, and sheep that had been pale islands in the green paddocks slowly melted away, disappeared in the sheep-coloured landscape. The flies of spring that had danced in the sunlit windows became fat, slow, sluggish flies of summer.

The boy had his seventh birthday. There were no candles on his cake, only red-headed Yank matches.

'It's a whole year,' he said, 'since Rick went away.'

'Uncle Rick's dead,' Didi said. 'Uncle Rick and Uncle Peter got killed in the war.'

'They did not,' cried the boy, furiously. 'The Japs are keeping them.'

'Then they'll torture them,' said Didi, awed and staring.

The Christmas trees flowered on the sandy land, a hard burning orange. The boy went with Harry round the paddocks where the soldiers had built their cubby-houses. The houses were made of fresh-hacked gum branches, pungently wilting. The boy could not understand why the soldiers left them while they were still green, before they smelled so beautiful.

'Why do they build them?' he asked, sitting in the stippled shade, watching Harry rake the leaf-strewn floor for souvenirs.

'They're just practisin' jungle warfare,' Harry said.

They tried out the wilting jungle-beds. 'Not a bad life, bein' a soldier,' said Harry, lazily.

The boy thought so too, and lost any anxiety about Rick. Rick was in the jungle. Rick was lying in a hot green cave, on a sweetly dying bed in the heart of the jungle. Rick lay smoking on his bed through the heat of the day, swapping jokes with the drowsy soldiers. The beauty of the jungle had tamed the war, had reduced it to a summer game, a gentle lassitude in a cubby-house of drying leaves.

6

The boy stood on the wall and brooded over the dry weeds of the tennis court. He spat into the weeds. He was a town kid again, and he did not care for it.

Once again it was a new year, a happy new year. It was 1943, and the boy was not happy.

He was going to have to go to school again, and be a town kid, and see town kids every day. He felt at once superior and inferior to town kids. He was superior because he knew so many animals. But there were kids in town who knew lots more soldiers than he knew, there were kids who were even getting coconuts in the post, with their addresses written on the shells in indelible pencil.

Rick had never sent him anything.

When he was learning by correspondence at Andarra he had written Rick a letter, and Rick had not answered.

The boy brooded. He suspected that his mother had not posted the letter, as he suspected that she had not posted his letter to the King. The King had not answered either.

A ginger kitten was rubbing against his leg. The kitten's name was Garrison D Coy Coram. His father had brought it home in a kitbag.

Kitbag. Ha ha. He ran his finger over the silky fur behind the kitten's ears. Then he picked it up, burying his face in the warm white belly. The kitten wriggled, biting his ear, and he laughed into the fur.

It was a soldier kitten. But it was not the same as a coconut.

Still, he had a soldier's dog-tag on a leather bootlace, and no other kid had one of those. He had found it under a tree in his grandmother's garden. 'What would a soldier be doing there?' he had asked, puzzled; and no one had been able to hazard a guess.

He set the kitten down on the wall. Moodily, he threw a

stone into a cypress tree by the windmill, and a cloud of white dust came out. Funny, that, he thought: how the tree seemed to make white dust in its leaves.

The sandy trench among the weeds was falling in. Nobody was bothered about air raids any more.

The war must have moved away. He felt a vague discontent, a sense of anti-climax. Less than a year ago small yellow monsters wearing spectacles had been coming to spit babies on their bayonets. Now, out of all that dread and excitement, nothing remained but the normal town, the hole among the weeds, the soldiers and the seaplanes, and the barbed wire along the beach.

There were some changes, some reminders. Tony Boldoni who used to cut the boy's hair, in the dim shop hung with sepia racehorses, had been interned for speaking too well of Italy. Sister Rosalie, the Anglican nun, still wandered at large in her grey habit and sandals, but was known to be a man and a German spy. A couple of Jap tomato-gardeners had left forever. And when two kangaroo shooters with rifles had stopped at Arnie Saarinen's farm, Arnie Saarinen had come out with his hands up.

Arnie Saarinen was a Finn, and confused about the war.

There were still blackout curtains, blackout hoods over the car headlights. But the urgency was gone.

Living at Andarra, a trip to town had been an event, a long venture through counted familiar landmarks. Now the town was nothing. A horizon of windmills, a sky for kites, a harbour for fewer and fewer sails. He knew all this. There was nothing left to discover.

He looked across the drab thorny scrub to where his grandmother's house lay hidden behind palms, under the dark dome of its Moreton Bay figtree. He had them, at least, in town, Grandma and Aunt Kay. And Aunt Kay was teaching him to play the piano, to play *Clementine* with one finger. Here at least he had Aunt Kay to talk to: Aunt Kay talking of hills and trees and horses, and dead small boys in various parts of the world. Now he and Aunt Kay pored over the atlas, learning capitals of countries where the war was, testing each other on capitals, looking at places where Aunt Kay had been and other places, like Mexico, where she had not been but had almost been, and so in some way established an interest in them. The nostalgia for places Aunt Kay had not succeeded in reaching, for Mexico and the redwood forests of California, was almost stronger than the nostalgia for Highland snow.

The quiet beginnings of the afternoon southerly stirred the peppertrees, and the windmill clanked a little, turning about. Far away a rooster crowed, a sleepy sound. Somewhere in the distance someone was hammering, but everyone else must be asleep, soothed by the sea, which was hushed and slow now, like people praying in church.

In the street a big Army transport pulled up, and three soldiers got out. It was Ian and two other soldiers from the camp near Andarra, come to see if anyone was going for a swim.

There was that, at least, in the town. On three sides of the town, the sea. At each end of the next street, the variable sea, hushed now and distantly praying.

He jumped from the wall and ran towards the soldiers, the kitten springing after him, and then stopping, staring with fascination at something in the grass. 'I bags going in the transport,' he shouted, listening still to the sea, distantly praying.

The southerly was blowing, dusting the sweaty faces of the children with grit and grey sand as they chased and scuffled by the wharf gates. Spiky balls of sea-grass rolled over and over in the wind. The wharf was hooting and clanging, sending up steam.

The band hooted and brayed against the wind. Every beat of the drum was like a blow in the stomach.

The soldiers marched like toy soldiers, stiff and staring. Rifles thrust up like blackboy spears. The rays of the rising suns on their turned-up hats were not light but bayonets.

The boy saw his father, marching alone.

'Daddy,' he shouted. 'Goodbye, Daddy.'

His father did not turn. Under the officer's cap his face

looked more than ever like the King, remote as the King.

His father was gone. The brown soldiers passed and passed and were gone.

The boy looked round for Nan. Together they walked back to the car where their mother was waiting.

'Just look at your faces,' she said, 'you're filthy.'

Her voice was very quiet, and they kept quiet too, in case she was cross.

The wharf was clanging and hooting, and the rusty, dirty *Chungking* was moving out into the blue water, moving towards the harbour mouth and the flat-topped coastal hills to the north. The bay was dark blue under the south wind. Once, in the Old Days, beautiful ships had been there, white-petalled ships coming for gold and sandalwood. Now, the rust-stained *Chungking* was taking the Garrison north to the Kimberleys.

The *Chungking* was moving north towards the Kimberleys. In the waters to the north it would sink a Jap submarine. That was the sort of thing that happened in the northern sea.

The bay was dark dark blue under the south wind. Once, in the Old Days, a little boat had come from the north, skirting the flat-topped range and beaching at last on the sand by the place where the merry-go-round now stood. Six bearded men had climbed from the boat and waited there, silent.

Then the officer in charge of convicts had emerged officiously from his barracks, and come to the beach, and said to one of the bearded young men: 'Are you the ringleader of this party?'

The young man, whose name had been Isham Coram and who had been the boy's great-great-uncle, had said: 'I am the *leader*, yes.'

'Then could you tell me,' the officer said, 'where you might be coming from, in a twenty-six-foot whaler?'

And Isham Coram, whose eyes still perhaps had shown traces of a great storm and many islands, had said quietly: 'From Escape Cliffs.' And watched, with a certain amusement, the blank surprise in the officer's face, because Escape Cliffs was Darwin.

Now the unbeautiful *Chungking* was taking the boy's father

77

to the north. The sea was dark dark blue under the southerly. The beautiful ships, the mysterious visitants, would never come again to the port of gold and sandalwood.

The tree above the drinking tap outside the boys' shed was called a sore-eye tree, because the seeds had little hairs that clung to the fingers and inflamed the eyes if one rubbed them. The flowers of the sore-eye tree were pink and waxy, smooth as lily-flesh. The boy stared at the flowers he could not reach: pink waxy cups around yellow waxy stamens.

Under the sore-eye tree, under the shining tap, three big boys were squatting. They were polishing pennies in the damp sand. The pennies shone like gold.

A bell rang, and they stood up and went. Rob went too, and joined the double line of boys at the door of the school.

The bell rang again, and they marched. They marched through the bare corridor and into the big bare hall, to the crash and tinkle of a piano. They lined up in the hall, boys on one side, girls on the other, and the headmaster mounted the dais.

The morning was fresh and cool, the floor was cool under the boy's bare feet. None of the boys wore shoes to school. Wearing shoes was sissy.

The school was old, with new bits added. The hall was funny, one side of it was the outside wall of the old stone schoolhouse, and the classroom doors opened on to the hall like doors opening into the street. The classroom doors had fanlights above them, like the front doors of old houses.

The headmaster was talking, he was talking about the war. Then the piano struck up, and the children began singing. This morning the song was *Australia Australia Australeeyah*. On another morning it would be *Advance Australia Fair* or *Waltzing Matilda*. The boy sang hesitantly, unsure of the words.

> There is a land where summer skies
> Are gleaming with a thousand eyes . . .

A thousand eyes. Was that right? It sounded a bit scaring. And the other children, evidently, were uncertain. The singing lagged behind the piano, then burst out at the end in a confident shout.

Australia! Au-australia! Austral-ee-yah!

The assembly was dismissed, the children marched to the classrooms. The boy beside Rob was Tommy Johnson. He was a blacknigger and had a great gobbet of pale snot on his upper lip.

Rob did not mind the blackniggers, some of the older ones he rather admired. But his mother was furious because Nan was sitting next to a blacknigger in school. 'They're dirty,' said his mother. 'They all have bugs in their hair.'

It was funny about blackniggers. They were Australian. They were more Australian that Rob was, and he was fifth generation. And yet somehow they were not Australian. His world was not one world.

Some people sent their children to the convent to keep them away from blackniggers. These people were despised. The State school kids hung over the fence as the convent kids passed, chanting:

> Convent dogs
> Jump like frogs
> In and out the wa-a-ater.

Rob chanted with them. He was a Protestant, and his world was not one world.

He sat in class beside Graham Martin, who was a white boy and lived in the next street to the Corams. The classroom smelled of chalkdust and children and the sour ink that was brought round in earthenware bottles. It was a different smell from the smell that school had had before he went away, when he had been in First Bubs. In First Bubs the smell had been of biscuits and oranges for play-lunch, mouldering bean-bags and paint-boxes and crayons. The desks had been different too, with green cloth bags on the backs of the seats for putting things in. These desks were wrought-iron and shiny wood, carved with people's names.

He sucked a new pen-nib and dipped it in the inkwell and

sucked it again. It tasted metallic. His copybook was open in front of him. In laborious copperplate he began to copy.

> What have I done for you,
> England, my England?

In the reading book there was a Little Bush Maid who did not even know what was on the other side of the ranges. He thought of Didi, happy and unsophisticated at Andarra.

He had fallen behind the other kids of his age while he was away. Now the kids he had started school with were in a higher class, and he was in a class with kids younger than himself. It hardly mattered, as his birthday was at the end of the year.

A little girl was reciting.

> Core of my heart, my country!
> Her pitiless blue sky,
> When sick at heart around us
> We see the cattle die . . .

It was about Australia. Bones and heat. He thought of Sandalwood in midsummer. Sheep-skulls in the dead grass.

> The drumming of an army,
> The steady, soaking rain.

The bell rang for recess, and they filed out into the playground. The girls played on one side of the school, and the boys on the other. Where the girls played, hopscotch lines were drawn in the dirt, and the skipping-ropes swished in the air: *Salt—mustard—PEPPER!*

Silly words they chanted.

> And wash him with milk
> And clothe him with silk,
> And write down his name
> With a gold pen and ink. . . .

Where the boys played the dirt was scored with rings for marbles.

'Want to play, Rob?' Graham Martin said.

'I haven't got any dooks,' Rob said. Dooks were hard to come by, with the war on, and the big kids had pretty well cornered the supply. Graham had inherited his brother's dooks, but the big kids would soon have those off him.

People were even playing Chinese Checkers with wooden pegs instead of marbles.

Rick must have had some dooks, he thought. Maybe at Sandalwood——

'Hey, youse kids,' Donny Webb called out. 'Gunna play branders?'

'Yeah. Who's got the ball?'

'Here,' Brian Carter said, throwing the bald tennis ball in the air and catching it.

They formed a ring in the sand and tossed the ball from one to another. At last Graham Martin dropped it.

'Yuh-hoo!' the others yelled, scattering.

The playground was like a First World War battlefield, with sand instead of mud. At some time there had been a lawn, but wind and boys' feet had eroded it into a series of gullies and sandy bottoms, the original couch-grass remaining only as a crown to the small hillocks that studded the terrain. Running from Graham, Rob caught his foot in a tussock, and sprawled in the dirt.

Graham was standing over him, the ball in his raised hand.

Rob squirmed in the sand, kicking his legs, feeling an unbearable giggling tension as he waited for the ball to hit. 'Hey,' he was saying, 'hey-hey-hey-hey-hey-hey!' Graham's arm was drawn back. He was really going to give it to him.

The ball struck him stingingly on the calf. 'Aw, —— you,' he said, using a new word he had tried with some effect on his mother.

He stood up, reaching for the ball. There was a round red mark on his leg where he had been branded.

He began to run towards Donny Webb, who was dancing up and down on a tussock, waving his arms and taunting.

It was a bit like the war, he thought. Like the newsreels of the war. He imagined Donny as a cheeky Jap, and himself as a soldier, charging with lowered bayonet.

'Yuh-hoo!' he shouted, flinging the ball. 'Beauty!' as the ball bounced off Donny's cheekbone.

Donny looked surprised and furious, a red mark on his face. 'Jesus, Rob, you're gunna get one in the face too.'

'You can't catch me,' Rob said. He bounded away towards one of the abandoned air raid trenches and sprawled there beside Graham Martin, listening to Donny's bare feet pad off after someone else.

'It's like the war,' he said. 'Donny's a Jap.'

'If it was the war,' Graham said, 'Donny wouldn't be the only one with a grenade.'

'I think he's gone over towards the woodwork shed,' Rob said. 'I'll have a look.'

Then the ball came down, smack, on Graham's backside.

'Oh, Gawd,' said Graham, half laughing, half sobbing. 'Gawd, what was that, a mortar?'

Brian Carter was laughing and laughing. He looked savage. It was really war, in the playground.

In winter, rain flooded the gravelled verges of the streets and made brown lakes where wooden and paper boats were floated. The soft mud squished up between the boys' toes. In winter they were forced into shoes and socks, but they took them off and paddled home from school in the delicious mud.

The stark grey berry-bushes on the vacant land grew green and soft-looking, and put out small, mauve-tinged flowers. Then spring came, loud with bees, and the red berries formed, and in many yards were yellow flowering cassias. When the petals fell, the flowers turned into writhing green snakes full of seeds.

The peppertrees bloomed. At Sandalwood the olives drizzled continually, the little green-white flowers and unformed fruit whispering down.

In the early mornings the harbour was polished like a blue mirror.

The boys walked home from school, arms linked, chanting the songs of the war. They discussed which branch of the Forces they would join when the time came, passionately arguing the merits of the different services. Rob clung to the Army, in the face of the others' scorn. He would go into the Navy if he could sail on a windjammer, but otherwise he would settle for a gumleaf cubby-house in the jungle.

Graham was going to join the Air Force, and Rob was curiously disturbed. He thought of Graham plunging in flames from the sky.

Donny Webb was going in the Navy. He thought of Donny disfigured with burning oil, watching the dark fins of sharks come closer. Sharks were so commonplace, so likely. Rob could not admit to Donny that he was afraid of the sea.

They felt no doubt that the war would last for another ten years, that it would last forever. The songs about peace were just songs. No one believed that peace could ever happen.

Yet the question would keep being raised. As for instance on one spring day when he and Graham were walking home with a boy called Kevin O'Hara. They had left Kevin O'Hara at his gate to go in for lunch, and were walking on when Kevin O'Hara suddenly ran out of his house again and called after them: 'Hey.'

'What?' they said, turning.

'The Dings have surrendered,' Kevin O'Hara shouted.

'Aw, they're always surrendering,' Graham said.

'No, this is dinkum, they've signed a treaty or something.'

'Gee,' said Rob. If Italy was really out of the war, then that might be after all the beginnings of peace. 'Maybe the Dings'll fight the Jerries now.'

'That's what they reckon,' Kevin O'Hara said.

'Gee, I dunno,' Graham said. 'Funny if it *was* the end of the war.'

They walked on in silence, and as they thought about Italy the possibility of peace became a stronger and stronger possibility, until at last it was almost a fact. They felt oddly let down, as if something had been taken away from them.

At the gate of his grandmother's house Rob said: 'So long,' and went in. His grandmother and Aunt Kay were sitting down to lunch, and he saw with surprise and with a feeling of omen that from somewhere or other they had got some rice. No one

83

had seen rice for ages. Being without rice was part of the war.

He tried some. He had forgotten what rice tasted like.

'I suppose Rick gets plenty of rice,' he said, 'in Malaya.'

'I expect so,' said his grandmother, sounding as if she did not wish to discuss it.

'Italy's surrendered,' he said, suddenly realizing that they would not know this, as they had no wireless.

'Good enough for them,' said Aunt Kay.

They were hopeless about the war. They just did not seem to be interested.

'Oh, well,' he said, 'I'd better go home. So long.'

He pushed his way through the palms choking the side gate, and followed the sandy, twisting path through the scrub that divided his grandmother's house from his own. Wattle was flowering in the paddock, and he reached out and broke off a spray of the fluffy yellow balls.

He held it in his hand, staring at it. The taste of rice was still in his mouth. Suddenly, very clearly, he saw a face he had forgotten. He saw Rick's face, the slow smile, the glint of gold.

He thought towards Rick with a yearning intensity like nothing he had ever felt before. Oh, come home. Come home, Rick, and Peter too. The Dings have surrendered, and it's going to be peace. Peace, peace, peace ever after.

The wet wood stank. It stank of rot, and worse.

What was in his arms was lighter than a child. How could a man weigh so little? How could a man shrink so small, and still be remembered and still be mourned as a man?

The tears would never stop. The flames of the bonfire danced distorted by tears into trembling stars.

The man who tended the bonfire, who was mad, was saying: 'Your mate?'

'Yeah,' said Rick, his voice choked and high. 'My——' But he could not find the words.

The body was so light, so dry. It should burn, it should burn like twigs.

'This is——' he started to say, and choked. 'A hell of a job,' he brought out, in a rush.

Around the body sparks rose, flames burst. 'Don't you——'
Rick cried to the madman. 'Don't you——'

He could not watch. He began to run, running from the crackling fire, and worse.

At the entrance to his own hut he stopped, catching his breath. The smallest exertion tired him now. He leaned on the doorpost, shaking his head to stop the tears, and panting.

The skeleton of Hugh Mackay lay on the floor. In the darkened skull the eyes and teeth were enormous. The eyes were burning.

Rick kneeled beside him. 'How're you feeling, fella?' he said.

'I'm feeling pretty good,' Hugh said, 'but I ain't felt nothing today.'

He tried a grin, and Rick dropped his eyes.

'Rick,' Hugh said, breathing painfully.

'Yeah?'

'I drank your water.'

'That's all right.'

'No, no—bastard of a thing to do.'

'Don't be stupid,' Rick said. 'What's a mate for?'

He kept staring at their two hands, lying on the floor. Only the hands were unchanged. The bodies were angled skeletons, loosely draped with skin. The hands were human.

'Pete Cooper died,' he said. 'I just put him on the fire.'

'Sorry, mate. He was family, was he?'

'Oh—kind of. He and my brother married a pair of sisters. He was—a good sort of bloke.'

The hands fascinated him. If he concentrated on them, if he tried not to see the wrists, then they were still the hands of Hugh Mackay and Rick Maplestead.

'Rick.'

'Yeah?'

'I think I'm gunna die, mate.'

He could hardly think, the hands absorbed him. 'No, you're not.'

'I reckon I've had it, Rick,'

'You're not going to die,' Rick said, suddenly angry. 'In a

85

pig's arse you're going to die. Get hold of yourself.'

The tears were coming again. And in another hut, a short distance away, men were starting to sing. The voices were strong, they were young. The voices were miraculous. The voices, the words, swelled his throat.

> There's a long, long trail a-winding
> To the land of my dreams. . . .

The tears flowed, dropping on to the clasped hands on the floor. The tears would never stop. 'We're young,' he whispered, looking down at the normal hands. 'Hughie. We're young. We're young.'

7

Donny Webb was reciting, sing-song:

> They shall grow not old, as we that are left grow old:
> Age shall not weary them, nor the years condemn. . . .

Rob felt a lump in his throat. His cousin in South Australia had just got killed in the war. He had never seen this cousin, but if he could be dead then Rick could be dead, Gordon could be dead, his own father could be dead, killed by a Jap bomb. Even the teacher was looking sad, although Donny was the fourth person who had recited the poem.

The cousin in South Australia had been eighteen. *They shall grow not old*.

'I don't think you learned that very well, Donny,' the teacher said. 'Now, Rob.'

He stood up, awkward. He hated reciting poetry, it sounded wrong, out loud.

> Break, break, break
> On thy cold gray stones, O Sea. . . .

Tony and Pete Minetti were a fisherman's boys, he was thinking. They laughed with their sister at play. Their sister used to push him on the merry-go-round, a long time ago.

Nostalgia.

'You've learned the words,' the teacher was saying, 'but try to say them with some *expression*, Rob.'

He sat down again, feeling sad.

It was hot. The air outside was burning. When his mother was a little girl the kids had got a holiday when the temperature went over a hundred, but now it had to be a hundred and ten. He knew that at lunchtime it had been a hundred and seven.

No, he had misjudged them. A bell rang, and the teacher

was saying: 'The headmaster has decided that school will finish now. Boys and girls who have to go on the school bus are to meet Miss Jones outside the boys' shed and she will take them for a swim.' It was only half past two.

The boys ran over the hot sand in the playground.

'You going to the beach?' Graham Martin said.

'I'm not allowed to go by myself. Are you?'

'Nuh. Not till I learn to swim.'

'We could go with the bus kids.'

'We've still got to go home,' Kevin O'Hara said, 'to get our bathers.'

On the burning footpath, under the Norfolk Island pines, they jumped from shadow to shadow.

'Ouch,' Rob said. 'I got a doublegee.' He stood in the road to pull the thorn out of his foot, and then danced with agony. 'The tar's melting. It's burning my feet off. Hoo crikey.'

'Come over here, you drongo.'

He leapt into the shade, and stood on one leg to pull the tar off the sole of his foot. 'Jiminy, that burns. Hey, that'd be a good way to torture someone.'

'I reckon the best way to torture someone,' Kevin O'Hara said, 'would be to make 'em drink petrol and then drop a match down 'em.'

'Aw, the match'd go out.'

'No, it wouldn't. They'd be breathing all those fumes.'

'What do you want to torture people for?' Graham Martin asked, bored.

'Aw, I don't, really,' Kevin said. 'Be interesting, though, wouldn't it, to have a Jap to mess around with?'

'D'you ever get a datepalm thorn stuck in you?' Rob said. 'That'd be a good way to torture someone.'

'No prize for second,' Kevin said. 'The Japs've been doing that for years.'

'How'd *you* like to be tortured?' Graham said. 'How'd *you* like to have all your fingernails pulled out?'

'I'd hate it,' Rob said.

'Why don't you shut up about it, well.'

'Don't get off your bike. No harm in talking.'

'I bet you wouldn't think so,' Graham said, 'if *your* brother was in Bougainville.'

'Aw, cut it out,' Rob said, feeling miserable suddenly. It was just a game, just theorizing; and here was Graham bringing real people into it. Now he felt sick.

'I'm gunna learn to swim,' Kevin said, 'this holidays.'

'So'm I,' said Graham.

'So'm I,' said Rob.

They jumped, and landed, teetering, in the narrow shade of a treetrunk.

'We might just as well wear sandals,' Kevin said. 'I'm not gunna have any feet left when I get home.'

'Softy,' Graham said.

'No nigger blood in me,' Kevin said. 'I got white man's feet.'

'Yeah?' said Graham, threateningly. 'Who d'you reckon's got nigger blood here?'

'I bet Rob's got nigger blood,' Kevin said. 'He's got a nigger mouth.'

'Yeah?' said Rob. 'You say that again.'

'All right,' said Kevin. 'You got a nigger mouth.'

Rob pushed him. They danced a few steps on the burning gravel, then jumped back into the shade.

'Hey,' Kevin said, 'd'you reckon they're black all over?'

'How'd I know?' Rob said. 'I never had a bath with a nigger.'

'Garn, I bet your old man's a nigger. Didn't you ever see him in the shower?'

'You shut up,' Rob said. 'My old man's a soldier.'

'All right, he can be a nigger soldier, can't he?'

'They reckon they're good soldiers,' Graham said, 'some of the noogs.'

'I bet Keith Johnson'd be a good soldier,' Kevin said. 'Gee, he's a tough kid.'

'I don't reckon he'd get into the Army,' Rob said. 'He's thirteen, and he's only in Third Standard.'

'Well, he hardly ever comes to school,' Graham said. 'They have a good life, these noogs.'

'I know what he does all day,' Kevin said. 'He's up in the

89

sandhills ———ing girls.'

'Gee, I dunno,' Rob said. 'I wonder what they get out of it.'

'Aw, they're just stupid,' Kevin said. 'Makes me sick, hearing big kids giggling like tarts.'

'They don't do anything,' Graham said. 'They just talk about it.'

'Hey,' Kevin said, 'did youse kids hear about Miss Jones?'

'What about her?'

'Brian Carter saw her doing it with a soldier in the sandhills.'

'Aw, go home. You think we believe that?'

'It's dinkum. Honest. Brian saw it.'

'Whyn't you shut up,' Graham said, 'you dirty cow.'

'Yeah?'

'Yeah.'

They pushed each other, and danced on the hot footpath.

'I'm gunna be eight next week,' Rob said.

'Hoh, Grandpa. You having a party?'

'I dunno.' Parties were starting to look like kids' stuff.

'I reckon if you go to some little kid's party,' Graham said, 'you have a better time than if you have a party of your own.'

'You don't get presents, but.'

'If you have a party, you never get anything except books and snotrags anyway.'

'I had some beaut parties before the war,' Rob said.

'*You* don't remember before the war.'

'I do. Before the Jap war.'

'You don't remember before Hitler.'

'I bet I remember more than you do.'

Suddenly he had a memory. Searchlights in a dark sky.

'I went to Perth once,' he said, surprised. He had forgotten that. Searchlights had been practising, and on the river there had been a pelican. 'Hey, you ever been to Perth?'

'Nuh,' said Graham.

'I went once,' Kevin said, 'but I don't remember.'

'I can remember,' Rob said. 'Gee.'

He was somehow startled by the memory. If he had been to Perth once, then it might be possible to go again, after the

90

war. Suddenly the horizons of the known world had moved outwards.

'Gee,' he kept saying to himself. He had been in a city. The only city.

When they went to Perth, that was when they went to get the car that his mother had now. They had gone to Perth in a little green car. There had been thick bush with small fires burning, and his mother had said: 'Look, Rob, look at the blackniggers.'

He felt uplifted, as if he had discovered something. A future.

They had come home from Perth in the cream-coloured car, which was new then, and had stopped at a hotel halfway to spend the night. He had even been in a hotel, or perhaps more than one.

'Gee,' he said.

'That's your car, isn't it, Rob?' Graham said.

He came out of his trance, and saw the car that he had been thinking about going past. He looked at the figure in the driver's seat, and then stared.

'Who's that?' Graham said. 'Who's driving?'

'I dunno,' Rob said, slowly. 'My mother must've lent it to someone.'

'Maybe that bloke pinched it,' Kevin said. 'You ought to tell the police.'

'No, I think it's—I think it's my dad,' he said, incredulous.

'Yeah, it looked like a nigger,' Kevin said.

'Shut up, Kevin. p'rhaps it *is* his dad.'

'It is,' Rob said, struggling to cope with this circumstance. 'He's come back. It must be the end of the war.'

'I don't reckon they'll stop fighting,' Kevin said, 'just 'cause your dad's not there. It's not his ball they're playing with.'

'It must be,' Rob said. 'It must be the end of the war. I gotta run,' he said, the hot sand spurting up under his feet as he raced after the car, watching it slow and pull up outside his own house, and open to release the tall civilian figure of his father, like a portent.

'Rob,' said his mother, 'don't say: "Yeah".'

'Don't say: "I'm gunna".'

'Don't say: "Eh?".'

'Don't say: "Shut up".'

'And don't ever let me hear you use that word again.'

'Of *course* I talk like a State school kid,' he protested. 'I'm going to the State school, aren't I?'

'And don't contradict.'

'Awwwww.'

She glowered at him. 'Have you ever heard your father speak like that?'

'Nuh,' he said. 'I mean, no.'

His father was a gentleman. He, the boy, was not a gentleman. He did not think that there would be any more gentlemen after his father's time.

The boy sat at the dining-room table eating cold mutton.

'Ergh,' he said.

'Rob,' said his mother.

'Aw, all right.'

Nobody was talking at the table, because the boy's father never spoke. Without meaning to, the boy's father emanated silence like a cloud. It made Nan nervous, and she clattered with her knife and fork.

The boy stared at the picture over the sideboard. His handsome young great-great-grandfather with the epaulettes who had known Byron in Greece. That was a romantic thing to have done, because Byron was a Poet, like Adam Lindsay Gordon. Other people wrote poems that made one cry, yet one did not even remember the names of those people. But Byron and Adam Lindsay Gordon were Poets, and it would not have mattered if they had never written anything at all.

The young man over the sideboard had left Byron his bed to die on, and gone back to England with a bit of a poem called *Don Juan* in his pocket. There was no copy of *Don Juan* in the house, the boy had discovered. But that, any way, was just poetry, and had nothing to do with being a Poet.

Rick would make a good Poet, he thought. He's just about

as good a rider as Adam Lindsay Gordon. I bet he can swim as well as Byron.

But then he'd have to die young.

No. That was no good.

'Why've I got so many great-great-grandfathers?' he said.

'Everybody has—eight, that's right, eight,' said his mother.

'You counted on your fingers,' the boy said. 'Baby.'

He had one great-great-grandfather he detested, a gaunt, white life-sized bust. They had taken that one out of his bedroom because it gave him nightmares. But it had been wearing a slouch hat for a year now, and he was getting used to it. It was a clergyman, and used to make its own wine in South Australia.

'Haven't you got any *live* relations, Dad?' he said.

'Mm?' said his father. 'Yes, hundreds.'

'Why aren't there any here?' the boy wondered. Sometimes he felt sorry for his father and for Uncle Paul, who had no family of their own and had to make do with the Maplesteads.

'I don't know,' his father said. 'You could find one in most places.'

It sounded an unsatisfactory arrangement to the boy, and he was sad on his father's behalf. That must be why his father was so quiet.

His eyes went back to the portrait. 'Did *he* know Adam Lindsay Gordon?'

'Probably,' his father said. 'My grandfather did, and wished he didn't.'

'Gee,' said the boy. 'Gosh.' When Aunt Kay and Grandma were young they used to swoon over Adam Lindsay Gordon like a dead film star. 'Did he know Henry Lawson?'

'You're being silly, Rob,' his mother said. 'Eat that meat.'

'Awww,' said the boy. It was intolerable, the way she would tear him back from thinking about Poets in order to concentrate on cold mutton.

Adam Lindsay Gordon shot himself, he thought. And some other Poet hanged himself with his stockwhip. He supposed that their bones were still out there, with Leichardt's, bleaching in hot tragic Australia.

Australia was a good country for Poets, he thought. It was sad, like Poets. It was a pity that Byron died on his great-great-grandfather's bed, because otherwise he could have come with his great-great-grandfather to Australia and died in the desert instead.

> Out where the dead men . . .
> Out where the dead men lie . . .

That was the one who hanged himself with his stockwhip. Gee, he thought, it must be *interesting* being a Poet, except that you've got to die.

'Was your father a Poet?' he said to his mother.

His parents looked at one another, and started to laugh.

'Poor Dad,' his mother said. 'Well, he did read Wordsworth in the train.'

'You said he was the best horseman people could remember,' the boy said, indignant, 'and he went near the desert after gold, and he fell off his horse and died.'

'But that doesn't make him a Poet, darling.'

'Awww,' said the boy, disgusted. 'It does so too.'

She didn't understand. Probably her own father's bones were out there in the desert, and she didn't even understand.

The only person who understood was Aunt Kay. She had a photograph of his grandfather standing up in a cloud of dust, called *Charles Winning Sulky Race*. Of course he was a Poet. He could probably thrash Adam Lindsay Gordon.

'Could Byron beat Adam Lindsay Gordon?' he asked.

'Rob,' his mother said, 'if you don't eat, I'll——'

'All right,' he said, surrendering. 'I'm eating.'

It was a silly question, anyway. Of course Adam Lindsay Gordon could beat Byron. Byron had a gammy leg. Australians could beat the Pommies any day, even right back in the Old Days, before Gallipoli.

Now the boy was beginning to discover blood.

Blood. The prize Merino rams with the huge neck folds. That was because of blood, because of breeding.

Blood was extraordinary. He looked at Nan, who was his

sister, as she bent over the cards. She was his sister, and had dark hair and brown eyes. And he was her brother, blue-eyed and fair.

'Nan even *looks* as if she's got Red Indian blood,' he said.

'Aren't the Corams odd?' said his grandmother. 'Imagine anyone *wanting* to be descended from a Red Indian.'

Blood. It seemed that all through his life there had been a chorus about blood. Couldn't you pick that one for Charles Maplestead's grandson?—He's his father's son—— If only Dr Coram had known Rob—— When you said that you looked *exactly* like our brother Jack.'

The cards were spread face-down on the dark red tablecloth with the ink stain, under the lowered light. Aunt Kay's thin hand with the bloodstone ring reached out under the light, turned up two cards, and then turned them down again.

'I think I know,' Mrs Maplestead said, 'I think I know where that other Queen is.' Her plump hand with the wedding ring reached out in the light and turned up a Queen and a ten. 'Bother,' said Mrs Maplestead.

'I know,' Nan said, standing on a chair and jumping up and down as she leaned on the table. 'I know, Grandma.' Her small brown hand reached out and turned up two Queens.

'Good for you, Nan,' Aunt Kay said.

The boy's freckled hand moved under the light, and turned up a two and a three. 'I knew where those Queens were all the time,' he said, sulking.

'Now, Rob,' Aunt Kay said, 'don't be a bad sport.'

Around the spread cards were newspapers, spectacle-cases, sewing baskets, velvet pin-cushions studded with bright-headed pins. On the sideboard, light glowed in the round sides of the silver kettle, under which a blue flame used to burn on Sunday afternoons before Pearl Harbour.

'Do you know what I heard on the wireless,' Rob said, 'on the Children's Session?'

'No,' said his grandmother. 'What did you hear?'

'I heard all about the Eureka Stockade.'

'Oh,' said Mrs Maplestead, looking pleased and embarrassed. She half-wished that she had not told him that her father,

as a gold-hungry youth, had been caught up in the Stockade.
She suspected that he would tell Mrs Ernest Maplestead, who
would not think it respectable.

Mrs Ernest Maplestead's relations were spotlessly respectable. The wildest ones among them were an uncle who had
hunted Ned Kelly, and another uncle who had fought the last
formal duel in Australia. The duel, which was staged in the
main street of Melbourne, had gone no further than Mrs
Ernest Maplestead's uncle's first shot, which had unluckily
struck him in the foot.

'Your father was Rebel,' the boy said, in a voice which
demanded that his grandmother admit it.

'He wasn't really,' said Mrs Maplestead, modestly. 'He was
just a silly wee lad.'

'He had a fearful temper,' Aunt Kay said. 'I suppose he was
a Rebel. He was always a Jacobite.'

Aunt Kay was a Jacobite, and so was the boy. They sang
Jacobite songs, and talked about Tearlach.

'You're all Rebels,' the boy said, firmly. 'All your family.'

'*Tearlach gu brath*,' murmured Aunt Kay, rebelliously.
Then, as always when anyone started a train of thought in her,
she began singing to herself, and drumming with her fingers
on the table. '*Come o'er the stream, Charlie, brave Charlie,
braw Charlie*,' she sang. '*Come o'er the stream, Charlie, and
dine wi' MacLean.*'

'Aunt Kay,' Nan complained, 'it's your turn.'

Blood, the boy was thinking. Blood was mysterious.

'Have I got any nigger blood?' he asked.

'Of course not,' his grandmother said, shocked.

'Have I got any convict blood?'

'Certainly not,' said his grandmother.

'If I had convict blood and nigger blood,' the boy said,
thinking it out, 'I'd be related to just about everyone in
Australia.'

'No,' said Aunt Kay, gravely. 'You wouldn't be related to
any Italian fishermen, or any Greek tomato-gardeners.'

'Or any Bog Irish Catholics,' said Mrs Maplestead.

'Uncle Paul's a Catholic.'

'That's quite different,' said Mrs Maplestead.

The mention of convicts had started Aunt Kay off again.
She was drumming and singing.

> 'Come all ye young dookies and duchesses,
> Take warning and heed what I say:
> Mind all is your own as you toucheses,
> Or you'll join us in Botany Bay.'

'It's your *turn*, Aunt Kay,' Nan said, crossly.

Blood was very odd, the boy was thinking. He had Rebel
blood, he was a Rebel. And yet his father was so respectable.
His father was related to things like churches and courts and
the Navy and something called the Constitution. And all this
blood was mixed up in him and in his sister Nan, whose hair
and eyes under the light were dark brown, while he was blue-
eyed and fair.

The children lay on their bellies in the damp sand by the
water's edge and kicked with their feet.

'Faster, faster,' the swimming instructor called to them
'Come on, pattercake.'

They pattercaked against the hard sand.

The whistle blew. 'Very good,' said the swimming teacher.
brown and strong in her dark bathers. 'Now, frogkick.'

They frogkicked, breaststroking, making cleared places in
the softer sand in front of them. The sand was hotter there,
and had little flecks of blue and purple in it, sea-ground shell.

The whistle blew again, and they got up and stood in a line
on the sand.

'Now,' said the instructor, 'we'll go out along the jetty to
the second trestle, and then we're going to swim.'

It was alarming. For the first time they were going to swim.
and in the deep deep water.

The timbers of the rotting jetty were seagull-grey, soft and
furred like an old stick that had been used for poking clothes
as they boiled in the copper. Great bolts stuck out of the
wood, staining like iodine.

It was terrible, at the second trestle. The water was deep, deep green, green as wheat, and fathomless.

The teacher was in the water, at the bottom of the ladder, waiting for him. The silver whistle still dangled at her wet brown throat.

He stood on the ladder with his legs under the water, green and pale.

'Now, Rob. Swim.'

'I can't,' he said, 'I can't——'

He felt her hands under his armpits. And suddenly he was swimming.

He could see the sky through the grey timbers of the jetty, and two or three gulls that were gliding on the wind. He could see the sunbathers on the beach, and the fences of the main street that turned its back on the sea. The sea underneath him was wheat-green and fathomless. The sea was holding him up.

'Oh,' he sighed, looking through the timbers at the timber-grey gulls. The sea was his. The sea was his.

In his backyard, by the woodheap, was a merry-go-round.

'Gee,' Graham said, looking at it, 'your dad's clever, isn't he?'

'Yeah,' Rob said, 'he's not bad.'

But the merry-go-round was not much use to them. It was meant for little kids like Nan. So they went back to the fire they had built, and to cooking potatoes in ex-Lieutenant Coram's dixies.

Later, they went to the tank and practised the Japanese water torture on themselves, emptying mug after mug of rain-water. It was a large mug, part of the equipment of ex-Lieutenant Coram.

'Here goes,' Rob said, running for the grass, and spouting a fountain of clear water.

'I'm not gunna be able to chuck,' Graham said, palely. 'Gee, why did we start on this? I won't eat any dinner now.'

'I beat you, anyway.'

'You can have it,' said Graham. 'Gee, we have some stupid ideas.'

'You gunna go home, then?'

'Yeah. Yeah, I'll see you,' Graham said. 'And thanks a lot for poisoning me.'

He turned the corner, and Rob wandered back towards the merry-go-round. It was true, he was thinking; his dad was clever. Not many people would have thought of turning an old windmill-head into a merry-go-round. That was what the merry-go-round was: the old head of the windmill in the tennis court. His father had sunk a log in the ground and bored a hole in it, and in that pivot the merry-go-round revolved, hauled on a rope tied to the spokes. Old linoleum covered the sharp vanes where Nan and the little girls sat and span.

Little kids like merry-go-rounds, the boy was thinking. Gee, I remember when I was a little kid, I was mad on that merry-go-round near the jetty.

The horizon was spiked with windmills. Merry-go-rounds, spinning in the sky.

I wonder what made Dad think of it, he thought. Gee, Dad's clever.

He trailed behind his tall father. Immensely long walks they went, never speaking, pushing through the sandhill scrub.

Stinging-bush lashed at the boy's bare legs, the couch-like leaves raising lumps. After he had been walking for a while, he got to like it; he would walk straight through a stinging-bush, feeling a pleasant tingle.

The scrub had a harsh, sweet tang all the year, and in spring he would hunt its meagre flowers; the scarlet horns of running-postman, the miraculous pure complexity of white clematis shrouding the bushes. He tore off festoons of clematis, fault-less as the white roses at Andarra.

They would come down through white passes in the dunes to the beaches where the surf was: clean and bare in the summer, in winter weed-littered and rank. On the beaches lay extraordinary mysteries: sea-slugs like lumps of liver on the sand, the soft white bones of cuttlefish. These things his father knew about: things like sea-eggs and castor-oil-bottles and

Portugese men-o'-war that seemed blown of blue glass. In the later afternoon, small yellow crabs began running in droves into the surf, disappearing as if they had gone to drown themselves.

He had no conversation with his father, except when he found something: a cartridge case on the rifle range, or some new sea-life. Then he would ask, trailing after the long-legged figure farther up the beach: 'What do they *call* this, Dad?'

'Mm?' his father would say, abstracted. 'That? I think it's called bladderwrack.'

Then the boy would fall back and wander along in silence, popping the small brown bladders between finger and thumb.

He was glad that his father was home, yet sorry that he was no longer a soldier. He was older than most soldiers, and not very well, and it was the Army itself that had told him to come home and be a lawyer every day. But it had been interesting when he was a soldier. The boy gazed sometimes with a certain nostalgia at the pencil portrait in Nan's room that showed his father in uniform, looking like the King.

But he liked the long walks over beach and scrub, and accustomed himself to hour-long silences. His father was a very grown-up man. So grown-up that it came as a revelation to find that his father was capable of pulling his leg.

But he had done that, one day at the beach. It was a day when they had been swimming, and the boy, half-buried in the warm sand, had called out to the long freckled back of his father by the water's edge: 'Dad, what's that country over there?'

His father had said, looking at the clouds massed on the horizon, and not turning: 'That? That must be Antarctica.'

And the boy was seized with enchantment. Antarctica. So near. A land of snow.

'When I can sail a yacht,' he said to Graham, 'I'm going to Antarctica.'

'Gee, you're dumb,' Graham said. 'You can't get to Antarctica with a yacht.'

'You can,' Rob said. 'You can see it from here. Look.'

'Awww,' Graham said, disgusted. 'That's clouds, you dill.'

'My dad says it's Antarctica,' Rob said, furious. 'D'you reckon my dad wouldn't know?'

'He was pulling your leg,' Graham said. 'Gee, I dunno, what makes you such a drip?'

'It is Antarctica,' Rob muttered, and fell into a brooding silence. Graham was probably right, and his father, incredibly, had been teasing him.

And yet it was still and always Antarctica. A country of cloud. A land of cloud and snow, a short sail away.

8

In an upstairs room of the palms, on a platform of branches and debris, the boys sat peering down from the tawny dimness on other unknown kids who passed in the sandy track through the scrub.

Pyeugh! they went, softly. *Peeowwww!* That was the sound of snipers.

Mrs Maplestead's palms had chambers and passages, reptile-haunted brown caves where secret societies flourished briefly and then died of boredom. At the risk of snakebite or impaling an eye, it seemed that boys might extend the labyrinth forever.

Pyeugh!

'I got that stupid tart,' Kevin O'Hara said, 'right through the neck.'

They felt such contempt for tarts that tarts were hardly worth shooting. 'Aw, tarts,' Rob would groan, puzzled that his mother flew into a rage whenever he used the word. 'Gawd, tarts.'

Yet deep inside him, inadmissible, there had been a certain respect for little girls, ever since a day in class when Athene Stratos had turned round in her seat and given him a bloody nose for pulling her pigtails.

Even through the blood and the humiliation he had had to laugh. Gee, that Athene was tough. He bet she could thrash her brother.

Pyeugh! He shot a big kid in the back. The stupid big kid had no suspicion that there were snipers in the palms. It must be interesting, being a sniper.

But it must be awful walking through the jungle and not knowing where the snipers were. There were awful things in the war, he had seen some awful newsreels at the kids matinée at the pictures. He had nine and a half years to wait till he joined the Army, and he rather hoped that the war would be over by then. But, of course, there would be another one. He had said to his mother: 'Do they have the News on the wireless when there isn't a war?' and she had said: 'Oh, there's always a war somewhere.'

'Hey,' Kevin O'Hara said. 'Someone's chopping this tree down.'

'Don't be mad.'

'No, they are. Listen.'

They cocked ears to the floor of their jungle-loft. Certainly someone was hacking at something.

'I can see who it is,' Graham Martin said. 'It's Mr Arden and Sister Rosalie.'

Mr Arden looked large, all in black, his face ruddy and warm under a wideawake hat. Sister Rosalie was shrouded in a grey nun's habit. Mr Arden and Sister Rosalie were the Church of England, and they appeared to be chopping down the tree with a tomahawk.

'Gawd, I dunno,' Kevin said. 'You get up a tree, and then some loony comes and cuts it down.'

Kevin was a Catholic. A bad State school Catholic.

'They're not gunna cut it down,' Rob said. 'They're just cutting branches. They're gunna make those little crosses for Palm Sunday.'

'You're s'posed to keep them and burn 'em on Ash Wednesday,' Graham said. 'Did you do that, Rob?'

'Nuh, I just keep 'em, like the poppies you get on Remembrance Day.'

'You s'posed to burn the poppies?' Kevin asked.

' 'Course not,' Graham said, scornfully. That was a blasphemous idea, anti-Anzac.

Down below Mr Arden and Sister Rosalie were going chop-chop and rustle-rustle-rustle. Rob stared at them through the fronds, thinking about Church. All that was very strange, very mysterious. He believed in God, he had a clear picture of what God looked like. God looked like the picture of Bernard Shaw in one of his father's books: He had a white beard and wore hiking shorts and long socks. But Jesus, Jesus was something different, and most curious. Even when he had first started going to Sunday school he had been able to feel no warmth for Jesus, and when they told the kids how Jesus had cursed the figtree, he had given up Jesus as hopeless. Heck, he'd like to hear what his grandmother would say if someone cursed one of her figtrees. Jesus was just bad tempered and wasteful. He would have made a lousy farmer.

It didn't seem to matter what religion people were. His father hadn't been to church since Nan was christened, and his mother only went to weddings and didn't really have any religion except being anti-Catholic. And he couldn't make out what his grandfathers had believed. Once he had said, puzzled by what was left of the late Dr Coram's library: 'Dad, was your father a Buddhist?' and his father had said: 'Mm? Well, I don't know. Perhaps.'

Among his other grandfather's books was the Koran, another foreign religion. And his mother had said that her father believed in reincarnation, which was something to do with a duck may be somebody's mother. It just didn't seem to matter about religion.

But Aunt Kay was very religious, and he liked to go to the Kirk with her, for one thing because they went at night, and for another thing because he liked sitting next to Aunt Kay and smelling the smell of the coats and gloves that she wore. He liked Aunt Kay's Kirk best. One night there had been a preacher from Scotland, from the Hebrides, and this preacher had said in his funny voice: 'There is a magical island in the river of time, where the harps are broken, and the lutes are cast away. . . .'

That was like poems, and on the way home he had kept imitating the preacher. 'There iss a matchical island in the riverr of tahim. . . .'

'You mustn't laugh,' Aunt Kay had said, laughing. 'He had a beautiful accent.'

'I wasn't laughing,' the boy said. 'I like the way he talks.' And he kept on reciting to himself, like a charm: 'There iss a matchical island in the riverr of tahim. . . .'

But the Hebridean preacher had only come for one night. And the Church, the true Church, always had been and always

would be these two figures down below, permanent and enduring in his world as Aunt Kay herself. Sister Rosalie, in grey
habit and sandals, climbing the steep sandhill to her house
full of orphans. Mr Arden, broad and black-clothed on his
bicycle, talking on Friday mornings of Scripture and England.

'In England,' he had told them, in mid-winter when no one
had been swimming for months, 'you children would be considered suntanned.'

Gawd, they had thought to themselves. What a life these
Pommies must lead.

'Wish they'd go,' Graham was saying, shifting restlessly. 'If
we come down now they're going to want to talk to us.'

They peered through the fronds at the two stooping figures.

'Agh,' said Kevin O'Hara. He drew a bead. *Pyeugh!* he
went, softly, and shot Sister Rosalie through the top of her
pointed head.

Like all the other ladies in Rob's world, Miss Mackay
MacRae practised the siesta. That was a good time for having
conversations with Aunt Kay, when she was resting, and in
the weekends he liked to go into her dark room and poke
around in her drawers and trunks and talk to her about the
things he found there: her jewellery, for instance, which
included a brooch made out of gold found by his grandfather.
'Poor Charles,' said Aunt Kay. 'It looks like a jockey's tiepin,
but he meant well.'

The boy thought it was lovely. 'Can I have it for a tiepin,
when I'm bigger?'

'Oh, you won't want to dress like a jockey,' said Aunt Kay.

Sometimes it struck him as funny, the way Grandma and
Aunt Kay had only one husband between them, and shared the
grandchildren. His mother said, darkly, that her father had
known what he was doing when he married Grandma and
Aunt Kay. She said that because when he came in from the
farm where he lived like a bachelor he would start living like
a king, and call out: 'Anne, where's my shirt? Kay, where are
my boots?' And Grandma and Aunt Kay would come running,
because he was a man, and they loved men.

The boy's mother and her sisters did not think very highly of men at all. They said that Grandma and Aunt Kay were doormats.

Aunt Kay's room was full of photographs, photographs of Charles Maplestead's children and Charles Maplestead's dogs and Charles Maplestead's horses and the Pool at Innisfail. And in her drawers, among the jewellery and the souvenirs, were more photographs of people Aunt Kay had not seen for a long time, and places where she had not been, like the redwood forests of California. There were also books which she treasured especially, or which she thought were too racy to go on public view.

Aunt Kay's most treasured book was about a horse. It was called *Wildfire*, by Zane Grey. Zane Grey had once passed through Geraldton to go fishing at Shark Bay, and the boy thought that that must have been an awesome occasion, but nobody could remember seeing him.

Aunt Kay's raciest book was about a girl who kept being found on the doorstep of a handsome embittered South African farmer: at first as an infant, and from then on regularly. 'Something within me has been resisting you,' said the handsome embittered farmer, at last, 'but this is indeed the moment I have dreamed of since one stormy night long ago when a tiny darkeyed child. . . .'

'Ergh,' said the boy, reading the last page. He was one of the kids who booed at the pictures when the hero finally got kissed.

He put the book back, picking up a photograph that had been lying beneath it. It was an old snapshot of a young woman in a bellskirt standing on a lawn.

That's Aunt Kay he thought, staring at the face. He had never seen a photograph of Aunt Kay, nor had anyone else. It was one of her eccentricities that she would never let herself be photographed.

He turned it over. On the white back of the snapshot there were dirty fingerprints, and someone had written something in pencil. He read the smudged letter with difficulty. *Fare well is just two little words, but they hold a deal of sorrow.*

Suddenly he felt ashamed at having seen it, and put it back quickly under the book. And he was very quiet and kind to Aunt Kay when they started talking again.

But the words ran round his head, and he had at last to ask his mother, when she came to say goodnight: 'Did Aunt Kay—ever have a boy-friend?'

'I think there was someone,' his mother said, frowning as she tried to remember. 'I think there was some awful rough fellow, and her brothers made him go away.'

He could not get out of his mind the grave face of the young woman in the photograph. A terrible sadness took hold of him when he thought of Aunt Kay. *Fare well is just two little words, but they hold a deal of sorrow.*

A falling picket fence divided the sandy yard from the street. The house was a narrow wooden house, iron-roofed, unpainted, like other houses all over the town. The peppertree that shaded the small front veranda smelled sharp in the sun.

Janet Cooper walked the sandy beaten track through the sparse couch-grass and mounted the wooden steps. On the veranda, a thin young man in shorts and singlet got up from the iron bed where he had been lying and stepped towards her in his bare feet.

'I suppose you know who I am,' she said, speaking very quietly, because she was nervous.

The man also was tense and shy. He said: 'Yeah, you'd be Mrs Cooper, wouldn't you?'

'I know you didn't really want to talk to me,' she said. 'But I did want to know.'

'Well, ah, won't you take a seat?' he said, waving awkwardly to a sagging chair. And she sat, and he sat down on the edge of the bed.

The floorboards, the bed, were strewn with shattered sunlight, strained through the leaves of the peppertree.

'This must be awful for you,' Janet Cooper said.

'No,' he said, 'no, I don't mind talking about it, it's just that—I didn't know how you'd take it, I thought you might be —you know?——'

'That was over long ago.'

'Yeah,' he said. 'Yeah, it would be.'

She was staring at the thin freckled arms. 'But you,' she said, 'are you quite well now?'

'Ah, I'm fit, I feel good.'

'It must be like a dream, to be home.'

'It was a dream, all right,' he said, 'at first. But now the other thing seems like a dream.'

'You were lucky.'

'You don't need to tell me. When we got on that ship, I was dead sure I was gunna die in Nippon. And when we got hit, all I could think of was I was gunna die in the water. Then suddenly—no more Nips, no more war—back to Mum and home cooking. That was luck, all right.'

In spite of everything, the tears pricked.

'I'd heard,' she said, 'that you knew something about Peter. That was why I came.'

He looked down at his hands, clasped between his bony knees.

'It's all right,' she said, 'I'm not going to be emotional. It's just that I—I heard that you'd said that Peter died in Thailand, and I wanted to—hear that from you. It's true, isn't it?'

'Yeah,' he said, still not looking at her. Sunlight spattered on his sandy hair, that she now intently watched. 'He—he died quite easy, you know, and—and Rick Maplestead looked after him real good, he couldn't of had a better mate than that. I wouldn't worry about him now, 'cause—well, compared to things that might of happened, what happened to Pete was —real easy, you know, real quiet. It couldn't of been better.'

He turned his head at last and looked at her. He saw that her eyes were full of tears, but that she would not cry.

In the street, wind stirred the dust, whistling a little in the skeletal Norfolk Island pines.

'And Rick?' she said.

'Rick was wearing pretty well, up to just before I left, but then he was pretty crook, I dunno how that would of turned out——'

'*Very* sick?' she asked, staring out at the street.

'You can't tell. I seen so many big strong blokes just drop, and so many little blokes come through what oughter've killed 'em. You can't tell how things are gunna take people.'

'Do you think Rick's dead?' she murmured.

'I dunno,' he said, watching his hands again. 'Yeah. Yeah, I reckon he is.'

She no longer saw the street, her eyes were unfocused. And now he began to talk, to describe the life he had come from, the life that had killed Peter, and it neither shocked nor moved her, it seemed so incredibly remote. He was racking his memory for every detail he could think of concerning Peter, and what he remembered seemed to have no bearing on her husband. He remembered some other Peter, some other Rick. They were people she had never known or seen.

The young man was looking at her, anxiously. 'I'm not upsetting you, am I?' he was saying. 'You don't mind hearing all this?'

'No,' she said. 'No,' rising from the sagging chair. 'I wanted to know. Everything. You've been very patient and very kind.'

He rose, and they shook hands. 'If there's anything I can do——' he said.

But of course there was nothing. She walked the street in a trance of memory, fences and hedges just registering in her physical view. She walked the red path of the Coram's house, and in through the open front door.

'Back already,' Margaret Coram said, rising from a chair. 'Let's have some tea, then.'

'It was true,' Janet Cooper said. 'I knew it was.'

'Janet——'

The windows were open to let in the sea-breeze. Beyond the flapping curtains was the street, the stunted gums. The street was Australia: sandy, makeshift, innocent.

'I feel so—so sticky now,' Janet Cooper said. 'I must just go and wash my hands, it's like summer——'

The thin trickle of water ran into the basin, over her wrists. She listened to the water, the wind in the leaves outside, the intermittent clank of the windmill, voices beyond the door.

'Who's that in the bathroom?'

'Aunty Janet.'

'Can I go back to Andarra with her?'

'No, Rob. Please—go away and play.'

The water flowed and flowed. Oh, why now? I said goodbye, I said goodbye two years ago. Why this now, why this?

The dunes were like snow, like hills of snow. Here and there a few bushes broke the drifts, but the slopes were bone-white, wind-rippled and smoking.

As Rob climbed to the top of a dune, someone shot him: *pyeugh!* 'Eow!' he screamed, and rolled to the bottom of the white slope. Sand filled his clothes and his hair as he lay dead.

Kevin O'Hara had taken off his shirt, and was rolling at tremendous speed down the dune. A fume of sand came with him.

'Watch out,' Rob shouted, getting up. But the juggernaut called Kevin O'Hara hit him behind the knees, and he fell flat.

'Aw—you,' he said, spitting sand.

At the top of the dune Graham Martin was standing, sharply drawn against the sky. 'Come on, youse kids,' he shouted. 'Stop mucking about.'

The other two picked themselves up and charged towards him. 'Charge!' they shouted. On the way, Rob grabbed Kevin by the belt and flung him revengefully in the sand.

Graham was looking into the white valley below, scanning the old stone cottage with the board-covered windows that peered out from behind a clump of tobacco-bush. The floor of the valley was hard sand, partly overgrown with a red-stemmed succulent like green worms. It was a very desolate, very Antarctic scene.

'D'you reckon there's anyone there?' Kevin asked, dropping his voice, although the cottage was a long way out of earshot.

'No,' Graham said, also low. 'I reckon it's safe.'

They began to descend into the valley, moving cautiously, and keeping an eye on the doorless doorway.

There was no telling when old men might be living in the cottage, and whatever old man was there was sure to be mad. Once there had even been a woman, a lady called Methylated

Myrtle, who used to come in to the fringe of the town and scream prophecies in the street where Rob lived. The inhabitants of the dunes were always crazy. Even the amiable ageless boy from the town, who roamed the dunes every day with a rifle, was half-witted.

The dunes and valleys were called The Hommoes, or Mahomet's Flats, after Mahomet the Afghan who had built the cottage. It was because of Mahomet that the boys were making this perilous reconnaissance of his valley.

Even barefoot, even in the sand, they still, for safety, walked on tiptoe past the cottage.

'Over there,' Kevin whispered, pointing.

'No,' Graham said. 'We tried there last week, and struck water.'

'You get water everywhere,' Rob said. 'D'you reckon the treasure might of rusted away by now?'

'Gold doesn't rust, you dill.'

'How do you know it's gold?' Kevin said. 'I reckon it'd be jewels, you know, pearls and emeralds and rubies and diamonds and moidores and things like that.'

'Moidores are gold,' Rob said. 'They're money.'

'I reckon it'd be sovereigns,' Graham said. 'That's what they used for money when Mahomet was here.'

'Why wouldn't he've put it in the bank, well?' Kevin demanded.

'Because he was a miser, dope.'

'Gee,' Rob said, 'I hope it's jewels and so on like Kevin reckons. I reckon it'd be in an old oak chest with a skull on top of it.'

'And a piece-of-eight between the skull's teeth,' Kevin said. 'Gee.'

'I reckon it'd be in a dirty old Afghan sock,' Graham said.

'Aw, pew,' they all said.

'Where we gunna dig?'

'Here,' Graham said. 'It's gotta be near the house somewhere. It's no good going right out there, that's where you get the water.'

They knelt in the sand, and began digging with their hands.

It was late afternoon, and the sun laid a sharp golden halo on the ridges of the dunes, glinting on the grey-green leaves of the scrub. Behind the line of dunes that closed the valley to the south, the sea was peacefully snoring. Blue shadow crept across the flat sand floor, and the air grew sharp.

'My Grandfather Maplestead,' Rob said, dreamily, feeling the tingling of his fingertips as he dug into the coarse sand, 'my Grandfather Maplestead knew where the treasure from the *Gilt Dragon* is.'

'Aw, I bet he did,' Kevin said. 'That's why you're a millionaire.'

'No, he did,' Rob said, 'dinkum. It's at Jurien Bay. He knew where to find it, but he never got round to going there before he fell off his horse and died.'

'Gee,' Graham said, sitting back on his heels, 'd'you reckon he might of left a map somewhere?'

Kevin was getting excited too. 'Hey, would there be any secret panels or something in your grandmother's house?'

'Heck,' Rob said, 'I never thought of that. 'Cause it's an old old house. Built by convicts. Yeah, I *bet* there's some secret panels in it.'

'Has your grandmother made a Will?' Graham asked, keenly.

'Yeah, I s'pose so. She's pretty old.'

'Well, then, she'd have to have a secret panel, wouldn't she,' Graham said, 'to hide her Will in.'

'Gosh,' said Rob.

'Gosh,' said Kevin.

They sat on their heels around the hole, looking at each other.

'The hole's filling up with water,' Graham said, slowly.

'Yeah, let's go,' Kevin said. 'Let's go to Rob's grandmother's before it gets dark.'

'How're we gunna get to Jurien Bay, but?' Rob wondered.

'We'll get a fisherman to take us,' Graham said. 'We'll give him a share of the treasure.'

'Gosh,' said Kevin.

'Gosh,' said Rob.

The blue shadow was creeping across the dunes.

'Yippee!' Graham shouted suddenly, jumping up and starting to run towards the high dune on the town side.

'We're gunna be rich,' Kevin shouted. He and Rob jumped up and pushed each other, and struggled to get a grip on each other's gritty necks.

'C'mon,' Graham called back.

They pushed each other away, and started to run.

From the top of the dune, where they stood for a moment, panting, the white hills set in grey-green scrub dazzled against the sea. Costa Branca, Rob thought, catching his breath. Aunt Kay had taught him that. The first name of his country, the Portuguese name. The White Coast.

The Portuguese had named the Abrolhos too: the keep-your-eyes-open islands. The Dutch had not changed that name. But Costa Branca had been forgotten, had become just a part of New Holland. Yet it had been the first, the oldest named land in Australia.

He thought about the Abrolhos, feeling a thrill of darkness. He had never been there, and the islands were too far away to be seen, though the fishing boats had gone back and forth as long as he could remember, bucking over the sea. He had never been there, but the name gave him a thrill of darkness.

Darkness and fires and massacre. The staid Dutch merchants and their wives from the wrecked *Batavia*, camping as best they could on the barren islands, must have settled down grumbling on that night. And then, the torches and swords, the blood on rock and sea, the mutineers prancing, in the richest clothes from the rifled chests, round their crazy peacock of a Captain-General.

Hundreds of men had died on that night. Hundreds of bodies had sunk through the night sea to the roots of the Abrolhos: the Graveyard of Ships, the graveyard of bones and treasure.

Fire and blood, and lace and velvet and steel. Never knowing that Pelsart in his tiny boat would reach Batavia and bring back retribution.

And then more blood on the Abrolhos: lopped hands and

dangling corpses feeding the gulls. And for two, the fate, equivalent to death, of becoming the first white settlers of Costa Branca.

The boy looked out across the white dunes. He thought of the two marooned mutineers who might have stood here, where he stood, watching the ship go away. He thought of them as night fell, at this time of afternoon, wandering in the greying dunes. They would have been scared then, thinking of blackfellows, too scared probably to light a fire. He thought of them plodding day after day along the White Coast, perhaps setting out in different directions, perhaps quarrelling, and then when night fell calling, calling to one another across the pale ridges of moonlit sand.

In the reddening sunset light he felt cold and lonely. He ran after Graham and Kevin, running between them, throwing an arm round each neck and swinging, until they fell cursing in the sand under the weight of his affection.

9

The town had its seasons and its sounds, like the country. Lying on the clover-sown lawn in the winter sun, or in a hammock under the cool peppertrees in the summer, the boy listened to the sounds of the town's seasons.

Always the sea, roaring or praying. Always, somewhere, a wind among leaves, a clank of windmills. Always, somewhere, a rooster crowing, someone hammering, the clop of the baker's horse in the street, a child calling, the whang of the circular saw in the distant woodyard, the far hoot of a lazy train.

In summer, in the hot east wind of the early morning, doves roocooed and dogs barked, a horse-drawn lorry clattered past, the milkman rattled his cans at the gate. And in the afternoons, when the southerly came in, the windmills whooshed in the air, leaves flapped and fluttered, sprinklers turned slowly, slowly, pattering spray on the parched grass.

The iceman came through the gate at a half trot, afraid that the block of bubble-speared ice that he held between iron claws would melt in the street. From farther away came the sad *Wollamulla!* cry of the Wollamulla man, who was trying to say that he sold watermelons.

At night the sea was loud, the easterly sneaked around corners. Suddenly out of the dark would come the eerie shriek of Susan's peacocks.

In winter, before rain, when the wind came from the north, sounds also came from the north, and the banging and the shouts of men working on the wharf were clear and sharp. Mudlarks hopped on the lawns, scratching the air with their calls like diamonds on glass. After rain the gutters gurgled, the tanks gurgled as the fresh water drained into them. Someone would be chopping wood; someone would be calling, playing football in a back street. In the warm Sunday afternoons of winter the siren wailed on the football field, marking the quarters.

The town had its scents and seasons like the country. In the dry, burning easterly of March, leaves wilted, grass dried. The southerly was damp and salt off the sea. And winter smelled of crushed winter-grass, crushed clover, crushed, sour and bitter weeds, fat-hen and mallows.

And spring smelled of capeweed and wattle, the pollen of capeweed and wattle, the green-white flowers of peppertrees, the flowering sandhill scrub. Spring smelled of wild jonquils in his grandmother's lawns, of freezias tended by Aunt Kay, of that elusive scent from the black-columned mauve-petalled sprays of Cape lilac. And autumn smelled of the first rain, bitter and clean; and bitterly, cleanly, of chrysanthemums in Aunt Kay's garden.

In every season the boy exulted in his senses, in his body. He exulted in the heavy sweetness of jonquils and in the frail scent of tomato leaves; in the harsh rasp of leaves on his skin as he climbed a figtree, and in the waxy dusty smoothness of the minute datepalm flowers; in the cold sea of early morning, and in the warm sea under the rain. He loved the rough taste of gumleaves and the sweetness in tecoma flowers; the red jewels in pomegranates, and the shells of rainbow beetles in the grey tuart bark. The boy then was little more than a body, a set of sense organs. To himself he had little identity, and to his friends none at all, as they had none to him. They knew each other by sight and hearing, by certain mannerisms. In absence, they ceased to exist for one another.

They exulted in their bodies, in their senses; in skills of movement that they were learning, in appetites that were new. Their bodies, their senses did not fail them. Only with the first sunburn of summer could a body be a liability; and when that was over it became a new fascination, as absorbedly they peeled the skin from each other's backs.

The boy exulted in his senses. The town had its sounds and its scents and its seasons. But at times he raged against the town, feeling dispossessed, feeling exiled from the country where he knew his body belonged.

116

Then he escaped from the town. On the school bus, singing.

> You are my sunshine, my only sunshine,
> You make me happy, when skies are grey . . .

The school bus rang with singing. The school bus was beautiful, a chariot. Or, to a less infatuated eye, a sort of cray-pot on wheels, a grey wooden vegetable-crate with flapping canvas instead of glass at the windows.

> You'll never know, dear, how much I love you:
> Please don't take my sunshine away.

He watched the flat land pass, the brown squares of tomato gardens fenced with brushwood, the wattle and banksia scrub. Then the bus was skirting the flat-topped range.

> **The oy-ul wells**
> **Are full of smells**
> *—Deep in the heart of Texas* . . .

In the shadow of the hills was the Witch's House, the abandoned stone cottage with a pointed roof like a witch's hat.

> **They remind me of**
> **The one I love**
> *—Deep in the heart of Texas.*

The country was green, green under winter, and the hills green and blue-dark. And the landmarks were children, the names of children getting off the bus. An orange side-road was Con and Athene Stratos. A pair of houses by a big gum was Bill Cook and Rosina Morelli.

The road was rising, climbing to the raw red cutting in the low range. Now, from the cutting, the view was immense: a huge green land, dark-splotched with scrub and cloud-shadow, sliding eastward towards the heart of mythical Australia.

The bus was descending, bumping on a corrugated road, crossing a bridge. Then it was halting at a fork, beside a clump of tall aloes.

117

Rob took his suitcase and followed the two other boys out. He felt a little in awe of them still. Whatever the town kids at school might say about country bumps, there was somehow a feeling that a country kid had a clear hereditary superiority over a town kid; and Rob had just discovered, with a certain surprise, that he was a townie.

Jack Moore was already tall, and nearly two years older than Rob. When he bothered to talk, he was full of sardonic fantasies about people who met with his scorn, which was all-embracing and impressive to behold. A few scathing witticisms from Jack could strip a grown man of all dignity in the other kids' eyes.

Rob thought Jack hero-material, but he was scared of Jack's tongue. And he was not much less scared of Jack's brother David, his age-mate, who already had a fair proficiency in the art of comic scorn.

It was their fantasies as much as their sardonic humour that kept him on his guard. He simply did not know when to believe them; and as soon as he had detected one whopper he was likely to fall for a bigger one. In the Moore's family grave-yard one day, looking down at the remains of a glass-domed floral ornament on their grandmother's grave, which seemed pretty to him, he had said: 'Pity that got broken.'

'Aw, that was Grandpa,' Jack said. 'He chucked a rock at it.'

'Gosh,' said Rob, 'that was a funny thing to do.'

'Grandpa's always chucking boondies at Grandma's grave,' said Jack, deadpan. And Rob would believe him for years, though the elder Mr Moore was a model widower.

Now they walked the climbing road to where the house stood, on a rise overlooking the gums and red breakaways of the shallow river. In the front garden, a billow of soft green starred with yellow sourgrass flowers, a stooping man straightened and leaned on his spade.

'G'day, Salvatore,' David shouted.

The man grinned and waved. 'Die, Dieveeda,' he said.

They all laughed at Salvatore, because he could not speak English. He was one of the Italian prisoners-of-war who had

118

been sent to work on the farms round about.

'You can go home now, Salvatore,' Jack called out, 'now the Allies are back in France.'

'Yeah, yeah,' laughed Salvatore, not understanding a word.

'He doesn't want to,' David said. 'He wants to stay here and do embroidery.'

'He doesn't, does he?' Rob said, shocked.

'Yeah, he does, he sits in his room and sews pictures. They're good, too.'

Rob was baffled: by the idea of a soldier, even an Italian soldier, doing fancywork, and by the Moores's tolerance.

'I've got a cousin who's a prisoner-of-war,' he said. He tried to think what Rick might be doing: working for a Jap farmer, maybe, drawing pictures for the farmer's kids. Perhaps Rick was happy. Certainly Salvatore was happy, and resisted going home; in fact, in the end would go home under protest, and immediately try to return to the Moores, who had always laughed at him affectionately.

As he had at them. 'Salvatore,' Mrs Moore had said once, in mid-summer, consulting her phrase book and approximating Italian. 'When the sun is shining, do not make water on the flowers, for they will die.'

And Salvatore had collapsed in wild giggles, while Mrs Moore stared.

'You mean Rick Maplestead?' Jack was saying. 'I bet he wouldn't mind swapping places with old Salvatore.'

'You don't *know* Rick Maplestead's a prisoner,' David said. 'I heard someone reckon he's dead.'

'I dunno,' Rob said, his voice trailing away, retracting from the subject. Once he would have denied the possibility. But Aunty Janet's husband had been with Rick, and now Aunty Janet was a widow. And Rick's face, Rick's person, kept fading and fading in his memory, until there was not much left to Rick but a name and a few jokes and certain places forever associated with him. He hoped that Rick was not dead; but Rick had been gone for so long that his death was already prepared for.

Kajarra was whitewashed and red-roofed, a plain, pleasant

house with dark wooden ceilings. Like most homesteads of its age it had been built with a kitchen block at a distance from the main house, and the boys slept in the old dining-room, at the end of a creeper-hung latticed walk. Mrs Moore was in the path when they came through the gate in the saltbush hedge, and greeted them with calm no-nonsense friendliness.

'You'd better change your clothes straight away,' she said, leaving them at the door of the old dining-room.

'Or else,' Jack muttered, sotto voce. It was one of the fantasies of the junior Moores that their mother was a savage and uncontrollable woman.

They changed in the big dim room, putting on battered old shoes.

'What are we going to do?' David said.

'I dunno,' Jack said. 'Will we go to the creek?'

'Yeah,' said the other two, following his lead, as usual, through a yard of rank mallows, across a fence and down a slope to the small creek that outlined the rise the house stood on. Dropping down a red clay bank, they stood under the gums in the sand stippled with late sunlight.

'The dam's gone,' Rob said. He stood in the sand in a sort of dream, soothed by the faint hush of the meagre stream, the moving leaves, the sound of mudlarks in the sunlit paddocks.

'You want to build it again?' David said.

'Yeah, let's do that.'

They began carrying dead branches and laying them across the creek piling green leaves and clods against them, until slowly the trickle through the barrier ceased. Now the water was silent, and the sand downstream soaked up what had passed before. The cold pool behind the dam grew deeper.

They ran back and forth from the bank, carrying more clods to widen the wall. Shoes were kicked aside, and the cold sand bit into their feet.

'Gee,' David said, standing in the water. 'Look at this.' It was up to his knees.

'Get on with it,' Jack ordered. 'It's going to go.'

That was the exciting part, when the water began to catch up with the wall. They tossed up sand feverishly, using an old shovel blade that was left down there for the purpose.

'It's going to go,' Jack said, panting.

'Gosh,' Rob said, looking at the sheet of water behind the dam. They had turned this miserable little creek into a river. Miles upstream people were probably saying: 'Where is all this water coming from?' and miles downstream they were saying: 'What made the creek go dry?'

It gave one a sense of power.

'D'you reckon we could dam the Chapman?' he asked. 'Gee, that'd make people wonder.'

'Don't be dumb,' Jack said, still breathless and wildly shovelling. 'Hey. Hey, stand out of the way.'

He jumped back. And with a burst of water and sand the dam wall broke, and a flood tore down the river, carrying sticks, grass, leaves and everything.

'All that for nothing,' Jack said. But they knew that the only reason they built the dams was for the satisfaction of that moment when the water proved too much for them.

The yellow, stick-strewn flood poured on. 'I wonder what people are thinking,' Rob said, 'down there.'

'I bet they think Jack Moore's having a leak,' said David.

'Aw, joke,' Jack said. 'Lend me a feather.'

They sneered at each other. 'Yok yok yok.'

As the land cooled, the pasture gave out an exhilarating sweetness.

'You want to see the horses?' Jack said.

'Yeah,' said Rob. They climbed back up the bank, and through the mallows, crossing the farmyard to the stableyard, and slipping under the rails to fondle the two horses that were in that afternoon.

While Bessy nuzzled at his hand, Rob looked carefully at her teeth. They were all there, he saw. He was terribly anxious about Bessy's teeth. Every time he came back from riding Bessy he counted her teeth, because Mr Moore had told him that if he let her hang her head her teeth would drop out. While he was riding, he started neurotically at any sound that might be the sound of a falling fang; and would ride, for years afterwards, with such a tight rein that most horses hated him.

Jack was fondling Dandy. Rob felt gratitude to Dandy. Dandy was the first horse who had ever cantered with him, and in some mystical way it was because he had fallen off Dandy then that he could ride now. 'You can't learn to ride without a fall' was a proverb of his world, like 'If it doesn't rain by May the tenth, it will rain after.' So it was Dandy who had initiated him.

He drank in the smell of horse, his face against Bessy's neck. It reminded him of Rick, the horse-smell. Rick had been going to teach him to gallop when he came home; but now there was no need.

'Where'd David go?' Jack said.

'I'm in the chaff,' David called from inside the shed.

They went into the dim shed. Sunlight was falling in spears through nail holes in the roof, making burning pools on the great golden hill where David sat. They stepped across the wooden barrier that kept the chaff from spilling out. Then David came down, whoosh, in a golden avalanche, and bowled Rob over in the slippery drifts.

Their jumpers were a mess of clinging gold.

'You'll be sorry,' Jack said. 'Wait till Mother sees you.'

'What are you fussing about?' David said.

'I reckon we better take our shirts and jumpers off,' Rob said, pulling his over his head.

'You'll get chaff-itch,' Jack said.

'Listen to him.' David said inside his shirt. He mimicked somebody unknown to Rob. ' "I get so worried about you boys".'

'Aaah,' Jack said, and started to laugh, after fighting the temptation for a while. Then he too stripped to his trousers and climbed the yellow hill to its summit below the roof.

'Well, goodbye, Rob,' David said, shoving.

'Hey,' Rob said. He grabbed David round the neck, and they rode the avalanche down together.

Chaff dust filled their throats and nostrils, and they lay at the bottom coughing.

'Sorry to do this to you,' Jack said, and came down in a yellow cataclysm that left them buried.

'Aw, jeepers, Jack,' Rob said, as they emerged and started to sort themselves out.

'Ssh,' Jack said.

'What?'

'Barney's in the milking shed. We better get out, or he'll tell Dad.'

They dusted each other off and put on their shirts. They looked crazy, Rob thought: their hair full of chaff, their faces coated with dust. Every time he blinked, sharp particles pricked him. David's eyes were watering, making damp trails in the dust.

Barney, the senior farmhand, was milking. They heard the low complaint of the cows, and the spurt of milk into a bucket.

They stole up behind him, in the big dim milking shed where he sat, head bent, on a stool. It was a sort of power they had over him, being there, watching him, without his knowing.

Then a jet of milk caught Jack full in the face.

'You cunning old so-and-so,' Jack said, wiping his face.

'That'll be the day,' Barney said, still without turning, 'when you can sneak up on me.'

'Gee, you're a good shot,' David said, enviously. 'How d'you do it?'

'You gotta be as old as me,' Barney said, 'to know how to handle a tit.'

They all gave a dirty laugh. Then a dreamy silence took hold of the shadowy shed, and they stood still, listening to the measured spurt of milk in the bucket, and the stirrings and murmurings of cows.

'What are we going to do?' David said, at last.

'I dunno,' said Jack.

'Let's go and fight, Jack,' Rob said, 'in the weeds.'

'D'you want to fight?' David said to Jack.

'I don't care,' Jack said, shrugging. 'If you want to.'

'Is Les home?' Rob said. 'It's good fun when the three of us get on to Les.'

'You don't mean to lose, do you?' said Barney.

'Old Les,' Jack said, 'he doesn't mind, he's as strong as a bullock.'

'But he ain't half the man his dad was,' said Barney. Barney was Les's dad.

'Aw, listen to the——' Jack started to say, and then got an eyeful of milk. 'You've got tickets on yourself,' he finished, lamely.

'Don't you give me none of your lip,' said Barney, 'or I'll come out and wrestle the lot of youse.'

'Gee, I'm scared,' they all said. 'Crikey, let's get out of here.' They scattered to the door, and to the red-earthed yard still warm in the last of the sunlight.

'Right, fight's on,' Jack said, jumping the fence into the smaller yard overgrown with weeds. By the time the other two had climbed in he was already armed, and the bombardment was beginning.

The game had no rules, but a certain shape. It began with both sides pulling up weeds by the roots, throwing the clods or beating each other over the head with them. The soil was gluey, the weeds were immensely tall, and the clods seemed to weigh half a ton. After the attack had gone on for a while and exhaustion was setting in, the parties would move in at close quarters and the game became a two-against-one wrestling match.

Now the clods were flying, and breath was growing short. Between bombardments came a frantic tugging at weeds as all re-armed. 'Oof,' Jack groaned, as a great lump of earth descended on his stooped back. Then his ammunition came loose from the earth, and Rob sprawled as it hit him in the chest.

'I dunno,' said a slow voice from the fence. 'D'you ever see such a dirty-lookin' mob?'

That was Les. Broadchested, bullock-like Les, who was fourteen.

'Hey, Les,' Jack said, 'which side are you going to be on?'

'I ain't gunna be on no side,' said Les. 'Whichever side I'm on everyone else is on the other.'

A small clod, thrown by David, donged him on the side of the head.

'By gee, young David,' Les said, vaulting the fence.

'Beauty,' Jack said. 'Get him.'

They jumped on Les. Fighting Les was a marvellous sensation, like throwing a bull. They struggled with Les, almost dancing with him, as they skidded on weed-stems and the clayey ground. Sometimes Les had Jack's head under his arm, till the other two managed to release it. Sometimes Jack got a headlock on Les, and then they climbed on Les's back. But Les would not fall.

'Pull his legs,' David whispered. He and Rob each grabbed an ankle, and dragged. At last, kicking, Les was brought down.

Then they let go his legs to jump on his chest, and in an instant he had got a scissors grip on Jack and was sitting on him.

'Choke him off,' Jack groaned to David, who obligingly tried to strangle Les from behind. But Les did not seem to notice.

'Give in?' he said to Jack.

'No.'

'Give in?' said Les, digging his thumbs into Jack's biceps.

'Aw,' said Jack. 'All right.'

Les stood up. Immediately, David and Rob jumped on him, then Jack joined them, and Les was down again, securely pinned.

'Give in?' Jack said, boring into Les's shoulders with his thumbs.

'Nuh,' said Les, smiling at the sky.

'Rub a lump of dirt in his face,' David suggested.

'All right,' Les said. 'I give in.'

'Who's a dirty-looking mob now?'

'You are,' Les said. 'You're a dirty mob of fighters, too.'

'Here,' David said, holding out a clod. 'Shove that in his mouth.'

'All right,' Les said, 'I'm a dirty-lookin' mob.'

'You're a dirty fighter, too.'

'An' a dirty fighter, too. Takes one Chink to reckernize another.'

They bounced on Les a bit, considering the problem of withdrawal. Somehow they had to get off him and to safety in a single movement.

'When I count three,' said Jack, meaningfully, 'I'm going to

rub this in your face for calling me a Chink. One—two—
three!'

On the signal, Les's tormentors rose from the carcass like
vultures and flew to the house.

Looking back, they saw Les still lying among the weeds,
smiling up at the twilight sky. It was a terrible anti-climax.

·'These big blokes haven't got the stamina,' Jack said, making
the best of it.

They took stock of one another. Their hair was full of chaff,
their legs were river-clay up to the shin, and their faces masks
of reddish loam. Their knees and elbows were bright green
from falling among the weeds, and they were sweating.

'Go on, you two,' Jack said, 'get under the shower before
Mother sees you.'

'I have seen you,' said Mrs Moore, coming out of the
shower room, 'you dirty-looking little monkeys.'

'You gunna let her get away with that?' Rob whispered to
Jack.

The water from the shower was river-water, it had its own
taste and its own smell. That had become another of Rob's
nostalgias, the Kajarra water.

They sat, clean and combed, in the smoking-room, reading.
Then they sat round the table in the new dining-room. When
first Rob started coming to Kajarra it had seemed unfarmlike,
because it had electric light. He missed the lamps of Sandalwood and Andarra, their flutter and their smell. But he liked
this room with the jarrah ceiling, and he listened to Mr and
Mrs Moore with fascination as they teased each other. He had
never heard grown-ups joking like this, it delighted him.
'Goodness,' said Mrs Moore, seeing him quivering with sup-
pressed giggles, 'if everyone thought we were as funny as you
do, we could go on the stage.'

Rick had said that, he remembered, still quivering. One
afternoon in the stableyard at Sandalwood, when the war
started.

When the lamp was taken away from the room where they
slept, in the old kitchen block which had no electric light, the
boys lay talking by the faint blue glow of a nightlight on the

mantelshelf. This was the time when Jack wove his most extraordinary fantasies, about the things he had seen and done, and the things that people like Les and Barney had seen and done. After a while Rob got tired of giggling: 'Aw, bulldust,' and let it flow over him.

The trees sighed in the road outside, and the generator put-putted in its shed. For a while a boobook owl visited the trees, very melancholy with its slow, measured *boo-book*.

He was soothed by the owl, by the tranquil breathing in the other beds. I'm happy here, he thought, sleepily. I wonder if Mrs Moore would adopt me if I was an orphan.

The boy liked the winter mornings, the silver and green mornings when the plovers called above the mist, when butcher-birds warbled in the first sun and the air was biting on hands buckling girths and gripping reins. He liked the silver dew on the grazed grass, the dew-hung spiderwebs from twigs and fences, the dew smoking from cantering hoofs, the smoke of breath and warmsmelling horseflesh. He liked, in the midst, above the smoking river, the fragile swaying bridge of wire and planks slung between two gumtrees, where one stood as if floating above the shallow water.

He liked the noises of morning, the cows coming in, dogs meeting their first humans for the day, roosters crowing. And in the growing warmth of the day, jerseys being shed, the long aimless rides (taking care of Bessy's teeth) and the long aimless walks, with a dog rushing back and forth on the scent of rabbits. He liked the wild races to catch a rabbit by hand, the tense waiting outside a burrow where a rabbit had vanished, hearing from under the earth the thump-thump of its alarm. Under the earth were other worlds. He watched ants and rabbits with fascination, wondering.

And there was one silver and green morning that would never be lost from his memory: one morning when he had stood with David beside the truck in a far paddock, idly watching the black shapes of the Aberdeen Angus herd in the mist. Near the dark shapes were small pale shapes, and he thought: That's funny, to see sheep in with the cattle. And he said aloud: 'Those sheep have got funny horns.'

'They'd be funny, all right,' Mr Moore said, 'if they were sheep.'

'Well—what are they?' Rob said, staring at them.

And Mr Moore said: 'They're deer.'

Then Rob could hardly breathe for enchantment, watching the alien visitants in the mist.

'Old Mr Mackenzie brought them from India,' Mr Moore was saying. 'He used to have them running round the homestead at Lochinch. Then these fellows struck out on their own.'

'Come and see them,' David said, stepping into the mist.

They moved forward among the black cattle, watching the wary, listening forms of the deer. For a moment Rob saw them with such clarity that their foreignness almost shocked him: the deep watchful eyes, the delicate horns, the tiny hoofs. Then they pranced about and bounded away, dimming in the mist.

'They're so little,' Rob said, breathing the words like a sigh. Inside him, the name kept reverberating like a charm. Deer, he kept saying. Deer.

There seemed no end to the apparitions his world might reveal.

Then he would go back to town: waiting on cold early mornings, by the tall aloes, for the school bus to appear in the light river mist.

He hated that. It was exile and demotion, making him again a townie instead of a bush kid. He belonged, he knew, to the country where his grandfather and great-grandfather had belonged. And yet he had no land.

He would be a farmer, he thought. He would be a farmer, some day.

At his grandmother's house Aunt Rosa and Aunt May came visiting: dressed all in black, big hatpins spiking their black hats, black velvet ribbons around their old white throats.

Aunt Rosa and Aunt May were having an argument. They were arguing about Aunt Rosa's age. Aunt Rosa said that she was ninety-one, and Aunt May said that Aunt Rosa was only ninety.

The boy felt choked with laughter, listening.

Then Aunt May said: 'Rob,' and he came to her. 'We are going to give you a present, Rob,' said Aunt May. 'We are going to give you a calf.'

His heart jumped. He could hardly thank her. They were going to give him a calf, and he could start being a farmer already, keeping his calf on the tennis court at home.

But he had misunderstood. He would never see the calf. When it was grown they would sell it, and give him the money. So he stammered his thanks, finding that easier now, because no one could be excited about money.

They gave him a calf, and another calf, and a third calf, and the money went into his bank account, and he ordered a pair of roller skates from Perth, something no other kid in the town possessed. But he never saw one of the calves that might have made him a farmer.

So he was doomed to be a townie. He was a Coram, not a Maplestead, and the Corams belonged to an old but other Australia. The Corams had no land. The land that they had had was a suburb of Adelaide, built over with houses, and now the Corams were people who lived in towns, owning no land, only the dew-frosted lawns that Rob's father, in his dressing-gown, traced with green footprints in the early mornings.

Under the shower, at Kajarra, Jack said: 'Old Val's going to have a baby.'

'What's she want a baby for?' Rob said. 'She isn't even married.'

'Aw,' said Jack, offhand, 'Old Jim's been —ing her.'

Rob knew all about *that*. *That* was no mystery, either to country kids or to town kids who roamed the sandhills. And Old Val and Old Jim, who were both about fifteen and lived on neighbouring farms, were a likely age for it.

Yet he was puzzled. 'What's that got to do with it?'

He could see Jack looking suddenly evasive, being responsible, a ten-year-old addressing an eight-year-old. He said, turning away: 'Aaah—you can't have a baby without that. You know?—like taking a cow to the bull.'

Rob thought about it in silence. Slowly, he began to burn with fury against Jack. Jack had gone too far this time, with his fantasies. He had accused the whole grown-up world of behaving like dirty kids, he had implicated. . . . The boy could not bear to think of the implications, but he felt a loyal rage against Jack, and would not speak to him.

No, he would not believe it. No one but larrikins and boongs had ever behaved like that.

But gradually, the new facts slid into place in his scheme of things, and though the world was changed by them, it made sense. In time he forgave Jack, and David too, which was harder, because David had gravely listened to Rob's theory that babies were manufactured under government licence by a sort of sausage-machine in Perth, and must have been laughing fit to bust inside. In the end he accepted. The mystery was to be explained by a greater mystery.

But one person he did not forgive. Life, it seemed, was not at all as described in *Cole's Funny Picture Book*, and he felt bitterly about Mr Cole, who must have been sniggering all the time behind his Burke-and-Wills beard.

Spring came, and Paris was liberated, and even grown-ups talked of the end of the war.

Summer meant the sea, every day the sea. It meant sunburn, and backs becoming a mass of freckles, and the walk to the sea over hot roads, jumping from shadow to shadow. It was good then to come upon the ice-cart standing outside a house and to crouch under the cold drips, sometimes even to pick up a lump of ice, not too much the worse for dirt and horse-manure. The west end of the harbour was delivered up to the children as the war moved away. Fences became mere rusting stakes, barnacled at the base, and the war bequeathed even a new plaything, the Yanks' Jetty, where younger kids learned to dive, spearing through the pale water after small bottles filled with Reckitts Blue, and rising among shafts of green light that trailed like ropes from the surface. The moods and colours of the sea were always changing: on some days still and burning blue, on others grey-green and swelling. The sea withdrew, till diving was dangerous; then flooded in, covering the beach to the tide-line of sea-olives, changing everything. The sea was never the same, but one could tell by the wind and the sky what mood it would be in: whether warm and grey-green under rain, or brightly burning like a blue gas-flame.

In the weekends there was another sea, the open sea where the surf was. The boy went there with his father, and stood hot and timeless vigils, up to his shoulders in the green water, waiting a wave. When a wave came and he caught it and came hurtling down he would have a moment of panic, wondering if it were going to dump him under itself, and roll and batter him against the sea-floor. But if he caught it, if he rode it right to the beach, as his father did, then that was a triumph, and a pure sensual joy like flying.

Rising from the water, he would toss back his wet hair, after the manner of his favourite book-hero, Jack of *The Coral Island*, and of all the lank-forelocked big kids at his school. Then he would find a white hollow in the scrub, and bury himself in the sand, and drowsily bake.

The open sea had wilder moods than the harbour, days when it crashed green mountains, and other moods when it lay flat and still, till the bored surfers complained and went home. And one grey day it tried to take the boy, as it had taken several soldiers, dragging at his body, drawing him away to where the dead soldiers had gone. He struggled in the water, and saw his father struggling towards him, and reached out a hand. Then together they swam and waded towards his mother and Nan, and linked hands all four, and emerged, linked, wading and struggling, from the sudden tug of the sea.

There were still, and would be always, times when he feared the sea.

School started again, and the walks on the hot roads, the furnace-blast of the easterly burning in the lungs. What one kid did, another kid must do. So he followed some of the kids into the Church of England choir, a band of freckled male sopranos in white surplices; and some other kids into the Wolf Cubs, where they learned bushcraft in a mouldering cellar under the half-ruined old courthouse, never leaving the cellar, seeing no more of the bush than an odd sunflower through the gratings near the ceiling. But the cellar was ancient and romantic, built by convicts, with 1868 carved above its stone arch, and whatever grown-ups might say about bond-stores, the boys knew that it had been a dungeon, where chained convicts had been flogged and tortured. Sitting under a naked light bulb, listening to Miss Ward read from the *Jungle Book*, they lost interest in Mowgli and dreamed about torture.

And Miss Ward, who had taught most of them in kindergarten, read gently on, holding the book in her lean painter's hand; for she was a painter, and had studied with famous painters. She would listen attentively to some anecdote about life or nature, and at times allow a just perceptible smile to touch her mouth: a smile that fascinated Rob, a bewildering smile. Only years later he would solve the riddle of Miss Ward's smile. Miss Ward, who had gravely listened to small boys for so many years, had been laughing fit to bust all the time.

Then some of the kids began to learn to play tennis, so most of the kids began to learn to play tennis, and Rob's father put his own derelict court into some sort of order so that kids could play there. At times he stood by the house watching them, smiling more enigmatically even than Miss Ward, as they fumbled on the lawn that they had marked themselves with lines as pale as milk and wild as snake-tracks.

At the dawn service on Anzac Day the boy stood by his grandmother in her light black coat and listened to the bugle. So huge the world grew, growing out and out to accommodate the trailing notes. The Last Post echoed in the dawn sky, touching the nerve of every forgotten grief.

He felt tears, singing beside his grandmother. The war was ending, the war would soon be done. *Lest we forget—lest we forget.*

The war was ending; and one evening, in the street, a voice called: 'Hey, youse kids. They reckon Hitler's dead.'

And one day bells rang, with cheering and crying and singing. The bell in the schoolyard started tolling, then from farther and farther away the other bells chimed in. At the Church of England Mr Arden watched with interest as a very respectable lady swung on his bell unbidden. In the town, in all towns, the grown-ups celebrated wildly, like big kids. And the little kids sang in the streets.

The bells chimed with the static-riven bells of London. It was victory in Europe; in faraway, hardly believable Europe, from which emanated the static-riven voices of Mr Churchill and the King.

But it was not the end of the war. And Rick did not come home.

10

Rob stopped dead in the middle of London Court. 'Look!' he called out. 'Nan, look,' pointing at Dick Whittington and his cat.

Nan stopped and stared, open-mouthed. People were jostling to get past them.

'You are a pair of country bumpkins,' Margaret Coram said, embarrassed. 'Don't just stand gawping.'

'I want to see St George kill the dragon,' Nan said.

'Darling, we can't just stand and watch the clock for a quarter of an hour.'

'Isn't London Court *romantic*,' Rob said, dragging against his mother's arm, which was trying to tear him away from Mr de Bernales's Elizabethan folly.

'Really,' Margaret Coram said, 'people will think you've never been anywhere.'

'We *have* never been anywhere,' Nan pointed out.

'Do come along,' begged their mother.

The children trailed after her, down the cobbled street of the Court, of which visitors were wont to say that there was nothing like that in London. In the Terrace they met a damp wind off the brown and choppy river.

'Perth's cold,' Rob said, shivering. He had never been really cold in his life before.

'People wear coats,' Nan said, studying the passing natives, 'even when it isn't raining.'

They were fascinated by the customs of this new country.

It was a mystery to them what they were doing there, how it was possible to be transported from the known world to a place so utterly foreign. Simply, their mother had said that they would go for a holiday, because they had never had that sort of holiday within their memory. And the holiday had been, first, a brown-panelled nineteenth-century sleeping compartment in the shuddering train, in which they had spent sixteen hours, and then this extraordinary, huge and ancient metropolis, which must be, Rob thought, as old as London, to judge from the romantic grime on the buildings near the railway station.

'It's really only about twenty years older than Geraldton,' his mother said. But that meant nothing, emotively. Perth was ancient, an ancient civilization. Soot-darkened buildings proved it, and the existence of a Museum, and the fact that it was a seat of government. And it was a very special city, cut off from other cities by sea and desert, so that there was not another city for two thousand miles. Among all Australian cities it had proved itself the most special, by a romantic act called the Secession, which the other cities had stuffily ignored.

Cinderella State, he thought, feeling indignant. That was the reason for the Secession. Because they had ignored his poor Cinderella State, all one million square miles of it.

Maybe after this war there'd be another war. Western Australia against the world, the Black Swan flying.

'We shouldn't have gone to Parliament House,' his mother had remarked, 'it seems to have made you political.'

'I'm a Rebel,' he had replied. 'I've got Rebel blood.'

Walking down the Terrace he dreamed of Eureka, the torn banner of the Republic of Victoria.

But not a republic, not in Western Australia. That would hurt the feelings of Princess Elizabeth and Princess Margaret Rose.

'When will Western Australia be free?' he wondered.

'I don't know,' said his mother. 'Perhaps when Bonnie Prince Charlie comes over.'

'Aww.' He grew disgusted at her flippancy.

The buildings in the Terrace were tall and clean and pale, and the small trees that grew there were so neat that they could never have suffered the south wind. At a corner a boy was shouting: 'Py*per*-her! Py*per*-her!' He was not much older than Rob, and Rob stopped to stare at him, admiring this loud-voiced insouciance. Then the newspaper boy noticed, and made a face like a Jap, and Rob moved away.

Turning the corner, he saw another set of jockey scales. He fumbled for a penny.

His mother was looking back. 'What are you doing, Rob?'

'I'm weighing myself,' he said.

'You weigh yourself about six times a day.'

'I'm saving the tickets,' he explained, patiently, coming towards her with a card in his hand. He still weighed the same, he noticed. It seemed that he could not catch the jockey scales out in an error.

Outside a newsagent's stall Nan was looking at postcards. 'Look,' the boy said, 'there's a picture of Kings Park.' He picked it out, and offered a sixpence to the newsagent.

'You'd better send that to Grandma and Aunt Kay,' his mother said.

'Why?' the boy asked. 'Why send it?'

'Well, it's a postcard. You write a letter on the back and post it.'

'Oh,' said the boy, intrigued. He had not heard about post-cards.

'If I send it to Rick,' he said, 'will you put the address on?'

His mother had started walking, and murmured, offhand: 'Yes, if you like.'

The city smelled exotic, extraordinary. It smelled of fruit in the greengrocers' shops and flowers in the florists' shops, of food in the cafés and something strange and pungent in the shops where the ladies had their hair done. The boy sniffed like a dog, following his mother up the street. A tram came scream-ing down Hay Street, spitting blue fire from its arm that touched the overhead wires. The sound did something to him inside, like the sound of sirens and drums.

The hotel smelled like a hotel. He followed his mother up the stairs and into the big room that they were sharing. On the table by the window lay the things he was saving: tram tickets, trolley-bus tickets, tickets for the South Perth ferry. He threw the card from the jockey scales among them, and sat down. 'Now I'm going to write to Rick,' he announced.

He sat listening to the noises in the street below. There was so much to tell Rick. He wanted to tell him about the trams;

about the trolley bus purring between brilliant flame-trees and bare planes round the bay at the foot of Mount Eliza, on early mornings when the river was flat and pale-blue as ice. He wanted to tell him about the brown river seen from the ferry, jelly-fish floating like parachutes under the water. He wanted to tell him about the bucking train, about the wild squirrels in the trees near the Zoo, about the ducks in the bamboo islands at Queens Gardens. And also about the gardens of the people he had visited, the damp green gardens with moss on stone walls and exotic plants like ivy and camellias and tree-fern, which made him look again at his own country and see it as dry and windswept and spare. And he wanted to tell Rick about another discovery he had made, which was that the only reason for going to a foreign country like Perth was the pleasure of going home again and bringing news.

There was too much to tell. He picked up the pen, and wrote in his smallest copperplate:

> Dear Rick,
>   We have come to Perth for two weeks on the train. I hope you will be home soon. I weigh 4 stone 6 lbs 4 oz. I have been sleeping often in your room and I have used your hairbrushes. I hope you don't mind.
>
> > > Love
> > > > from
> > > > > Rob.

On the way to school the boys were very quiet.

'I s'pose they were asking for it,' Graham Martin said. 'I s'pose so.'

'Yeah, 'course they were,' Kevin O'Hara said. 'Look at what they done to all the prisoners.'

'But that was the soldiers who did that,' Rob said. 'These people were just civilians.'

'I dunno why they didn't drop it on Tokyo,' Donny Webb said, 'an' get bloody old Tojo and Hirohito.'

'Would it be big enough to wipe out Tokyo?'

'They reckon it's big enough to wipe out anywhere,' Donny said. 'Just one of 'em'll wipe out a city.'

'Gee, it makes you think,' Graham said.

'There can't ever be another war,' Rob said. 'There wouldn't be anything left.'

'I bet there will be,' said Kevin. 'If they want to have a war they'll have a war, and bugger everyone else.'

'Who's *they*?'

'Ah, the bloody generals and the politicians.'

'Well, we won't be getting called up,' Donny said. 'We'll be dead before that happens.'

'Gee, one of those'd wipe out the town and a lot of the farms as well,' said Graham.

'There wouldn't be any town left,' Kevin said. 'The sea'd come up and cover it.'

They thought about that for a moment: their drowned blue town.

'I dunno,' Graham said, 'there's something—something *terrific* about it. Just think of wiping out a city with one bomb. I wish I could've seen it.'

'And they *were* asking for it,' Donny said.

'Yeah, and we couldn't just refuse to win the war,' said Kevin.

'I dunno,' Rob said. 'I wish they could forget how to make it.'

For the first time in his life he began to read the newspaper, poring over the dark photographs of Hiroshima and Nagasaki, of the Bomb itself, and the mushroom cloud that had now taken root in the world like an upas tree. They were saying that they would make a Bomb as small as a tennis ball.

It had poisoned the war, poisoned the talk of peace. The negotiations over the surrender dragged on, and the peace to come was tarnished: not a quick, clean, joyous peace like the peace in Europe, but a quibbling guilty peace, too clearly man-made and not God-given.

On VJ-Day bells were rung again, and there were official celebrations for the children. But the peace had been stained.

'I hope they torture that bloody old Tojo,' the kids said. But nobody really cared. Bloody old Tojo was not only less than a monster, but less than a man. And the Emperor was just a funny little drip.

'When is Rick coming home?' the boy kept asking. Out of this débâcle he would rescue something.

'I don't know,' said his mother, said Aunt Kay, said Grandma. 'Not all the Japs have surrendered yet.'

It was Didi's birthday, and they drove to Andarra through the green and golden spring country. The slopes and ditches by the road were a dark-pink mass of rustling everlastings. The boy breathed deep from the car window, breathing heath and wattle and spring.

The house was full of children, and many of them were cousins. The aunties came and went along the verandas, bearing a monstrous banquet. For a while Didi disappeared, then returned mounted on the huge draughthorse that Harry used to ride before he was a soldier. Didi sat in her party dress on the bare brown back of the horse, inviting the children to throw stones; and they threw stones, and the horse pranced and pig-rooted, while Didi shouted with laughter.

Then, in the lamplit dining-room, they sat down to eat, eating heartily, needing no example from the Starving Children of Europe. Jellies and cakes and ice-cream and meringues and cool drinks poured on to the tables; and as the twilight faded feeble voices rose from one corner and another, crying: 'Mum, I feel sick.'

'What's wrong with you?' Rick said, laying a hand on the skeleton of Hugh Mackay.

'I feel sick,' said Hugh.

'What have you been eating, you stupid bastard?'

'A fella gave me half a pound of sugar,' Hugh said. 'Wish I'd told him to keep it.'

'I dunno,' Rick said. 'Here have I been running round like a cut snake to get you some tucker, and you go and ruin your appetite.'

'Gee, sorry, Mum,' Hugh said. 'What did you find?'

'You won't believe it. I got a pound of cheese.'

' 'Struth.'

'I've eaten half of it. You want the rest?'

Hugh shuddered. 'No, thanks. How do you feel?'

'Crook, slightly.'

'It's a rotten shame, isn't it,' Hugh said, 'when food starts falling out of the sky and you don't enjoy it.'

But in the darkness around them, the camp had gone wild with joy.

'Where are we going to sleep?' Rick said. 'I'm not going back inside.'

'What's that shed?'

'Dunno. Looks like someone got impatient and busted the wall in.'

'Looks empty,' Hugh said, sticking his head through the hole. 'Shall we take it?'

A voice in the dark said: 'Yeah, come in.'

'Who's that?'

'Nobby Clark.'

'Never heard of you,' Hugh said. 'D'you keep a clean house?'

'Good enough for the class of person you get round here.'

'Yeah,' Rick said, lying down on the floor, 'they're a bit ordinary.'

'You want a smoke?' Nobby Clark said.

'Jesus,' Hugh said, 'what hasn't been dropping from the clouds? You bet I do.'

'One smoke,' Nobby Clark said. 'You can share it.'

'That's okay,' Hugh said. He went towards the glowing butt he could see against the wall, and then stumbled. 'Hell, who's that?'

'Ah, that's me mate,' Nobby Clark said. 'He's crook, silly bastard.'

'What did he eat?'

'He found a whole lot of flour.'

'I dunno,' Hugh said, 'all the years I've been dreaming about food, I never once dreamt about flour.'

He lit the cigarette from Nobby Clark's butt, drawing deep, and then took it back to Rick.

'Hey, what's-your-name, Nobby,' Rick said, 'do you want some cheese?'

'Gawd, no,' Nobby Clark said. 'Thanks all the same. I just et a tin of powdered milk.'

'You lucky bastard,' Hugh said. 'I've dreamt about powdered milk.'

'It fills you up,' Nobby said, complacently.

The cigarette end lit Rick's face as he drew on it. 'Once upon a time,' he said, dreamily, 'there was a couple called Mr and Mrs Vinegar who lived on cheese. I'm stuffed if I know how they did it.'

'I bet they was constipated,' Nobby said.

'Aaah,' Hugh said, 'why does the conversation in this place always get round to shit?'

' 'Cause that's all a human being is here,' Rick said. 'Just messed-up bowels.'

'Shut up about bowels,' groaned the man who was full of flour.

'Yeah,' Hugh said, 'forget about bowels. The war's over. People don't have bowels in peacetime.'

'They do where I come from,' Nobby Clark said, 'in New Guinea.'

'Well, you can go home and roll in it.'

'Yeah—home,' murmured Nobby Clark.

'Home,' said Rick, passing the cigarette to Hugh.

'Take me home quick,' said the sick man on the floor.

'You coming home with me?' Hugh said.

'What about your grandma?' Rick said. 'Will you have room for me?'

They knew every room in one another's houses, every member of one another's families. Rick knew all the people in Hugh's street as well as Hugh knew all the horses at Sandalwood. They could, at times, correct one another's memories.

'Listen,' Hugh said, 'if I've got to sleep on the veranda, you've got to sleep on the veranda. Don't start acting the rich cocky with me.'

'I'd like to hear you tell my mum she was married to a cocky.'

'She'd be too polite to say anything,' said Hugh, who was well acquainted with Mrs Ernest Maplestead.

'She'd freeze you, mate, she'd freeze you.'

'Hey, Rick,' Hugh said, thinking. 'When I come home with you, she's not going to like me being the son of a butcher.'

'She's going to like you,' Rick said. 'She's going to know a lot about you by then.'

'Like the ninety-seven times I saved your life?'

'Yeah, all that. We'll make it good for her.'

The cigarette passed again in the dark.

'So,' Hugh said, 'I'm going to sleep in that room with all those phony silver cups you bought yourself. And please, can I use your hairbrushes?'

Rick started to laugh, puffing red-tinged smoke in the darkness.

'I've got to use those hairbrushes,' Hugh said. 'Those hairbrushes are famous. Gee, that was the nicest letter anyone ever gave me a share of.'

'I suppose everyone's still alive,' Rick said. 'I suppose the kid would have said if anyone had died. No, perhaps he wouldn't.'

'We can't be worried, sport.'

'There's half a drag left in this smoke. Want it?'

'No. Finish it.'

The cigarette end glowed for a moment, then Rick ground it out. He stretched out on his side on the floor.

'Where are we going to live, Hughie?' he wondered.

'I dunno,' Hugh said, from far away.

'What are we going to do?'

'Dunno.'

'Well, think of something, quick, the war's over.'

From the darkness came sounds of Hugh Mackay's skeleton spreading itself on the floor.

'Rick,' he said.

'Yeah?'

'We won't be doing the same thing, mate.'

'Funny,' Rick said. 'I knew you were going to say that.'

'I'm just facing facts. Peace is different.'

'It doesn't have to be.'

'We're not so young,' Hugh said. 'We're twenty-four. You've got to go back to Uni, and I've got to find a job somewhere.'

'Do you want to?'

'I dunno. Yeah.'

'I thought we were going to bum round the world together. Hell, we talked enough about it.'

'Talk's cheap,' Hugh said, shifting in the darkness.

Outside in the camp were voices, movement. Nobby Clark and his mate were breathing deep and loud.

'Well, I can live without you,' Rick said. 'But it seems a pretty stupid idea.'

He lay listening to Hugh's breathing beside him. Now Hugh was moving, sitting up and panting. 'Rick, Rick,' he whispered.

'What?'

'Where's the door, mate? That sugar. I'm going to chunder.'

'Lucky you,' Rick said, guiding him, solicitously. 'Wish to Christ I could.'

One afternoon, stopping by his grandmother's back door, the boy heard a voice coming from inside, and stood listening in a flood of nostalgia, remembering early mornings in the dry red country, remembering night roads and the sweetish smell of an old car, a smell that had something to do with oil. The voice, the accent was unlike any other voice. The accent was a Maltese accent! So Uncle Paul, who had this accent in four languages, had come home to the clan.

And Gordon came home, tall and calm as a tree, though looking shy when the old ladies fussed around him.

'When is Rick coming?' asked all the children who remembered.

Rick was on a ship. He was getting well, and sunbathing.

'Where is Rick now?'

Rick was in a camp, a sort of hospital. He was getting well, and eating.

'When is Rick coming?'

Soon, soon, they said.

The boy's mother said, looking shy: 'Rob.'

'Yes?'

'If Rick is—different—you mustn't say anything.'

'How, *different*?' he demanded.

'If he's very thin—and perhaps hasn't got all his teeth—or is just *different*——'

'No!' the boy cried, between temper and tears. 'He *mustn't* be different.' He could not permit any change in Rick.

'Where is Rick now?'

Rick was in Perth, and Gordon had driven Aunt Mary down to meet him. Rick was getting well, and seeing the doctor. He was staying with such a funny boy called Hugh Mackay. And Aunt Mary was having to call on Hugh Mackay's mother, who was a butcher's wife.

'Why doesn't he come now?' Rob persisted.

'I expect he wants to get well,' Aunt Kay said, 'and look nice.'

'Aw,' said the boy. 'Sissy.'

It was growing dark in the paddocks at Andarra, and the children were a long way from the homestead.

'Come on,' the boy shouted back. Didi and Nan and Jimbo were trailing far behind.

'You're going the wrong way,' Didi called.

'I'm not,' he said. 'This is the quickest.'

'You'll get lost.'

'*You*'ll get lost,' he said. 'I'm not waiting for you.'

He jumped into a sandy creek bed and scrambled up the other bank. Now he felt self-righteous. As soon as he got to the top of this rise he would be able to see the lights of Andarra, and he would be home hours before the others.

The drying paddocks smelled sweetly as they cooled. He crunched the dry tussocks under his shoes, skirting the darkening scrub. The sky towards which he was mounting was softening and deepening into the colour of the darkest sea.

From the top of the rise the land spread out lightless. There was no Andarra, and the sun was gone.

I must be lost, he thought. He began to run downhill, slithering on the small stones.

In the darkness he tripped in a dry runnel, and fell, cutting his shin.

Lost, he thought. He moved forward, cautiously, and ran into a fence, the barbed wire of the top strand tearing his arm.

With great care he climbed over it, and began to trudge up the hill behind. From there, surely, he would see lights. Dark trees reached out at him. He could no longer see what sort of trees they were.

It was no longer his country. There was nothing familiar there, it was simply darkness.

From the top of the hill there was nothing; only darkness.

Then he began to run, going nowhere, simply running, stumbling and falling. He shouted from time to time. And as the hours of darkness went by he shouted more often and more feebly, with less and less conviction, because darkness was another country, which was now his country, and it grew difficult to believe in the country of light.

He told himself that some day it would be dawn, and that he would discover a place he knew, and go home. But this he no longer believed, because he belonged in a new country now, and if light should ever come it would come when he had wandered far away from Andarra, and he would go on walking, on and on into the heart of perilous Australia, where his bleaching bones at last would lie.

That was the most terrible thing about the darkness, that it destroyed one's memory of the light.

He ran, panting and stumbling, up the stony slopes. Once, fallen on the ground, he called into the ground: 'God. God.' But God did not reach out a hand.

In time he grew tired and cold, stumbling along with head bent. He was in a paddock of stubble. A white shape jumped up in front of him and crackled away. 'Oh,' he groaned with the pain of his bounding heart. But it was a sheep, and then there was another sheep, a paddock full of sheep, and he grew calmer.

He tried to lie down beside a sheep to sleep, but they bounded off when he came near them. So he lay in the stubble, shivering, and tried to bury himself with handfuls of straw, cold piercing him from the ground and from the sky.

I must sleep, he thought. Sleep, and perhaps die. Because he knew now that it was possible to die of darkness.

For a while he did sleep, but woke shivering, knowing that the darkness would not take him that way, but while he was walking, while he was afraid. Among the sheep he was not afraid, because they were alive.

He plodded with head bent through the stubble, knowing that this was what the darkness intended.

He could hardly believe, raising his eyes, the light he saw. Long ago he had ceased to believe in light. But a light was coming: he stood with a sort of indifference watching it as it grew in the distance, and then stopped.

Light had come, but would go away. With no real belief in it he began to run towards it, shouting: 'Hey, hey, you with the light,' panting. And then the light was moving again towards him, the light was shining full on him and stopping, car doors were opening and people were coming out.

He felt dull surprise, seeing his mother and Aunty Jean. They should have been strangers. After the darkness, it did not seem possible that anything from the old life could remain.

He sat in the warm cab of the pick-up, between the warm women. They were cross with him, and he was cross with his mother, because she reckoned that he had been crying when he ran for the light. It was true that he had sobbed in his shouting, earlier, long ago. But his mother was stupid not to know that one did not cry when one had discovered that it was possible to die of darkness.

Mrs Charles Maplestead and Miss MacKay MacRae sat in wicker chairs on the dark lawn. They breathed the evening cool, the faint breeze that sent an occasional withered fruit of the Moreton Bay figtree clattering on to the roof. Inside the house, someone was bashing the piano.

In the street behind the plumbago hedge a car pulled up and turned off its lights. Two doors banged.

'Now who could that be?' said Mrs Maplestead.

With practised ease, the sisters called the roll of the Maplestead clan. At length they decided on the Misses McDermott of Innisfail and their niece.

'I must put on the veranda light,' said Miss MacRae. 'Poor Rosa is getting quite blind.'

Then she stopped. 'Oh,' she said, pleased. 'It's a man.'

'It's Gordon,' said Mrs Maplestead, as he crossed the lawn. 'You wretch, you've been standing there listening and laughing at us.'

Gordon's teeth showed white in the dimness. 'I wouldn't laugh at you, Aunt Anne,' he said. 'Hey, who's that chopping up the piano.'

'Oh, Rob,' said Mrs Maplestead. 'We find it quite an advantage to be deaf.'

'Who is that by the gate?' Miss MacRae said. 'Anne! Look!'

And the sisters, sudden tears in their eyes, exclaimed.

In the drawing-room the boy stopped hammering on the piano and sat with his head bent in the pool from the crystal lamp, cocking an ear towards the voices in the garden. For some time he had been hearing them, through his own noise, and now they were moving closer. Footsteps sounded on the veranda, going towards the dining-room. Then other footsteps, a man's, broke away from them, and were coming towards the open front door.

He turned in his seat and watched the drawing-room door, which he had closed to keep in his music-making. The white china doorknob with the gold rose on it, like the iris of an eye, was turning. He slipped down from the stool and stepped towards the door as it opened.

The blue eyes that looked at him from the doorway were like the light through a magnifying glass, when it is at its brightest and smallest, when paper and leaves begin to smoke.

'Hey,' said the man in the door. 'Remember me?'

'Yes,' the boy said, whispering. 'Rick.'

He almost winced under that blue gaze. All of Rick seemed to be concentrated in the eyes, with an intensity that ought to have hurt him.

'You knew me,' Rick said. 'You hadn't forgotten.'

'You're—just the same,' the boy said, and felt a gush of gratitude.

He seemed even to be wearing the same clothes, the same

blue shirt and grey trousers. He was thin, but he was built to be lean; and he was still, or again, sunburnt. After everything, the slow white smile still showed the glint of gold.

'Let's look at you,' Rick said, dropping into an armchair. Gradually, the fixity of his stare diminished, and he became once more just Rick, as if nothing had happened. There were lines and shadows about his eyes, and deeper lines tracing the hollows of his cheeks, but he looked like just Rick, lined by sunlight and smiling.

'When I look at you,' he said, 'you remind me of me.'

'Yes,' said the boy, eagerly, 'they reckon we both look like my grandfather.'

'Well, you might say welcome home,' Rick said. 'You might shake hands with your deadbeat cousin.'

'Aw, sorry,' the boy said. He gripped Rick's lean hand, and said formally: 'Welcome home.'

'So. How old are you these days?'

'Nine. Nearly ten.'

'Rising double figures. Well, now.'

'I can ride,' the boy said, with ill-concealed modesty. 'And swim, and play tennis.'

'You any good?'

'Nuh.'

'That's fine. I like to win.'

'Can I come and stay with you,' the boy said, 'and sleep in your room?'

'You bet you can. And you can go on using my hairbrushes till you're as bald as a goanna.'

'Did you get that postcard?' the boy said. 'Gee. Everyone said you wouldn't.'

'I got it, all right. It was the only mail I got in three and a half years.'

'Were you pleased?'

'I bawled,' Rick said.

'You bawled?' said the boy, mistrustfully.

'Yeah. Then I showed it to a fella called Hughie Mackay who didn't get any mail all through the war, and he bawled too.'

'Gosh,' said the boy. 'I didn't mean it to be sad.'

'So you weighed 4 stone 6 lb 4 oz,' Rick said. 'And Hughie and I weighed five stone apiece.'

'Five stone,' the boy said. 'Gee. You must have looked funny.'

'You'd have got the giggles,' Rick said. 'Hey, d'you still get the giggles?'

'Yeah.'

'So do I. I just got the giggles talking to your grandmother.'

'Why?'

'I dunno. Just being home makes me giggle. And all the people.'

His hand was resting on the boy's schoolbooks that lay on the arm of the chair. 'How's school?' he asked.

'All right,' Rob said, shrugging. 'It's just school.'

'What's this? Ah, it's an autograph book. So you've got to that stage.'

'It's got everyone in it,' the boy said. 'All the family, and all the kids in my class, and the teacher.'

Rick was grinning over the book. 'Some of your little mates have got an earthy sense of humour.'

'Will you write in it?' asked the boy, shyly.

'Sure. What shall I write? Something really rude?'

'No, something—something nice, like Aunt Kay.'

'Something homecoming?' Rick said. 'Right. First chance I've had to use this pen my old mum gave me.'

He took the book over to the piano, and wrote, in the pool of light from the crystal lamp. Then he turned, and the boy reached for the book.

'That's something really nice,' Rick said, 'from the *Muses' Favourite Treasury of English Verse*, which I happen to know off by heart 'cause I had it with me when I was captured.'

'What does it mean?' asked the boy, staring at the clerkish copperplate on the green page.

'I dunno. It's just poetry. You're the one that used to be keen on poetry.'

A voice called up the passage: 'Rick.'

'We've got to go, mate,' Rick said. 'We've got to drink a

glass of whisky from the bottle Aunt Anne bought to celebrate the relief of Mafeking.'

'I don't understand it,' the boy said, following after, watching Rick, with a sudden conscious jerk, straighten his bent shoulders. Under the hall light he stopped, puzzling over the meticulous writing.

> Thy firmness makes my circle just,
> And makes me end, where I begun.
>
> Richard Maplestead
> 1945

2
Rick Home
1945-1949

11

Rick was standing in front of the mirror, admiring himself.

He was always admiring himself. He would stand on the mat in his underpants, looking down at his arms and legs. Then he would lean forward into the mirror and sneer with his lips and examine his teeth. He even admired the whites of his eyes.

'Do you think you're beautiful or something?' said the boy, from the bed where he lay.

'Yeah,' said Rick. 'Don't you?'

'Awww,' said the boy; and added, not to let Rick get away with it: 'You're pretty skinny.'

'I'll live forever,' Rick said. 'I really believe that.'

He sat in his pyjamas on the edge of his bed, rolling cigarettes. As he stuck out his tongue to lick the paper, he thought of something. He got up and looked into the mirror and admired his tongue.

'Say *Ah*,' said the boy.

'You may laugh,' Rick said, 'but I think I'm a bloody marvel.'

He sat down again, and went back to rolling cigarettes, while the boy watched him in the yellow light of the lamp. Rick was remembering something: he knew the signs. Rick's face was changing, almost changing in substance, growing clenched and closed, and his eyes had that dead look that the boy hated, because there was nothing he could do about it.

'Rick,' he said.

'Mm,' Rick said, looking up, slowly, and staring through the boy with his empty eyes. 'What?'

'Nothing,' the boy said. 'Just—I like being here.'

'You know something?' Rick said. 'So do I.'

'Rick—don't look like that.'

'How was I looking?'

'Oh—sad.'

'Sorry,' Rick said. As he reached out, laying a cigarette beside the others on the chest-of-drawers, the muscles moved over his tight jaw.

'Why do you make so many cigarettes every night?'

'I don't sleep too well,' Rick said. 'I'll probably smoke all these.'

'That's bad for you.'

'Hey, Pollyanna,' Rick said, 'why don't you drop off?'

'You've got the lamp on.'

'Right,' Rick said, blowing it out. 'Now, die, will you?'

He listened to the sounds of Rick getting into bed. Outside, the night was moonless. Through the door, against the stars, he could faintly pick out the black shapes of the olives.

Rick lay so still when he got into bed. The boy never heard him move, never heard him breathe, like other people. He never sounded asleep.

The boy moved, comfortably, and breathed, easily, falling asleep.

After a long time, sounds faintly penetrated his sleep, and he turned on his back, waking. A hand was fumbling on the chest-of-drawers, then a match flared. He saw Rick's face above the match.

Rick was crying. Tears shone on his face.

A cigarette end glowed, and the match went out. The glow of the butt followed Rick back to his pillow.

The boy listened, feeling shocked, feeling helpless. Rick was quiet. He wanted to go to Rick, to comfort him; and yet he wished that it had never happened that he had seen Rick cry.

He sat up in bed and strained his eyes against the darkness. 'Rick,' he whispered.

And Rick's voice, Rick's other voice, said: 'Mm?'

'Are you all right?'

The cigarette glow grew and faded. But Rick said nothing.

The boy got out of bed and padded across the room. He reached out a clumsy hand and patted Rick's hair, roughly, as if Rick were a puppy. 'Don't cry, Rick,' he said. 'Don't cry.'

The cigarette momentarily lit Rick's face. And Rick was grinning. Miserably, the boy supposed that it was something stupid that he had said and done, and that Rick was laughing at him.

'I'm not crying, matey,' Rick said. 'Well, I mean, when I was crying I was still asleep.'

'What were you dreaming about?'

'It doesn't matter, does it?'

'Was it sad?'

'Yeah, pretty sad.'

'Was it a nightmare?'

'Uh-huh.'

The boy watched the glow come and go on Rick's face. Rick smoked very fast.

'Sit down, Rob,' Rick said. 'I want to talk to you.'

That was a formula that the boy hated, and he sat on the bed feeling tense.

'Now listen, fella. Wouldn't you rather sleep somewhere else?'

'No!' said the boy, firmly.

'You see, I have these dreams, and I yell out in my sleep, and that must wake you up. I must make you nervous, I reckon. Wouldn't you sleep better somewhere else?'

'No,' the boy protested. 'I don't mind, honest. I just couldn't sleep anywhere else.'

'Well, you're a stubborn little offsider to have,' Rick said.

'When you have bad dreams,' the boy said, 'I'll come and talk to you, like they used to do to me, and then you'll forget about them.'

'Right,' Rick said. 'If I yell, you come and wake me.'

'And I'll tell you a story or something.'

'Fair enough. Or just say: "Don't cry, Rick", like you did then.'

'You thought that was funny, when I said that.'

'That's just it. I want to wake up laughing.'

The boy said, half resentful: 'I never know when you're kidding.'

There were times when he was almost afraid of Rick, of the

155

effect that things he said might have on Rick. There had been terrible moments when he had said things to Rick that had changed Rick's face. The time, for instance, when he was talking to Rick and Rick was smiling and the boy had said: 'I thought the Japs would have pinched that gold out of your tooth.'

Then very slowly, remembering something, Rick's face had set, congealed, and the empty look had come into his eyes.

And another time he had said to Rick: 'Doug Maxwell's father brought him back a Jap skull and now all the kids are going to Doug's place to see it and Doug thinks he's a hero or something.'

'Mm,' Rick had said, in his other voice.

'Why didn't you bring me a Jap skull? You never brought me anything.'

Then Rick's other voice had said: 'I wasn't a —ing soldier, mate, I was a —ing slave.'

And he had said something even worse to Rick, one morning when Rick was lying on his bed in his pyjamas, as he did often now that he had got so lazy. He had looked at Rick's bare feet, and had come across the room with pleased interest to touch the scars on Rick's ankles. 'Gee,' he said, 'you *did* get tortured, then.'

When he looked up, he could not meet Rick's eyes. Rick seemed to hate him.

After a time Rick said, in a small strained voice: 'You'd have been disappointed if I hadn't, wouldn't you?'

'No,' the boy said. 'No, Rick.'

'Ah, go on. I bet none of your bloodthirsty little mates has got a cousin who was tortured.'

'Please,' the boy said, 'don't go crook at me, Rick.'

He had wanted to run away. He could not stand that terribly quiet voice, which cracked like the voice of a big kid just getting whiskers. Yet he did not like to move.

After long moments he dared to look at Rick again, and saw that Rick's face was normal.

'Come here, buster,' Rick said.

He went and sat by Rick on the bed, sitting tense.

'You want to know the story, don't you?' Rick said. 'So you can tell the other kids.'

'No,' the boy said. 'No, I don't want to hear it now.'

'Well, I don't care about you,' Rick said, 'I want to tell it.'

It was a redhot bayonet that had made the scars. The boy felt sick suddenly, glancing down at Rick's face on the pillow. But Rick was looking happy by then, he looked proud. 'I was a bloody good thief,' he was saying, 'even that time they didn't have anything on me, they just hoped I might be what they were after.'

'How could they do that?' the boy said, faintly. 'How could you stand it, Rick?'

'Well,' Rick said, 'I had this happy knack of passing out cold if anyone laid a finger on me.'

'Agh,' said the boy, shaking his head, and feeling wretched now. How could this have happened to Rick when everyone in the world would have wished to prevent it? How could anyone torture a Maplestead and an Australian?

'Cheer up,' Rick said, pushing the boy on the shoulder. 'It never was anything very spectacular.'

He was sitting up by that time, cross-legged, admiring his own scars, which seemed to please him.

The boy reached out and touched them, and said, through his nausea and his dread: 'Gee, that's really something to have, to show people when you're old.'

And Rick said, grinning, and looking at the boy as if he did not hate him after all but quite the contrary: 'Aren't you the slimy little diplomat?'

Now he sat in the lightless room, watching Rick's face come and go in the glow of a second cigarette. Things were going wrong with Rick; he was not, after all, the same Rick who had gone away, and at times the boy felt bewildered and helpless. There had been a day when they had gone to Andarra together, and on the road to the house had seen Gordon working in the yards. They had pulled up and waited for him by the fence, and Rick had smoked a cigarette.

Gordon had been castrating pigs. Watching the sheepdogs dart about, gobbling down the pale severed organs, the boy had felt uneasy in his stomach. He had turned to say something to Rick, and had seen Rick white and sweating, his eyes closed, momentarily poised before he swayed and fell.

Rick had lain in the grass staring at the sky, while Gordon and the boy knelt beside him. 'I can't take it,' he had kept saying. 'I can't take it—mutilation—oh Christ, Gordon——'

But afterwards he had slung off at Gordon, because Gordon was so tall and quiet and had been an officer. 'Pull yourself together, man, have a nip of this what is it a scorpion yak yak.'

He never knew when Rick was kidding. And he did not know how to respond to these weaknesses of Rick's, which disturbed him and left him without bearings. If there were any need in Rick, if Rick had made any demand on him, he could not have met it. He had nothing at all to give: only a promise as casual as an agreement to wake Rick in the morning.

But the habit of caring for Rick was strong. And he watched over Rick with a wary, half-critical solicitude.

There was no glow now on Rick's face. The cigarette had gone out, and Rick was sleeping. The boy reached out in the dark and took the dead butt from between Rick's fingers, dropping it in the ashtray on his way back to bed.

'Why don't you play with me?' Jane Wexford said. 'I'm not very good, either.'

'No,' the boy said. 'If you're not very good you ought to play with Rick. He's good.'

'He's a terrible partner,' Jane said. 'If you miss a shot, he looks ready to murder you.'

'Aw, he doesn't mean it,' the boy said, defending Rick.

He looked sideways at Jane as she sat on the low bench, her hands and chin resting on top of her racquet. Jane was beautiful. He had a thrill on Jane. Jane's brown hair was like a curly cap on her head, and her eyes were the colour of sherry. And below the short white tennis skirt her legs were smooth and brown like a kid's back in summer.

'Anyway,' Jane said, 'Rick won't play again. He looks tired.'

'He's very lazy,' the boy said. 'He lies around all day.'

'Well, of course,' Jane said, 'he's not really well yet, he's still resting.'

The boy supposed that she knew what she was talking about, since she was a nurse, but Rick looked well enough to him as he darted about the court and waited, knees bent, for the ball. The new watch flashed on Rick's wrist. That was a present from all of them. Rick had got a lot of presents for his twenty fifth birthday, because he had had nothing at all when he came back, only a few bits of paper with his drawings on them.

'He looks all right,' the boy said.

'Isn't he good-looking?' Jane said. 'I think he's terrific.'

'Aw, I dunno,' Rob said. 'He's not *pretty* or anything.'

'He's marvellous,' Jane said, on a sigh.

'Yeah,' said Rob, 'that's what he reckons.'

It occurred to him to hope that, as he looked like Rick, Jane might think him good-looking too.

'Game and set,' Rick called out. He had just thrashed Jane's brother John, and they were coming off the court, wiping their wet foreheads with their wrists.

'He walked over me,' John said, flopping on the grass beside his wife. 'Heck, Rick, you must be used to playing for sheep-stations.'

'I hate to lose,' Rick said. 'I even hate it when this kid beats me at draughts.'

'I only ever beat you once,' Rob said.

'I won't forget it,' said Rick. 'I sulked for days.'

'I suppose that's natural,' Jane said, 'after——' Suddenly she bit her lip and looked shy.

'Well, who does like to lose?' Julie Wexford said, jumping in quickly.

'Natural, after losing the war?' Rick said. He was smiling, rather tightly. 'That what you meant, Jane?'

'I forget what I meant,' Jane said.

' 'Cause you're right. I was on both sides, and both times my team lost.'

The boy scuffled in the grass, feeling uncomfortable, and noticing that John Wexford looked uncomfortable too. For

159

some reason it was the men rather than the women who felt awkward when Rick talked like this.

'Are you and Jane going to play?' John said to his wife.

Julie got up rather eagerly, reaching for her racquet. 'Come on, come on,' she said to Jane. 'What are we sitting around for?'

'Is there any water down here?' John asked.

'Only the sheep trough,' said the boy.

On the court Jane and Julie were hitting up, going *pong! pong!*

'I think I'll go up to the house,' John said. He went away up the paddock, his tennis shoes quiet on the summer-tawny grass.

'You want to watch these girls?' Rick said.

'Aw, no,' the boy said. 'They play too slow.'

'Come for a walk?'

'Okay.'

The orchard was a green island in the summer country, soft underfoot. I wonder what it looks like to the birds, the boy thought. They must see it for miles, that must be why they're always here. Galah's screeched away from stone-fruit trees, rose and silver against the sky, as he and Rick walked by.

'Jane thinks you're good-looking,' he said to Rick. 'She says you're terrific.'

Rick slashed with his racquet at the tall asparagus fern. 'Ah, the stupid bitch.'

'She's not,' the boy said, affronted. He looked at Rick, who was sort of smiling, half irritable and half amused. He supposed that Rick meant nothing by that, he was just swearing because he was always swearing. He was the only grown-up in the whole family who swore, and he swore enough for all the rest put together, using some of the really dirty words.

'Why do you swear so much?' he said.

'Ah, habit,' Rick said, idly. 'Matter of fact, when I first went into the Army I promised myself I never would. These bloody camps, you know, they sound like a chook-yard. All you can hear for miles around is N.C.O.s going: *Fahhhk-fahkfahk-fahk-fahhahk!*'

The boy laughed and laughed until his belly-muscles ached.

160

'*Fahhhk*,' he murmured, under his breath, like a chook. '*Fahk-fahkfahk-fahhahk!*'

'You dirty little bastard,' Rick said, 'shut up.'

'Why is Jane a stupid bitch?'

'Ah, the way she talks,' Rick said. He mimicked Jane, grinning. ' "How can you possibly justify the mass-murder of all those innocent children?" And I say: "Lady, if I'd had the use of that Bomb there wouldn't be a city standing in Nippon right now." '

'Are you kidding?' the boy asked, uncertain.

'No, I'm not kidding. I'd have wiped Japan off the map, and given it no chance to make a comeback against us. Because that's what the little yellow insects will do.'

'No,' the boy said. 'They're our friends now.'

'Balls,' said Rick, slashing with his racquet.

'If you feel like that,' the boy said, 'why wouldn't you talk to the War Crimes people?'

'What's the use?' Rick said, shrugging. 'You can't cure a cast of mind.'

'Is this what you dream about?'

'Partly. Partly the past, and partly the future.'

Uneasily, the boy listened to the peaceful sounds of tennis, the self-absorbed birds. 'No one else thinks like that,' he said.

'I know,' Rick said, indifferent. He mimicked Jane again. ' "You may not realize it, but you talk just like *Hitler*." Ah, forget it.'

The hill beyond the orchard was a copper-pink now that the grass-heads caught the light. The sheep hardly moved, the trees hardly moved. Very faintly in the afternoon heat the boy smelled old sheep droppings in the dry grass.

'When's Hughie coming?' he asked.

'Tuesday.'

'Is he going to have my bed?'

'Now, look,' Rick said, 'you're not going to be jealous of Hughie, are you?'

'No, I just wondered.'

'We'll put a campbed in the room for you. Hell, you could sleep a dozen blokes in a room that size and it'd still feel empty to Hughie and me.'

'All right,' the boy said. 'Good.'

The giant figtree rustled, and a sheep came out of one of the green tunnels, wrinkling up the silvery nap on its nose, sniffing the air.

'You don't want me to go home?' the boy said.

'Ah, no,' Rick said, turning to look at him, deadpan under his rumpled, sweat-damp hair. 'No. You're the only person of my age I've got to play with.'

'I never know when you're kidding,' said the boy feeling happy.

Passing a trellis of roses, the boy heard voices on the other side, and stopped to listen, grinning.

'I really did appreciate that,' Hugh Mackay was saying, 'you getting out all those books about painting. I dunno, people nowadays don't seem to have that feeling for Beauty that people had a while ago, when you can remember.'

Aunt Mary's quiet, vague, courteous voice replied: 'Yes, I do sometimes think that with all the roughness of life when we were young, there was a sort of fineness, too.'

The boy slipped past the roses and went up the broad stone steps to the veranda, where Rick was lying flat on his back on the bare boards.

'You ought to hear Hughie,' he said. 'Gor'struth.'

'Why, is he buttering up my mum again?'

'Is he ever.'

'Hypocrisy's Hughie's best sport,' Rick said. 'Pity they don't give cups for it.'

'He should be winning cups for tennis soon. He's been beating you.'

'Isn't that the rottenest thing you ever heard of?' Rick said. 'The bastard had hardly had a racquet in his hand till I offered to coach him. You'd think he'd have the decency to lose.'

'He's coming,' Rob said. 'He heard that.'

Hugh Mackay was mounting the broad steps. As he ascended, a change came over his lean black-Celt's face. The

boy watched fascinated. It was like watching Dr Jekyll turn
into Mr Hyde. At the bottom of the steps he was a grave and
dependable young man. By degrees, on the way up, he under-
went a transformation, and arrived on the veranda a friendly
junior pirate.

'You bitching again?' he said, kicking Rick in the ribs.

'Ah, go and sell someone a gold brick,' Rick said. 'I hear
you've been charming the pants off my mum.'

'She likes me,' Hugh said, sitting down on the edge of the
veranda. 'She knows I'm a soul. Hey, kid, what you know
about Beauty?'

'Not much,' said the boy.

'Don't they teach you about Beauty at school?'

'Nuh,' said the boy. 'Only poems.'

'When are you going back?'

'I've got four weeks yet,' said the boy.

'It's not long. Still, you'll see all your mates again.'

'I haven't got any mates now,' Rob said. 'I was too old for
the class I was in, so they shoved me up one, and now I don't
know anyone.'

'What,' Rick said, 'your old mates reckon you reckon you're
too good for them, do they?'

'Yeah,' said the boy, 'I s'pose so.'

'Poor little bugger,' Hugh said. 'It must feel like they made
him a corporal.'

'My dad used to be a corporal,' the boy said. 'We've got an
old broom in the shed that's got *Cpl Coram* carved on the
handle.'

'Gee, eh,' Hugh said. 'What did he do with it, fly?'

'Uh?' said the boy.

'Hughie doesn't like corporals,' Rick explained. 'We didn't
rise very far in the Army.'

'Ah, we just didn't have initiative,' Hugh said. 'We were
happy just sitting at home knitting socks for Nippon.'

'Can you knit socks?' said the boy, shocked.

'You bet. Just give me a couple of sticks and an Imperial
Japanese Army pullover and I'll knit you a layette for your
first baby.'

'Aw,' the boy said, laughing. Then he wondered: 'Where did you get the pullovers?'

'Pinched 'em.'

'And you knitted them into socks?'

'That's right. And then we sold 'em to the Nips.'

'Aw,' said the boy.

'You may laugh,' Hugh said, 'but they thought very highly of our socks. Hey, mate,' he said to Rick, 'why don't we go into business? Something sort of, you know, masculine, like *MAPLESTEAD & MACKAY—Hairy Socks for Phoney Englishmen.*'

'He's off again,' Rick said, 'white-anting the Empire.'

'No, I like the Poms,' Hugh said. 'They've got a sense of Beauty. Only I'm stuffed if I know where they get it, 'cause they all seem to live in rabbit warrens.'

'They sit in their rabbit warrens reading D. H. Lawrence,' Rick said, 'that's what does it.'

'How disgusting,' said Hugh.

He got to his feet, picking up the racquet that was leaning against the veranda rail. 'Where are all the balls?' he asked.

'In the Blacks' Camp,' the boy said. That was what Aunt Mary called Rick's room.

'You game to take me on, sport?' Hugh invited, poking Rick with the racquet.

'I don't play with you,' Rick said. 'You cheat.'

'Well, I'm going to go and hit up against a wall, and I'm going to get so good that you're going to be embarrassed about all those cups you bought yourself.'

'That was joke Number 98A,' Rick said. 'Yak.'

'Some day,' Hugh said, 'you're going to feel lousy about the way you used to talk to me.'

He went away down the veranda towards the Blacks' Camp.

Rick lay on his back with a hand across his eyes. By his side was the new sketchbook with the old tattered drawings tucked inside the cover. The boy had been watching him pore over the drawings, trying to copy them in the book, and then swearing and tearing the copies up.

He reached out for the book. It seemed to be full of frag-

ments, meaningless lines. On one page the lines were over-
written with words, and he lay on his stomach, chin on his
hands, to read them.

War is a different country, Rick had written. *It doesn't
matter which side you were on, or if you won or lost, if you
fought a war you became a citizen of another, extra nation,
not on the map. It has its own language and its own litera-
ture, its own art (caricatures and battlescapes) and its own
music (brass bands, nostalgia, bawdy). When you have belonged to that country you do not really go back to the
known nations. You never lose your citizenship. In that
country everything dies and nothing breeds, but somehow
it never ceases to exist, because while it is flourishing its
language and its songs become part of the experience of
children, growing into a heroic nostalgia, so that once every
twenty years or so that nation is refounded, and begins
enthusiastically to die.*

'Are you reading my book?' Rick said, still with his eyes
covered.

'Yeah,' said the boy. 'Can I?'

'I don't know why you'd want to. It's a lorry-load of bulldust.'

'Why did you write that,' the boy said, 'instead of drawing?'

'Just to remind myself what I wanted to draw.'

'It's like——' the boy began, and then stopped, unable to
find a tactful way of saying that it was like the passages he
skipped when he read a novel.

He pulled the old drawings out of the book and spread
them on the boards. The papers had torn edges and were
smudged and smeared. On one of the drawings was a signifi-
cant brown stain.

'This one's got blood on it,' he said, intrigued.

'Yeah, I know,' said Rick.

'Whose blood?'

'Mine.'

'Gosh,' said the boy. 'What happened?'

165

'Well, my good friend Mackay and I,' Rick said, 'were giving the Emperor a hand with a railway he was having trouble with, and one day while I was holding a spike and Hughie was holding a hammer, Hughie landed the hammer on my thumb. Which was a bit careless, but Hughie wasn't really interested in building railways.'

'Gee,' said the boy, 'I bet you swore.'

'I bet I did. I bet I would have booted him in the ring if he hadn't run.'

The boy was staring at the drawings. They made him uneasy, they were so nearly comic: a dark skeleton in enormous boots, a grinning skull in a slouch hat. Everything was blurred and smudged, drawn with charcoal and pencil and something resembling faded ink.

He picked up a picture of a body lying propped against a wall. It was like a sheep's carcass after weeks in the sun. The staring eyes, the grinning teeth, had a look of awful cheerfulness.

'Ergh,' he said. 'Was he dead?'

Rick looked sideways at the drawing. 'No,' he said. 'That's Hughie.'

'Ohh,' the boy said, a soft groan.

He shuffled the drawings together and put them back in the book.

'You're shocked,' Rick said.

'Yeah,' the boy muttered. 'Yeah.'

'Perhaps you should be, while you're still young.'

'Did you look like that?'

'Most of the time. Except once, when I had dropsy or something, and swelled up like a dead cow.'

'I've seen some awful things,' the boy said. 'For a while, if you went to the pictures you always saw newsreels of the German concentration camps. But not—people you know.'

'You didn't believe those newsreels, did you? You didn't believe those people had ever been human.'

'No.'

'I wonder what you'd have felt if you'd seen me in Singapore.'

'I dunno.'

'I think you'd have run away. I bet Jane, who thinks I'm so good-looking, would have run away. I think everyone would have run away. Except Hughie, of course; he's permanent.'

'We wouldn't have run away,' the boy said, 'but we would of felt different.'

'Mm. Sick and sorry.'

'I s'pose so.'

'That's what's stupid,' Rick said. 'Because what's left when everything else is gone is what matters. And nobody knows what was left in Hughie and me except Hughie and me.'

'That's—that's lonely,' said the boy.

'Yeah, it is. Because I've got a soul, and I know it. Which is more than you could say, buster.'

'P'rhaps I'll get a soul,' the boy said, 'later on.'

'P'rhaps you will. Or p'rhaps, if you're lucky, you won't need one.'

The skull of Hugh MacKay lingered in the boy's mind, distracting him. He knelt, looking down on Rick, whose eyes were still covered by his hand. 'I'm going to see Hughie,' he said.

'Be nice to him,' Rick said. 'Tell him he's big and beautiful and the stars say it's a good week for being elected President of the R.S.L.'

'Sometimes,' the boy said, thoughtfully, 'I reckon you're round the bend. Sometimes I reckon you don't even know you're talking, let alone what you're talking about.'

'If you'd just stop listening,' Rick said, 'I might be able to control myself.'

'Heck, it's not my fault.'

' 'Course it's your fault,' Rick said. 'How can I help pouring out my confidences when you're always waiting round like a gurgling drain?'

'Oh, *ari*-bloody-*gato*,' said the boy, bitterly, as he stalked off.

Behind the kitchen block Hugh was knocking a ball against the wall, crouching and darting out with tigerish energy, as surprising in him as it was in Rick, since he was quite as lazy as Rick. The boy stood and watched him, seeing all the time under the taut, dark, youthful skin the age-old skull of

167

Hugh Mackay that Rick had drawn.

He felt an aching pity for Hughie. He wished he had something to give Hughie, some present. But he had nothing to offer, only a halting invitation to Hughie to hit up with him down on the court.

Under the galloping hoofs sand spurted, yellowish in the late sun. The sandplain scrub that had been cleared and was now springing again revealed, in the slanting light, highlights of copper and bronze. Against that sheen and the pale sand the emus looked very dark as they raced before the horses. Their bustles agitated, their stiff-held necks nodded like blowfly-grass in the wind. As they streaked on their huge legs across the sandplain they looked frantically, idiotically busy.

The boy was laughing, his mouth open in the wind, as he galloped behind Rick. 'Can't they go!' he was saying. 'Can't they just go!' The emus were drawing away from the horses already, now only the long necks were showing above the scrub. Ahead of him, old Gay's great bounding gallop slackened, and Rick reined in and waited.

The boy came up breathless on the piebald mare, and wheeled around him. 'Ohh,' he sighed, catching his breath. 'Ohh, that was terrific.'

'Look at Hughie,' Rick said, glancing back.

The aged Goldie was standing stockstill and resigned, trying not to notice her rider, who had his face in her mane and his arms round her neck.

'He's hopeless,' Rob said. 'He's scared of her.'

'Well, he's only a townie.'

'I'll race you to him,' Rob said, kicking the mare as he spoke, and bounding off. He was cheating, because Rick had still to turn his horse. But even then, it was hardly a minute before the big bay gelding lóped past him.

They circled Hughie, waving their hats rodeo-style and shouting: 'Yah-hoo!'

'Don't!' Hugh said. 'You'll make her nervous.'

'She hasn't got a nerve in her,' Rick said.

'She's a terrible high-spirited horse,' Hugh said. 'She tried to gallop or canter or something.'

'So in return you tried to strangle her,' Rick said.

'I only wanted to stay on,' said Hugh, pathetically.

The boy watched the grass, which was waving like the sea, surging west towards the bare and golden-tawny hills. The grass was like a yellow tide-rip which might draw everything after it. The windy sky was tiger-striped white and blue.

'Hell, I never claimed to be Lance Skuthorpe,' Hugh was saying. 'It's you two bastards who put me on this animal. Now I'm going to be walking like Donald Duck for a week, and all because you feel inferior 'cause you can't play tennis.'

'You ought to try, Hughie,' the boy said. 'That was terrific, chasing the emus.'

'Suppose you caught one,' Hugh said, 'what would you say to it?'

'Alistair Scott's got a tame emu,' Rob said. 'It runs after the horse when he goes mustering, and rounds up the sheep like a dog.'

'What's he want a horse for, then?' Hugh said. 'Why doesn't he ride the emu?'

'Aww,' said the boy, laughing.

'No, listen,' Hugh said, 'I'm being practical. Hell, think how long a horse is pregnant for, and then the colt's got to be broken after that. But emus, you'd just have to put a clutch of eggs in an incubator and you could have a whole fleet of 'em in a few weeks. You wouldn't even need saddles, with all those feathers. I dunno, I think it's shocking the way we waste our natural resources.'

'But how'd you feel about riding something that could turn it's head and look you straight in the eye?' Rick said.

'What sort of man would you be,' Hugh said, 'if you couldn't outstare an emu?'

From the high plain the country was rolling, sad-coloured, immense. Red creek-beds and runnels cracked the land's straw-sandy fur, and the slopes of the sudden hills. The stems of jam and mallee stood out dark and sharp under their drab leaves which, catching the sun, flashed like mirrors. The rounded bushy wattles glowed malachite-green.

'I love this place,' Rick said, as if he had surprised himself.

They were skirting a paddock of dead lupins, the seed-filled pods rattling against the horses' legs.

'What I can't understand,' Hugh said, 'is why you're not a farmer. Oh, excuse me, I mean grazier.'

'You know my feelings about manual labour. I'm not ever going to get my hands dirty again.'

'But you were doing Law even before you joined up.'

'I dunno why, exactly,' Rick said. 'I suppose I wanted to get away from the monotony of the life, and just take from it what did me good. It still seems a fair enough arrangement—to be a holiday pastoralist, and work with your head for a living.'

'But why Law, for Christ's sake?'

'Dunno,' Rick said, shrugging. 'If you're brought up to the land and you want to do something else, it pretty well has to be one of the learned professions. I hardly even thought about it, I just did it.'

'Are you going to go back?' the boy asked.

'Yeah. In March.'

'I think you're nuts,' said Hugh.

'I think you're nuts too,' said the boy.

'You could be right,' Rick said. 'But it gives me a few years to get sane in.'

The homestead was a green oasis in the tawny paddocks, complete with palms. Frank was walking away from it, going to his camp.

'That's a happy old man,' Rick said. 'I think.'

'Well, he's not a model I'd pick to follow,' said Hugh.

'He seems to have got everything he wants, just by not wanting anything.'

'You're going to throw one of your dewy-eyed fits,' Hugh said. 'So just remember that when you had nothing you hated it.'

'Not all the time,' Rick said. 'Nor did you.'

'Aw, let's go back, mate,' Hugh said. 'Let's grab a boat back to Thailand. Jesus, didn't we have some good times there, eh?'

'All right, all right,' Rick said, 'you don't have to bury me with sarcasm.'

170

'I reckon I do. I reckon you're such a sentimental bloody maniac you're getting homesick for the Old School already.'

'That's it,' Rick said. 'That's it exactly. The Old School.'

'Well, you matriculated, sport, whether you like it or not. And it's compulsory to grow up now.'

'I grew up,' Rick said. 'And so did you. And we outgrew everyone. We lost our innocence. Only, you seem to've got yours back again.'

'You ever heard about doing in Rome as the Romans do?'

'It's not doing, it's knowing. Un-knowing, in the case of the Romans. Un-knowing what human beings are capable of. Un-knowing themselves.'

'Un-know thyself,' Hugh said. 'Yeah. Yeah, I like that. That's a good motto for any returning warrior.'

The boy stretched and yawned, letting the reins hang loose on the neck of the walking mare.

'We're boring the mascot,' Hugh said.

'Uh?' said the boy.

'I said, we're boring you.'

'I wasn't listening,' the boy said. 'I was thinking, how could you use a bridle on an emu?'

'Let's all consider this problem individually,' Hugh said, 'and we'll have a meeting on it tonight.'

The boy's eyes wandered back to Rick, who was staring into the distance. The late low sun reddened his brown face, which the wide hat-brim now no longer shadowed. His eyes looked deep, and blue as a Siamese cat's.

What's Rick looking at, the boy wondered. Rick's face was immobile: not with the congealed look that it had when he thought of bad memories, but with a trancelike calm.

In the gumtrees along the dry creek that wound almost to the river at Innisfail, cockatoos swirled like torn paper, catching the light. Rising from one tree, they flashed and screeched across the tiger-striped sky to another a quarter of a mile away. They infested the tree like migratory fruit-blossom, flapping, tearing, quarrelling. The cockatoos were a tribe, a clan, whose country had no boundaries. Their colony was the sky, and they had never heard of fences.

12

The fire of dead mallee branches died down, and eggs sizzled in the pan. Rick was whistling as he squatted beside the fire. He was whistling *Lili Marlene*, which he had not heard until the war was over.

'Hurry up and feed me,' Hugh said. 'I'm dying.'

'Gee, I'm tired,' the boy said, stretched in the grass.

'Couldn't you sleep in the caboose. kid?'

'The dogs kept waking me up,' Rob said. 'They kept licking my ears.'

'They must have some kind of deficiency,' said Rick. 'Which trace elements do you keep in there?'

The boy looked round him at the drab mallee-scrub, the red stone-littered soil. 'Heck, we've come a long way,' he said. 'Two hundred miles.'

'And you're now in the ancient continent of Yilgarnia,' Rick said, 'after living on the beach of it all your life.'

'Is it old?' said the boy, hungry for history.

'They reckon it's the oldest land in the world. Once it came up, it never went down under the sea again.'

'Can't say it's any prettier for it,' Hugh said. 'All red and flat.'

'So would Betty Grable be flat, after a few million years of erosion.'

Rick was fishing eggs out of the pan, and handing them on enamel plates to the men sitting round the fire. Ted Barnes, the manager of Bogada, was still rubbing sleep out of his eyes. He had got up before dawn to bring the truck to the siding. The two farmhands from Sandalwood, Alan Lamb and Barry Bailey, had hardly spoken since they rolled up and went to sleep on the floor of the caboose the night before. They had only opened their mouths to yawn, and to shout *huht! huht!* and *book-book-book-book!* as they untrucked and yarded the sheep.

The sheep from Bogada that had come down to Sandalwood and Andarra during the drought inland were going home again now that it had rained. And the boy was filled with excitement about the whole proceeding. The yarding and trucking at the Andarra siding had been, in his eyes, big, heroic, like the Overlanders in the Australian film, and he burst with pride to think that that whole long train was filled with Maplestead sheep. And the endless night in the rocking guard's van, lying rolled in a blanket between Rick and the chained sheepdogs, had seemed fraught with portents, as if the forever-postponed Great Trek that they had been going to make to Bogada when the Japs were coming was at last taking place.

He forked the broken-yolked fried egg into his mouth. Rick wasn't much of a cook.

The sheep complained in the siding yards. They were going to Bogada, and the droving was going to take three or four days. The boy melted with gratitude to Rick and to Uncle Ernest, who had let him come droving like a man.

'Any more tea in the billy?' Ted Barnes asked, sitting with his mug clutched between his khaki knees.

'There's more brewing,' Rick said. 'Half a minute.'

Hugh picked up Rick's mug and drained the tea out of it. 'I see a dark lady,' he said, looking at the tea-leaves, 'with waving raven locks sticking out of her stockings.'

'You have some disgusting daydreams,' Rick said.

'She's got an R.S.L. moustache and her name's Gladys.'

'And am I supposed to get off with this sheila?'

'You watch yourself,' Hugh said. 'She's a respectable married woman with nine kids.'

'Read mine, Hughie,' the boy said, holding out his mug.

'This is a funny one,' Hugh said, frowning into it. 'I'm not sure I can read this one. There's something here that looks like—it looks like three dark balls.'

'King Billy,' said Ted Barnes.

'A Manchester pawnbroker,' said Rick.

'No. No, it's not that,' Hugh said. 'It's coming clearer. Now I see it. It's three sheep turds. How was your tea, kid?'

'Awww,' said the boy.

Hugh lay on his back in the early sun. 'This is beaut,' he said. 'How can you talk about sheep being manual labour?'

'If you feel like that, sport,' Rick said, 'come back for the dipping.'

'And the crutching,' Ted Barnes said. 'That's really pretty.'

'And the shearin',' Alan Lamb said. 'I'll teach you, if I can find a real maggot-ridden one for you to learn on.'

'And what about tailin' lambs,' said Barry Bailey, 'and what about cuttin' 'em?'

'You ought to try picking grass-seeds out of sheeps' eyes,' the boy said. 'Then you wouldn't think it was so beaut.'

'Aah, all you hardened old veterans,' Hugh said. 'You reckon you're tough just 'cause you've had your hands on a bit of daggy wool.'

'Listen to him,' Ted Barnes said. 'He sounds like a Kimberley cowboy.'

'You ever killed a sheep, kid?'

'No,' the boy admitted. 'But I've killed chooks.'

He would rather not think about that. He had had to chop the heads off the fowls that his family ate at Christmas and New Year. His mother had held the chooks' legs, and the chooks had looked at him as their heads lay on the block. When he had chopped the first chook's head off, the headless body had run and flapped around the yard. Even when it was hanging up on a cypress tree and the blood was draining out of it, it had kept on twitching and quivering.

He hated killing things. Uncle Paul hated killing things, too. When Uncle Paul killed a sheep he sent the kids away, though they sometimes peeped around corners, watching the bright blood gush from the slashed throat.

'I've killed sheep,' Hugh said, 'and calves. My old man taught me. He's a butcher.'

'D'you ever kill a man?' asked Barney Bailey; interested because he was too young to have been in the war.

'Shut up, son,' Alan Lamb said, quickly.

Suddenly Hugh's face had the sort of set look that Rick's face got, but darker. And he said, rather quietly: 'I reckon the Nips knew they were safe with me.'

Rick was looking angry.

'Let's get going,' he said, standing up, and gathering the cooking gear together.

'Yeah,' Ted Barnes said. 'Come on, you two bludgers.'

Alan and Barry got up, stretching, and followed him to the yards.

'Lend 'em a hand, Hughie,' Rick said.

'Who d'you reckon you are,' Hugh said, 'giving me orders? Anyone'd think you were the boss's son.'

But he roused himself, yawning, and went to the yards.

'What's wrong with Hughie?' the boy wondered.

'Ah—something worried him. What that kid said.'

'You mean he's worried 'cause he didn't kill anyone?'

Rick was scrubbing at the greasy pan with newspaper, head bent. He said: 'You like Hughie, don't you?'

'Yeah,' said the boy, with enthusiasm.

'Well, don't ever say anything like that to him.'

'I won't,' the boy said. 'I never have.'

'Maybe I can even tell you why,' Rick said, looking up.

'Yeah, tell me,' the boy said. 'I won't tell anyone.'

'He feels bad,' Rick said, 'because when he was first captured, before I met up with him, he let someone die. An Australian. A bastard of a man who went off his head in front of a firing-squad and said he loved the Emperor.'

'What happened?' the boy said. 'How did the man die?'

'Well, Hughie was pretty near dead himself, and he refused to carry this sod. And so the Nips shot him, while he was lying on the ground, complaining.'

'I don't know why he worries about that,' the boy said. 'I wouldn't.'

'Maybe you would,' Rick said, 'if someone asked you: "Did you kill anyone in the war?" and the only person you knew for sure you'd killed was on your own side.'

The sheep from Sandalwood and Andarra, and the horses from Bogada, stamped and stirred in a temporary yard by the mill. The fire blazed up bright, reddening the faces of the men sitting and lying around it. In the small dome of firelight in the huge dark bush Barry Bailey played his mouth-organ, sad and low.

The boy, lying beside Rick, drank in the lonely music. The tune was *You Are My Sunshine*, and it sounded heartbroken.

'What a night, what a night,' Hugh said, stretching his arms towards the stars. 'It makes your nuts tighten.'

'Poetic bastard,' said Alan Lamb.

'He is, you know,' Rick said. 'Say your poem, Hughie.'

'Ah, no,' Hughie said. 'No, I couldn't.'

'Come on, be a sport.'

Hugh cleared his throat. '*The Highwayman*,' he announced. speaking towards the stars. 'By Hugh Mackay.'

'She twined a dark-red loveknot in her hair like mouldy hay,
She read the *Women's Weekly*, then she read the *Woman's Day*,
She ate a box of chocolates, between half past three and four,
And the highwayman kept riding,
                    *Rid*ing,
                         RIDing,
The highwayman kept *RID*ing—and the queue banged on the door.'

'Gee, you're a dirty cow, Hughie,' the boy said.

But he laughed, because it was the poem some girl always recited at school break-up concerts.

'Hey,' Hugh said, 'he understood that.'

'That'll be the day,' Rick said, 'when you know so much you can surprise a kid.'

'I think that's shocking. Whatever happened to childish innocence?'

'Were you ever innocent?' Risk asked, 'that way.'

'Come to think of it,' Hugh said, 'no.'

The boy blushed, wishing that he were innocent. Looking back, he realized that he must have been seven when he first started hearing about *that*.

Clouds were beginning to rush across the stars, silver-trimmed by moonlight. A wind was rising, whistling in the stiff leaves of myall.

'You know, I reckon we might have a storm,' said Alan Lamb.

Barry Bailey's mouth-organ was playing Tex Morton's song, *Move Along, Baldy*, and the boy sang with it.

> 'I've never wanted to live in the towns,
> Never been past Alexandria Downs,
> When I get lonely I tell myself lies,
> And sing with my mouth shut to keep out the flies.'

'I wish I could yodel,' said the boy, wistfully.

When Tex Morton had come to Geraldton with the rodeo he had waited for three hours outside the tent to see him face to face, but had had no luck. He had only seen him in his official capacity, in the ring, shooting and stockwhipping cigarettes and cards from a lady's lips and fingers.

> 'Move along, Baldy, there's work to be done,
> Got to get home by the settin' of sun;
> Nobody's waitin' to welcome us back,
> Just an old cow and a broken-down shack.'

'Gee, you know,' Hugh said, 'I can remember when I was a soprano.'

'If you want to be one again,' Alan said, 'we could fix it.'

'Where did Mr Maplestead find a crude peasant like you?'

'In the Walkaway pub,' Rick said, 'dead drunk.'

'That's a lie,' Alan said. 'I was havin' a sleep in the shade under 'is truck.'

Silence fell as Barry Bailey knocked the mouth-organ against his leg.

'You know,' Rob said, 'when they have Church at Balladyne, Mrs Pearse plays the mouth-organ for them to sing hymns, and they have to stop while she shakes the spit out of the mouth-organ.'

'You people are really rural,' Hugh said.

'It's funny having Church like that,' said the boy. 'When

177

they have Church at Kajarra, Mr and Mrs Moore go and have Communion off the hall-stand.'

'Well, I don't s'pose they're fussy,' Hugh said, 'so long as they get a drink.'

'Ted reckons some of the local yamidgees really go for being confirmed,' Alan said. 'They get a shot of Full Cream Port in their bellies and they think God's talkin'.'

'What's yamidgees?' said the boy.

'Boongs. Noogs. Coloured folk.'

'I like them,' the boy said. 'There's some nice boong kids at school.'

'He's gunna grow up to be a gin-jockey,' said Alan.

'What's a gin-jockey?' said the boy, and then realized. 'Aw, you dirty cow.'

'Hey, look,' Rick said, 'maybe the kid's not innocent, but we don't have to educate him.'

'Sorry,' said Alan.

The boy felt uncomfortable. It seemed that grown-up men liked to talk dirty all the time, and he just got in the way. 'I don't mind,' he said, earnestly. 'You can talk dirty if you like.'

'As the actress said to the bishop.'

'Hughie,' Rick said, 'I'll have your skin for a saddle in a minute.'

'As the bishop said to the actress. Yah, gotcha there.'

'Ah, you know no language but a boot,' Rick said, kicking him.

The boy laughed, feeling happy. That was what he liked, grown-ups kidding each other. And the sad reedy mouth-organ quavered on, playing *Red River Valley*.

'I'm turning in,' Alan Lamb said. 'Where are the blankets, Rick?'

'Back of the truck. Bring the lot, will you?'

'Give us a hand, Barry.'

'Right.' The mouth-organ stopped, and the whistling of the wind in the stiff leaves took over.

'This is beaut,' the boy said, flat on his back. 'Isn't it beaut, Hughie?'

'Sure is.'

'You glad you came up here?'

'Couldn't be gladder. It couldn't be more like what I needed.

'Why don't you stay?'

'Well, I wouldn't mind it.'

'I wish you'd stay. I wish you were going to be here while Rick's away.'

'You're a nice little bugger,' Hugh said. 'But it can't be done, sport.'

Blankets plumped on the ground between them.

'Better clean your teeth, Rob,' Rick said.

'Listen to Mum,' Hugh exclaimed. 'I'm seeing a new aspect of you, Maplestead.'

'I was told to say that,' Rick said. 'What's it to me if his fangs start falling like autumn leaves?'

The boy, at the trough by the mill, gathered water in his cupped hand from the ball-tap, and filled his mouth, and foamed. He scrubbed and spat, watching the cloud-dark sky.

When he came back, Rick and Hugh were grey cocoons by the low fire. He shrouded himself in a blanket, and lay down by Rick, and fell asleep, listening to the wind sweep across country, hissing in the leaves.

In his sleep, the sky cracked open. He woke, and jumped to his feet. The sky cracked open with blue fire, and enormous thunder rolled.

The horses were blundering around the yard, maddening the sheep. Another clap of thunder and an explosion of lightning came together.

Rick and Alan and Barry were at the yard, hammering the iron stakes firmer against the thrust of the frightened animals. The boy saw their dark figures by the lightning, and Hugh staggering back from the truck under the weight of a green tarpaulin.

'Is it a storm, Hughie?' he asked.

'I'd accept that diagnosis,' said Hugh, 'for the time being. Give us a hand to spread this tarp.'

Huge fat drops of rain began to fall, and the three men by the yard came running back.

'Dive under, kid,' Hugh said, getting beneath the tarpaulin.

The boy followed, and found his own blanket, and lay down on it, while rain splattered on the fabric above. The edge of the tarpaulin kept lifting, letting in wind and lightning and the dark figures of the two farmhands and of Rick, who lay beside him.

Rain beat on the canvas, and a small stream began to course the ground below it. The tarpaulin lay on the ground like a coverlet. Every now and then someone would raise the edge to let in air.

The edge lifted, and let in blue fire, and the sound of a rocking explosion overhead. 'Oh,' said the boy, his heart jumping.

'You scared, Rob?' said Rick, beside him.

'No, just—sort of excited.'

He felt Rick's arm go round him, and burrowed against Rick's shoulder. He was scared, a little.

'Aunt Rosa and Aunt May will be under their beds now,' he said, 'with blankets over all the mirrors.'

'I doubt if they're having a storm at Innisfail.'

He lay beside Rick, feeling his fear go. The air under the pattering tarpaulin was thick and hot.

'Jesus, Maplestead,' Hugh complained, 'you need a bath.'

'If you don't like the atmosphere, stop breathing.'

The boy lay with his face against Rick's sweat-and-wood-smoke-and-sheep-smelling shirt, feeling grown-up and happy.

'Your arm'll go to sleep,' he said, drowsily.

'Doesn't matter, kid,' Rick said. *'Tidak apa.'*

Blue steamy smoke rose from the wet wood, and as Rick stood over the fire his face had its other look, its bad-dream look.

The two farmhands had ridden off to look for the fifty-odd sheep that had broken out in the storm, and Hugh was away in the bushes. Hughie had gone to the benjo. There was nothing confidential about Hughie's natural functions.

The boy looked at Rick, and knew that there was nothing he could do about whatever it was that Rick was remembering.

'What's the matter?' he said. 'You worrying about the sheep?'

'No,' Rick said, waking up, slowly. 'Just the smell of the wood. It reminded me of something.'

He shook his head suddenly, and looked round the camp. He was lonely, the boy saw. He was lonely for Hughie.

There was nothing Rob could do about it.

He went off into the bush to scout for dry wood, and met Hugh coming back. 'I think Rick wants you,' he said. 'He's thinking about Thailand or something.'

'The way you watch us,' Hugh said, 'it makes me quite nervous.'

'Well, he's got that funny look.'

Hugh's hair was all over the place, and his jaw was dark with three days' growth of beard. It seemed unlikely that anything could ever dim the clear shining light of jemenfoutisme in his black eyes.

'What will he do, Hughie, when you're not around?'

'Let him worry,' Hugh said. 'He's a bigger boy than you are.'

He stooped, helping the boy to gather wood, and they went back laden to the fire.

'They find the sheep?' he said to Rick.

'They're not back yet.'

'Well, they can't get out of this paddock, can they?'

'You know how big this paddock is?' Rick said. 'It's twelve miles by nine.'

'I dunno,' Hugh said, 'you bloody squatters and your delusions of grandeur. Every paddock has to show up on a map of the world. Just so you can wear a big hat.'

'It works the other way,' the boy said. 'They say: The bigger the hat, the smaller the property.'

'Now I get it,' Hugh said. He pointed at Rick. 'Now I understand why this broken-down bum staggers round under a sort of beach-umbrella.'

Rick's hat was stained and bent and had a strip of kangaroo-skin for a band. 'I wouldn't part with this.' he said, spinning it on his hand. 'I've had it since I was at school. I shot that roo myself.' He looked very seriously at the hat. 'The things that have happened to me since that was new.

' "A few more treasures rest," ' Hugh crooned, ' "within my treasure chest." Ah, you're making me sick. I bet your great-grandma wore it on her wedding day, and washed it with Velvet soap for ninety-two years. Bloody thing ought to be condemned by the health inspector.'

'I wish you were one of those people,' Rick said, 'who never speak before lunch.'

'Those people suffer from night starvation,' Hugh said, 'and they're being slowly poisoned by the natural toxins of the body. But my regularity worries are over, thanks to your lousy cooking.'

'I've seen the day when you wouldn't turn down a nice steak of snake cooked by me.'

'Ergh,' said the boy.

'Hey, this kid's never tasted snake,' Hugh said. 'Or cat, or dog. How about we barbecue that useless old Jock tonight?'

'No,' said the boy, indignant. Jock was one of the fixtures in his world.

He looked to Rick for support, and saw that Rick had stopped remembering whatever it was that he had been remembering, and was gazing down at the fire with a faint smile that meant that he was enjoying himself. Hughie's beaut, thought the boy, feeling a surge of affection for Hughie, who was looking around the camp now, wearing his unique and paradoxical expression of sardonic gentleness.

I want to be like Hughie when I grow up, he thought. Hughie was unbreakable.

'They're coming back,' Hugh said. 'Better put the breakfast on.'

The horses pushed their way through the myall with a swishing sound, Jock prancing ahead with lolling tongue. He came to the boy, and the boy fondled him, promising him that he would not be barbecued.

'Can't find a trace of 'em,' Alan Lamb called out, as he dismounted by the yard.

'Well, let's just go on,' Hugh said. 'What's fifty sheep to a rich cocky like Mr Maplestead?'

'I reckon we'll have to,' Rick said, breaking eggs in the pan.

'Ted can come back for them.'

'What a thrill for Ted,' said Alan. 'He'll be ropeable.'

'So will my old man,' Rick said. 'Ah well, too bad.' He laid out the plates on the ground around him. 'Funny, I keep forgetting I'm over twenty-one.'

'Same here,' Hugh said. 'It's as if those four years didn't count.'

The boy sat on the tarpaulin and smelled wet red earth, wet leaves, wet wood. It was the first rain on this part of Bogada, and white stones, washed clean, stood out sharp against the darkened soil. Now I'll find some gold, he thought. He would find a nugget worth four hundred pounds, like the one the man on the next property had found when he was walking behind sheep. He would find a nugget, and buy Hughie a wristwatch like Rick's. That would make up to Hughie for the four years that didn't count.

The air smelled of wet woodsmoke, wet sheep and the sizzling frying pan, as he sat daydreaming in the sun.

The long, slow trek went on. The boy walked behind the sheep, and rode Rick's horse behind the sheep, and drove behind the sheep beside Hugh in the truck. What had been tracks had become reddish creeks, and the truck rocked and strained, while Hugh swore, bumping in hidden runnels and labouring in red gluey clay.

In one of the rare fences they found a trapped emu. Its leg had caught in the wire, and it had toppled, and now lay still, the giant leg poised, as they stood around it.

' 'Struth,' said Hugh, with awe. 'Imagine getting a kick from that.'

'What are we going to do?' asked the boy.

'I'm not going to do anything,' Rick said. 'We haven't got a rifle, and if anyone's going to untangle it, it's not going to be me.'

So they left it there. But they all felt guilty.

Emus were rather nice, the boy reflected. Dozing in the shade after the midday meal, he woke to find a semi-circle of emus staring down on him. Their long necks craned, their idiotic eyes rolled, as they commented to one another on their find. Then the boy laughed out loud, and they ran. Everything about them was exaggerated, including their agitation.

Another sunset came, and they staked out the yard by a mill, and set up camp, and Ted Barnes came from the homestead in a pick-up bringing an iron pot of stew from his wife. 'Thank God you thought to get married,' said Hugh.

In the sunset light the earth was burning red, and all the heat of the day rose concentrated from the pale stones. The land was strangely limited in colour. It had nothing to set against the bright earth but the grey-green of myall, the grey of dead wood, and the tender peacock-green of the empty sky.

At the trough by the mill Rick was stooping, skinny and naked, washing himself.

'Hold it, Rick,' Ted Barnes called out. 'I want just one more photo for *The Western Mail*.'

Rick made a signal like Mr Churchill in reverse.

'I want to swim in the tank,' Rob said. 'Can I?'

'Yeah, I reckon,' Ted said.

'You want to swim in the tank, Hughie?'

'That's a thought,' Hugh said, beginning to unbutton.

They clambered naked up the rungs of the corrugated tank, and lowered themselves into it, circling like pale frogs in the greenish, green-scummed water.

'If I was a sheep,' Hugh said, spitting. 'I wouldn't drink this. I bet those ones we lost have gone looking for a better billet than Bogada.'

They dropped down the warm side of the tank and stood against it, drying themselves.

'You poor little drowned rat,' Hugh said. 'Why don't they feed you?'

'Hoh, look who's talking,' said the boy. 'Old Gandhi Mackay.'

'We should live forever,' Hugh said, comfortably, 'if I don't knock your block off for giving me lip.'

In the darkening camp, Rick was heating up the cooking pot, and the stew bubbled. They ate, and pushed their plates and mugs aside, and lay on blankets near the fire. The talk of Hugh and Rick and Alan Lamb went on and on. Every now and again they would stop arguing with one another and launch some sort of leg-pulling attack on Barry Bailey or the boy.

'Heck, you talk a lot,' Rob said, half admiring. 'You sound like my mother and Susan on the phone.'

'How'd you like a clip over the ear?' Rick enquired.

'Leave him alone,' Hugh said. 'He's right, we do bash the drums a bit.'

'Yeah, but hell, you haven't heard my sister on the phone. She's like an epidemic of galahs.'

'*Why* do you talk so much?' the boy wondered.

'Well, for a few years,' Hugh said, 'that was the only entertainment there was. So we all became brilliant conversationalists.'

'In self-defence,' Rick said. 'Otherwise the other brilliant conversationalists would have pounded the ears off us.'

'You're like a lot of wirelesses,' Rob said, 'all on different stations.' He fell asleep on his blanket, the talk still flying in the air above him.

In the morning they reached the country where the earlier rain had been, soft under green, the drab leaves of myall now brilliant with green light thrown upwards from the grass. Turpentine-weed was trampled by the passing sheep, and filled the air with its medicinal sweetness. 'Ah, that's beaut,' the boy said, breathing deep.

'Maybe we ought to go and roll in it,' Hugh said, 'then we wouldn't smell like we've been sleeping in these clothes for five days.'

'I can't get used to the way this delicate bugger complains,' Rick said. 'Times have changed.'

'I want to feel beautiful,' Hugh said, 'like an American Mom in Paris. Hey, Rick, remember when we were unloading that go-down and we doused ourselves in Eau de Cologne?'

'Crikey, you don't look beautiful,' Rob said. Hugh's face was black with beard, and his hair was like the feathers of a dead shag washed up on the beach.

'I'm beautiful inside,' Hugh said. 'You just haven't got enough soul to see it.'

Alan Lamb said with a sort of wonder: 'I dunno, I reckon you must really be round the bend. No one could keep up an act this long.'

In the late afternoon they reached a floor of flat grey rock holed with shallow pools, and let the sheep wander off. Ted Barnes was waiting with the Andarra pick-up that had come on the train. They unsaddled the horses and roped them in on the back of the Bogada truck and watched it bump away towards the homestead.

'You know what I'm going to do,' Hugh said, 'I'm going to have a shave. Oh brother, it's going to hurt.'

They sat about on the warm flat rock, washing themselves in the pools, and shaving.

'Want a shave, kid?' Hugh said.

'No, thanks.'

'I remember when I was about thirteen, I shaved myself all over to make my hairs grow quicker. I could hardly wear clothes for a month after that.'

'You know what you are, Hughie?' said Rick. 'You're a bloody narcissist.'

'I bloody well was not. I was learning the ropes from a girl of fifteen.'

'That doesn't stop you from being a narcissist.'

'What's a narcissist?' said the boy.

'A fella who's in love with himself,' Rick said. 'A fella who keeps swooning over himself in the mirror.'

'Heck, you're the narcissist,' Rob said. 'Hughie doesn't stare at himself in the mirror like you do.'

Rick looked uncomfortable suddenly, and the boy was surprised.

'Well, anyone who looked like we did at the end of the war,' Hugh said, 'and looks as pretty as we do now, couldn't help being a bit of a narcissist.'

'Aw, I dunno,' Alan Lamb said, looking at his own white horseman's legs with wet ginger hairs on them, 'you buggers are lucky. I fail to thrill me.'

Rick is a narcissist, Rob thought. He knows it.

He studied Rick with revived interest.

'I feel shy about asking for the mirror now,' Rick said, 'but I've got to shave.'

'What are we doing, getting all dolled up?' Barry Bailey wondered.

'Oh, I thought we'd go and eat in Magnet.'

'The bright lights,' Alan Lamb said. 'The big smoke. Here we come.'

'What's at Magnet?' the boy asked.

'Three gins and a goat,' Alan Lamb said, 'most days. And a street about half a mile wide.'

'They're kind of pathetic,' Rick said, 'these goldfields towns. They all started out with the idea that they were going to need streets built for ticker-tape parades.'

'I thought the idea was so camel teams could drive six abreast,' Barry Bailey said. 'That's what it looks like.'

'I wish they had camels now,' the boy said. 'It must have been beaut when they had camels.'

'My old man was with a camel team,' Hugh said, 'up round Peak Hill. He liked the things.'

'They're nasty bastards,' Rick said. 'I remember seeing a few around when I was a kid.'

'They have wild camels in the Northern Territory,' Rob said. 'Gee, I'd like to go there.'

'Why don't we?' Rick said. 'Hughie. Why don't we go to the Territory?'

'Because I'm going to get a bloody job in a bloody shop in bloody Perth,' Hugh said. 'So forget it.'

'Awe, Hughie,' the boy said, shocked, 'you're not going to work in a shop?'

'Yeah, I am. I'm going to sell tennis racquets and golf balls.'

'I think you're nuts,' Rob said.

'I don't take risks, kid. Risks are for the birds.'

'Gawd,' said Alan Lamb, looking depressed. 'A shop.'

The boy saw that Hugh looked depressed too, and felt sorry for him. 'Well, you'll be able to start playing golf,' he said, 'as well as tennis, and p'rhaps you'll get good at that too.'

'Yeah,' Hugh said. 'Yeah, I'll learn to play all the rich buggers' sports and finish up in high society.'

'A shop,' said Alan Lamb, looking across the green and fragrant country in the afternoon light. 'That beats me.'

Rick dried his face on the communal towel, and stood up. 'You all ready for civilization?' he said.

'Yeah,' they said, 'yeah,' following him to the pick-up and stowing themselves away in it here and there. The boy sat cramped in the cab between Rick and Hugh, with his legs twisted sideways to leave the gearstick free, and brooded, as the car bumped through the green bush, about Hugh's job and Hugh's future. It was all wrong for Hughie. There was something brilliant and buccaneering about Hughie, that ought not to be shut up in a shop, that ought to be out in the Territory hunting camels among the legendary gallant bones, or pearling, or shooting crocodiles in the wet North. But there was nothing Rob could do about it. How could Hughie have failed to know this about himself?

Rick wanted to go, he knew, to go off and do something brilliant and buccaneering. But he would not go without Hughie. Rick was not really tough, not like Hughie, though he was cleverer.

He felt a spasm of irritation against Hughie, who was condemning Rick to a dull life. Then it faded, and he watched the waterlogged country in a mindless content.

It was dark when they reached Mount Magnet, and there was no one in the broad street but one small man who sat on the edge of the footpath under a store veranda with his boots in the gutter.

The small man looked round and saw Hugh studying him as he passed. 'Who d'you think you are?' he said.

'Who do *you* think I am?' Hugh asked, stopping dead.

'I know who y'are,' said the drunk man, standing up. 'You're a rotten lousy Catholic capitalist bastard. To hell with the Pope.'

'How'd you like a mouthful of knuckle?' Hugh enquired.

'Come out of that, Hughie!' Rick said, like calling a dog.

Hugh turned back reluctantly and joined the others. 'He can't talk like that about the Pope,' he complained. 'Any mate of Mrs Murphy's is a mate of mine.'

'Who did he think you were?' the boy wondered.

'He didn't think I was anyone. He was trying to find out.'

'He must have Northern Irish blood,' Rob mused, 'like Rick and me.'

Rick said, grinning: 'This kid's grandfather used to wear an orange rosette on St Patrick's Day. He really believed in trailing his coat.'

'I hope these quaint old customs like Christianity die out some day,' said Hugh.

They sat around a table in a cafe, eating steak and chips. Barry Bailey ate like a grain elevator, and Rob stared, fascinated.

'You must be a growing boy,' Hugh said. 'I'd hate to be cast away on a raft with you.'

'Aah,' said Barry Bailey, embarrassed, and refused to eat any more.

They paid the bill and went back to the pick-up, where Alan and Barry rolled up in blankets and lay down among the camping gear.

'You want to sleep in the back, Rob?' Rick asked.

'No. I'll stay in the front with you.'

He sat staring at the red road in the headlights, the whizzing roadside scrub. The tunnel of light through the dark bush hypnotized him and he drowsed. Once he woke with a start as the pick-up braked suddenly, and saw four pale wavering kangaroos in the road. Then he leaned back again, and fell asleep.

When he woke, he was lying across the seat, with his head in Hugh's lap and his feet in Rick's. Hugh and Rick were talking, after having been quiet a long time, and that was what had woken him. He lay, cramped but warm, across the seat, and smelled the smell of Rick's cigarette and Hugh's dirty old clothes.

'You really do want to?' Rick was saying. 'Still?'

'Yeah, of course I do, you drongo.'

'It's not just this she-waited-all-through-the-war-for-me crap?'

'You know bloody well there's nothing chivalrous about me.'

'Well, good on you,' Rick said. 'And good luck.'

'Will you stand up for me, mate?'

'Be your best man, you mean? Yeah, of course.'

'You're a good bloke,' Hugh said, pushing him lightly on the shoulder.

'Hell, it's no trouble. You're the one who's got to do the hard work.'

The boy sat up and stretched. The tunnel of light ran now between dense gumtrees festooned with pale clumps of mistletoe. 'I know where we are,' he said, yawning, 'we're nearly there.'

'Thank Christ you woke,' Hugh said, stamping and stretching his legs. 'I was thinking I was going to be permanently paralysed from the waist down.'

'Bad time for it to happen,' Rick said.

'This is sacred,' Hugh said. 'Let's have no rough military jokes.'

'Hughie's going to get married, Rob,' Rick said, 'to a gorgeous blonde called Joy.'

'She's not, actually,' Hugh said. 'She calls herself a brownette.'

'Oh,' said the boy. 'Oh. Good.'

He stared out at the whizzing gravel. He felt sleepy and irritable, and he could not remember, offhand, ever hearing of a more rotten idea than that Hughie should get married.

'What's she like?' he asked.

'She plays hockey,' said Hugh.

'Oh.'

The lights picked out the white gate of Balladyne, the station neighbouring Sandalwood.

'*You* won't get married, will you, Rick?' the boy hoped.

'Not me. Risks are for the birds.'

'That's good,' the boy murmured. Then he remembered his manners, and said: 'Oh. Congratulations, Hughie.'

13

Mrs Charles Maplestead's house was full of family. The boy's Aunt Judith and her husband, Uncle Michael, and the girl cousins belonging to them were staying with Mrs Maplestead, and other forms of family came and went continually.

Rob came through the palms and into the shadowed cemented place between the stone and wooden houses where Uncle Michael and Gordon Maplestead were sitting on the wood-box, wearing long white trousers and drinking beer. They said: 'Hullo, Rob.'

'Hullo,' he said. 'Have you been playing cricket? Did you win?'

'We won,' Uncle Michael said, 'but we're getting old.'

Rob was puzzled when people said that. Uncle Michael and Gordon must be thirty-something. and they were getting old. Aunt Kay was seventy-four, and she said that she was getting old. When did people decide that they had actually *got* old? He wondered if Aunt Rosa, who was ninety-two, supposed that she wasn't quite old yet.

'Did you bring Didi in?' he asked Gordon.

'No, they're all out at Andarra.'

The porch of the house with the rough stone walls smelled sweet with roses. Dark-red and yellow and pink roses were standing in a bucket of water on the porch table. Aunt Molly must have come to town, thought the boy.

In the big kitchen Aunt Kay was darning socks at the table by the window, in the cool of the southerly. On the window ledge, weighed down under a round flintstone, a long letter from Aunt Kay to the milkman flapped in the wind. Aunt Kay was great mates with the milkman, because they were both mad about the milkman's horse.

In the gravel drive outside the window dead leaves of the Moreton Bay fig were blowing.

'Did Aunty Molly bring those roses?' the boy said.

Aunt Kay started at his voice, though she had not heard what he was saying. She was very deaf now, and that was why she sat so much alone, darning socks or playing Patience in the sewing room or the kitchen.

'Oh, Rob,' she said. 'I didn't hear you coming.'

'Are those Aunty Molly's roses?'

'Isn't she clever?' said Aunt Kay. 'And they've only been at that farm a few months.'

'Are they here now?'

'They went to see a man about some sheep.'

Something went *thunk!* on the underside of the table. 'What the heck?' Rob said, leaning down to look beneath it, and encountering the stony blue gaze of a three-year-old cousin, the property of Aunty Molly and Uncle Paul. 'He must have a head like a rock. Any other kid would of bawled.'

'What was that?' Aunt Kay said. 'Did Rob bump his head?'

'His name's Peter,' Rob said. 'I'm Rob.'

'I keep forgetting,' Aunt Kay said. 'There are so many children now.'

In the drawing-room up the passage someone was playing *Happy Birthday To You* on the piano with one finger, over and over again.

'Whose birthday?' Rob asked.

'It's nobody's birthday,' said Aunt Kay, who always knew.

'Then why do they keep playing that?'

'It's the only tune they know,' Aunt Kay said, sighing.

'Ah, they're dumb kids,' Rob said. 'I'm going to play.'

He walked up the passage into the drawing-room and was hit in the face by a cushion.

'Hey, you shouldn't do that,' he said. 'You'll break something.'

'Bossy,' said his sister Nan. 'I s'pose you'll go away and tell now.'

'Telltale tit,' chanted his cousin Jenny, who had thrown the cushion. 'Your tongue shall be split.'

'Silly kid,' he said, flooding her with ten-year-old scorn. She was only five, and belonged to Aunty Judith and Uncle

Michael. She had straight hair which was almost white, and everyone said she looked like one of the little white-haired boongs from farther north, that were supposed to be descended from the marooned Dutch mutineers.

Her sister Helen, who was seven, was still industriously banging out *Happy Birthday*.

'Can't you play anything else?' he asked, with exaggerated distaste.

Helen turned on the piano stool and flashed her blue eyes at him. 'Go and jump in the lake,' she confessed.

'Gee, you're a little larrikin,' he said, virtuously. But she had won, obviously, so he withdrew, and went out through the big front door with the wolf's-head knocker to the people sitting on the lawn.

His grandmother and his mother and his Aunt Judith and Susan were talking and talking. They talked very quietly, but couldn't they go. They were talking about tennis, about gardens, about children's clothes, about the golf season. Susan's youngest boy, his cousin Johnny, with yellow curls like a juvenile Harpo Marx, sat on the grass at her feet, consumed with boredom.

'Rob,' Susan said. 'Just the boy I was looking for. Will you climb the figtree for me?'

'Yes,' he said, gladly, feeling his self-esteem revive a little after the blow it had received from the little girls.

Greeneyes sped from the rough leaves as he climbed the tree, and the shiny tins that were supposed to scare them away from the fruit rattled and flashed. His mother and Susan and Aunty Judith stood on the ground below, still talking quietly. It annoyed him that they would not concentrate. 'Catch!' he shouted, dropping ripe figs. But nobody caught, and the figs squashed on the ground.

'Well, it doesn't matter,' Susan said, brushing the dead grass off them and putting them into the figleaf-lined basket. She went on talking.

A car came up the drive and stopped by the figtree. Susan's husband, Edgar, got out, wearing his fishing clothes.

'You must make those hats he wears,' Aunty Judith said to

Susan.: 'No one would sell things like that.'

'Did you have a good day?' Susan called out to Edgar, who was pulling something out of the boot.

'Have a look,' he said. And she went and joined him, and exclaimed.

'These are for Aunt Anne,' Edgar was saying, holding up a dripping sugar-bag full of fish.

'Goodness,' said Margaret Coram, 'aren't you clever? We must get our share of those.'

'Catch,' called the boy. And Aunty Judith caught, and put the figs in Susan's basket.

'Where shall I put this lot?' Edgar asked.

'In the ice-chest,' Aunty Judith said. 'I'll show you.' They went away into the house with the dripping bag.

'Catch,' said the boy, patiently.

'I think that's enough,' Susan said. 'Yes. Thank you, Rob. Now, where has Johnny gone?' She wandered off with the basket of reddish-purple-sheened fruit, calling: 'Johnny!'

The boy looked through the leaves at his mother. 'Aunty Judith's getting fat,' he said.

'Ssh,' said his mother.

'Well, she is. She usen't to be fat.'

'Aunty Judith's going to have another baby,' his mother said, and looked up at him, cautiously.

'Oh,' he said, interested. And she saw that no further explanation would be necessary.

'Grandma and Aunt Kay will be pleased,' he said. 'Now they'll have six grandchildren, and Aunt Mary's only got five.'

'I expect she'll win in the end,' his mother said. 'She's still got Rick to marry off.'

'Rick's not going to get married,' Rob said. 'He says it's too risky.'

'Well, we all know what happens to these sour old cynics,' said Margaret Coram.

'Do we want some figs? Dad likes them.'

'Yes, throw down a few.'

He clambered across to another branch, prospecting for ripe figs. Down below, Aunty Judith had come back again.

and was talking to his mother.

'I suppose one oughtn't to say this,' his mother was saying, 'but really, I do think Rick's awfully immature.'

The boy sat back among the leaves, thinking and feeling angry. He had no idea what 'immature' meant, but if it was something that she ought not to say, then why had she said it?

He felt depressed suddenly. It was one more thing that was wrong with Rick. Everything was wrong with Rick, and in his mind he worked out a catalogue of Rick's offences.

Rick was immature.

He was lazy.

He was a narcissist.

He used dirty language.

He was not a gentleman to Jane Wexford, and had lost his temper with her while arguing about the Bomb.

He talked like Hitler about the Bomb.

He fainted.

He cried in his sleep, and when he had got drunk at Andarra on New Year's Eve.

He had stayed at the very bottom of the Army.

He had given his campaign ribbons, &c., to a kid in the street as soon as he had got them.

He had not given his campaign ribbons, &c., to Rob.

He looked bored and miserable when he was with people Rob liked.

He refused to be a farmer.

Everything was wrong with Rick, and there was nothing Rob could do about it. He stared down from a gap in the leaves towards the sewing-room window where Aunt Kay was now framed, hunting in the sewing-machine drawers for cotton. Aunt Kay would not say things that she supposed she oughtn't to say about Rick. Aunt Kay thought Rick was wonderful, and she loved Hughie too, because he was both a man and a Mackay, even if he did mispronounce his name in the Australian fashion.

Everything was wrong with Rick. And yet, he was still the most beaut bloke Rob had ever known, and the next most beaut bloke was Hughie. Sitting among the leaves, he felt melancholy about Rick, and wished that there was something he could do.

Now that Rob had skipped a class at school a barrier had risen between him and his old friends, and he had to look around for new ones. And in the strange class he found another stranger, a boy called Mike Ashcroft, who had come from the goldfields to the north-east of Bogada, and Mike became his mate.

Mike had come to Geraldton because his town had died. It had died in the night, Mike said. He had woken up one morning and everything was quiet, because the gold mine had shut down suddenly and everyone had gone away. The thought of Mike's dead town haunted Rob. He thought of Mike waking in the morning, listening for familiar sounds in the broad red street and hearing none, going out in the morning sun to the broad red street and finding that his town had died in the night. It seemed to Rob a terrible and poetic thing that had happened to Mike, who was now a sort of refugee, among kids who did not understand his foreign slang, filled with terms to do with goldmining and aboriginal words from the boongs of the dead town.

In this first year after the end of the war, all the kids were full of war stories, and Rob grew prouder and prouder of Rick's scarred ankles. But some of the stories were shocking. 'There was this Jap,' one kid said, 'that was washing his clothes in a creek, and this bloke with Uncle Dick run up with his bayonet and shoved it right up his——'

'Ergh,' said the other kids. 'Stop bulldusting, you dirty cow.'

Everybody knew that Australians could not behave like that. But the thought was shocking.

At other times they talked about the Russians. 'I just couldn't fight the Russians,' Rob said. 'In the war, my grandmother took me to a picture called *Song of Russia,* and gee, they're beaut people.'

'You're not going to have any say about who you fight,' Mike said. 'I reckoned for a while the Poms were going to fight the Yanks over those atomic secrets.'

'It's like my mother said,' Rob mused. 'There'll always be a war somewhere.'

He had a bike now, and so had Mike, and they rode everywhere together, foully cursing the south wind when it was so strong that they had to get off and push. From the top of the big sandhill called Mount Misery, beyond which the coloured population lived, they surveyed their town, looking out for new places to explore. From Mount Misery the town looked clean and tidy and pretty, the iron roofs of the houses small and neat, the harbour blue as New Guinea butterflies, the dunes to the south blinding white against the sea. It was not at all the sandy spit of land that a lady, nearly a hundred years before, standing with fluttering veil on Wizard Peak, had pronounced a dismal situation for a settlement. Even the blacks had said then: 'Wittacarra no good.'

'Gee, you know,' Rob said, looking at the brown-and-white-ringed lighthouse at the Point, 'when my mother was a kid, they used to go to the lighthouse in a spring cart, and they always stayed the whole day there. And we've ridden round there three times this week.'

'Let's go to the wharf,' Mike said. 'I feel like fishing.'

The wharf smelled of the wheat-dust that always coated it, drifting out of the great bins and dropping from the elevator, lying hardpacked in the concrete beds of the railway lines. Underneath the wharf, where they clambered or sat quietly fishing, the water was of the deepest green, and fathomless. They sat for hours staring down in the green water, watching the useless fish, the black-and-white footballers and the flame-blue-striped yellow-tails and the stonefish like animated rocks that they did not really want to catch at all but only to study. They hauled up blowfish, swearing, and let them swell, and then stamped on the white balloons and kicked the burst bodies back into the water. They rarely hoped for anything much better in the way of fish than a trumpeter. But one day Rob hauled up from the bottom a great silver fish with a curious insecticidal smell, and was for a while speechless with achievement.

'Mike,' he shouted, 'Mike, look.'

'Oh, no,' Mike groaned. 'You know what that is?'

'Nuh. I've never caught a fish this big.'

'It's a poisony. My dad caught one last week.'

'It's no good, then?' Rob said, forlornly.

'It's no good, all right. You watch out you don't spike yourself on the fin.'

'I already have,' Rob said.

'Oh boy, you're going to be sorry.'

And he was sorry. His finger swelled up like a sausage, and he passed three hours of agony, which the doctor told him to grin and bear.

'There's some funny things in the sea,' he reflected, bitterly.

At times he and Mike went to the wharf by night, when there was no ship in, and fished for herring, throwing out handfuls of greasy meal called burly, and watched the moon rise glistening on the oil-streaks. They rarely caught anything, but it was peaceful on the wharf in the moonlight, hearing from farther along the quiet, intermittent talk of the other fishers.

Maybe I'll be a fisherman, Rob thought, watching Eric Larsen, one of his heroes, unload his boat by the dinghy-slip.

The wharf was a fascination, especially when a ship was in and grain was being loaded, or sheep, or even, for a time, goats. The ships went so far, to Singapore and Darwin and even to England. One night Rob and Mike stole up the gangway of a freighter and peered down the companionway. The lighted ship was hot, like an oven, and smelled of bitter grease.

'What if we went down there,' Mike whispered, 'and stowed away?'

'I dunno,' Rob breathed. 'Would you be game?'

Then they looked down on the head of a man climbing the ladder and ran.

One of the boys from school who played around the wharf was killed by a ship, crushed against the piles as the ship drifted gently in. It meant nothing to the other boys. The dead boy had simply ceased to come to school. Life beneath the wharf went on.

And life went on at school, and on the beaches, and in the

streets and dunes and country roads, and Rob fell in love with a tall, green-eyed girl, to whom he gave an old brooch of Aunt Kay's, and received in return a photograph of his girl on her bicycle. It was the first time that he had felt this way about a real girl, though he had been in love with a little girl called Elizabeth Taylor, who was in a film called *Lassie, Come Home*. He wrote letters to his girl, wanting nothing of her but that she should say that she was his girl-friend, which she, for some reason, would not do. Somehow it happened that their lengthy courtship was carried out without exchanging a word, at that time or ever after.

The red-brick Norman fortress of the college was green under Virginia creeper, and pink oleanders flowered around the tennis courts. Behind the college was the wild bush of King's Park, and in front of it, beyond the sloping lawns, the broad blue moody river. The noises of the college were noises of peace: people yarning on the balconies, people singing in the showers, voices in the quadrangle calling the names of people wanted on the telephone. The chapel bell tolled in the morning and in the evening, and when his turn came to read Compline, Rick found himself wishing everybody, with unexpected sincerity, a quiet night and a perfect end.

On the balconies, in the high panelled Hall with great windows on the river, in the showers and the Junior Common Room and the bedroom-studies, the talk went on and on. The war was refought daily, on every front; Europe and Asia were anatomized, ideologies were disembowelled and publicly examined. Rick felt old and young at once; old and yet irresponsible beside the youths who had just come from school, young and yet disillusioned beside the men who had fought the war right through. His room-mate was an old school friend, a rowdy lunatic who had been a Commando sergeant in New Guinea, and was relaxing now from that responsibity in a bout of irresponsibility that would go on for years. On nights when Tom Anscombe came in, half drunk and talkative, to sit on his bed and commiserate with him on the humiliation of being a prisoner, Rick came close to rebellion. It was after

Tom's tête-à-têtes that the dreams came: dreams from which he started cold and sweating, knowing that he had called out, and wondering if Tom in the next room had heard him; and other dreams, quiet and almost pleasurable, from which he woke with tears on his cheeks and on his pillow.

The university was bursting at the seams, and behind the pale sandstoι e colonnades and Spanish tiles of its Australian-Moorish nucleus an ugly clump of temporary buildings sprouted. But on the green lawn of Whitfield Court, fringed by poplars, young bodies decoratively dowsed in the sun, and the semi-tropical garden behind Winthrop Hall was festooned, as summer fell away, with scarlet vines. On the Ovals and paddocks near the river, the university flock peacefully grazed.

Sheep May Safely Graze. Someone was always playing that on the organ, the sound echoing faintly among the creeper-grown arches of the College quadrangle.

He sat in lectures and made dutiful notes, and dutifully discussed the affairs of the world in the refectory. He drank occasionally, and went to dances and parties occasionally, and once, when a girl with a car offered him a lift home, found himself in that girl's bed. When it was over, they told each other that they felt strongly attracted, but. And the girl confessed, with a little irritation now that the effect of gin and everything else was wearing off, that he was not at all her usual type, he was so withdrawn. He stroked her loveable back, feeling contented and at peace, since the war was now without question over, and his body was cured of the war. But he did not love her, he felt no more than a tender gratitude to her, and he wondered whether he would ever have any stronger feeling than tender gratitude for anyone.

In the brick-and-tile and conscientiously gardened suburb of Nedlands, Hugh had rented a run-down wooden house near the river, and installed his fresh-faced Joy, who was expecting a seven-months baby in six months' time.

The house became a sort of club, a caravanserai for all ex-prisoners within range, where the lithe and brownhaired Joy handed out beer or tea with lumps of fruitcake, calling everyone a mob of hoboes, and appearing to believe that they had surrendered to the Japanese in a last burst of boyish high spirits before surrendering for life to the Australian suburbs. Under Joy's influence the reminiscences came cascading, the experiences transformed unrecognizably by humour and nostalgia, so that Joy was continually reminded of things that she and the girls had got up to when they toured with hockey teams.

Rick watched her with bewilderment and admiration, trying to fathom what it was in her with which what he knew was in Hugh must make contact. Somewhere in this healthy girl were guarded depths of understanding, another Joy, the antithesis of all the girls Rick danced with and talked with, resenting their blank incuriosity. Or perhaps Hugh made no contact with her at all at that level; perhaps he was tough enough, and in the midst of his gregariousness, solitary enough, not to need to share the dark inside. Perhaps that was even gone now, healed like a clean wound.

In Rick, as time passed, the grief and the anger, the emptiness now that danger and the need for endurance had passed, swelled to a helpless anguish.

'You happy, fella?' he said to Hugh.

'Mate, I worship her wet footprints on the bathmat.'

'Do you dream?'

'Only about golf.'

'Ah, you insensitive ape,' Rick said. 'You lucky, lucky moronic bastard.'

'Take up golf,' Hugh advised, earnestly. 'You'll dream about it, too.'

14

In the kitchen at Marsa, the boy sniffed with pleasure. It smelled just like the other farm that Uncle Paul and Aunt Molly had had before they went away to the war. He could not identify the smell. It had yeast and vanilla in it, and jamwood burning in the stove, but the smell of the whole, the combination, was just the smell of nostalgia; though Marsa looked and smelled prettier than Dartmoor, with the sweetness of roses drifting in through the window.

'Gee, it's nice,' he said. 'It smells nice.'

'Please?' said Lisa.

'Oh, nothing,' he said. It was hopeless trying to talk to Lisa, who spoke hardly any English. Lisa was a Balt, and when you asked her where she came from she said Litauen, though Aunty Molly said the real name of her country was Lithuania. Lisa had no country any more, the Russians had taken it. So Lisa had come to Australia, to the migrant camp at Northam, and Rick, who had done part of his military training there, said he didn't suppose she even noticed that she had left her refugee camp, unless maybe because of the blowflies.

Lisa was sitting at the kitchen table, sewing something for her little boy, who was called Tad. The Russians had taken Lisa's husband as well as her country.

'Do you like working here?' Rob asked.

'Please?' said Lisa.

'Good country, Australia?'

'Oh, yess,' said Lisa. 'Yess, yess, very—hospitable.'

It was funny, the words that Lisa picked up from reading. She hadn't even known what to call a baby cow, yet she called the bucket it drank from a 'receptacle'.

'You talk funny,' he said, laughing.

'Yess,' said Lisa, also laughing. 'I know I am very droll.'

Lisa and Uncle Paul often talked in French, and Uncle Paul

said that Lisa was an educated woman. Uncle Paul talked French to Lisa, and Italian to the farmhand, and Maltese to the boy from Tardun farm school, and English to everyone else. It was a mystery to Rob how Uncle Paul ever kept track of himself.

'We're very international here,' the boy said.

'Oh, yess,' said Lisa. That was the sort of long word that she would know.

Aunt Molly was washing her hands in the sink outside, earthy from gardening. 'Lisa,' she called.

'Yess, Mrs Rohan?'

'I think we'll have lunch out in the paddocks where Pietro's working. Will you pack up some chops?'

'Please?' said Lisa.

'*Je crois,*' said Aunt Molly, laboriously, '*que nous aurons le déjeuner sur l'herbe.* I know that was terrible French, but you understood, didn't you?'

'Oh, yess,' said Lisa, getting up and going to the refrigerator.

'Can I ride Bob down there?' the boy asked.

'Yes, if you like,' said Aunty Molly.

He went out through the separator room and under the trellis of roses with the rough bark still on the jamwood posts. The Border collie pup, whose name was Gyp, danced round him as he ran to the stableyard.

He grabbed the bridle from a hook in the corrugated iron shed, and went gently towards Bob, holding out a handful of chaff. Bob put his nose to the chaff, and *prrmph*ed, and blew the lot away.

'Ah, you drongo,' Rob said, pushing in the bit, 'Well, you're not getting any more.'

Bob champed on the bit, irritably.

In the small green paddock nearby the pup was yapping and dancing. It was teasing the young bull, who was showing a dull sense of outrage, handsome head lowered. 'Come out of that, Gyp,' Rob shouted. But the cheeky pup went right up to the bull, and licked his running nose.

The bull roared, and the pup yelped and fled.

The boy buckled the girth, and swung into the saddle. He

rode much more stylishly at Marsa, because Uncle Paul had been in the Indian Army.

He cantered down the red track, exulting in the green early winter country, spreading out and out, soft under wheat and pasture, to the drab high plain on the horizon scarred with an orange road going no one cared where. Little rocky pimples of hills, grown with sandalwood and jam, rose out of the green. The small creeks were running in their red sharp-sided channels.

In the road behind him Aunty Molly was following, driving a battered khaki ex-Army pick-up. He left the road, and galloped across the paddocks to the clump of trees where Uncle Paul and Pietro were clearing. The sharp clip of the axes came to him as he reined in, and the smell of cut sandalwood and mallee and jam.

Ah, it smelled pretty, his country.

He dismounted, looping up the reins, and let old Bob wander. His country was so clean-smelling and pretty. He had never heard anyone say it was pretty except Aunt Kay and Uncle Paul; and once, almost unwillingly, Rick. It seemed that everyone took it for granted. Only Aunt Kay, remembering the flat dull Wimmera where she had grown up, and Uncle Paul, remembering stony, crowded Malta, saw beauty in its hills and trees.

He gathered dry wood, and carried it to the pick-up where Aunty Molly and Lisa were unloading sons and food. 'Shall I build the fire here?' he asked Aunty Molly.

'Yes, that should do. Make sure there's no sandalwood, though. It makes the meat taste as if it's been kept in mothballs.'

'Mothballs,' murmured Lisa. 'What is mothballs?' She was always ready to learn a new word.

Rob spluttered, lighting the fire. It reminded him of a joke about how Little Audrey laughed and laughed and laughed. Hughie had told him that. He missed Hughie.

His cousin Peter and Lisa's Tad sat on a tartan rug, a present from Aunt Kay. The fire blazed up, and Aunty Molly came with an old kerosene tin with no ends to it and a gridiron, and beat the fire down a bit with her foot, and set the tin upended in the flames. Lisa was unpacking meat, ready for grilling, and Uncle Paul and Pietro were coming up from the trees.

His country was pretty, he thought, sitting down on the rug, and would be prettier with spring, and Aunty Molly was cleverer than most grown-ups to know that people didn't always want to eat in houses.

'Ah,' said Uncle Paul, sprawling, tired, on the drug. *'Sono benvenuti,* eh, Pietro?'

Pietro nodded, sitting to one side of the grass, looking shy.

Lisa was talking to Tad, in Lithuanian, presumably.

'On devrait parler anglais devant l'enfant,' Uncle Paul suggested. *'Il faut qu'il l'apprend.'*

'Peut-être,' murmured Lisa. But she went on talking her foreign language.

The grilled meat was being forked from the fire.

'Pietro,' Uncle Paul said. *'Mangia. Hai lavorato molto.'*

Pietro came to the fire and took a plate, muttering: *'Grazie, signora.'*

'Prego,' said Aunt Molly.

'It's a pity Guzepp's gone,' Rob said. 'There's no one to talk Maltese to.'

'I can talk to you,' Uncle Paul said. *'Kif inti,* Robert?'

'Tajjeb, grazzi,' the boy said. 'But it's not much good just being able to say hullo to people. *Ma nafx nitkellem bil-Malti.'*

'That's not a bad imitation,' Uncle Paul said. 'I could almost guess that you've been talking to a Gozitan.'

The boy stared into the green distance. He wondered if he would ever go as far as Malta, and hear people talking foreign languages in the streets. His country was pretty, yes, but impossibly far from other more beautiful, more soul-filled countries, that had earned the right to be written about in books.

Yet Lisa and Pietro and Uncle Paul had come from those countries, and it should not then be impossible to retrace their steps, and Aunt Kay's steps, and arrive, not completely as a stranger, in legendary Europe.

205

He looked with sudden dissatisfaction at old Bob, quietly grazing in the heart of the green land. Obviously, he was not going to get very far on Bob; not even as far as the orange road on the scrub-dark horizon.

Sometimes on Sundays he went with his father to his office, and played with the typewriters while his father sorted out papers for burning. The office always smelled like typewriter-ribbons. The late Mr Justice Coram, bewigged and aquiline, stared down on him from the top of a bookcase packed solid with the late Dr Coram's law books. He supposed that there was some history there, but it did not interest him. It was not like the land.

In a dinghy with Mike he looked across the green sea to the flat-topped hills, dominated by Mount Fairfax like a decapitated sphinx. 'My grandfather used to own that,' he said.

'Lot of good it does you,' Mike said. 'You don't own it, do you?'

Owning things did not seem to be important to Mike.

They went for long rides on their bikes, poking around among the disused scrub-grown cemeteries, intrigued by the indecipherable headstones of long-ago Afghans and Chinese. They developed a taste for ruined houses, and for ghosts. A house by the sea at Bluff Point was haunted, and a friend of Mrs Maplestead's had been visited by the ghost of her husband. At Bootenal there were phantom lights, and at Mount Erin the mundane ghost of Michael Morrissey's hurricane lantern. And every crumbling cottage offered the possibility of another, unrecorded apparition.

They stood among the sheepdroppings under the rotting reed roof and sagging sailcloth ceiling of the old homestead near the sea at Drummonds Cove. The bare, grazed paddocks stretched around them. It seemed unlikely, looking out from under the twisted gumtree at the door, that in those paddocks had once been vineyards, and that in that house in 1865 Isham Coram had tasted an excellent wine, savouring somewhat of the Shiraz.

And on the windswept Greenough Flats were big houses, a two-storied barracks that had quartered the soldiers who protected the first settlers against the blacks, a two-storied corn chandlers', a solid-looking church which suddenly, startlingly, disgorged a congregation of sheep. The Greenough was full of ruins and history and agreeable reminders of the world's vanity.

'It doesn't feel like a young country,' Rob said. 'It feels *old*.'

They were fascinated to know that a house near the school called The House With The Morning Glory had been a Chinese opium den, and was said to be still something funny.

'Gee, you know,' Mike said, 'if I'd been born a hundred years ago. I wouldn't have minded being born here.'

'You couldn't have been,' Rob said. 'There wasn't anyone here till 1849. That's when the lead-mining started and Governor Fitzgerald got speared.'

'Well, I could have come up when I was three,' said Mike.

'My grandfather came up when he was three months,' Rob said, 'in a covered wagon.'

'I thought he was born at Sandalwood.'

'No, they didn't reckon it was safe.'

'It must have been tough on the women,' Mike reflected. 'But I s'pose they were tough women.'

'Not like my grandmother,' Rob said. 'My grandfather used to have Mount Galena Station, and she made him buy her a house in town.'

'Ah, you're always going on about land,' Mike said, growing bored.

'Sorry,' Rob said, embarrassed. The truth was that he was fascinated by his dead grandfather, who seemed to have tried his hand at everything, from selling horses to mining gold in partnership with a man who struck a reef a few days after Charles Maplestead pulled out, and ended up rich and knighted. He had even once stood for Parliament and lost.

'But once again Dame Fortune refused her smile,' said the *Cyclopedia of Western Australia* on the subject of Charles Maplestead. The straight-looking questioning eyes of Charles Maplestead gazed out from the page, and one knew, even from the black-and-white photograph, that they had been of a piercing blue.

207

The boy's other grandfather had denied his photograph to the *Cyclopedia*, and neglected to mention that he was a husband and father. It seemed that he too had desired, like Rob's father, to be invisible.

'I wonder what I'm going to be when I grow up,' Rob asked himself.

'Well, not a film star,' Mike said. 'And not an all-in wrestler. Why don't you be a drunk? You don't need any talents for that.'

'It's got to be something in your blood,' Rob said. It was his view now that all history was a matter of blood.

'That's a lot of bulldust,' Mike said. 'Hell, Australia was built by people who didn't know who their grandparents were. You can be anything you want to be, and you ought to be what you want to be, not what your grandpa was.'

'Well, what are you going to be?' Rob demanded.

'A drunk,' said Mike. 'I haven't got any talents.'

Without question Mrs Charles Maplestead's house harboured some interesting junk. Poking around in a box in the play-room Rob discovered an old exercise book which proved to be an account of the first Maplestead's arrival and early years in Western Australia. Then one of his grandmother's recipe books turned out to contain a journal of his grandfather's lone ride from the port of Cossack to the goldfields at Nullagine; and a box couch yielded immemorial photographs, including one of Charles Maplestead on his celebrated (by Aunt Kay) steed Mazeppa. And at last, in a rusting trunk in the cow shed, he discovered his grandfather's collection of stones.

'I think I'm going to be a geologist,' he announced.

'Oh, really?' said Mrs Maplestead. 'I thought you were going to compose hillbillies.'

'Not now,' he said, impatient.

The body of Australia and the past of Australia had him enthralled, and he besieged Mrs Maplestead for her memories of the district he lived in.

And she remembered, and had heard other people remember, extraordinary things. Darkness.

'You mean he was *hanged?*' breathed the boy.

'Well, they said he was hanged,' said Mrs Maplestead, darkly. 'But everyone believes that he escaped on an American whaler with some Fenian convicts.'

'Gosh,' said the boy. 'Oh, gosh.'

'They say he was a very nice man,' said Mrs Maplestead, on a different story now. He was a half-caste, but nice. He lived in a camp at Innisfail, and Aunt Rosa was very kind to him. They were rather like Aunt Mary and Frank. Then one day she went down to see him with a young English jackaroo they had at Innisfail, and just as they turned their horses to go, Jacky picked up a gun and shot the jackaroo dead.'

'Gosh,' breathed the boy. 'Why?'

'I think he was just insanely jealous.'

'And what happened then?'

'Well, then he ran away into the bush, and they had a great manhunt. Everyone was terribly scared, of course, especially Aunt Rosa and Aunt May. Uncle Ernest and Aunt Mary came over from Sandalwood to stay with them, and they were quite scared too, driving the sulky through the bush.'

'And what about Jacky?'

'They found him in the end, and he was quite, quite mad by then. They put him in the asylum at Claremont.'

'Heck,' said the boy, sighing with bliss. 'Fancy that happening to Aunt Rosa.'

At home he disgorged Mrs Maplestead's narratives to his parents, and his father, who perhaps felt rather out of things, said: 'I should think my relations in Virginia could beat anything that was done here.'

'What did they do?' asked the boy.

'I'll lend you a book,' offered his father.

The boy accepted the novel with suspicion, since the last time his father had lent him books they had been Chapman's *Homer* and *The Confessions of An English Opium-Eater*, and his father moreover had made him a present of the Complete Works of Honoré de Balzac in Translation. But the book was fascinating, it was pure darkness, and parts of it were not very

209

nice at all. And these were his relations. He had dark blood.

Before long there was no one left to whom he could impart all this history, and he jumped on Rick like a dog on a bone when Rick came home for the vacation. He told Rick about the half-caste and Aunt Rosa, and Rick, who had heard the story at his mother's knee, listened with visible patience.

'You're like your grandmother and Aunt Kay,' he said, when the boy had finished. 'Gaélic through and through. Just a fey old Highlander.'

'Well, what's wrong with that,' demanded the boy, who had grown up believing Highlanders to be the crown of Nature's effort.

'Ah—violence is boring, fella. Boring. More boring than anything. Except, maybe, peace.'

Rick looked bored as he said it. He was always looking bored now, and the boy felt depressed.

Then he thought of something else, and cheered up. 'Did you know,' he asked, portentously, 'that Great-grandmother Maplestead hid Moondyne Joe under her bed?'

'You're not getting starry-eyed about poor silly old Moondyne, are you?'

'Why not?' the boy asked, rather forlornly. 'He's the only bushranger we ever had.'

'Some bushranger. Bush-burglar's more like it. Just a housebreaker and a horsethief who liked to hole up in a romantic cave in Great-grandfather Maplestead's back paddocks.'

'Well, if he wasn't a bushranger,' Rob said, 'he was a sort of what-d'you-call-it, a Houdini. Heck, the governor built a special cell for him at Fremantle gaol and bet him that he couldn't get out of it, and he got out with a spoon.'

'He was a pathetic nut,' Rick said, 'and he ended his career peddling aphrodisiacs.'

'What's aphrodisiacs?' asked the boy.

'Jane Wexford's an aphrodisiac,' said Rick. 'No! No more questions.'

The weed-strewn beach was sharply black-and-white in the moonlight, and the foam-lines in the shallows crawled like cream. Farther out, the black-and-white rollers folded over their hollows and shattered with an echoing boom.

Dry seaweed crackled under the passing feet, and hair flapped loose in the wet wind.

'It looks so dark and wild,' Jane said. 'How can fishermen bear to go out at night?'

'Are you cold?' Rick said.

'I don't feel cold, but it looks cold.'

'Jane——'

'Don't be silly, Rick. I'm not cold, and if I was, one hairy arm wouldn't keep me very warm.'

'Try two hairy arms,' Rick said.

'Oh, stop it. It's not *compulsory* to behave like this on the Back Beach.'

'I feel a compulsion,' Rick said. 'Jane, stop walking for a moment.'

'Why?' she asked; stopping, however, and turning towards him.

'I want to look at you.'

Her eyes gazed back at him darkly from shadowy hollows.

'You're beautiful, Jane.'

'That was a rather automatic remark.'

'Will you let me kiss you?'

'No,' she said, beginning to turn from him. But he caught her shoulder, and kissed her soft closed lips, which began to open, and then pulled away.

'No, Rick, I——'

'What?'

'I forget. I think I was going to say that you're not such a nice boy as everybody's mother thinks you are.'

'I only kissed you.'

'I'm not the village idiot, Rick.'

'Jane—why not?'

'Because—I don't like being taken out for a drive and then —vamped, or whatever the male version of vamping is. I suppose you and your friends have some revolting word for it.'

'I'm not that sort of lad,' Rick said. 'I'm much more like everybody's mother thinks I am.'

'And besides, I don't think I trust you. To care, I mean.'

'But I do.'

'And I'm not even sure that I like you. I don't see how I could like you, when I don't trust you. Though I do think you're very good-looking.'

'You're the only person who thinks so. That must mean something.'

Her feet shifted in the sand, popping dried bladderwrack. 'Take me home, Rick.'

'Am I really as bad as all that?'

'No, but—oh Rick, don't make me walk home in these awful shoes.'

His face in the moonlight had its set, now slightly craggy look.

'Jane,' he said, 'tell me something.'

'Well, ask.'

'What's wrong with me?'

'There's nothing wrong with you, and I love dancing with you, but this—this just makes me feel awkward.'

'Why?'

'Oh—because I think you want awfully much for someone to love you. And I don't want to. I don't think you'd love me back. I think you think you'd be very gentle and protective, and you probably would be, but I can't imagine you in love. I think you're—I don't know, frozen.'

'There's nothing there,' Rick said, quietly staring at her. 'That's what someone told me. There's nothing there.'

'Rick—what I've said doesn't mean that I don't care. I do want you to be happy.'

'And you'll follow my future career with deep interest?'

'Don't be sour with me. Just admit that you tried something that didn't work, and we don't care much, and we'll laugh it off.'

'I think I really do make you nervous.'

'Yes. That's why I want to go back to the car.'

The short curls of her hair fluttered in the wind, pointed with moonlight.

'Suppose I said I loved you?'

'I wouldn't believe you.'

'Jane, you know what I want. Give it to me, for friendship's sake.'

'No,' she said turning away. 'No, no, no. You're not my responsibility, and you've no right to tell me I ought to give you something that won't mean a thing to you tomorrow. I don't owe you anything, nobody owes you anything. Only babies can get things just by sounding hurt.'

Her footprints, going away from him, made pits of darkness in the moonlit sand.

'There's nothing there,' Rick repeated, dropping in the sand. 'Nothing there.' Cool sand trickled out of his clenched fist, and the black sea curled over its hollows with a hollow boom.

15

Mrs Maplestead's palms had chambers and passages, reptile-haunted brown caves where secret societies flourished briefly and then died of boredom. At the risk of snake-bite or impaling an eye, it seemed that boys might extend the labyrinth forever.

Then the bulldozers came, and the palms went down in a roar and a fume of sand. Flames leaped, and the palm-trunks lay under sun and rain in the devastated paddock like black-scaled basking dinosaurs.

Mrs Maplestead had sold her palms, and people were going to build houses. The town was growing in a sudden spasm. It was going to be a *real* town, everyone said.

Fury reddened the boy's face, and choked his speech. 'Oh, you conservative old thing,' said his mother, surprised.

She could not understand, and he could not explain to her, that the bulldozers were worse than the Japs.

The sandy town shook with explosions as the piles of the jetty, the first of the two rotting jetties to go, were blasted from their bed. There was more sea without the jetty, but still the boy was resentful. Huge grey timbers washed up on the surf beaches, and the boy stood on them, thinking that he had probably stood on them before.

He supposed that some day, in South Africa or somewhere, other boys would stand on the timbers of the jetty and wonder where they had come from, as he always wondered about drift-wood and bottles.

He walked in the town and watched the town change: the empty, dirty-windowed shops restored, the poky, shabby shops growing Yankee-flash, the swinging doors coming off the pubs, the verandas and wrought-iron balconies over the street torn down by order of the council. In time, the whole run-down haunted town would be reborn, remade, according to standards of beauty and elegance proper in a nation which had done its pioneering in hovels.

Bushfires and clearing stripped the Sandalwood paddocks to the bare bone. Andarra was refurnished and revived. The house where he had seen the ghost grew unremarkable behind balconies of louvred asbestos. Only Innisfail was as it had always been, an eroding island in the river of time.

Bungalows spread into the dunes, the service stations blossomed. The old courthouse was razed to become a field of sunflowers. And in the north, the tower of Geraldine fell.

So he walked the streets, and then rode his bicycle through the streets, and at last drove his car through the streets, asking himself how a country town on the sea had become a provincial seaport, how a world so congruent, so close-knit by history and blood and old acquaintance, had become fragmented into a mere municipality. But he knew the answer, by that time.

The sea at each end of the next street roared or shone, and the dunes to the north and south remade themselves, smoking.

In the dark water under the sunken deck something moved.

'Ergh,' said Rob, stepping back from the hatch.

'What is it?' said Mike.

'Something alive down there.'

'Prob'ly a squid.'

'No, something pale. I dunno——there's some bloody funny things in the sea.'

'It's not a body, is it?'

'After all this time? Don't be silly.'

'When did it get wrecked?'

'Oh——ten or fifteen years ago. When they built the wharf and the breakwater.'

They paddled through the water up the sloping deck to the end where the planks were salt-caked and dry, warm under the sun. The wreck lay against the grey rocks of the breakwater, commanding a view of the Bay and the hills, which were now brown and grape-dark with summer.

The stump of the mast still stuck up from the deck.

'When I was a little kid,' Rob said, 'the mast and the what-

215

d'you-call-'ems were still here, and I used to think it was a merry-go-round. A merry-go-round in the sea.'

'That'd be rather good,' Mike said, 'a merry-go-round in the sea. It'd be more fun than the Dolphins. You'd have to make it good and high, though, for diving.'

'I just thought of sitting on it,' Rob said, 'and dangling my feet in the water. I couldn't swim then.'

'You can't bloody well swim now.'

'How'd you like to go down that hatch?'

'Gee, I'm scared,' Mike said. 'Well, what are we going to do now? Go out to the end of the breakwater?'

'Ah, no, the rocks are too hot.'

'Will we go to the P'lice Boys' Club, well?'

'All right.'

They jumped from rock to rock along the breakwater, making their way back to where their bikes lay on the sand.

On the way, an argument started.

'Listen to you,' Mike said, exaggeratedly mimicking. ' "Mrs Grahnt's got ahnts in her pahnts".'

'Oh, listen to you,' Rob said. ' "Mrs Graent went passt very fasst to plaent tomattoes." '

'Shall we dahnce?' said Mike.

'Drop dead.'

At times Rob's accent seemed to infuriate Mike, and his scorn made Rob uneasy. His world was not one world after all, and might fall apart over an issue as simple as the way to say Mrs Grant's name.

'You talk like a bloody Pommy,' Mike said.

'I bloody well do not,' Rob said, angrily. Nobody wanted to be like a Pommy. Pommies might be gallant in wartime, but they had an unfortunate ancestry. They were descended from all the people who had declined to found America and Canada and South Africa and New Zealand and Australia. They were born non-pioneers.

At the Police Boys' Club, which was Wainwright's historic store slightly remodelled, they put on gloves and climbed into the ring and hit out at each other, unconvincingly. It seemed to Rob rather pointless. He did not want to hit Mike, and he

216

wanted even less for Mike to hit him. The shuffle of their feet on the canvas grew more and more aimless, until at last Mike said: 'Ah, bugger this.'

'Yeah, let's give the gloves back to the cop.'

The cop sat behind his table with furrowed brow. Rob supposed that he was hoping he would not be shot by anyone he was persecuting, or forcibly exported to New Guinea. Though he seemed a nice cop.

Mike was swinging on the Roman rings. 'Yuh-hoo,' Rob yelled, grabbing his legs, and he fell down cursing on the mat.

'You got your bathers on?' Rob asked.

'Yeah.'

'Let's go swimming.'

'Okay.'

The sand burned their feet, and they hopped as they pulled off their shorts. Against the still blue water the new Dolphins, two wooden platforms rooted in the sea, stood out raw and dark. Between the Dolphins and the shore was a raft of planks and iron.

'Race you to the raft,' Mike said.

'Okay.'

They ran for the water, and started racing. Mike was winning, but before he reached the raft he stopped, and waited, treading water.

'What's up?' Rob asked, swimming beside him.

'Ah, that girl's there. Jane Wexford.'

'Well, she won't hurt you.'

'She goes out there and reads, and when you dive off she starts screaming and cursing because you've splashed her book.'

'How the hell does she get a book out there?'

'She swims backstroke with one arm and holds it over her head.'

'She must be nuts,' Rob said. 'I always thought she was rather a nice girl.'

They circled the raft, breast-stroking noiselessly.

'Hullo, Rob,' said Jane, standing up and pulling on a white bathing cap.

'Hullo,' he said. 'Haven't you got a book today?'

'I'm not studying now,' she said. 'I don't need to, for a while. I've got a new job. In Perth.'

'That's good,' he said. 'You'll be able to go around with Rick. Rick reckons you're an aphrodisiac.'

'You horrible little boy,' said Jane, laughing, and plunged into the green water.

'What's an aphrodisiac?' asked Mike.

'I dunno,' Rob said. 'But Jane's one.'

'You want to be careful what you say. It might mean a moll.'

'No. Rick wouldn't say that about Jane.'

Aboard the raft, they lay on their bellies on the warm planks, watching Jane rise from the water and pull off her cap and dry herself.

A tall man in bathers with a towel round his neck came out of a gate in a fence, and sat down on the grey rocks to smoke and stare out to sea.

'There's my dad,' Rob said. 'He must've been playing tennis.'

'What's that place he came out of?'

'That's the Club. He goes there after work and drinks whisky.'

'Is he a drunk?' Mike asked, interested.

' 'Course he's not a bloody drunk.'

'He sounds like a drunk. Why doesn't he drink whisky at home?'

'He does.'

'Well, hell,' Mike said, 'and you reckon he's not a drunk.'

'He drinks whisky with milk,' Rob said. 'How the hell could you be a drunk on whisky and milk? You'd get sick drinking that much milk.'

'All right,' Mike said, disappointed. 'So he's not a drunk.'

They lay with their chins overhanging the edge of the raft, studying the sea-floor. A small stingray drifted across a patch of pale sand, then was lost against a pasture of stingray-coloured weed.

'Nasty bloody things,' Mike said. 'My brother's mate Finney nearly died after one got him.'

'There was a bloke who did die,' Rob said, 'a couple of years ago. He died of heart failure or something.'

'There's some lousy things in the sea. Sharks and things. They saw a Grey Nurse in the harbour yesterday.'

'They reckon there's a swordfish around, too.'

'Gee, I'd like to see that. Not while I'm swimming, but.'

'Did you see that whale that was washed up near the old jetty?'

'No. Before my time,' Mike said. 'I bet it stank.'

'Yeah, it did. I forget what they did with it. Towed it out to sea, probably.'

Rob's father was in the water, swimming with long over-arm strokes.

'Hell, what's the time?' Mike asked.

'After five. I heard the Brewery whistle a while ago.'

'I've got to go home,' Mike said, standing up. 'Race you in.'

They dived, and swam underwater, skimming the dark weed, and rose at last, among trailing ropes of light, halfway to the shore.

'Look what I found,' Mike said. It was a girl's hairclip, a blue plastic bow.

'Who're you going to give that to?'

'Dunno. I might try giving it to Elizabeth, but I bet she won't take it.'

'Once I found a brooch with MOTHER on it,' Rob said. 'Heck, you should have heard my mum when I gave it to her. You'd have thought it said FLOSSIE or something like that.'

On the beach they picked up their clothes, and wheeled their bikes to the dressing-shed. The floor of the shed was strewn with strips of sunlight falling through the slatted ventilators, and in the middle of the floor stood a bronzed tough guy drying himself. His chest swelled, his biceps flexed, as he scrubbed the towel across his back. Then he became aware of the eyes of two small boys fixed studiously on his private parts, and suddenly deflated and turned away.

'He thinks he's really something,' Mike whispered, under the shower. 'He ought to see Eric Larsen.'

'Hell, you've got no right to criticize,' said Rob.

'Just wait,' said Mike magnificently, 'till I finish growing.'

219

Outside the dressing-shed, strapping the rolled towel with his bathers in it to the carrier of his bike, Rob looked up and saw the merry-go-round. It seemed that he had not noticed the merry-go-round for years. The broken seat had vanished long ago, and the bent stays dropped down against the iron centre post. It looked curiously forlorn.

'I was mad about that,' he said, 'when I was a little kid.'

Perhaps he would do something about the merry-go-round when he was grown-up and rich. Perhaps he would restore the merry-go-round, and put a plate on it, like the people who had given the town the horse-troughs. He would build the merry-go-round again, and put on it a plate saying.

Presented

to

The Children of Geraldton

by

The Hon. Sir Robert Coram Esqre

D.S.O., M.L.A., LL.D.

A.D. 2000

And since a merry-go-round was something that people ought to think about, like a sundial, he would put a thoughtful motto on it, like a sundial. And he knew what he would write on the merry-go-round, his tribute to the merry-go-round. It would be the lines that Rick had written in his book on the night he came home from the war.

> Thy firmness makes my circle just,
> And makes me end, where I begun.

Mrs Maplestead's house was full of family, because it was Christmas Eve, and in the house and on the verandas and lawns outside people came and went continually, to have a drink with the other people who had come to have a drink

220

with Mrs Maplestead (who did not drink) and to leave presents for Mrs Maplestead's grandchildren.

In the drawing-room, hemmed in by children, Miss MacKay MacRae played carols, and the children sang. Miss MacRae's long fingers with the bloodstone ring plunged on the yellow keys, and the children's voices came out in the hot night high and tuneless and clear.

'Oh, please,' said Lisa, standing in the doorway, 'please, can you play *O Tannenbaum?*'

'Play *O Tannenbaum,*' Rob shouted to Aunt Kay, who had not heard.

The bloodstone ring winked in the light of the crystal lamp, and Lisa in the doorway sang sweet and pure, singing alone.

> 'Du grünst nicht nur zur Sommerszeit,
> Nein, auch im Winter wenn es schneit:
> O Tannenbaum, O Tannenbaum,
> Wie treu sind deine Blätter.'

The voice went out high and true into the hot summer night. Then Lisa bent her head, rubbing her wet cheek against the brown hair of the boy sleeping in her arms.

16

At Marsa, in the draining heat, Rob roamed the bleak gullies through the drab and prickly summer scrub. He chose the gullies because they were desolate, and while he tramped there was always at the back of his mind an expectation. He thought that in the gullies he would some day meet someone, and his life would be changed. But no human being ever visited the gullies. He met nothing but a few kangaroos, that crashed away from him, making great bounds through the scrub.

There was a boy of thirteen working at Marsa now, and when he was free he came with Rob exploring. In the paddocks of another farm they found a cave, a hollow under a rock, and wriggled into it on their backs, lying on the sheepdroppings and the bones that foxes had left. On the roof of the cave, an arm's length above, were silhouettes of hands and spear-throwers and kylies, outlined in dull clay.

'I wonder what they reckoned they were doing,' Rob said. He thought of the dead dark nomads who had lain where he and Jimmy Bryant now lay. Mysterious, haunting people.

On the way back to Marsa, Jimmy Bryant got sick. He had a touch of heatstroke, and lay on his bed draped with wet towels.

It was hard, hard country, Rob thought, looking at the summer paddocks. How hard it must have been, even in summer, when no wheat and pasture grew, when the Scots song was written that Aunt Kay sang:

> New Holland is a barren place,
> In it there grows no grain,
> Nor any habitation
> Wherein for to remain. . . .

'Gee, the abos are funny people,' he said to Jimmy Bryant,

as they sat in a gumtree by the creek.

'They're funny, all right,' Jimmy Bryant said. And then he was off. What interested him about the coloured population was its sex life, and he had spied on it with a devotion that might have made him a hero in time of war. Rob listened with half an ear. He couldn't see anything very amusing about having carnal knowledge of a duck, and he couldn't see either why anyone should go to gaol for it.

Something moved in the grass below. A yellow lizard, three feet long, with brownish markings.

'Jimmy,' he said. 'Look. A racehorse.'

'I wonder if I can hit him,' Jimmy said, breaking off a bit of dead wood.

The wood hit the bungarra on the back, and it started, tilting its head, and looked at them.

'You fool,' Rob said, 'he'll come after us.'

Jimmy was looking slightly nervous. And the bungarra was approaching the tree in which they sat.

'I reckon we'd better climb farther up,' he said.

'That won't be any use. They can run up anything. They run up people and horses and down the other side.'

'Hell, I wish he'd nick off. It's no good trying to shoot through, they go like lightning.'

'Aren't you a clever bloody kid?' Rob said. 'I suppose we're going to spend the rest of our lives in this tree.'

'Well, hell,' Jimmy said, 'they can't hurt you much. They only give you a bit of a nip, and the sore comes back once every seven years or something. On the anniversary.'

'They can't have much strength in their jaws,' Rob said, 'if they're anything like bobtails. We've got a goanna at home that comes every summer, and I give it grapes, and its jaws are so weak it can hardly break the skin. Hey, you know something, it'll only drink out of a red cup. They like anything red.'

'You got anything red on you?'

'Yeah,' Rob said, pulling out a red bandanna. 'This.'

'Give us it,' Jimmy said. He broke off a piece of wood and tied the handkerchief around it. 'Now, when I lob this near the old goanna we drop and run—get it?'

The red bundle padded on the dead grass, and the boys jumped and fled, leaping the garden fence overgrown with Mexican rose.

'Come to think of it,' said Jimmy, 'what are we scared of? Let's go back and kill it.'

'Ah, no,' Rob said. 'We're always killing things.'

They were, in fact, killing birds and animals all the time, roaming the paddocks with a .22 after cockatoos and galahs, picking out twenty-eights in the fruit-trees of the garden. Sometimes Rob felt pangs of blood-guilt. Once there had been two galahs flying alone, and he had dropped one, and the other had turned back and circled over the body in the grass, screaming and screaming, until he thought he would never get the shrieks of the widowed bird out of his mind. So he had shot it, out of charity.

Another time he had wounded a Major Mitchell cockatoo, and the bird had stood at bay on the ground, bleeding, its dawn-coloured crest on end, screaming and screaming in terrible defiance. He had felt sick then, as he smashed it with a dead branch.

And once they had seen a wedge-tailed eagle sitting on a fencepost: a perfect shot. 'Oh, boy,' Jimmy had said. 'A wedgie. I reckon we'll get a bounty for this.' But his first shot had missed, and the huge bird had sailed away, rising up and up in the blue air until it was as small as a crow. And Rob had felt strangely glad, because it was majestic, and because for some reason he did not wish to meet an eagle, even a dead one, face to face.

But most of their killing was done with traps and their bare hands. Every evening they went across the paddocks to a rocky hillock mined with rabbit warrens to see what was in their traps and to reset them. Grabbing the rabbits by the ears, they opened the iron jaws of the traps, then broke the lean necks with the edges of their hands or with a stick. In the shed, stinking skins stretched on wires, waiting to be sold in Northampton. Knives eased through the silvery membrane connecting the skins to the pale flesh; and at times, slitting up bellies, they would find litters of minute rabbits never to be born.

Traps were cruel, Rob thought, knowing it well, as he had trapped himself once and lost several fingernails. But rabbits have got to be killed. He had spent half his life on farms, and did not question that some cruelty was necessary. But at times his own cruelty disturbed him; he would hear the birds screaming inside his head, and see again the huge bungarra that had been caught in one of his traps and left to die, taking weeks perhaps to die, because he had been afraid to go near it. That callousness was only later recognized as cowardice, and took on in his memory the proportions of a major betrayal.

Sometimes at night they went to the hillock with Jimmy Bryant's foxwhistle, and crouched in hiding behind the rifle, sending out the thin sound that was meant to imitate the cry of a trapped rabbit. But the light was poor, and the foxes were quick, quick and elegant and beautiful, and the boys never killed one, and Rob was glad.

In the blazing paddocks with Uncle Paul the children hunted poisonbush, and grubbed out the roots with mattocks, receiving a bounty for each plant they found. The engine turned in the yard, cutting chaff, crushing oats, and Jimmy and Rob lumped the bags of oats on and off the truck. In the ramshackle house, a battler's house, begun in stone and continued in weatherboard and iron, Aunt Molly and Lisa glistened over the stove and the petrol-iron. In the stunning heat of the afternoons the children, the cousins, squatted on the veranda round heaps of lupin seed, picking horseradish pods from the seed, and receiving, again, a bounty for each bag they purified. In the stunning afternoons, and in the breathless evenings by lamplight, they lay on their beds arguing, reading, dreaming. Rob pored over the picture-books, over the Greek gods in marble, over the picture-books of Malta. Malta was ancient and incredible, older than Greece, filled with bleak and terrible temples where people no one knew anything about had worshipped gods that no one could imagine. Malta was ancient, and inexplicable as the clay-painted cave in the paddock. Dreaming in the heat, he thought what memories Aunt

Kay and Uncle Paul must have, memories they could not impart of the feel and essence of times and places that they had known and that he would never know. On the flyleaf of the picture-book of Malta Uncle Paul's mother had written her name. Uncle Paul's mother's name had been Elise. Her name had been the Most Noble Marchesa Rohan de Pinto Xaghra and she had lived in a palace. Her name had been Elise, and she had walked in beauty, on a high terrace above the sea.

Rick and Gordon came to Marsa to see a horse that Gordon was thinking of buying. The wild-eyed chestnut mare took one look at them and reared.

'I don't think I like her,' Rick said. 'She looks a real prima donna.'

'She has a good pedigree,' Uncle Paul said. 'She was a race-horse, but she was too neurotic even for that. And quite useless for stockwork. I'm not really recommending her.'

Gordon accepted the challenge, and mounted the mare, who propped and pigrooted all round the paddock.

'If you want that,' Rick said, 'you shouldn't be allowed to handle your own money.'

But Gordon was charmed. 'I think I can knock her into shape.'

'And I've got to ride sixty miles on that?' Rick said. 'Well, no one could say you lose sleep being your brother's keeper.'

'You'll be all right,' Gordon said. 'Treat her gently.'

Rick approached her with a sugar-bag containing his gear, which he meant to fasten on the saddle. Immediately the mare shied away from the bag. He handed it to Gordon, and swung into the saddle. The mare gave a token rear.

'She's a sweetie,' Rick said, as Gordon tied on the bag. 'I'm going to have a lovely time. Well, remember that I want to be buried deep down below, where the dingoes and crows can't molest me. *Out there where the coolibahs grow,*' he concluded, in song, and let out a yodel.

'I didn't know you could yodel,' Rob said. He looked up at Rick worshipfully.

Rick did it again, and the mare, plunging forward, was off at a canter. 'Well, so long,' shouted Rick, and vanished in no time at all in the direction of the boundary gate.

'I hope she's not going to kill herself on the way,' Gordon said.

'Kill *herself?*' said Aunty Molly. 'What about Rick?'

'I haven't got any money invested in Rick,' said Gordon.

Rick was beginning to have fun with the mare. She had a beautiful gallop, and he allowed her to demonstrate it for a while. But at the first gate she reared, trying to drag the reins out of his hand, and reared again when he remounted.

'I don't think you like human beings, do you?' he said, speaking into her ears which were permanently turned back towards him.

They settled down to a walk, and the slow miles went by. Oh God, he thought suddenly, Northampton. I'll have to go down the main street, and she'll throw a fit at the traffic.

But in Northampton she seemed to enjoy herself. She clopped down the street with an air of hauteur, ignoring the small boys who came runing after, shouting: 'Give us a ride, Mister?' She trotted over the bridge like a queenly baker's horse.

'You know what you are?' Rick said to her. 'You're a narcissist. And aren't we a handsome couple?'

He turned off on to the long back road that led to Andarra. Now, in the sunset light, the bush felt lonely. Gordon passed, waving, in the pick-up, and faded in his own dust. After he had gone, the world seemed uninhabited.

The mare kept listening, her ears back, trying every now and again to turn her head. She's keeping track, Rick thought, in a trance now from the gentle motion. She hears the country she's leaving. It must be like music, growing fainter. As I keep listening, to the music of the war.

When he let her turn her head, she immediately wheeled and started back toward Marsa. 'Poor old girl,' he said, setting her right. 'Memories can be a bloody nuisance.'

The slow miles went by, and he grew stiff and tired. It was nearly dark. He reined in for a rest, and dismounted and tied her to a tree with the halter. She reared and snapped it, effortlessly, and started off again for Marsa.

'Come back, beautiful,' he said, grabbing the reins near the bit. 'Ah, you're a trial to me, you bitch. It's a bit rough when a man can't have a leak without a lady looking over his shoulder.'

He got back in the saddle, and she made her resentment known. The ride now seemed interminable, as the light faded and the loneliness grew, and the mare made it more apparent that the only way to control her was to keep her moving forward. He stopped, in the twilight, at a farm, and without dismounting let her drink at a trough. 'Come on,' said the man of the place, 'have a cuppa tea. We don't see many horsemen these days.' But: 'I can't get offa my horse,' Rick had to confess. 'Some dirty dog put glue on the saddle.'

With the darkness his weariness became overpowering, and the mare was almost done. The Nabawa pub, he thought, like a Bedouin remembering an oasis. There should be a yard, and I can get a drink. But at the wayside pub the mare reared in terror at the sound of the generating plant, and they went on.

The bush-road was pitch-dark, and the footsore mare alternated between fear and apathy. She touched him now, as she plodded along. Sometimes her head hung low with utter exhaustion, and she forgot everything, forgot Marsa, forgot the road, simply moved her legs like an automaton. But at other times she revived, starting at sounds in the bush, shifting her head from side to side and listening, tremulously. He talked to her, tenderly. 'Someone's treated you badly some time, you poor hysterical bitch. But everything's going to be fine, after tomorrow night. So forget the bad things that happened, the past won't hurt you, and we can't be worried about the future.'

At times he sang to her.

> 'Eyes like the morning star,
> Cheeks just like the rose:
> Laura was a pretty girl,
> God Almighty knows.'

She grew calm at his voice, listening, listening with her turned ears.

> 'Weep, all ye little rains,
> Wail, ye winds, wail,
> All along, along, along
> That Colorado Trail.'

She listened, alert and soothed.

'Ellenbrook,' he murmured to her, wondering what she thought of her imposing name. 'I know what it feels like, Ellenbrook, having to walk when you think you're done. I reckon I know what it feels like being you, Ellenbrook. But we can't shy and rear at memories.'

In the distance he saw the lights of the Mackenzie homestead where he was to spend the night. Colin Mackenzie met him at the gate with a torch and led him to the yards.

'Well, old girl,' Rick said, fondling the mare, 'you'd better sit down and soak your feet, 'cause we've got another thirty miles to do tomorrow.'

She looked touching and beaten, all the histrionics ridden out of her.

'I think we'll put her in here,' Colin Mackenzie said.

Over the gate of the bull yard was a bar of railway iron, wreathed in barbed wire.

'I don't think the stupid bitch'll go under that,' Rick said.

'We'll try it,' Colin Mackenzie said. He gave her a slap on the rump, and the mare, starting, trotted meekly under the bar.

'Well,' Rick said, 'I'll be buggered. Obviously all she understands is a hard hand.'

But in the morning they had to dismantle the gateway before she would come out.

The Lowes, which was the collective noun for Aunty Judith and Uncle Michael and the impertinent small girls, were staying in the town, and Rob grew infatuated with the new cousin. When he had first seen her, in the old stone Maternity Hospital behind the oleanders where he and most of the other cousins had been born, she had been a boiled-looking deformity. But now he felt a tenderness for her, and made her crude toys, pasting pictures of animals on three-ply and cutting round them with a fretsaw. She was so blue-eyed and white-haired and small; and she was bright, too. Playing with an old envelope she kept saying: 'Deff, Deff.' 'Huh,' he said, realizing, 'she's trying to say Uncle Jeff.' She thought the face on the stamps was his father, who looked like the King.

The Lowes' house was full of cheeky small girls, and men who had come home for a drink with Uncle Michael after tennis or cricket or fishing, and female Maplesteads quietly and ceaselessly talking. He liked the Lowes' house. He liked any house that had people in it. His own house grew quieter and quieter with his father's increasing depression.

And now he was in love again; and so, this time, was Mike. Mike was in love with Aunty Jean's niece Elizabeth, and Rob was in love with a brown-eyed girl called Miriam, and they were both losing sleep because the girls would not confess themselves to be their girl-friends. In their last year at the primary school the barrier between the sexes was being lowered; with the curious result that the girls invaded the boys' playground and competed with them in gymnastics, whizzing around the horizontal bars in the muscle-grinder, or dropping from the sky in the arm-tearing rooster-chute. It was slightly alarming how tough they were, with their skirts tucked into the elastic legs of their pants. There were times when Rob had fits of disillusionment. Miriam had no soul. She cared about nothing but the development of her biceps.

And all the kids now were learning to dance, attending decorous social evenings in the Parish Hall, where the small boys circled with small girls who gazed intently at the corner of the ceiling and never spoke. The small girls had backs as hard and muscular as the boys'. Sometimes the big girls, when they could find no one better, condescended to dance with Mike and Rob in their short pants, and even to make conversation. And once one of the big girls said, staring at the ceiling and speaking out of the side of her mouth like a gangster: 'Someone just told me I look like Olivia de Havilland.' Rob replied: 'Uh?'

'I suppose he's growing up,' said Margaret Coram. 'I suppose we'll have to think about sending him away.'

'Yes,' Rob said, 'send me away.' But the circling days went on, and the possibility of leaving his country, never easily imaginable, was sorted away with the other possibilities, such as his project for sailing to Antarctica.

It was autumn in Perth, and in Jane's flat were vases of great bitter-smelling chrysanthemums. Jarrah blocks were burning in the fireplace, and the firelight, which was the only light in the room, shone red on Jane's smooth skin, and on Rick's.

'I didn't want this to happen,' Jane whispered. 'I didn't.'

'Why not?' Rick's mouth was against her neck, in the hollow of her shoulder.

'I don't know you.'

'But you do. You're my lover, Jane.'

'No, still, even now, I don't know you.'

'No one can know anyone better than this.'

'I wish it hadn't happened. Not here, not just now. Suppose Lucy's awake. She could have heard everything from the bed-room.'

'I don't care about Lucy. I love you, Jane, and Lucy's welcome to hear it.'

'Ssh.'

'You're so scared,' Rick said, in a trance of firelight. 'And the back of your neck's so innocent, and I won't let anything hurt you, not a thing.'

'Oh Rick——'

'Oh, Jane.'

'I love you so much. I'm so frightened. Rick, be good to me.'

In the green winter country Mike and Rob rode farther and farther afield, learning the country, till its creeks and hills and bigger trees became as familiar as the houses on the way to school. Their billy-fires smoked on the sandbanks of the rivers, and they plunged into shadowy places, places where paper-barks were engulfed in leafless creepers, and dark pools turned round and round, twisting debris in their hearts. The country seemed immense and wide-open and empty, their own property. So that it was a shock, like finding a hostile Man Friday, when they emerged from swimming in the Chapman to find that some bastard of a kid from school had made off with their clothes. The indignity of having to chase after him, naked, worried them less than the impertinence of his being there at all.

And the green winter country turned to spring country, the last of the wild Geraldton wax plant flowering along the Chapman, and the dune-scrub flowering with white clematis, and the country paddocks and the town lawns with yellow cape-weed. Spring turned their fancies to thoughts of love, and the girls turned them back again to thoughts of body-building.

And in Jane's flat, drunk-sweet with boronia masking the frailer scent of daffodils, Rick said something into Jane's hair, and Jane said: 'Would you mind mumbling that again?' and Rick said: 'Will you marry me, 'cause I'm getting awful sick of this hearthrug,' and Jane said: 'Oh, mate.'

17

'Lisa's engaged, too,' Rob said, 'to a man in the Customs.'

'I hope he's a good man,' Rick said. 'The poor girl deserves a break.'

'Aunty Molly says he's nice, and he likes Tad. They're going to change Tad's name.'

'That all sounds pretty all right for Lisa.'

'When are you going to get married?' Rob asked.

'God knows. What's this, 1948? Just. Probably not till this time in 1950, at the rate I'm going.'

'What's the good of getting engaged, then, if you can't get married?'

'What's the good of ordering a car if you won't get it for a couple of years? Hell, I wish the old man had got in quick and ordered one as soon as the war finished.'

The aged Sandalwood wagon was sitting under a sheoak near the river. It was the Murchison river, greenish and brackish by the bridge, winding through the red myall country and wild-goat-haunted limestone gullies to the sea.

'That's the North, over yonder,' Rick said, pointing to the other bank. ' 'Least, I always reckon the North starts at the Murchison.'

'Gee,' Rob said. The North was romantic.

'I come from north of the Murchison,' said Mike.

'That was a pity, what happened to your town,' Rick said. 'It makes you practically a D.P., like Lisa.'

'I don't mind,' said Mike, bravely. 'I'd sooner have the sea.'

'How old are you buggers now?' Rick wondered.

'Twelve,' Rob said, 'just.'

'Twelve,' Rick said, drawing in his breath. 'Time's certainly got his skates on. *You* were six, Rob, when I left for Malaya. D'you remember kissing me a weepy goodbye?'

'Aww,' said Rob, embarrassed. 'No, I don't remember.' But

he did. 'How old are you, Rick?'

'Ancient,' Rick said. 'Twenty-bloody-seven, this month.'

'Twenty-seven,' Rob breathed, with a kind of horror. Rick was getting old. And he didn't want Rick to get old. What was the point of Rick's enduring so much, and surviving all that the Japs could do to him, if he was only going to get old at the end of it? He didn't want Rick to be twenty-seven, he wanted him to be twenty again, and the difference in age between them to go on shrinking. 'Don't get old, Rick.'

'I won't,' Rick said, 'if I can help it. I don't think I could grow old gracefully, any more than I could die gracefully.'

He grinned suddenly. It was, after all, a bit comic, to be lamenting his age to a pair of twelve-year-old boys on the banks of a river running through the oldest stretch of land on the globe.

'Shall we go and look for this place, then?' he said, getting up.

'Yeah,' the boys said, eagerly, following him to the old car. Rick's explorations, since he had taken to drawing ruined houses and abandoned lead-mines instead of ruined men, excited them like a journey in a time-machine, and everything was touched with deep nostalgia, Mike remembering the gold-mines around which he had grown up, and Rob dredging out from somewhere in his memory, fresh and new, a picture of a disused mine where someone had taken him when he had been a very small child, which had been an unfathomable pool in a cleft of grey rock, the water green as verdigris from lead or copper.

The mines too were history, and not dead history yet. The Cornish names of farmers around Northampton were a reminder of the first Cornish miners; and one of his father's clients was called the Wheal of Fortune, a dazzling and romantic pun, a wheal being a mine in Cornish.

Rick was taking strange back tracks, jolting on the red dirt through country where the low scrub had been cleared here and there for grain and pasture paddocks, now brown and sere. From time to time he consulted an old survey map he had brought with him. 'It's here,' he kept saying, pointing on

234

the map. 'But how the hell do you get to it?'

They were on private property now, bumping across rough paddocks, just like Uncle Ernest, who tore around Sandalwood in the old car as if he had never heard of roads.

'There,' Mike said. Something curious projected above the scrub half a mile away.

'That's it,' Rick said. 'And it looks like we walk.' He pulled up by a fence, and they got out and climbed through. The myall scrub was sparse, the earth red and bare between the fanning stems, and after a time they struck what seemed to be a track.

'Hey,' Mike said, kicking at the red dirt. 'What's this?'

Short wooden posts had been laid, a great many years ago, side by side through the scrub like a roadway.

'It must have been a road surface,' Rick said. 'Or maybe some kind of wooden railway that the poor buggers hauled trucks along.'

'Gee,' Rob said, enchanted. 'Just imagine.'

'I can imagine pretty well,' Rick said. 'I've been a slave myself.'

Then they came out in a clearing. And on a small hillock, like a crumbling keep, the Shot Tower of Geraldine stood red-brown and sharp-edged against the sky.

'Oh,' Rob sighed, blissfully. It was old, it looked old as the Tower of London, and desolate. Desolate.

Two roofless stone houses stood nearby, young wattles springing out of the floors. The red-brown walls were solid, and still handsome.

'It must have felt like the end of the world,' Mike said.

'It *is* the end of the world,' Rick said, 'isn't it?'

In the side of the hillock, as they mounted towards the tower, they saw a tunnel piercing the hillock to the core. A sort of stony sluice ran out of it, towards the clearing and the wooden road.

They stood inside the tower looking up at the square of sky high above. At their feet, a well dropped down, ending in a rubble of stone and brick fallen from the tower.

'What was it for?' Mike wondered.

235

'Far as I can make out,' Rick said, 'there must have been a convict or two standing up there dropping spoonfuls of molten lead into this well, and the other fellas picked up the shot as it washed down the sluice.'

'What a place to work,' Rob said. 'Gosh, they must've been lonely.'

'It must have given them a giggle,' Rick said, 'knowing that one of the main uses for the shot was keeping convicts in order. Still, if it hadn't been for the lead, we probably wouldn't have grown up here, buster.'

'The Tower,' Rob murmured to himself. 'The Tower of Geraldine.'

'The locals call it the Chimney,' Rick said. 'But it's marked Shot Tower on the map.'

The Tower of Geraldine. It had a noble and desolate sound.

Rick was sitting down by the wall of the tower to sketch, his hat pushed back, and the book resting on his drawn-up khaki legs. He stared at the clearing and the houses with the faraway blue look that was like Uncle Ernest and Gordon. For a long time he was not there; in that place, but not in that century. He had gone back nearly a hundred years.

The boys clattered in the tunnel, looking for lead. When they came out again, Rick was sitting by the houses, the book lying on the ground beside him. He had just finished a rough sketch of the Tower, which the boys did not greatly admire.

'I dunno,' Rob said, turning back to the other drawing. Crudely drawn shirtless men were hauling trucks of rock, and a soldier stood by with some kind of firearm. 'Everything you draw turns into prisoners-of-war.'

'It's my gimmick,' Rick said. 'Like being a Catholic or a Commo.'

The Tower rose tall and sharp against the sky, commanding an endless view of nothing at all.

'I tell you what,' Rick said, getting up, 'I'll take you to Lynton, if you like.'

'Yeah,' they said. 'Yeah, that'd be good.' And followed him away, down the old roadway or railway or whatever it was, to the fence and the car. In the clearing, the remembering houses and the gallant tower stood forgotten by the world, perhaps crumbling just a little in each puff of breeze which stirred the surface of the monotonous scrub.

The car bumped in the paddocks, and on the rough back tracks, and came out at last on the Carnarvon road, turning south towards Northampton. 'By the way,' Rick said, 'you can say now you've been on the other side of the rabbit-proof fence. *That* was the rabbit-proof fence.'

'Heck,' said Rob, feeling like a celebrated voyager. It was a proverb of his country: The most something-or-other this side of the rabbit-proof fence.

'And there's a bit of history for you,' said Rick. 'Just about as historic as the Maginot Line, but funnier.'

They drove down the broad main street of Northampton, lined with wooden stores, verandas over the footpath. 'Gee, I like Northampton,' Mike said. It made him homesick for his own dead town.

The car took the road to Lynton, rattling over the corrugations. 'What are we going to see?' Rob asked.

'Just wait a bit,' said Rick.

Sheep wandered on the road, and stared apathetically at the crawling, hooting car.

In a fold of the barren hills the old prison stood, roofless, rubble-strewn, its faded greying stone merging into the limestone landscape.

'It's lonely,' Rob said, slowly, feeling a sense of desolation no longer pleasurable. The cells with their little high gratings were so small; the manacled convicts had lain alone, unable even to see the sky, which was nowadays the roof of their gaol. 'Awfully lonely.'

'I can't think of anything worse than that,' Rick said, his voice quiet. 'To be a prisoner, and alone as well. Speaking as an old gaol-bird, it shocks me.'

'I hate this place,' confessed Mike.

'Okay,' Rick said, turning away. 'Let's go to the nice clean sea.'

The car passed between the buildings of the old homestead,

and followed the road through the paddocks towards Port Gregory. Now the road was passing by a strange country, skirting the whitish sandy shore of a sheet of water which was dark red, red as congealing blood, the weirdness of its colour sharply emphasized by the blinding white salt floes that edged it.

'D'you ever see anything like this?' Rick said. 'It's an end-of-the-world landscape, like something Poe might have dreamed up.'

'Yes,' Rob said, eagerly. 'Like *The Fall of the House of Usher*. Like a tarn in the sunset before a storm.'

Rick laughed, watching the twisting track. 'I bet Aunt Kay got you reading that. She fed it to me, too.'

The car struggled through the sand among the handful of shacks that made up Port Gregory, and arrived on a sandhill above the sea. The sea was of the deepest blue-green, stainless and calm.

'Well, I don't know about you,' Rick said, 'but I'm going for a swim in my underpants, and if any lady wants to scream she can scream.'

In the brilliant water they dolphined and ducked each other, panting. 'I wish there was four of us,' Rob said, 'so we could cockfight.' He loved fighting with Rick.

'Well, we can do a what-d'you-call-it,' Rick said. So Mike and Rob climbed one on each of his shoulders, and joined hands and struck an acrobatic pose, and then were surprised at their own naïveté in not realizing that he had only got them up there so that he could toss them off.

'The sea's terrific,' Mike said, floating on his back. 'The sea's better than old prisons.'

'What miserable bloody beginnings this country had,' Rick said, 'when you think of it. First, half-starved abos, then marooned mutineers, then lead-mining convicts. And at last, respectable folks like us Maplesteads, kid.'

It changed, and yet it didn't change, the boy was thinking, looking along the endless grey-green and white shore. Java the Great became New Holland, and then Western Australia. Costa Branca became Edels Lands, then the Northward, and at last Victoria District. Wittacarra became Champion Bay, and finally Geraldton. But the coast of Costa Branca was the same White Coast; and the Tower of Geraldine, like an edifice from the history of another tribe, thrust up still from the unvisited scrub.

The folds of the bare silver-brown land were marked with green wattle, and the farthest hills and the patches of cloud-shadow were dark sea-blue. Wattle suckers glowed malachite-green in the late light, and the driven ewes gathered around them, nibbling, like piglets round a sow.

The ewes climbed the slope to the yards, and the randy rams came prancing to meet them. Light pierced the tawny dust in the air above them, and every head and horn and rounded rump wore a nimbus of furred silver.

'Oh,' the boy said, sighing, 'why don't you paint that, Rick?'

'I might try,' Rick said, sitting bent-shouldered and easy in the saddle. 'But it's too good, really. It needs Turner.'

'Turner,' the boy repeated, storing the name.

Aunt Mary was getting out all his picture-books for him now, and he pored over them in the lamplight, sometimes looking up to ask a question. 'What's *Annunciation* mean, Aunt Mary?'

'That's just a posh name they gave it,' Rick said. 'Originally it was called *It Came From Outer Space.*'

'Oh, you unbeliever,' said Aunt Mary; and Rob felt uncomfortable, because for the time being he was a believer, having just been confirmed.

What he liked best were the coloured picture-books, or magazines, called *Art in Australia.* There he saw the fabric of his country and its plants and its people curiously transfigured, hardened or softened or elongated, made craggy or delicate and rich. He dreamed over the pictures, and Aunt Mary, in her silver-rimmed glasses, sometimes came to look over his shoulder.

Aunt Mary liked the Australia of George Lambert. She remembered the days when Andarra and Balladyne and Lochinch had been rough-elegant manors, and Uncle Ernest had been a young man celebrated for his beauty.

Uncle Ernest stood, tall and vague, over the boy as he squatted on the lawn skinning cockatoos for the cook to put into a casserole. 'Mm?' said Uncle Ernest, from far away. 'Yes. Yes. That's the way.'

The white cockatoos infested the orchard and stripped the gumtrees, and the boy and Rick roamed the trees by the creek with a shotgun, bringing them down. They were fat and well on the seeds of the dry paddocks, and dropped with plump thuds in the grass.

'You know something?' Rick said. 'I don't like killing things.'

'Nor do I,' said the boy.

'Well, let's go and play tennis,' said Rick.

But on the tennis court old Frank, who was getting a bit ga-ga, crouched over the bull-ants' holes and donged them on the head with a hammer as they came up. 'You've got to kill things,' the boy admitted, 'or they'll mess things up for you.'

The lights of the homecoming car shone on the yarded ewes, and the eyes of the ewes were a wall of green jewels.

'Oh,' the boy said, 'paint that, Rick.'

'I wouldn't have a hope,' said Rick. 'That's Pre-Raphaelite stuff.'

Rick's paintings leaned against the veranda rail, drying. They were all of jungles, slashes of greens and yellows and purples and blues, with dark shapes that might have been tiny men.

'You don't like my pictures, do you, mate?' said Rick.

'Oh—ye-es,' said the boy. 'But they're all the same.' And jungles didn't look like that, not those colours, he was sure.

'Well, I'm only learning,' Rick said. 'I'm just a potterer.'

But he did a self-portrait which Rob and Aunt Mary liked. 'I could have guessed,' said Margaret Coram, when the boy told her, 'that he would do a self-portait.'

'Why?' asked the boy. 'Why could you?'

'Oh, just because he's Rick,' said Margaret Coram.

And the boy felt unhappy. Apparently painting a self-portrait was one more thing that was wrong with Rick.

There were so many things wrong with Rick. He would not play polo, or ride in the gymkhana, although Rob begged him to go in the rescue race and rescue Rob. He would practise polo and polo-crosse with Rob on the sandplain near the house, and tilting at the rings, and he was good, too, but he refused to come out in public and do these things in places where Rob could feel proud of him.

'What makes you so sulky?' Rob demanded. 'Why won't you go anywhere where people are?'

'Ah, I'm just a home body at heart,' said Rick, lying on his back in the shade of a tree.

'I dunno,' Rob said, defeated. 'You must be the laziest man in the world.'

'Yup,' said Rick. 'That's what keeps me young.'

But there were things that were right with Rick, too. He was interesting to talk to, and to argue with, at nights in the long lamplit room. It was his intolerance that made him interesting. 'There's not a bloody leader in Australia,' he would pronounce. 'Why can't we produce a Churchill or a de Gaulle?'

'Or a Hitler,' Rob said, trying to prick him.

'Well, Hitler had one or two qualities we could use. He wasn't a nonentity.'

'What's a nonentity?' asked Rob. And Rick rattled off a list of the Federal Cabinet.

'What you want's a Hero,' Rob said. 'The sort of bloke I used to reckon a Poet was, when I was a little kid. Someone like Adam Lindsay Gordon.'

'But Gordon was a nonentity as a politician.'

'I know,' Rob said. The Corams did not think very highly of Gordon as a politician, for family reasons.

'But he was,' Rick said, 'the right kind of Hero for Australia. Gloomy and romantic. And a good person to represent Australia in Westminster Abbey. He had a handsome head.'

'Lord Forrest was a Hero,' Rob said. 'I don't suppose he'd have been a politician at all if he hadn't been a Hero first as an explorer.'

'Yeah,' Rick said, dubiously. 'He doesn't excite me much.'

'Gee, I wonder if that J.F. on the Moreton Bay fig opposite

241

the Geraldton Hotel really is Lord Forrest. Some of the kids reckon Johnny Field carved it there.'

'It probably was Johnny Field, then, whoever he is. The less interesting version's always the truth.'

'Who could be a Hero?' Rob wondered. 'I don't know any Heroes.'

'I reckon C. Y. O'Connor was a Hero,' Rick said. 'A Hero like one of the abos' Heroes, the ones that went round the tribal country creating the animals and waterholes, and then vanished into the ground. He engineers this huge scheme to bring water to the goldfields, and then just before it goes into operation he shoots himself. Vanishes into the ground. That was Heroic.'

'They're all so sad,' Rob said, 'all the Australian Heroes. They always die in the desert or shoot themselves or something.'

'I reckon it's the Celt in us,' Rick said. 'I reckon you could define Australia as an Anglo-Celtic vacuum in the South Seas.'

'Gee, you're rude about Australia.'

'I don't mean it. It was a good country to be a child in. It's a childish country.'

'If you think like that, why don't you go to England and live in a rabbit warren, like Hughie says?'

'Because I'm engaged,' Rick said, shortly.

The summer wore on, and Rob and Mike went back to school, to the High School now, and Rick went back to College, and Aunty Molly disappeared into the Maternity Hospital and came out with a yellow-haired blue-eyed boy who would give Aunt Kay joy for the rest of her days. Going to school in the mornings, the kids sometimes would find the roads littered with romantic sheepdroppings. Sheep from the inland passed in the night like ghosts.

The year wore on, the merry-go-round of life revolved. In Asia there was war, and in Geraldton the profoundest peace.

In Jane's flat, branches of cotoneaster stood in a large white jug, the berries brightly orange against the grey wall. And the gramophone was playing Vivaldi's *Autumn*.

'This is good,' Rick said, drowsily. 'Why don't we arrange for Lucy to be on night shift permanently?'

'I can't see that it would make much difference,' Jane said. 'Lucy knows damn well what goes on.'

'Do you tell her about me? In intimate detail?'

'Don't be disgusting. As if a nurse would be interested, anyway.'

'You're interested, aren't you?'

'I've never known anyone like you,' Jane said, 'for fishing for compliments. Would you like some coffee?'

'Oh, yes. I dunno. No. Stay here.'

She lay against his shoulder, her hair tickling his chin. 'Do you love me, Rick?'

'You don't really doubt that.'

'I do, sometimes. When you just sit, not talking, and looking grim.'

'It's the music. I can't help listening to it.'

'No, not always. I hate it when you sit like that. It makes me feel—boring.'

'Aw, Janie,' Rick said, against her hair, 'you are a nit.'

'Why don't we get married?'

'Well, there's a little thing called money, that newly-weds seem to set some store by.'

'We could if you wanted. Lots of ex-Service students are getting married.'

'I want it to be fun,' Rick said, 'not hard slogging labour. And I don't want you to go on nursing.'

'But I want to.'

'You'll do what you're bloody well told.'

'I don't know,' Jane said, sitting up. 'I don't understand you. I don't think I ever will. So, let's have some coffee.'

She rattled in the kitchen. 'This is a nice flat,' Rick called out to her, lying back on the divan. 'I like these old high-ceilinged joints, and that fireplace. Shall we boot Lucy out and live here when we're married?'

'I'll bet Lucy's married herself, before then,' Jane called back.

'Don't be sour, honey.'

'Oh, stop it. Don't be charming to me.'

'You are having a lousy, aren't you?'

'Yes, I am,' Jane said, coming back into the room. 'And I give you fair warning, Rick Maplestead, if I get another proposal that doesn't mature like a Savings Bond, I'll bloody well take it.'

'Don't you talk like Eliza Doolittle to me,' he said, grabbing her.

'Oh, Rick. You are annoying.'

'Is this annoying you?'

'No.'

'Then shut up.'

'So much for the coffee,' said Jane.

Mike and Rob sat on a path, their backs against a wall of the High School, warm with winter sun. The air smelled of fresh-mown lawns.

'What are we going to do?' Rob wondered. 'What the hell will we do when we grow up?'

'I dunno,' said Mike.

'I know what we ought to be. What we've grown up to be already, really. Farmers or fishermen.'

'I don't reckon we will be, though,' Mike said.

'Everything we know that's got any sort of—dignity to it, is mixed up with the land and the sea.'

'But it's hard work,' Mike said. 'And we don't like hard work.'

'But there's something about—oh, my cousin Gordon out mustering, and Eric Larsen getting his boat ready for the Abrolhos. Something that makes a man sort of fill up. They're like trees, Gordon and Eric.'

'Yeah,' Mike said. 'I'd reckon I was getting on well with the world if I felt like they look.'

'So—what are you going to be, son?'

'A drunk,' said Mike. 'Join me.'

'Sometimes I think I hate you,' Jane said, with flashing, sherry-brown eyes.

'What have I done now?'

'Do you know what time it is? Do you realize I've been waiting two hours?'

'I'm sorry,' Rick said. 'I met Hughie.'

'I don't know why you didn't marry Hughie while you had the chance.'

'He didn't ask me,' Rick said.

'Rick, I'm serious. I want to break this.'

'Janie, just because I'm late——'

'It's not that. You don't love me.'

'Jane——'

'And don't come near me. You reek of beer.'

'I'm a bit drunk,' Rick confessed.

'A bit.'

'All right, I'm so drunk I couldn't scratch myself. I'm paralytic. But we're still engaged.'

'No. We're not.'

'I'll ring you in the morning.'

'I won't be in.'

'All right, I'll come and wait on the doorstep.'

'If you come here,' Jane said, 'I'll make you look such a fool in front of all the other people who'll be here that you'll be glad to crawl home.'

'Okay,' Rick said. 'I'll get good and drunk before I come, and bring Hughie.'

'Oh, Rick——'

'Oh, Jane.'

'Now, go away and sleep it off, like a good boy.'

'And we're still engaged?'

'I suppose so,' Jane said. 'Damn you.'

The yacht sped on the moss-green water, and gybed. 'Oh, hell,' Rob said, as he fell overboard. He swam furiously behind the yacht, and after a time was hauled in.

The hills were brown and grape-purple and blue, and the gently heaving sea was like moss or wheat. The yachts and the gulls and the necks and breasts of the shags were a dazzling salt-white against the sea and sky.

'You didn't do that very well,' said Kenny Beaton's father, whose boat it was.

'No,' said Rob, shivering in his wet clothes. 'I know I didn't.'

They anchored outside the breakwater, and dangled lines and feet in the water. 'Hey, Kenny,' said Kenny Beaton's father, 'Rob, watch out a shark doesn't get your foot.'

'We're watching,' they said, gazing entranced into the deep green.

'I thought that was shark fins back there where I fell in,' Rob said, 'but they were craypot markers.'

'I wondered what was making you swim so fast,' said Kenny.

Oh, the sea, Rob was thinking, kicking his feet in it. The terrific sea. White sails and the sea. And some day—Antarctica. A fishing boat passed them, laden with youths in bright shirts, who were waving beerbottles and singing and shouting. 'Shark! Shark!' they called at the boys with their feet in the water. 'Aw, go home,' Kenny yelled back.

'New Year's Eve goes on all day for some people,' Mr Beaton said.

The fishing boat came back again and headed for the beach. 'Heck,' Rob said, 'if I was as drunk as those kids are, I wouldn't go out.'

'If you were as drunk as that,' said Mr Beaton, 'you would, you know.'

The boats skimmed like swallows on the green water. It was another summer, and all children exulted in the sea.

The boy trudged beside Aunt Kay in the hot sandhills. They were going to St John's to see Aunt May, who was dying. The boy stood, feeling wretched, in the hospital-smelling room. Aunt Rosa and Aunt May had always been kind to him, and had given him three calves, even though they had feuded with his grandfather and had told him, after Margaret Coram's wedding, that they would not darken his doorstep nor break bread at his table again. Aunt May had been kind to him, and now Aunt May was dying; her hands like claws on the hospital sheet, her eyes large and curiously bright, with pale spots of blindness in the pupils.

He stood at the balcony door staring out across the white dunes to the summer sea. In that same room, one day, Aunt Kay herself would die, praying to die, after a year of pain. How long that year would seem: an interminable goodbye. *Fare well is just two little words,* he would think then, blinking at the dunes, *but they hold a deal of sorrow.*

The choir sang the anthem, the voices of the trebles soaring high and clear in the pale arch of the chapel. Rick listened with closed eyes. The voices were firm and strong and not quite sweet, a little rough; boys' voices, human voices.

He knelt beside Tom Anscombe in the pool of light falling from a copper-shaded lamp. All the schoolboys were kneeling too, in their circles of light, but they did not seem to be praying. Half the congregation, on the other side of the aisle from Rick and Tom, had hardly ceased for a moment to stare at the two strangers.

Well, so did I, Rick thought, covering his face with his hands. And I wonder how many hours I've spent in this place, if you counted them up. Six times a week and twice on Sunday. A feast of religion.

And it meant nothing, nothing. Not the prayers. The music, perhaps, but music one could find elsewhere. He wondered if Tom Anscombe got anything out of it. It was Tom who had dragged him back to Guildford on this sentimental pilgrimage.

Lord, now lettest thou thy servant depart in peace: according to Thy Word.

Almost without thinking, he sang the bass harmony, habit was so strong.

All so familiar: the music, the words, the intricately carved woodwork, the pale soarching arch. And as for God, had the idea ever crossed his mind?

The organ boomed in the loft, and the gowned masters left, striding rather self-consciously over the black and white flags. Then the boys marched out, House by House.

'Prepare for an ear-bashing,' Tom said, as they walked down the aisle.

On the lawn outside masters whom they had known, or half-known, before the war stood talking in the dark. And all the talk was of the war, who had died and who had done well, and what memorial the school should provide to keep the war in the minds of the young.

Rick felt uneasy, meeting them for the first time as a grown man. He did not feel like a grown man; and yet he felt centuries older than the masters.

Under the broad plane-trees Tom's motor-bike stood. He sat down on the pillion with a weariness of relief. Yet he still liked the place. Lights had gone on and boys were coming out on the School House balcony, and he felt that he knew everything they were doing and saying, the slang they were using, the whole dull safe routine.

'Well, d'you feel better for that?' Tom asked.

'I dunno,' Rick said. 'Maybe.'

The chapel rose tall and narrow and pale behind the Cape lilacs. Cape lilac flowers, in spring, would pile in drifts in certain corridors, drowning the school-smell with sweetness, floating even in ink-wells.

'Did you ever read *The Young Desire It?*' he asked, idly.

'Quiet,' Tom said. 'You don't mention that round here.'

'It's good,' Rick said. 'It feels young. He was young. So I suppose they can't forgive him.'

The motor-bike roared, the yellow light tunnelling under the green planes. 'What do you feel like doing now?' Tom shouted back.

'I feel like swimming the river,' Rick said, 'and pinching a bagful of Diego's grapes.'

'Oh, you lawless bastard,' Tom said. 'And right after Chapel, too.'

'Yeah, it's not a good time,' Rick agreed. 'We'd probably meet the whole school over there.'

18

By an outcrop of grey rock in the Sandalwood paddocks a picnic was going on, among the capeweed and everlastings, under the gold-dropping wattles. The Maplestead women and a few of the men stood about the leaping fire. And the cousins clustered round Rick.

'Uncle Rick,' Johnny Bradley asked, 'why aren't you married?'

'I'm going to be married,' Rick said, 'next year. To Jane, over there.'

'When?' asked Jenny Lowe.

'Oh, I dunno. Ask Jane.'

'Can I be a bridesmaid?' asked Didi Maplestead.

'You're a bit young. It's up to Jane to say.'

'Can I be best man?' asked Rob.

'What, in short pants?'

'I'll be in long pants by then.'

'You will look stupid,' said Nan Coram.

'You shut up.'

'Hey,' Rick said, 'I never talked to my sister like that.'

'I just heard you tell Susan to drop dead,' said Peter Rohan.

'Ah, but she's grown up now. She can take it.'

'Hey,' Helen Lowe said. 'Hey, look.' Jill Lowe, aged three, had discovered Charles Rohan, aged three months, in his basket, and was making off into the bush with him. 'Jill, put the baby back.'

'No,' said Jill Lowe. 'I want him.'

'Come on,' said Rick, 'give him to Rick. You wouldn't refuse Rick anything, would you?'

'He's my little cousin,' said Jill, at bay.

'Well, he's my little cousin too.'

'He's everybody's little cousin,' said Mark Bradley. 'How many darn cousins are there?'

'Twelve,' said Jimbo Maplestead, 'not counting grown-ups.'

'Have we got any more?' asked Patrick Bradley.

'Yes,' Didi Maplestead said, 'there's all the McDermotts.'

'Isn't that nice for you all?' Rick said. 'Like having a thousand brothers and sisters.'

'I wish I was an only child,' said Johnny Bradley, wistfully, 'like Elizabeth Fox.'

'Why?' demanded his brother Mark.

'So I wouldn't have to wear your mouldy old pants.'

'I know how you suffer, fella,' Rick said. 'I used to feel like dropping a match in Gordon's wardrobe.'

'It must be beaut, being the oldest,' mused Jenny Lowe.

'I don't know if it makes much difference,' said Helen Lowe. 'I'm wearing Nan's dress.'

'I'm wearing Didi's dress,' said Nan.

'I'm wearing Elizabeth's dress,' said Didi.

'I'm wearing Rob's pants,' said Peter.

'I'm wearing Patrick's jumper,' said Jimbo.

'So am I,' said Mark.

'I'm wearing Rick's pants,' said Rob, with some pride. They were his riding trousers, Rick's old moleskins cut down.

'Well, you'll hardly believe this,' Rick said, 'but I'm still wearing Gordon's pants. So don't imagine that things get better, 'cause they don't.'

'Uncle Paul's wearing my dad's pants,' said Rob.

'Oh, look,' Rick said, 'don't let's start on the grown-ups.'

Silence fell for a moment, as they watched the grown-ups grilling meat over the fire.

'Let's fight Uncle Rick,' said Patrick Bradley, suddenly.

'No,' said Rick, starting to jump up. 'No, fair go.'

But they fought him, all eleven of them, and won.

Rick lay among the crushed capeweed flowers with as many of the cousins sitting on him as would fit. 'I've never been so brutally treated in my life,' he complained. 'You must hate me.'

'Alison Mackenzie reckons,' Rob said, 'that the funny thing about the Maplesteads is that they all like each other.'

'Well, God save me,' Rick said, 'from demonstrations of affection from the Maplesteads.'

Over the fire, Susan was trying to persuade Rob's mother and Aunty Judith and Aunty Molly to go to Sydney with her to play golf in a championship. 'A Maplestead quartet,' she was saying. 'You know, like the Marx brothers.'

Susan was captain of games among the female Maplesteads, who all played tennis at Susan's place, while the geese and peacocks stood about booing and the kangaroo embraced the ladies as they served.

'What about me?' asked Aunty Jean, who alternated with Aunty Susan as the best golfer. 'I'm married to a Maplestead.'

'Well, a quintet, then,' said Susan.

'I wonder if we'll ever manage a Maplestead football team,' said Gordon.

'A polo team should be easy enough,' said Uncle Ernest. And in fact there would be one, within a few years.

'I think togetherness is being carried a bit far over there,' Jane said. 'Rick must be suffocating under all those children.'

'Isn't he good with children?' Aunt Mary said. 'It's odd, really, because he's not at all a patient man.'

'I think he's like the hound-dog sitting on a thorn,' Gordon said. 'Just too darn lazy to get off.'

'Gordon,' said his mother, reproachfully.

'He's awfully nice,' said Aunty Judith. 'And he was an absolutely horrible little boy.'

'He was not,' said Mrs Charles Maplestead, wounded on Mrs Ernest Maplestead's behalf. 'We were all very fond of Rick.'

'He *was* horrible,' said Susan. 'He was damnably spoilt.'

'Susan,' said her mother, 'I won't have you criticizing the way I brought up my children.'

'Do you remember,' Gordon said, 'we used to call him Benjy. Little Benjamin, the last of the tribe.'

'You were very unkind to him,' said Aunt Mary.

'I wasn't, you know,' Gordon said. 'I thought he was rather an interesting kid.'

'He's still interesting,' Aunty Molly said. 'It's still impossible to see what he's going to be like when he grows up.'

'Molly,' said Mrs Charles Maplestead. 'You seem to be

going out of your way to hurt Aunt Mary's feelings.'

'No,' said Aunt Mary, 'I rather agree with Molly. He's not really grown-up, although he's twenty-eight.'

'You keep considering Mary's feelings,' Uncle Ernest said. 'What about Jane's?'

'Oh, I don't mind,' Jane said, vaguely. 'I don't want him to be middle-aged. And what does grown-up mean, anyway?'

'Responsible,' Gordon said. 'And he's not.'

'I suppose he will be,' Aunty Jean said, 'when he needs to be.' Aunty Jean was always in favour of people being young, and the younger the better.

'I feel sorry for Rick,' Uncle Paul said. 'We've really torn him to pieces, and all this time he's been lying buried in children.'

'I haven't been tearing him to pieces,' Uncle Michael said. 'I think he's a good bloke.'

'I think he's a very likeable boy,' Margaret Coram said, 'in a rather conscious sort of way.'

'After this conversation,' Jane said, 'I think he's a cross between the Mona Lisa and the Sphinx. I wonder if anyone knows what he's like.'

'Oh, yes,' Aunt Mary said. 'Hugh Mackay does. But I don't.'

'I think perhaps Rob does,' Margaret Coram said. 'He seems to be trying to turn himself into a carbon copy of Rick.'

'Poor wee lad,' said Mrs Charles Maplestead. 'They are funny, at that age.'

'Children!' Susan called. 'Leave Uncle Rick alone, and come and eat.'

The children rose in a flock from Rick's body and swarmed to the fire, where food was being doled out on paper plates.

'Will you take this to Rick?' Mrs Charles Maplestead said, handing a plate to Jane.

Jane took it, and walked over the spongy pasture to where Rick was, still lying on his back in the crushed flowers.

'Oh,' he said, reaching out. 'Food. Thanks.'

She sat beside him with her knees drawn up under her skirt, staring out across the green-and-pink and green-golden hills.

'Rick,' she said, from a distance.

'Hadn't we better admit it, and call the whole thing off?'

He was eating a chop, and kept on eating, grease on his chin.

'All right,' he said, at last, with a shrug.

'Somehow,' she said, 'I knew that you were ready for me to say that.'

'Things were running down,' he said. 'Perhaps we've found out all there is to know about each other.'

'I still know nothing about you,' she said. 'Nothing.'

'It could be there's nothing to know.'

She watched the cloud-shadows moving across the land, varying in blueness between open grass and scrub.

'I feel so awfully sad,' she said.

'Well, it's been a long time,' Rick said. 'But we had fun, didn't we? And tomorrow to fresh woods and pastures new.'

'I hate you,' she said, dropping her head to rest on her knees. 'Oh, *God*. And whose *bloody* idea was this, anyway?'

Beyond the lead-lighted windows of the college, beyond the fresh new leaves and tendrils of Virginia creeper, the river was a misty blue, flat and still.

'Come in,' Rick shouted towards the door, from the lumpy armchair where he lounged reading.

The heavy jarrah door swung in, and Jane was there.

'Oh,' he said, getting up. 'You know, you were just about the last person I expected.'

'Yes,' she said. 'I do realize that.'

'Well,' he said, 'won't you sit down? Sorry about the bed. I slept in till lunchtime, so the maid couldn't make it.'

She sat tense on the edge of the one armchair, while he pulled out the chair from the desk for himself.

'I know I shouldn't have come,' she said. 'Everyone stared, and a boy in a pink towel screamed and ran.'

'Pity you missed Tom Anscombe,' Rick said. 'He always wears his towel round his neck.'

'Rick—I wanted to see you one more time.'

'Well?'

'To say—oh damn it, that I love you, Rick.'

'Oh, you don't,' he said. 'No, you don't. It was your idea

to break it off.'

'I broke it off because—you were bored with me.'

Across the desk, through the open window, he stared at white yachts moving on the blue river.

'No,' he said. 'That's not true. But perhaps it was a relief, some ways. I want to go.'

'Where?'

'Anywhere.

'Do you really know what you want to do? Have you ever had any idea?'

'I want to be young,' he said, low. 'I don't seem to have had the chance. No, that's not right. I don't seem to have taken the opportunity.'

'Can't you be young with me?'

'It's four years,' he said, turning to look at her, 'since Hughie and I came back from the war. And oh God, Jane, if you could imagine what sort of life we'd imagined for ourselves. Heroic lives. And what came of all that? Hughie sits in his little suburban house listening to the wireless, and I swot for a career that bores me stiff in anticipation, and somewhere out in the big wide world people younger than me are getting everything out of life that I promised myself that I was going to have as soon as the war stopped. I'm too young to rot. Not very young, but too young for the suburbs.'

'Rick,' she said, 'just kiss me once.'

He stood up and came to her, dropping on his knees beside the armchair. 'I haven't shaved for two days,' he said. 'This'll be horrible.'

'No,' she said. 'No, you can't be horrible.'

She had never looked more beautiful to him than now, with her brown eyes full of tears.

'Jane,' he said, 'I will marry you. Marry me.'

'No,' she said. 'No, Rick. Just kiss me.'

Her open lips were soft, and her back was soft, and her hair soft. 'Oh, Jane,' he said, stroking her hair, 'I do love you, I always will. Oh, Jane,' he said, laying his cheek against her breasts, 'I've been talking a lot of rot, and I do love you.'

'No,' she said, 'you knew what you were saying.' And she

stood up, pushing him away.

'What will you do now, Jane?'

'Go home,' she said. 'And go to work. And try to marry a doctor.'

'Marry me, Jane.'

'No,' she said, at the door. 'I wouldn't marry any man because he got tired of running. You got all you wanted from me, and you know now you're lovable. So keep running, Rick, and don't get caught.'

'Jane,' he said, 'don't be so hard on me.' But the door slammed as he stepped towards it.

He stood at the window and saw in the drive below her spring-clad figure climbing into the ramshackle little car. Jane, he whispered towards her; but felt even then a shamed sensation of release. On the blue river white yachts were moving, and the river flowed to the blue sea, which flowed everywhere.

The spring storm lashed the trees, and drove black rain into his face. The river was black and lightless, reflecting nothing, a black hole in the city, whose far lights shimmered and dimmed behind the rain.

He opened his mouth to the wind and the rain, shouting without voice.

Hugh's house was dark, and on the dark veranda he stumbled on a tricycle. His godchild, Ricky Mackay, was three years old now. Who am I kidding, he thought, when I say I'm young?

He knocked on the door, and heard from the bedroom window near-by bodies stirring. There was a pause, then Hugh's reluctant voice said: 'Go and see who it is, honey, before I go crazy wondering.'

The light came on behind the stained-glass door, and a dim pink shape appeared. The door opened on the shape, which was Joy Mackay, in a pink candlewick dressing-gown. 'Oh—Rick,' she said.

She was not the sort of girl to put curlers in her hair, or grease on her face. She looked as if she had just come from swimming, and he felt affection for her, though her strident

Australian voice jarred on his ear. 'Could I see Hughie?' he said.

'Well, he's in bed,' Joy said, rather coolly, and he wondered, not for the first time, whether perhaps she disliked him. But with Joy it was impossible to tell.

'Is that Rick?' Hugh called out. 'Put him in the lounge. I'm coming.'

The light flicked on in the lounge, illuminating the china animals in the glass-fronted cabinet, the three-piece suite in autumn-toned Genoa velvet. 'It's cool for the time of year,' Joy said. 'I'll put on the fire.' She stooped and pressed a switch, and in the red-brick fireplace electric logs began to glow.

'Sit down,' she said, and he sat, on a blond-wood divan. 'I'll say good-night, I think. Hughie'll be in in a minute.'

'Yes,' he said. 'Good-night, Joy. God bless.'

'God bless you, too,' she said, rather surprised, and went away, passing Hugh in the passage.

Hugh was wearing a vari-coloured satin dressing-gown, and rubbing his wild hair. 'What's up with you?' he demanded, sinking down in an autumn-hued chair.

'I wanted to see you,' Rick said, vaguely.

'I look better by daylight.'

'Sorry. I didn't—I didn't need to before.'

'What's wrong?' Hugh said. 'Tell Uncle. Is it Jane?'

'Yes. Yes, it is.'

'So. What have you done to her?'

'I don't know,' Rick said, staring at the wine-coloured Feltex at his feet. 'Well, yes, I do. She's tried to kill herself.'

'Rick,' Hugh said. 'Tell me more, mate.'

'She's not dead, she's not in danger, she just—— Oh, she took an overdose of something, these nurses can always lay their hands on anything they want. She's not going to die, but she did try.'

'And how do you feel about that?' Hugh asked.

'Well, how do you think I feel? I feel bloody awful. And then I think: The rotten bitch, she just did it to make me feel lousy, and I feel worse still.'

'And what are you going to do about it?'

256

'Nothing,' Rick said. 'What can I do?'

'And where do I come in?'

'Would you go and see her?'

'And tell her good-bye from you?'

'Yeah. Something like that.'

'Okay,' Hugh said. 'It won't be the first time I've cleaned up after you.'

'Don't say it like that, as if it was my fault. Am I supposed to've guessed that this'd happen?'

'Well,' Hugh said, 'if it'd been my affair, I'd have kept it in mind as a possibility.'

'Ah, it's no use,' Rick said, lying back on the divan. 'I can't cope with peace. I don't know where I stand. People keep asking you for things you can't give. I was a good mate to you, wasn't I, Hughie?'

'Yeah,' Hugh said, 'you were. But you can't live on that for ever.'

'I wish things were as simple as that still,' Rick said.

'Well—what are you going to do now, mate?'

'I dunno. Leave Australia, I reckon.'

'For where?'

'England, I suppose. I don't know. But I know a fella who's got a booking on a boat for England, and I think I could talk it out of him.'

'Why this mad yearning for overseas?'

'I'm so bloody bored,' Rick said. 'This country. It's so bloody boring.'

'It could be that that's not the country's fault.'

'Uh-huh,' Rick said, hardly listening. 'Oh Jesus, Hughie, I wish you weren't wearing that dressing-gown.'

'What's wrong with it?' Hugh demanded.

'It's so bloody awful. Especially against that chair.'

He had never before said anything to Hugh that had hurt him, and did not recognize for a moment the look on Hugh's face.

'Listen, Rick,' Hugh said, rising and coming to the divan, 'if you like me, you've got to like my dressing-gown and my lounge suite and my wife and the lot.'

257

'Yeah,' Rick murmured. 'Hughie. I'm sorry.'

'You've been on the sherbet,' Hugh said, 'haven't you? Well, you'd better sleep here. Let's just get that tie and those shoes off.'

He stooped over the divan, fumbling with the knot of Rick's tie.

'Hughie,' Rick said, reaching up and gripping the hard shoulders under the sleazy dressing-gown. 'Oh Christ, Hughie, I think you're a marvellous bloody bloke.'

'Hell, you are in the grip of the grape.'

'I'm not,' Rick said, sitting up. 'And I'm not going to sleep here, either. Funny, you know, I've only had one or two drinks, but it seems to get me in the head now. I can't take it.'

'Listen, mate,' Hugh said, pressing down on his shoulders so that he could not stand, 'tell me something. You're not cracking up, are you?'

'I don't know,' Rick said, shaking his head. 'I'm dreaming again, after a couple of years of good sleep. It feels like something's going wrong.'

'Why don't you marry Jane, you galah?'

'No. No, I couldn't face her again, I just feel so——'

'Have you got any idea what you're going to do?'

'No. I suppose I could try kidding myself I'm a painter.'

'You're a sad case,' Hugh said. 'I wish I could go with you.'

'I wish you could, too.'

'But boys grow up, and they marry girls.'

'That's hell, isn't it? We should have married the same woman, Hughie.'

'What relation would that make us?' Hughie wondered. 'Husbands-in-law?'

'Ah, you clown,' Rick said, getting to his feet. 'Right, I feel better now. I'm going home.'

They stood at the front door in the darkness, the wet black wind thrashing in the trees.

'Which way are you going?' Hugh asked.

'Ah, round by the river.'

'Don't fall in,' Hugh said, unsmiling.

'I'm not the type,' Rick said. 'You know that.'

258

'What type are you, though?'

'The type that's only got one instinct,' Rick said, 'and that's the instinct of self-preservation.'

A pink light came on in the bedroom, as a hint from Joy and Hugh noted it. 'Well, sport,' he said, 'good-night and good luck and take care of yourself.'

'Yeah. And give my love to your wife, 'cause I reckon she's a bonzer sheila.'

'She heard that,' Hugh said, 'with any luck. So, happy travelling.'

The wet black wind tossed the branches, and Rick opened his mouth, shouting without voice, feeling stinging rain on his tongue, as he walked by the river like a hole in the lighted city.

At Marsa, Rob's cousin Peter was driving him round the bend.
A deep artesian gush of questions burst from Peter as he discovered the world. 'What would you rather be: a Red Indian
or a boong? A cowboy or a bushranger? Joe Louis or Frank
Sedgeman? The Duke of Edinburgh or Randolph Scott?'

'For Gawd's sake,' Rob cried from the heart.

'Peter,' said Uncle Paul, at the table, by the light of the
hissing Coleman lamp, 'comparisons are odious.'

Peter replied: 'Who's the best fighter, you or Uncle Jeff?'

The spring country flowered in stunning profusion, flowered
like chintz with flowers whose multitudinous names one could
never hope to learn, flowers whose names were 'that mauve
one with three petals' and 'that pink one like the ones Little
Red Riding Hood was carrying in the picture-book'. As a
grown man Rob would discover that the pink ones were
trigger-plants, but he would never know the names of more
than a fraction of the flowers of his country, which would
continue to be called by different names by different individuals
within different families.

In the spring pasture and among the maturing wheat red
and blue wild geraniums flowered. Unflowering wild straw-
berry leaves draped dead wood and lichened rock, and everlastings rustled in one-coloured drifts of pink and white and
yellow.

By rock pools and creeks the delicate mauve-petalled wild
hibiscus opened, and the gold-dust of the wattles floated on
water. Wild duck were about, and in trees and in fox-holes by
water he looked for the nests, staring in at the grey-white
eggs, but touching nothing. Climbing a York gum, he was
startled when a grey broken-off stump of branch suddenly
opened golden eyes at him. He gazed into the angry day-dazzled
eyes of the nesting frogmouth and felt that he had witnessed a
metamorphosis.

Under the wattles, between the flowering shapes, he plunged in the cold rock pools. But his cousin Peter, when he was there, would not take his clothes off. Peter said it was a mortal sin or something. He was boarding now at the convent, and learning boxing and football from someone called Sister Catherine, who was in the habit of beating kids around the head with her empty beer bottles, according to Peter.

On the small, rocky hills, among the keening flowering sheoaks, Rob walked old Bob and drank in the country above Bob's ears. For the first time in his life he knew that he was young, and knew, with agreeable sadness, that he would not be young for long.

Time and death could stain the bright day, and the leaf-brown foxes that traced green paths in the dew could die poisoned and in agony among the flowers. He stood by the body of a young fox, and watched the capeweed and horse-radish flowers bend in the wind against it, pollen clinging to the stippled hide. Furry-silvery fingered leaves of lupins dipped and swayed, and the new blue flowerheads nodded. Out of the tender blue sea of the lupin paddock a windmill rose, sandy-tawny with rust, spinning against the lupin-blue sky. Lupins withered and foxes rotted, and the windmill whirled and whirled against all seasons of the sky, drinking from the filled dark caves below the earth.

In the garden behind Jane's flat in Mount Street, the garden which once had run down to the river, a green lawn sloped to a thicket of bamboo. Bamboo overhung the cane lounge on which Jane was lying, so that Jane was striped with long leaf-shadows and sunlight.

'It was awfully nice of you to come,' Jane said. 'But then, you are an awfully nice man, Hughie.'

'Everyone likes me this week,' Hugh said. 'Has the word got round I'm changing my Will?'

He was ill at ease, and rubbed his lean dark jaw.

'How d'you feel?' he asked.

'Angry,' Jane said. 'Ropeable.'

'He's pretty cut up, you know.'

'I'm not angry with him,' Jane said. 'Well, yes, I am. But

more with myself. What a stupid, girlish, film-starrish thing to do.'

'Are you still—you know—in love with him?'

'No,' Jane said. 'No, I don't think so. I really only worry about myself now, and what an awful embarrassment I've been to Lucy.'

'What *do* you think about him?'

'Goodness knows. I think I like him, in a funny sort of way. I rather hope he doesn't get married. He's more interesting as he is.'

'And what about you?' Hugh said. 'Will you get married?'

'Well, I'll have to be asked,' said Jane. 'But I think I'm the sort of girl who does get married, don't you?'

'You know something?' Hugh said. 'I think you're a smashing sort.'

'I like you, too,' Jane said. 'Awfully much.'

'Isn't that Maplestead a lucky bugger?' said Hugh. 'He's got such charming friends.'

The mown track smelled sweet in the dry air as Rob ran up and down on the spot. He had butterflies in his stomach, waiting for the baton. On the inside lane next to him was Kenny Beaton, in the yellow singlet of his team, and Rob felt certain that Kenny was going to make him look silly.

He started running forward, holding back his hand for the baton. Kenny was way out ahead of him, Kenny's team was winning the relay. Kenny had the baton and was sprinting away.

Rob's fingers closed round the baton, and he went. Kenny was getting closer, he was passing Kenny. Kenny was behind him, and the hand of the runner ahead clenched on the baton. The runner was sprinting off, and Rob's team was winning now.

He stood by the track to catch his breath, back bent and hands on his knees. Then, slowly, he walked back to the pavilion. By the time he reached it, the relay was over, and his team had won.

He heard kids saying: 'Did you see Rob Coram? Heck.

would you think he could run like that?' And big, quiet Bruce James, the faction captain, said: 'That was pretty good, Rob.'

His captain's hand on his shoulder smote, he thought; but was moved under his cynicism. He hadn't known he could run, either. He had been a last-minute replacement.

Gee, he thought, growing excited now, perhaps I'll be a runner. He began to build a new career for himself, in which he figured dressed in a singlet with AUSTRALIA written across it.

Then he looked up and saw Mike watching him, Mike's rather good-looking young face grinning with friendly and understanding malice.

What's the use? he thought, relapsing into cynicism. Whatever he did, Mike would never take him seriously. No one would take him seriously, no one wanted him to be anything but ordinary predictable Rob Coram. So he would be Rob Coram, and no more.

On the bank overlooking the Oval grown-ups were wandering. They were talking about the champion girl athlete, who was an aboriginal called Barbara Johnson. She was a very remarkable girl, they were saying, to have got as far as fourth-year High School, and they hoped that she would make something of herself.

He watched Barbara Johnson talking to the white people, her perfect teeth flashing, and could almost feel the cynicism behind her smile. He bet that she would not make anything of herself at all, not after that kind of encouragement.

He wandered in the desolate stony gullies of Marsa, in the summer silence, broken perhaps once a week by the crashing in the scrub of rat-faced young kangaroos the colour of new boots. He wandered, dreaming of an extraordinary encounter. In the house at Marsa was a half-caste girl of fourteen, who never spoke, who never spoke particularly to Rob, but who would sometimes momentarily meet his glance with large dark eyes holding a curious moonlike luminosity. He dreamed that in the gullies he would meet Nonie, and they would take their clothes off and he would do *that* to her. If he did that to Nonie then he might start a child. He was thirteen, and he knew now that he might start a child.

In the paddock by the house was a colt whose concupiscence was unceasing. The colt was feeling himself, said the grown-up men. The boy watched the colt continually, with shamed fascination.

He dreamed of Nonie in the hot night. But he was not in love with her He was in love with the fair-haired girl from the goldfields, and he wanted nothing of her, nothing, but that she should say that she was his girl-friend. And this she refused to do.

He hardly knew what was happening to him. There was no reason, no development in his now perpetual unhappiness. Mike's tongue tore strips off him, because of his accent, because his father practised a shameful profession, and in general because he was Rob. The fair-haired girl he loved would not speak to him on the way home from school.

On the salty planks of the Dolphins. in the middle of the sea, he lay sunbaking, listening to the talk of the older boys. They made jokes at him that he thought at first he did not understand. and then realized that he did understand, and blushed, but felt relieved at the same time that he was not the only person to know such things His life was shamed; and standing on the spring-board of the Dolphins he plunged into the clean sea, skimming the sand and weed of the sea-floor, wanting to stay down there, wondering what it was like to drown among the trailing ropes of watery light.

20

On the lawns in the summer dark Mrs Charles Maplestead and
Miss MacKay MacRae sat in cane chairs, telling tales of
glamourie and darkness; whose tone the shy and bony boy
sprawled on the grass at their feet would never forget and
never, except in the Border ballads, find again. Dried fruits
of the Moreton Bay figtree clattered on the roof, and in the
lighted drawing-room, behind the dark creeper with its large
white cyclamen-throated flowers, one or other of the cousins
would be banging on the piano. Mrs Maplestead and Miss
MacRae talked on the cooling lawns, spreading their thrall of
glamourie and darkness.

The Maplestead clan came and went, bringing flowers and
fish, bringing novels and cream, and all the gossip of the town
and district. 'It's a window in Thrums,' said Miss MacRae
to her sister, who alone understood the reference. At the
centre of the merry-go-round stood the Weird Sisters, and the
family revolved about them.

'Good for Rick,' said Mrs Charles Maplestead to Rick's
mother. 'So he has his degree at last.'

'But Heaven only knows what use he'll make of it,' said
Mrs Ernest Maplestead.

The boy brooded on the fresh lawn. There were more and
more things wrong with Rick, and now people were not even
speaking to him. John Wexford had walked out of the Club
when Gordon Maplestead walked in, and Maplesteads were
being cut dead by Wexfords all over the place, in accordance
with the country convention that one member of a family was
responsible for all other members of a family. Even Mrs
Charles Maplestead, who never had much idea what was
going on if it was disagreeable, reported that Julie Wexford
had been so strange when they met in the greengrocer's that
she feared that Julie had picked up this wog that was about.

265

It was not right that there should be unhappiness at Sandal-wood, the boy thought, out of his own profound and un-reasonable unhappiness. And Frank had died at last, washed and pyjamaed and unhappy at Nazareth House, and a part of everyone's childhood was gone with him.

In the house, children banged out tunes on the piano, and gift-bearing Maplesteads came and went. On the lawn, dark-ness failed to dim the shine of Mrs Maplestead's washed and dune-white hair. Mrs Maplestead too would die one night, very gently, after asking her granddaughters to bring her a new comb.

At the bridge over the Murchison was desolation. Flooding rains in the north had brought the river down, and the red fabric of the ancient continent was rushing to the stained sea.

'All that topsoil,' mourned a farmer, on the wooden bridge. 'The country's just washing away.'

In the road were clumps of people, come to see the moment when the bridge must go.

'It's not really deep yet,' Rob said to Nan, farther down the river. 'I'm going across.'

'You'll drown,' Nan said.

'No, I won't,' Rob said. 'I reckon it'll be rather a good feeling, swimming in this.'

He waded out, treading submerged grass and weeds, into the broad red river, which had long ago flooded its flat banks. The river felt so strong. He swam and floated with it, enjoying its strength like the strength of a big easy wave under a surf-board.

He was crossing the river at an angle. Then the river seized him and drew him under, and rolled him over and over in its darkness, banging him against rocks, and at last cast him up against something painful, which he embraced.

He rose from the darkness half-drowned and trembling. He was clinging to a sheoak in a flooded rocky gully, and the river was tearing at him.

He knew that he could not last out long against the river. His arms were not so strong as the river, and the boiling

266

brown race ahead would stun him against the rocks and drown him within five minutes or so.

I'm going to die, he thought, with awe. Oh, poor Rob Coram. Poor Mr and Mrs Coram and Nan. They came to the river for a picnic, and went home without poor Rob.

A centipede on the treetrunk above him was going mad with terror.

I'm such a nuisance to everyone, he thought. They're going to have such a job finding my body. No, they'll never find it. It will just float out to sea.

The centipede danced round and round his hands, almost pleading.

I don't mind dying, he thought. Everything's got so sad. But poor Aunt Kay. Poor Grandma. Poor Rick.

I mustn't die, he decided suddenly. Poor Aunt Kay.

He turned his head, looking across the broad, broad river which had increased even while he was clinging there. On the far bank stood his father, with the tow-rope from the car in his hands, searching the water.

'Here!' he shouted. 'Here!' But only his head and shoulders showed above the water, and they could not see him. They could not hear him, either, through the rush of the flood. 'Here!' he shouted, without hope, tensing his tired muscles against the tug of the river.

Nan had heard, she was pointing. And his father came slowly wading and swimming through the tearing water, the rope in his hands.

'Don't come near,' the boy shouted. 'Oh, don't come near.' Poor Mrs Coram, to lose a husband and a son in one day.

But his father had found an outcrop of rock under the water, and was clinging there, tossing out the rope.

'No, no,' the boy said, hopelessly. The rope would not reach.

But his father was clever. Gee, his father was clever. His father had broken off a gum-branch and knotted the rope to it, and the branch was falling through the air. It hissed in the air, falling on the water, and the boy leaped and seized it before it washed away.

He was being hauled through the roaring river like a fish. And at last he stood, shivering, on the rock by his father.

'Gee,' he said, weak with anti-climax. 'Thanks, Dad.'

'I think it's a pity,' his father said, 'that you've got too old for the razor-strop. Here, tie this round you.'

They roped themselves together, swimming and wading back across the river, which was now deep, and so strong that they finished up on the bank a hundred yards downstream.

Margaret Coram was furious. Nan Coram was triumphant.

'I don't think you'd even have been sorry,' said the boy, aggrieved, 'if I'd got drowned. You'd just have had a worse lousy than you're having now.'

'And don't use that revolting slang of Rick's,' said Margaret Coram.

When the sun set, it set on a waste of brown water, spiky with the black tops of trees. It set red and burning on the miles of scrub-dotted river, among black, thundery clouds.

'I think we'll go,' the boy's father said. 'It will be dark when the bridge gives.'

The boy sat in the back seat, watching his father. He felt grateful to his father, who had just saved his life, and as if he should now be closer to him. But he was not, and would not be, and he gave up, after a time, any hope of understanding this melancholy man: who would die one day, well fore-warned, reading Omar Khayyam.

The horses plodded single file along a track through the prickly dryandra scrub that masked the river, and on the clean sand under the gums the riders reined in and dismounted.

Rick had not shaved for days, and the golden stubble on his face glinted in spangles of light falling through the leaves. His eyes had a blue, smouldering look, and it was half an hour since he had spoken.

The boy stood by Rick in the sand, haltering the piebald mare to a horizontal bough. He watched Rick sadly out of the corner of his eye. He had just turned fourteen, and hardly knew what was happening to him, but he loved Rick heart and soul.

268

The water by the reed-and-gum-fringed bank was almost black, green-tinged, and mirrored farther away the sudden pink cliff that reared inexplicably out of it.

'Well,' Rick said, sitting in the sand, pulling off his boots. 'Aren't you going to swim?'

'Yes,' the boy said, slowly undressing. His riding pants dropped in the sand, and he tightrope-walked gingerly, bony and naked along a branch overhanging the river. He felt awkward now about going without clothes. He felt gawky and uncoordinated, and he walked like a drunk cowboy, according to Margaret Coram.

He dived, burying his nakedness in the murky water.

From below, the water was yellow, almost brown, flecks of river-stuff like dust motes spinning in the yellow shafts of light.

He came up, shaking back his hair, and saw Rick beside him.

'Race you to the cliff,' Rick said.

'I can't keep up with you,' the boy said. 'Let's go slow.'

They breast-stroked in the dark unfathomed water.

'People say it's bottomless,' Rob said. 'How could anything be bottomless?'

'Figure of speech,' Rick said, spitting water. 'Though some of your favourite cowboys are pretty bottomless. How does Randolph Scott keep his pants up?'

'They used to tell me there was a bunyip in it, too.'

'Look behind you,' Rick said. 'Here he comes.'

'What *is* a bunyip, Rick?'

'God knows. Probably some sort of fertility spirit, like the rainbow serpent in the Kimberleys.'

'It wouldn't hurt you, then?'

'I dunno,' Rick said. 'It might make you pregnant.'

'Aww.'

They reached the cliff, and clung one-handed to a ledge of rock. The pink clefts above, that in spring sprouted with everlastings, were now bare, and on the bend of the river beyond the cliff the gravelly ground under the York gums was red-brown and glaring.

'It was a sacred place,' Rick said, 'that's certain. And I

suppose the local yamidgees had the usual ideas about the spirits of unborn children being in the water. That ring of stones, you know, that our boundary fence runs through, that could have been something to do with fertility. Hey, it's probably making new men of us, swimming here.'

'I *am* a new man,' said the boy unhappily.

'So am I,' said Rick. 'Gone are the days when I chewed up all the hibiscus bushes round Changi to get a bit of Vitamin E.'

'Were you sterile?' asked the boy.

'Since you're rude enough to ask,' Rick said, 'yes.'

'Did you feel bad about it?'

'It didn't matter much. But hell, that's old history.'

'It's four years since you came home,' the boy said. 'Since you wrote that bit of poetry in my book.'

'Have you worked out yet what it means?'

'Yeah,' the boy said. 'It means us, the family. We stayed still, and you came back to where you started from.'

'It was more the idea,' Rick said, his wet, brown hair overhanging his eyes as he squinted up at the cliff. 'More the idea than the fact. It was remembering you for three and a half years that kept me circling.'

'Were you disappointed?' the boy asked, glancing sideways at him.

'I dunno,' Rick said. 'Dreams are awful glamourizing things.'

'I dream—ugly things,' the boy murmured, shivering.

'Poor kid,' Rick said. 'What, sex?'

'Yeah,' the boy whispered.

'So does everyone, fella. Don't worry.'

'I wish I was a kid again,' the boy said.

'You'll have the time of your life, matey, in a few years, so think about that. Hell, I'm cold now. Shall we take in a bit of sun on the rocks?'

'I'd sooner get dressed,' the boy said.

'Right. Let's go.'

They glided back across the pool, and clothed themselves, shivering a little in the light breeze, in the shade by the horses. 'Ah, you're warm, Splash,' the boy said, embracing the piebald mare. 'And we're going to be hot as hell again by the time we get home.'

Rick sat on a low branch with his back to the boy, smoking and gazing at the river. Small bushflies clustering on his lean blue back, glistening a little in the shifting spangles of sunlight.

'Rob,' he said.

'Yeah?'

'You knew I was going away, did you?'

The boy dropped his arms from the mare's neck suddenly.

'Where?' he said, with dread.

'London, to start with.'

'When?'

'A fortnight from Friday.'

'Rick,' the boy asked, unsteadily, his adolescent voice cracking, 'why?'

'To start living again,' Rick said. 'Because I'm dying of boredom.'

'Oh,' said the boy, and could think of nothing else to say. He felt like crying.

'That makes you sad, does it?' Rick said, without turning.

'Yeah,' the boy said. 'A bit.'

'Well, maybe you'll turn up on that side too, some day.'

'I don't want to go away,' the boy said. 'I want to stay here with you.'

'That sounds familiar,' Rick said. 'I think you told me that eight years ago.'

And the boy said, with sulky recognition: 'All right. I know I'm not a kid now.'

He broke off a spray of gumleaves, and swished aimlessly in the air. The little flies glittered on Rick's blue back, and he approached Rick and switched them away.

'You are a kid,' Rick said, 'but not for much longer.'

His love for Rick was like an ache in the boy. He leaned against Rick's back and put his arms round Rick's neck and hugged him, roughly, as the kids sometimes hugged each other when they felt affection. He hugged Rick, with his face against Rick's wet hair.

'Ah, fella,' Rick said, moving his shoulders, impatiently, 'I don't want to fight you.'

'I wasn't trying to fight you,' the boy said, dropping his arms, and went and sat down in the sand.

The reeds swayed along the sand, and the river had an old bitter smell of rotting reeds and rotting branches and black mud.

'I'm going away, too,' the boy said, with his chin on his drawn-up knees.

'You are! Where are you going?'

'To Guildford,' the boy said. 'In February.'

'Ah, well, you should like that,' Rick said. 'I did.'

'Is it like the schools in the English boys' books?'

'Not really,' Rick said. 'It's more like Changi. I enjoyed it.'

The boy felt in a way that Guildford was part of his world, because Charles Maplestead had gone there, to read Horace among the vineyards and olives, at the Reverend George Sweeting's Academy.

'I'm going to wear long pants,' he said.

'You're getting ancient, aren't you,' said Rick. 'Hey, is that a trace of bumfluff I see on that manly lip?'

'Aah,' said the boy, rubbing his fist across his mouth. He felt ugly. And a crop of pimples had broken out on his jaw.

Rob isn't handsome, Aunty Judith had said, but he would be pretty if he had a good skin.

'I wish I was a kid again,' said the boy, wretchedly.

'What was that?' Rick said, turning his head. 'Come round on the other side of me.'

'Why?' asked the boy

'Ah, I'm going deaf in this ear.'

'You can't be going deaf,' the boy said, shocked. 'You're young.'

'Well, they tell me I got bashed round the head by the Nips a few times too often.'

The boy got up and stood in front of him and stared intently into Rick's blue eyes with his own blue eyes, which were the same eyes, coming from their great-grandfather. 'Aw, Rick,' he said, 'you're not getting old, are you?'

'Don't be morbid,' Rick said. 'Hey—d'you reckon we ought to go?'

'Yeah,' the boy said, slowly, dragging himself away from examining Rick for signs of age. 'All right.' The examination, at any rate, had been reassuring. There were no visible signs of age in Rick, he looked young; and when he dived naked from a gum-branch he had what people meant when they said a boy's figure, unlike the skinny boy.

But time was like a river in flood. Heck, thought the boy, walking his mare behind Rick in the track through the prickly thicket, it's nearly 1950. And Aunt Kay's nearly seventy-seven, and Rick's nearly twenty-nine, and the town's getting ready to have a big birthday party for being a hundred years old. And Aunt May and Frank are dead, and Aunt Rosa's dying.

The horses clopped on the red road, by the red gashed banks of little hills grown with jamwood and York gum and grey-green sandalwood. 'Rick,' the boy said, 'don't go.'

'I've got to, kid,' Rick said. 'And I've earned it.'

'Why do you want to go?'

'I want to be young before I'm old,' Rick said. 'Hell, when I was half-dead in Thailand I was more alive than I am now. I had nerve-ends then that I don't seem to use any more. And I reckon that maybe, out there in the big world, I might use 'em again.'

'How long will you go for?' the boy asked. 'When will you come back?'

'Never,' said Rick.

The boy stared, unbelieving, from the back of the walking mare. 'And leave *us*?'

'Look, kid,' Rick said, 'I've outgrown you. I don't want a family, I don't want a country. Families and countries are biological accidents. I've grown up, and I'm on my own.'

'Why?' the boy asked, begging urgently to know. 'What's wrong with us?'

'I can't stand,' Rick said, 'this—ah, this arrogant mediocrity. The shoddiness and the wowserism and the smug wild-boyos in the bars. And the unspeakable bloody boredom of belonging to a country that keeps up a sort of chorus: Relax, mate, relax, don't make the pace too hot. Relax, you bastard, before you get clobbered.'

The boy stared at the road, aching with uncryable tears. 'I thought you liked us,' he said. 'If you liked us, you wouldn't mind those things you're talking about.'

'Hell,' Rick said. 'It's Hughie's dressing-gown all over again.'

'We always liked you,' the boy said, angrily. 'Don't you care if people like you?'

'Oh, kid,' Rick said, reining the old gelding in, and riding knee-to-knee with the boy, 'I know how you feel. I was your age myself. And I try to be the sort of bloke you think I am, but I'm not.'

'I don't know what sort of bloke I think you are,' the boy said.

The road was going through a yellow stubble field, like a courtyard between walls of grey-green scrub.

'We're being pretty honest with each other,' Rick said. 'You love me, don't you, Rob?'

'No,' said the boy, bitterly. 'Not if you're going to leave me to grow up all by myself.'

He kicked the mare, and plunged away, cantering and then galloping through the stubble, beside the whizzing scrub. Ah, his country was pretty: spare, bare, clean-smelling country. His country was grey-green and golden under the fairweather sky. And the blood of his country would go on and on, the blood of his country would never end, and there would be Maplesteads at Sandalwood for ever, and the one apostate would be forgotten.

He came to the boundary gate, and wheeled, and dismounted. From the high land Sandalwood stretched out like a relief map: pale brown under dead barley grass, silver under dead rye grass, yellow under stubble; the folds of the bare hills marked dark green with wattle and gum. Sandalwood and young gums looked almost grey in the silver-brown paddocks, but the trunks of York gum and christmas tree stood out dark and stark against the brown-purple hills, and the farthest hills, and the cloud shadows, and the far clumps of scrub were dark blue, and the east wind was dry as fire, and the whole huge land smelled of eucalyptus and dry grass and a harsh sweet smell like the stems of everlastings. The huge, huge land rolled out like a blanket under the world-enlarging cry of the crows, which made the screech of a snowstorm of white cockatoos in the river-gums by the creek sound busy and trivial and frail.

He held open the gate, and Rick passed through. He looked up at Rick, wondering why Rick looked angry. Rick's eyes were a smouldering blue under the shadow of the broad hat.

'I think I'll let him have his head,' Rick said. 'See you at the house, kid.'

'Yeah,' said the boy.

'Mate—*tidak apa.*'

'Yeah,' said the boy, though it did not feel like nothing to him. '*Tidak apa,* mate.'

Then Rick was gone, carried away by old Gay's great pounding gallop, over the bare, rounded paddocks of Sandalwood.

The boy chained up the gate and mounted the piebald mare. He let her have her head, too, but she could not keep up with Gay. He watched Gay grow small in the distance, and let the mare leave the track and gallop to the crest of a stony rise, where he pulled her in and looked out over the land.

By the fresh green patch in the dam paddock, which was a rose-tree, dead Maplesteads lay. And on the rise beyond was the old stone shearing shed, with slits in the walls for rifles, where dead Maplesteads, led by John Maplestead with the spear-scar on his hand, had withheld or expected to withhold dead aborigines. And beside the shearing shed were the grey timbers of the stableyard, where a blue patch, which was Rick, was now unsaddling.

He stared at the blue patch of Rick, feeling bitter, uncry-able tears. Rick was going, although everyone had loved him. Rick was going, although the boy loved him, and he had taken back the lines that he had written in the boy's book at the end of the war. The world the boy had believed in did not, after all, exist. The world and the clan and Australia had been a myth of his mind, and he had been, all the time, an individual.

The boy stared at the blue blur that was Rick. Over Rick's head a rusty windmill whirled and whirled. He thought of a windmill that had become a merry-go-round in a back yard, a merry-go-round that had been a substitute for another, now ruined merry-go-round, which had been itself a crude promise of another merry-go-round most perilously rooted in the sea.

Another Penguin book by Randolph
Stow is described on
the next page

TO THE ISLANDS

Randolph Stow

Set in the far north-west of Western Australia, *To the Islands* is no simple clash between the old and the new. Instead, Stow has chosen for his hero an old white, man, Stephen Heriot, who for many years has run a mission station for Aboriginals. He has reached a crisis in his life where the simplicity of his ideals has exploded into chaos and love has been twisted into hate.

His journey towards self-discovery and the islands of the dead, accompanied by the faithful Aboriginal Justin, bring Heriot through suffering to a greatness he had always been capable of but had never reached.